™

Also by Nancy Niblack Baxter

THE HEARTLAND CHRONICLES:

Hoosier Farmboy in Lincoln's Army
Gallant Fourteenth: The Story of an Indiana Civil War Regiment
The Miamis!

CHARMED CIRCLE

Indianapolis 1895: A Mystery

by

NANCY NIBLACK BAXTER

The Heartland Chronicles

Guild Press of Indiana
Indianapolis, IN 46208

PREFACE

This is a work of fiction, rooted in careful reconstruction of the past. Two Chinese tong-related murders occurred around the turn of the century in Indianapolis. They were never solved, though a tong chief for all of the Eastern U.S. was implicated.

Woodruff Place existed, of course, as shown at the height of its period of good taste and lovely living in the city; the commercial districts of Indianapolis, as described, were newly important parts of life.

Research in any of several books about Indianapolis establishes details of life in 1895: new electric streetcars and electric lights, the fledgling telephone service, bike mania, mass marketing of products familiar to us today. I have tried to recreate an atmosphere, complete with buildings and popular customs of the time. I have, in a couple of cases, used a 1990s neighborhood name; Lockerbie neighborhood was not called that in 1895, but that is the recognized title today.

Readers of earlier Heartland Chronicle books will be able to trace the ongoing saga of real McClures in the chapters where visits are made to Southern Indiana; John R. McClure, Susan Brooks Niblack, Nancy McClure and John H. Niblack are historical figures—though certainly not prominent, as some of their ancestors were.

I did not at all invent the scrappy and often intolerant relationships between groups who made up the city's melting pot.

We have come together, but it hasn't always been very easy and our successes in this modern, wonderful city should be, finally, a source of pride in the unending processes of community spirit and cooperation.

I need to clearly say that the intrigue in this book surrounding one of our city's most wonderful spiritual historical landmarks, Central Avenue United Methodist Church, the beloved church of my own childhood, DID NOT HAPPEN.

Building process, architecture, and details of worship and prominence are accurate, intrigue not! It's fiction, folks!

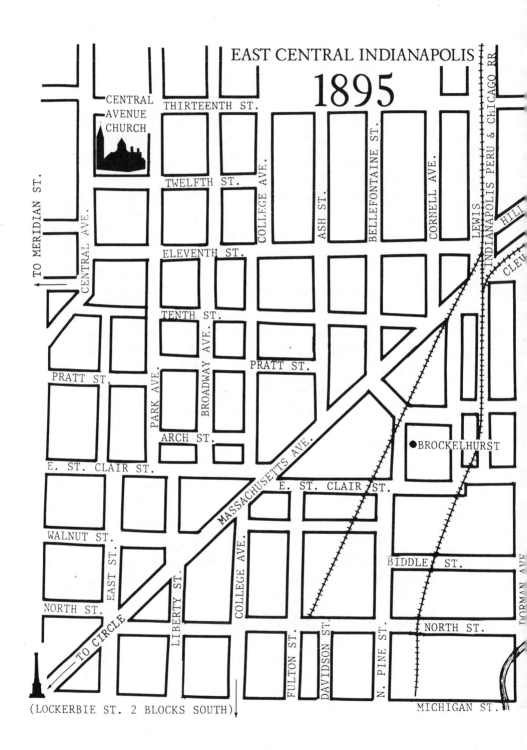

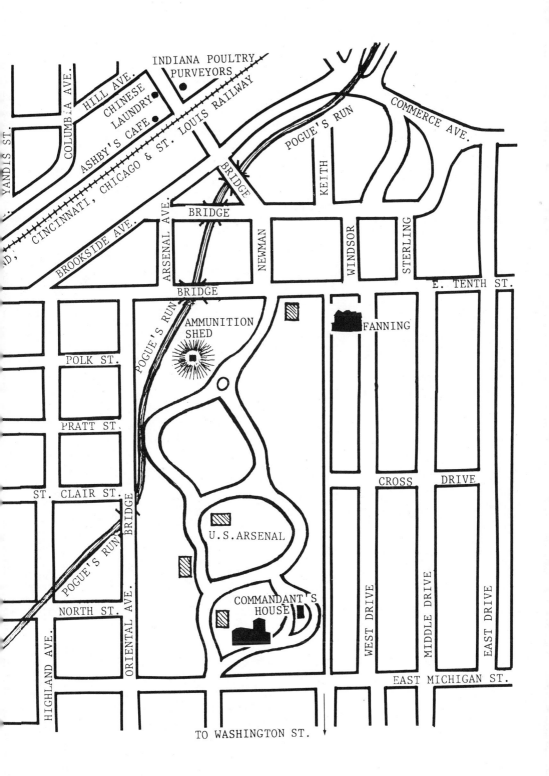

Chapter One

There are times when a spur-of-the-moment decision can change the direction of an entire life. Thus it was for McClure L. Scott as he made his way through the stifling, heat-baked brick and cedar-block streets of Indianapolis, Indiana in late July, 1895.

This visitor to the "Crossroads of America" was only twenty-four, fresh off the train from northern Michigan, and seeking the Christian Men's Hotel on East Michigan Street. The man in the ticket window at Union Station had told him the hotel was close enough for him to walk to. He was to go along the main north and south artery, Meridian Street, past the crowded business district, to Michigan Street, about a mile north of the station.

He complied with instructions, his small striped grip swinging at his side. But when he got through the business district and through the area of stately residential houses, many with wrought-iron fences and gardens full of larkspur and roses, and came to Michigan Street, perspiration dripped down his forehead and his eyes began to smart. He couldn't see very well, or perhaps he was too excited to look carefully. At any rate, he turned west on Michigan instead of east. And west was a very different direction from east on Michigan Street in Indianapolis in 1895.

Hesitating, he took out his handkerchief and wiped his forehead.

The sun was just setting on this humid July night, sending low shafts of light through the maple and elm trees that lined the street. It was almost eight o'clock. The train had been late leaving Traverse City—well, he would soon be able to sink into a bathtub at the hotel and scrape off the cindery dirt. Then he would hang up his trousers and the fresh shirt his mother had so carefully folded into the grip for the interview. He wondered if they would have a Remington typewriting machine in the employment office here in Indianapolis so he could show how well he could type, error-free for at least two pages, with two carbons underneath.

He stopped after walking three blocks, and looked up. Where was the hotel? He took the letter from the employment agency out of his pocket, looking at the address they'd scribbled at the bottom. The hotel was supposed to be in the three hundred block of Michigan. But instead there was a large, three story house with many curtained windows. Music was coming from it; probably a small orchestra was entertaining. The violins were out of tune because of the damp heat, he thought. He should know. It had happened often enough to him.

People were coming out of the house, walking across the lawn and to the boardwalk, obviously going somewhere. Mostly men they were, strolling and laughing, their line stretching like a gaggle of geese back to the portal of the big house. A fat man with huge mutton sleeves bound with garters came through the doorway, with a girl in a swishing dress clinging to his arm. "Paris Pleasure Palace," a sign near the door said.

He joined the crowd; all seemed to be hurrying, pointing at some sight along a street which ran in back of the place. They rounded a corner and walked just ahead of him, murmuring with the excited anticipation of curiosity-seekers. The sounds of the orchestra jangled out behind them like a music box which had run down; ahead, though, there was more music.

He craned his neck only a little; he was, after all, a good two inches taller than most of the men and certainly the few women in the rushing group. There, ahead and to what he now knew must be the north (obviously the sun was setting to the left—why hadn't he noticed the direction, how stupid of him)—they were entering a different section of town. Huge houses with fenced yards and carriage houses and turreted garrets were left behind and they were in a block of small shops and frame, two-story dwellings. A stench drifted off what must be a fetid river nearby; he glimpsed a ribbon of water through the trees. The crowd was backing up against itself, like dominoes falling in on each other, and the few women were shushing the men. McClure, called Mack since he was a boy, finally saw what had drawn the crowd out of the house of bright lights and music and into the summer street.

It was a small funeral procession, but unlike any he had seen, and as it came to the cross street, the crowd watched. Someone was playing a guitar-like instrument and singing a wailing dirge-song. The mourners were Chinese, six men dressed in chemise-like black coats over wide-cuffed black trousers, and two women in linen dusters, wearing turbans. The iron-eyed mourners marched in front of a hearse pulled by a white horse draped with scarlet silk. Three of the men wore queues but a third, with head held high, wore a Western haircut that stopped just below the ears.

The proud-looking man held high a banner with Chinese characters on it and a glaring lion. Behind him marched an old, stoic-looking woman in a long, silky-looking coat, trousers, and tiny silk shoes. She bore a platter on which had been placed a roasted chicken and cups which could be tea. Offerings for the dead? The hearse rumbled by, followed by the women in linen dusters and turbans, screaming and beating their breasts. One of them played the instrument Mack had heard earlier.

"Professional mourners," a voice next to Mack intoned knowingly. Mac turned to see who had spoken, and saw a man almost as tall as he, with a soft, but strikingly handsome face and a neatly-trimmed brown mustache. Although the man was not looking directly at him, Mack sensed he was observing his reactions to the funeral in an offhand way while the smoke from his cigar formed circles around him in the still air.

"Who are these Chinese?" Mack asked.

"Laundrymen and a grocer or two. Some live here near the canal." So that was what Mack smelled. A city canal in summer. "And some live on the east side of town. But it's rumored they're all members of the tongs."

"Tongs? You mean the Chinese extortion gangs? I thought they were only in San Francisco."

The mourning parade was past now, marching and wailing down the street and towards the cemetery on the other side of Washington Street. Mack looked the handsome man full in the face.

"They've spread out from there to New York and Chicago and Boston and Detroit—and here. Where have you been?" the man said with a patronizing smile. His eyes coolly appraised Mack's Sears and Roebuck suit, his too-kinky blond hair which now stood on end in sweaty curls.

"In northern Michigan. Lumber country," Mack said a little uneasily. He had never felt a lack of confidence before. He was proud of his hometown, The Queen City of the North, with its new opera house and fancy mercantile, and a few showy homes built from fortunes made overnight through the milling of white pine. But this man, who could only be three or four years or so older than he, made him feel like a hick.

Mack watched as, in twos and threes the men were beginning to stroll back. To what—gambling, he supposed, in the Paris Palace, tête-à-têtes with the handsome-looking women on their arms; little suppers in the back rooms, with squab and champagne served behind red velvet curtains. The two men joined the movement of the drifting group, but before they had walked far, the man stopped in the road and extended his hand.

"Walt Fanning," he said.

"McClure Scott," Mack said, shaking the hand with a smile.

"Now tell me who you are and what in the name of Jehoshaphat you're doing fresh out of the north woods in the middle of the street watching a dead Chink go by here in Indianapolis."

And so Mack Scott told his story of how he had been born and bred on the shores of Lake Michigan, where trees shot sixty feet in the air until men cut them with huge saws and skidded them out over winter snows, and floated them down the rivers to sawmills. He spoke of growing up where the air and water were as clear as the glass of a fine goblet; of how he had grown restless and wanted to go, not to college, but to do something practical, and how his doting mother and gentle, schoolteacher father had suggested the new typewriting school in Chicago. There he would train to be a business stenographer. And so he had gone to Chicago and stayed among its squalid smells and beautiful high-rising buildings for six weeks and learned how to be the best typist in the class, because he was good at mechanical things.

And how, when he needed employment, he had settled on Indiana, the home of his father, who had fought in the War Between the States from the Eightieth Indiana Regiment.

"I spent a week in Michigan to say goodbye. My business college wrote an employment agency in this town. So now I'm here to interview for a position as a business secretary," he finished as they reached the corner where the Paris Pleasure Palace stood.

Fanning lit another cigar, puffing the tip to a glowing ember. "With what sort of company do you wish to be placed?" His voice was slow and rumbling. Mack wondered which of the pleasures Fanning was attracted to in the house of many gaslights which loomed before them.

"Oh, an up-and-coming company. Not too large, with contacts nationally. Civic minded—" he shrugged. He really was still too at sea to have a clear-cut idea of exactly what he did want. Fanning motioned him to a concrete bench, where they sat under a catalpa tree. Long, white blossoms, now turning into seed pods, trailed above them.

"Think I might have something for you," Fanning said, taking the cigar out of his mouth to tap off the ashes. He put an arm confidentially on the back of the bench behind Mack. "I'm the owner of a company here in town, on the near east side. We serve the hotel industry, purveyors of fine fowl."

Lights were flickering on in the downtown, towards the Circle which marked the center of the town. "You—kill chickens and sell them?"

Fanning sucked on a tooth with an expression midway between bemusement and irritation. "Different kinds of fowl. Many passenger pigeons. We have them shot, well—right up where you come from." Mack nodded. He did recall that. His friends back home had been earning money shooting pigeons. "Quail, pheasant, ducks of all kind—they're shot all over the Midwest and shipped to the big hotels in Chicago, Louisville, as far away as New York by train."

"And you need a secretary in the chicken—fowl—plant?"

"Not in the plant, in the office. The office is near my home, near Tenth Street. I can walk to it. I need a secretary to take care of correspondence, make contacts for the business, keep copies for our files. I can give you eight dollars a week." The figure was not high; neither was it insignificant.

Fanning stubbed out his cigar and stood up. He brushed off his immaculate summer suit. "You can live with my wife and me, free room and board. We have a nice house in Woodruff Place, and you can have quarters on the third floor. In the time you aren't at the office, you can help tutor Chad, our seven-year-old. I suspect you can read and write well enough."

Mack nodded his head uneasily. The man projected an aura of prestige and power. But how could he take a position on such short acquaintance? That's what his mother would ask him.

Fanning began hurrying him toward a buggy parked near the back of the building. "At least spend the night at our house tonight. It's too late to get a hotel, anyway. We can talk about the details tomorrow, when you've seen the office."

As they climbed into the buggy and Fanning prepared to drive away, Mack asked him, "What kind of town is Indianapolis anyway?"

"Up-and-coming. With a good strong community spirit. Patriotic too. Did you see our Civil War Monument?" Mack said he had seen the scaffolding around the tall splinter of stone rising into the sky in the middle of the Circle.

"It's almost finished and Miss Victory's going up on top, although we almost lost the chance to put her up there. There was a controversy."

"Controversy?"

"Well—General Lew Wallace lives in Indiana. He's the author of *Ben Hur*. He told the committee he'd tell 'em all what's the matter with the memorial." He smiled gleefully, as if he were savoring the story he was telling. "Well, the general said it was ridiculous to put a woman on the top of the monument when it had been men who had fought the war. But nobody listened to him and he resigned from the committee in high dudgeon and she's going up as planned."

"It's the age of the new woman."

"You don't need to tell me that," Fanning frowned and sent an arc of spit into the street at his side. He cracked the whip, sending the smart little bay out onto Michigan Street. The horse seemed to shy a bit.

"Just got the buggy," Fanning conceded. "I'm not used to driving it, always used the cabs. I don't really like horses—have hired the boy next door to see to it. But it's important to keep up appearances, and that means a carriage in this town."

The horse picked its way across streets torn up for paving. "This is a Christian town," Fanning continued. "We have eighteen churches right within the downtown area. Eighteen."

"About the—select poultry," Mack said. "If the office of your company is near your home over east, where are the fowl processed? I was just wondering."

Fanning jerked his head north and west, near the area where the funeral procession must have originated. "The only fowl we buy locally are chickens for hotels. We bring in fancy fowl on the railroad cars for city restaurants. They're handled over across the railroad tracks near Niggertown. Lots of immigrants live there, too, like the Chinks you saw.

Mack was suddenly curious. "The man who was killed—the Chinese. How did he die?"

"His head was chopped off with a hatchet. Li Ting was his name."

"That's horrible! Who would do such a thing?"

"Probably a member of another tong gang, who maybe brought the hatred from San Francisco or even China all the way here. Or maybe even an Irishman or a nigger who had gambled with him or argued over one of the slave women the Chinamen keep." Fanning reached Tenth Street and turned in an easterly direction. "They're all alike," he went on. "Chinks, Irish, Hunkeys—come here wanting to get something for nothing. Maybe they'll all take off each other's heads and leave the city to Americans." He laughed in a baritone voice as rich as melted butter, then stood up and gestured at an odd turret tower rising to the south like something out of an English Saxon tale.

"That's my church over there," Fanning said proudly. "It cost one hundred thousand dollars to build and has fireplaces with butternut mantels. And we're already planning an addition—an auditorium for religious pageants, complete with a balcony. Finest church in the city."

It was only after the steeple of the church was out of sight that Mack Scott realized he had left his suitcase sitting on the lawn of the Paris Pleasure Palace on Michigan Street. He was too tired to even think of how he would get it the next day and he settled down to doze for the rest of the ride to Woodruff Place, whatever that was.

The next morning Mack woke up to the sound of several children playing. He went to the window to see little girls in bathing dresses with shoulder straps and bloomers, boys with short trousers and blouses, sailing boats and throwing water from huge, splashing fountains on each other, under the watchful eyes of mothers. He put his hands on the sill and stuck his head out the windows. This Woodruff Place, he decided, was like a park. The street had an island of green grass and flower beds in the middle, while lanes for the buggies stretched on either side of the island, and then more houses on either side, beautiful homes with upper stories crowded with gables and turrets and bay windows.

And there she was, the beautiful woman he had seen as if in a dream last night when he arrived from the buggy ride and came into the house. His heart pounded as he remembered her, as she had floated down the stairs, her hand barely touching the rail, in a long, modest robe, to see who was talking to her husband in the hall. Her fine, blond hair had shone around her head like a halo in the lamplight; a small, sharp nose and generous mouth defined her face. Now she stood in the sunshine petting—there was no other word for it—a frail child with thin arms sticking out of his sailor blouse, who splashed at the edge of the fun in the fountain. Chad. His charge.

Suddenly he was aware that it was later in the day than he'd wanted to sleep. Quickly going to the dry sink, he poured water on his face and hands before he pulled on his trousers to go downstairs.

A breakfast spread was arranged on the sideboard of the rather somber dining room, and as he sat alone eating eggs and sausage and cold toast, Alice Fanning entered. He looked at her, above the plate of food and found, in watching her hover like a butterfly near the buffet table, that he spilled applesauce over the plate edge. Well, he would ignore the appeal in her face and figure and think about the little boy, who was rubbing a large towel around his thin shoulders and asking for food. "Go out to Cook," Alice Fanning said, opening the door to the kitchen hall for Chad.

"We've had the best romp in the water," Mrs. Fanning said. "They open the fountains to the children on the hottest of days in Woodruff Place." She sat down beside him at the table, her long, oval nails resting on the lace tablecloth.

"This is a separate town?" he inquired. He recalled Fanning telling him something about it last night on the buggy ride.

"Yes. It was built in the last twenty years from a site they used to call the Dark Woods. The man who built it, Mr. Woodruff, travelled abroad and saw Venice and the Rhine Valley. He was so impressed with the beauty of the Continent that he wanted to build an area of European houses here, with statuary and fountains and formal flower beds."

"And I think he has done it," Mack smiled. She opened her little clasp pocketbook and took out a mint, which she placed under her tongue. She told him more about the town of Indianapolis which surrounded Woodruff Place now, of the up-and-coming character of the families who lived there, of the brand new streetcars which brought the children of Woodruff Place to the high school downtown. She took him to the screened back door, where she pointed out, just past their property line, the Civil War ammunition arsenal with grounds which ran alongside the boundaries of Woodruff Place on the west side, and the alley beside the Arsenal, which provided a fine, leisurely walking path just behind this house. He returned to finish breakfast; she sat beside him.

"Am I to go to the business today?" Mack asked, giving his plate to the small sturdy woman with a black bun of hair who had come through the door to take it.

"Walter said he would take you to the office after dinnertime," Alice Fanning said, rising. "Why don't you explore a little until then?"

"I'll see you later," he said, putting his napkin to his lips and following her departing form with admiring eyes.

He went out the back door to take the air on this heavy, hazy July day and walked around the house. It was one of the new "eclectic" mansions with a ruler-straight center hall downstairs, two parlors (fine and family) kitchen and dining room. Completing his circle, he came back to the carriage house. This old, barn-like building standing almost at the back of the property held a horse and new livery, the equipment strewn casually around instead of being hung up, as if the master of the stable was, indeed, careless of his duties. A boy of about thirteen with a sifting of freckles across almost every inch of his face lifted the latch of the gate at the back alley; he had come to tend the horse. Mack made arrangements with him to pick up the suitcase he had left on the lawn in town.

Then Mack walked about the beautiful island known as Woodruff Place. The sweet, spicy scent of stock flowers, the musky sharpness of marigolds drifted in the air from the flowerbeds. He knew them—well he should. Dora, his mother, spent all summer cultivating long beds of flowers, trying to make the cool wetness of Michigan yield the profusion of the gardens of her girlhood home in Louisville.

He read magazines in the parlor and then it was time for the midday dinner, with Walter Fanning home. Mack watched the domestic scene with detachment, as if he were seeing it in a magazine: the little boy sitting on a tall-legged chair with a huge bib around his neck, being coaxed to eat green beans and applesauce. The two adults genteelly eating five courses (he tried to find the right forks and spoons), soup in a real silver tureen, fish with tartar sauce (he did recognize the fish fork in the row after all) chicken croquettes with vegetables and a floating island, thin custard with meringue swirls on the top. The last was a triumph, with the sweet Alice serving it up into crystal bowls. This was the first thing the languid Chad ate.

"I worry about him," Alice said, passing nuts and chocolates. "Rheumatic fever, and the doctors wonder why we even have him today. Truly, the grace of God." She lifted her eyes to Mack. He could tell from their intensity that it was not a perfunctory statement with her; if she was a Catholic she would have crossed herself.

After lunch he and Fanning were off, walking down the streets of the town past houses with lawn tennis and croquet courts. They waited to cross the lanes where several men bent intensely over the handlebars of the new two-wheeled bicycles, peddling as if their futures depended on it. They crossed Tenth Street, passed over a bridge, through a couple of narrow lanes and over railroad tracks to a newly built commercial district of four streets. There were stores and a Chinese laundry, and across from them Indiana Poultry Purveyors, Inc., two stories of brick with a longer one-story recent addition.

Inside, Fanning introduced him first to the bookkeeper, a fortyish man with a handlebar mustache named McCloskey, who looked like pictures of Civil War general Burnside. Then Mack offered his hand to the office manager, a prim-looking woman behind a desk. Her name was Ermina Farquharson and she wore a blouse with a very high, starched collar and mutton-leg sleeves.

"This is our new secretary," Fanning said heartily, clapping Mack on the back. "Fresh out of Remington school." He showed Mack the new typewriter, sitting on a table, tall, black and impressive with a box of square paper and carbon sheets beside it. Looked like a brand new machine, Mack thought. This is where he would begin his duties. Then he went out the office door to the back section where were lodged the livery and the office of the dray man who carted supplies and equipment from the railroad nearby to the chicken factory a mile and a half away.

Fanning excused himself to answer some question the bookkeeper posed, and Mack walked about looking at the supply wagons, from which emanated the faint odor of decaying fowl. He cast his eyes over at the railroad tracks, where a boxcar sat. Crates and processing supplies came in by rail to be unloaded here, but the fancy fowl for this city apparently arrived at the plant on the other side of town. "Why didn't they just put the processing plant here?" he muttered to himself, thinking about the trip across town to the factory.

"And bring the rotten chicken smell into the best neighborhoods? I think not!" Someone had come up behind him. Mack turned around to see a short, wiry young man with dark skin and black hair parted in the middle—was he Jewish?

"I'm McClure Scott, from Michigan, the new secretary to Mr. Fanning," he said extending his hand.

"And I'm Abby—Abraham—Nessing from East Street. I drive one of these wagons." He was quite short, with the wiry physique of a thirteen-year-old, but he had the wise eyes and confident tone of someone older. Abby was seventeen, as it turned out, a fourth-year student at the Indianapolis High School downtown. He worked as a dray man, he said, afternoons, after going to classes all morning. He needed to raise money to send himself to Jewish seminary in Cincinnati. He was going to be a rabbi.

They were standing in the dust of the yard.

"And you? How have you ended up at the Crossroads of America?" Abby asked with a smile.

"I have Indiana connections," Mack answered. "And Michigan air was getting a little heavy for me. I have parents who still like to decide the style of trousers I wear."

"I know what you mean," Abby said, jumping back up on the wagon to arrange some boxes. "Only in the neighborhood I live in there are eight aunts and four grandmothers to give an opinion on the trousers. And all of them do." He paused a moment. "Well, welcome to the town. It's a wide-open place. I doubt in your case if anybody will care what kind of trousers you wear. Anything goes right now in this town." The young man bade Mack goodbye and went inside the livery stable.

It was time for Mack to find his way back to the Woodruff Place house. He strolled through the little commercial neighborhood of which Indiana Poultry Purveyors formed the large and imposing corner. A small, cozy-looking restaurant, a grocery store with a handsome display of Campbell's soup cans and Aunt Jemima pancake mix boxes stacked high in the window, and a Chinese laundry occupied the buildings facing the offices. Briefly he thought of the funeral last night. The odd emotional tone of it was still with him. The Chinese in that mournful parade seemed stoical but—what else did they feel? Frustrated? Angry? Could it be afraid? A horrid murder, decapitation. He peeked through the windows of the laundry. A Chinese man and a woman sat with their backs to him, working behind the counter—no customers. And there, in the corner ironing in this awful heat, was a young man about his own age. He did not stop to wipe his brow, but doggedly pursued his job. Well, there was much to ponder in this big railroad and agricultural town, really a smaller replica of someplace like Chicago or Cincinnati, not much like his northwoods small town.

And later that evening, he was still pondering as he climbed into the small, stuffy bedroom on the third floor which Fanning had assigned him the night before. As he stared at the ceiling, sheet pulled up around his sweaty body to keep the mosquitoes away, he realized this was no ordinary household he had stumbled into. He had learned some things about them during the evening.

It seemed the husband of the house slept in the second-story in a grand salon of a bedroom. Here he smoked his cigars and did whatever else he did in there. The wife of his bosom slept up here on the third floor in a small nun's cell by the servant stairs, where at least tonight she seemed to be crying, from what he could hear. And their son slept in a room by the cook near Mack's own little room. And, if what the cook had told him was correct, both husband and wife had their own pursuits, their own worlds, and the child was being raised by the cook. Well, maybe that was what Abby had meant when he said that in this town anything goes.

CHAPTER TWO

The next day was Thursday, and Mack began his new job at Indiana Poultry Purveyors. It consisted of typing replies to inquiries, filing carbons and taking letters dictated by Fanning. First was a letter to the Palmer House in Chicago. Yes, they could supply weekly shipments of canvasback ducks during the season, shipped by train by Indiana Purveyors' supplier direct from the Illinois River Valley. Yes, ordering from Indiana Purveyors instead of the duck hunters was a much more secure procedure because the company was bonded and could insure a consistent supply.

Two dozen ducks were to be shipped on Tuesday and again on Thursday. Wild rice to be included free. Addresses and correct spellings for the names in the letters were established by getting up from the typewriter desk in the front office several times to ask Fanning. When Fanning seemed busy, Mack asked Miss Farquharson, who answered his questions with her eyes closed and mouth pressed into a firm line, as if she were some sort of martyr. Obviously both she and McCloskey resented a typing machine in an office where until now their good, round script had been something to be proud of.

At noon he ate the lunch the cook had prepared for him: cold fried chicken and a little bowl of coleslaw and some tea biscuits, and then went out back. Fanning wanted him to go across town on the last run of the week to learn about the chicken supply division of the business. Abby Nessing, the dray man, was sitting on the seat of the wagon, eating from a little brown bag too, cold fish, a roll and a huge apple.

They drove through busy carriage traffic to an area almost two miles directly west, and he saw the factory for the first time, its odor definitely discernable several blocks away. The two-story ramshackle affair seemed to be left over from the Civil War period. After picking up a load, they drove to the back entrance of the English Hotel on the Circle, where Mack helped carry several iced crates of chickens and quail in through the huge back door of the kitchen.

"One more order," Abby said. "It goes to the Paris Pleasure Palace." They rode in silence up Meridian Street, the horse clomping along the cedar block pavement, past what seemed to Mack to be an inordinate number of churches, as Fanning had told him.

"I think almost every denomination is represented once or twice in this three-block area," Abby told him. Mack nodded. John Calvin, John Wesley, Roger Williams and Henry VIII gathered comfortably all together here in Indianapolis, and their descendants were prosperous indeed, if one were to judge by the huge stained glass memorial windows, the bell towers, and the size of the sanctuaries.

There was a little more time today to note the details of the elaborate houses along this main street of town, with the wrought iron fences, bandstand porches and flower gardens he had seen the night he came in. Around all of them, like the backgrounds of eighteenth century landscapes, were clumps of trees, while across the street was the park with the bandstand.

"I was there the other night," Mack said, nodding toward the palace as they turned onto Michigan Street.

"You?" Abby demanded. Was it skepticism or admiration in his voice.

"I—got lost. That's where I met Mr. Fanning. I wonder what he was doing there."

Abby laughed. "Probably anything there is to do. Gamble, eat dinner in one of the back rooms with the velvet portières. Drink a little rosé or champagne, eat a little squab." Somehow the vision of the squabs they were themselves delivering entered Mack's mind and he saw them lifting on free wings, across the bay at Honor, Michigan and then shot down by men, agents of Indiana Poultry Purveyors aiming shotguns straight up in the air. Hundreds, sometimes thousands, fell at a time at the hands of the market hunters, and now these beautiful creatures, carried here at freezing temperatures in ice-bed railroad cars, would grace the hidden tables of adulterers.

"There's a whole palace devoted to these things?"

"Full every night, even during the week. Well, every night but Sunday."

"That seems awful to me."

"And to me. What's your church?"

"I was raised a Christian Scientist."

"You don't believe in doctors?"

"That's what everybody always says. Yes, I believe in doctors and Santa Claus too, but not in ghosts."

They had tied the horse and started carrying the squab cases down the ramp into the cellar of the Paris Pleasure Palace. "Sorry," Abby said. "We do tend to view religions other than our own through old caricatures. Presbyterians believe in a strict God of predestination. Catholics do mumbo-jumbo and obey the Pope. And Jews—" He shrugged, obviously a little embarrassed as they both thought of the cliches.

"I've never known anyone who's Jewish," Mack said. "Well, close up, anyway." The few Jews in Traverse City had the oldest synagogue in Michigan, but they stayed to themselves. Everyone in Traverse City who was "different" tended to stay to themselves: Bohemians, Indians, the few black people.

"We're powerful enough here to have a rich ghetto. Most Jews here came from Germany, or their families did, fifty years ago. They own about a third of the major businesses in town. Over there is where I live," he gestured to the east. "I'll take you home sometime if you'd like to go."

They were nearing the end of their mission. Water ran out of the crates, which had been carefully re-packed with ice from the company's own ice house only an hour and a half ago at the plant. Keeping everything absolutely cold and getting it to the customers within three days was the secret of the new special fowl purveying business, and that's how Fanning was making his fortune, Abby told him. Until ice storage was perfected on railway cars, restaurants had to depend on local hunters' successes or failures. Well, Mack thought, the cooks who'd taken these birds had better put them in a large hotel icebox right away and keep them there till they were called for, from behind the portierés.

Mack asked one last question about their boss as they drove back to the office. "Well, if he spends his time going about to the Parisian orgy mansion and other places like it, what's his wife Alice do? Do you know?" It was rather bold, but it had struck him as very odd that the cook had told him Alice Fanning was out on many a night.

"Goes to spiritualist meetings. I know one of them she visits."

"And Fanning lets her?"

Abby seemed uneasy with the direction of the conversation. "I suppose he has no choice. She must know of his free living. Maybe it's a sort of barter system."

"Anything goes? Even for women?" Mack thought of Fanning's negative reaction to the "new woman" idea the night he had arrived in town. They were both lost in thought as the wagon headed back to the office.

The next morning there were even more letters, these dictated by Fanning, smoking his cigars, sitting on the edge of his new, mahogany desk and leaning forward to tap the ashes into a cuspidor whenever Mack needed to catch up on his not-too-expert shorthand.

"Umm—to J. S. Sidlow Company, 221 Michigan Avenue, Chicago, Illinois. Dear Sid: In the matter of the Palmer House, I am well aware that you are to have rights on your home territory as agreed at the Canadian lodge meeting, but I have reserved rights on the squab market exclusively. That was to be mine, although it is not in our document. I have earned this; it was I who travelled north and lined up the suppliers, and I intend to keep them. And I will continue to keep the canvasback market in Illinois as well. You must remember you are a new entrant in this business and your share of the apple pie is going to be limited. Let us who have been here a while make the decisions, and most of all, know your limits. It would not be wise to strike off on your own. As you know, in union there is strength, is good not only for the Communist labor organizers; it works for business too. I rely on your good judgment, which can only benefit you. Yours truly, Walter A. Fanning, President, etc.

"(Harumph, umm.) Letter Two: B.J. McGonigal, 421 St. Paul Street, Detroit Michigan. Dear Bartram: I have written Sidlow a stern letter reprimanding him for trying to move in on my Palmer House trade. This young upstart had better watch his step. It was clear at our meeting that he would have domestic fowl rights only in Chicago, that his sales territory went as far as Grand Rapids and that you picked it up from there for the Great Lakes as far as you wanted to ship on the iced cars. We must stick strictly with these limits. I, for instance, cannot sell south of Columbus, Indiana because we've agreed that's Whistel in Louisville's territory. That's the only way it will work. We do not want to get to the situation we got in last year. Some risks are necessary, but let us steer clear of them if possible. I look forward to the fall meeting at French Lick. But let's avoid that stinking water they want you to drink from the spa, for the sake of both our noses and inner plumbing, eh? Yours truly etc."

As Fanning paused in his dictation, looking up, Mack thought, How much older is he than I? Three years? Five? He seems worlds beyond me with this sort of stuff, but there's a sad look in his eyes. What is it?

Fanning stubbed out his cigar. "Scott, all work and no play makes Jack—a lot of money." He smiled like a contented tabby. "Seriously, sometimes I take lunch out on Friday. Suppose you and I just have a little sandwich together, over here at the cafe."

"Mrs. Fanning won't be expecting you?"

"Well, perhaps, but she and the boy can eat by themselves today. I'll ring her up on the phone to our next-door neighbors, here." He went to the mounted box on the wall and wound it up. "Hello, Miss. Get me 249." Command, rather than request. Mack could still not get used to the little wooden square with the hooked receiver, which interrupted the privacy of home life. Still, it was here to stay, annoying as it was sometimes, with its anemic, jangling bell.

They walked across the street and around the corner, to the last building in the small commercial district, Ashby's Cafe; beyond it lay cozy bungalows and two-story houses with tiny squares of yards, the homes of working people who were making good wages. Red and white checked curtains were hung in the cafe windows, and inside tables could be seen, with the same checked tablecloth pattern. A sign was in the corner of the window: "Position Available: NINA."

"No Irish need apply?" Mack asked, almost to himself.

"They aren't welcome on our side of town. But I do hire some of the better class from Irish Hill at the factory. There's not much you can do to botch a chicken." He laughed heartily as they seated themselves at the table.

"We'll take two hamburg sandwiches," he told the waitress after getting a nod from Mack. She was a spunky looking redhead with hair piled high on her head and a green bow above the bangs. "I've grown to like the hamburgs since we went to the Exposition."

"Ah, I wish I could have been there," Mack said, thinking of the restrictions of his parents' income in 1893, of the need for his wages from the lumber camps to help them pay the mortgage on their small house. His father was a good man, a kind and decent man, but teachers did not earn enough to more than squeak by. But to have seen the foreign pavilions, the new and exotic foods, the ferris wheel! Yes, the ferris wheel!

When the food came, Fanning leaned towards Mack. "Scott I want us to get acquainted a little more. We struck up fast; I'm that way, can tell a man's character from his face." He smiled a self-satisfied smile, but Mack felt a kinship to that idea; he liked to read faces too. "Tell me about yourself."

Mack put mustard on the hamburg sandwich. "Well, I grew up in Northern Michigan, but my family are from Indiana. My father's father and mother were both Scotch-Irish. His great-grandmother Jane McClure is supposed to be a legend in Southern Indiana. Are you interested in genealogy?"

"Well, only a little. The Fannings came from Connecticut, and I left the family back there. I'm a self-made man, so I don't know too much back before my parents, but go on."

"Dad never tires of telling the stories—Jane McClure coming with her husband and small children from Northern Ireland before the Revolutionary War. Two more children, including my great-grandmother Jenny were born in Pennsylvania. After the new nation was formed, they came down the Ohio in a huge flotilla to Kentucky seeking new land, where Great-Grandmother Jenny was married. Then, they came on to Indiana."

"Your family's been in Indiana a long time?" Fanning asked studying his own fingernails as the waitress refilled their glasses of Coca Cola.

"Since 1803, they say. My father and mother met during the Civil War, married and moved to Michigan. And now I'm completing the circle by moving back here."

"Good for you, good for you," Fanning said, losing interest in the history lesson.

Mack wondered if it would be all right to pursue what Fanning had said. "You said you were a self-made man? I admire that." It was true; he did. In fact, that sort of freedom and opportunity were exactly what he was looking for when he made the break from his parents and their circle up north.

"Well, yes. My family lived in Connecticut, around Stamford. But both my parents died when I was young. And I left my home town to come over here to live with an older sister who had married. Made my way selling Bibles door-to-door in the one-horse towns of Indiana." He adjusted an already straight tie. "And one day, when I came to Delphi, Indiana, I took my Bible to the door of a cottage in the wildwood and found a wildflower by the doorstep. I knew a good thing and married her."

Wildflower. Mack nodded. That wasn't too bad a way to describe Alice Fanning. But Fanning was rambling on, gesturing expansively with his hamburg sandwich in his hand. "I went into boiler sales and when I was made vice president of Benham Boilers over on Massachusetts Avenue, I found a way to buy into the Newman Street company and then built it up. Whatever it is, is because of me." His eyes grew vague, then he brightened. "It's a great land we live in, Scott, where a poor boy like me can rise to the top, well—near the top—in only eight short years. And be married to a princess from a fairy tale on top of it."

He leaned close to Mack. "Do you believe in the free market Scott? Really believe in it?" Mack thought he did and nodded affirmation. He certainly didn't believe in the Communists or Socialists.

"I do. You could say it is my religion—well, after Christianity of course. Have to put that first, naturally. You say your father was in the Civil War. Mine was too, so they say, though he was gone of TB when I was a small child. Hardly remember him." They ate for a while, savoring the ground beef, mustard and toast which made up the sandwiches, and then Fanning looked up with veiled excitement in his eyes. "After the war everything changed. A continent to tame out west, and wide open everywhere else."

The waitress came; Fanning stood to check the bill and pay her. They left, passing tables of neighborhood mothers and children, workers with caps on chairs beside them and businessmen. Outside Fanning began again. "Scott, we live in the garden of the gods. Fruit everywhere." He gestured across the horizon, towards the downtown of the city. "There are one hundred and twenty new businesses which opened up here in the last eight years. And medium-sized businesses are turning into big ones, big ones buying small ones. We're beginning to pave all the roads downtown. Why, Colonel Eli Lilly and some others—I was one—formed a city booster club. The Commercial Club. It has a beautiful new tower building downtown that's not like anything around here. Did you see the building that looks like the Waldorf Astoria when you came in?"

"No, but I noticed the smoke stacks, the railroads. And all the impressive stores downtown. They're crammed full of merchandise and some of the mannequins in the windows actually move. Business must be good."

Fanning nodded. "Garden of the gods, as I said. All you have to do is reach up and pluck—" his voice trailed off and he reached his arm up towards invisible trees, smiling enigmatically. "Different, of course from the Bible garden. In our garden of the gods you sometimes have to get your shoes dirty. Wade through the muck now and then. Which brings up what I want to say to you. You are now in my confidence. You have to be, because you will be typing the innermost strategies and business policies of the company."

"I feel honored, after so short—"

"I can read character in your face. But if I take you into confidence, you must honor your obligation." They stopped walking and stood in front of the grocery, and Fanning looked him full in the face. "You are in a delicate position, and your complete discretion is required. Business secrets—" He put his finger to his lips.

"I understand," Mack said solemnly. "I'm not much of a gossiper anyway, but I will be discreet. Whatever I type, I'll forget. Do we file the carbons?"

"Of course, of course. But lock the file." He reached into his pocket and handed Mack a key. They reached the end of the street; Fanning was preparing to return to do some more work and Mack was to head home to help Alice Fanning with Chad. "Nothing wrong with what we do anyway, perfectly good business policy. The free market means shrewd deals, some close calls. We just need to keep our cards close to our chest in general."

Fanning waved him goodbye and strode across the sidewalk towards his business, and Mack headed past the last shop on the commercial block. He peered casually into the Chinese laundry's large glass window; a man was looking out past him at Fanning as he crossed the street. For a brief unguarded second Mack could see the hatred, or maybe it was fear, that distorted the man's face. Then the Chinaman turned on his heel slowly to return to the steam-filled interior. That face—Mack realized with a shock that it was the man who had led the funeral parade, the man whose back had been turned to him when he'd last looked into this window—who seemed to be a leader in the Chinese community from the place accorded to him in that parade. Fanning must know this hard-eyed man; how could he not, working in this block, and hadn't he overheard something about the company owning a couple of these buildings? Why was this frowning Chinaman scrutinizing Fanning as the man went across the street? It was a question for which he had no way of getting an answer.

And so he found his way back along the narrow streets to Woodruff Place to be with the beauteous Alice and the boy for the first time alone that afternoon. He found her sitting on the front porch, with a little satchel on her arm, watching Chad playing in the front yard. They were waiting for him, ready to get on the streetcar to go to Fairview Park. "It's only 1:30," she said brightly. "We can transfer downtown and be out in the park by the canal in time for two or even three hours and then get back in time for cook's dinner. No one special is coming tonight." Did they usually?

He went in the house and changed his trousers, then joined them in the front yard. "May I carry the satchel?"

"No, thank you, I like to do my own package-toting." Ah, the new woman.

By two o'clock they were on the streetcar. The air blew at them, tousseling hair and rumpling collars as they sped along towards the downtown. In the center of town they boarded the transfer car northwest. "Nothing like a streetcar ride on a hot afternoon," Alice Fanning shouted across the aisle to him. Her cheeks were rosy. Mack was holding Chad on his knee as they lurched along, and Chad, who in spite of being seven was as light as a four-year-old, joyously bounced and leaned first to the left, then to the right. They came, at last, to Fairview Park along the canal.

"How serene it looks, like glass," Mack murmured as they stood on the canal's towpath, studying the gently rippled, green-brown surface. They had taken Chad for a ride on a splendid carousel and had now decided on a walk.

"I grew up along the Tippecanoe River and the canal wasn't far from our home. The Wabash and Erie Canal," Alice said. "This is the Central Canal, though. It was a white elephant. Do you know the history of Indiana canals?" They were carrying lemonade she'd brought in a canning jar down the path. Chad stepped like a soldier along in front of them looking energetic enough today. Some days were worse than others, Alice had said.

"Didn't the state go bankrupt from the canals fifty years or so ago?" Mack asked her.

"We were supposed to be cornering progress with the whole state traversed by canals, but they cost millions of dollars, and by the time they were done, the trains had already replaced them." Alice pushed at her blond hair, trying to straighten the mass of curls. A boy in overalls was fishing in the canal and Chad sat down beside him to watch him put worms on the hook.

"A relative of mine, some cousin from my grandfather's generation by the name of Jim McClure was involved in the canal projects. He was supposed to have lived in Indianapolis when it was still a little town." Mack pointed south, towards the downtown. "And after the canals went bust, he was found dead under the Central Canal bridge, so they say, a few miles—I guess—that way." He pointed south-west.

"How sad," Alice said, with sympathy in her eyes. "Did he—take his own life?"

"I don't think it was ever known. It might have been cholera. It was forty years ago."

Chad was up now, brandishing a stick. "Squirrels and chipmunks, *en garde*," he shouted. Meet your fate!"

"Well, at least he's remembering some of his French lessons," Alice laughed. She said that his rheumatic heart did, indeed, seem better in the last month or two, but that he still needed rest. She or Mrs. Bascomb, the cook, spent a couple of hours each day reading to the boy the pirate and adventure books he loved. After a pause, she turned to Mack.

"How do you know so much about things in your family that happened so long ago?"

"My family—well, the McClure part of it anyway, which goes a long way back, is very dramatic. Talk about adventure—they were evidently famous, or notorious, in Indiana. Their life stories read like a book. And my father has kept up with his McClure kin above all others. He fought with some of them in the war. They're the odd chickens in the barnyard, I'll say that. Don't you think it's like that—you have eight grandparents, but only one or perhaps two of these lines of ancestors will catch your eye?"

They walked slowly down the towpath. Chad had sat back down again, and the boy was letting him use the pole to fish. Alice had not responded. He looked at her, standing beside him, gazing into the glassy waters. She was as slight as a girl. Her waist could not be twenty inches around, and she did not even seem to be corseted. Her mouth was pursed a little, her eyes thoughtful.

"I really don't know. My mother's people in Delphi were genteel but poor. Mother taught school. And my father—he deserted the family. I know nothing about his folk except they lived in Ireland. I sometimes wonder. . ." Suddenly she whirled around and walked to the edge of the canal, to catch Chad up by the hand. He pulled back from her, trying to break free, then came along. The three of them walked a good long way, around bends and into clumps of trees that lined the winding path. Groups of bicyclists overtook them, and Mack could not help but marvel still at the caps, knickerbockers and hose of the women, as he had the first time he'd seen them last year in Chicago. Women in pants!

Alice saw him watching. "Don't they look wonderful? I long to do that. I don't have a bicycle yet. Walter doesn't approve."

"I can see how women's trousers are necessary. So many bicycle clubs around now, and the women's skirts get caught up in the machinery."

Then, almost to herself, Alice said, "I can see me now. Bicycle and bloomers. That would show him!" She laughed with a merriment that made him wonder; it was a little odd in a wife.

Finally they sat on the lawn in front of the bandstand. She brought out the cloth satchel she'd carried over her shoulder and they ate cucumber sandwiches and lemon cookies. A band was practicing for the Sunday afternoon concert.

"There's nothing I like so much as hearing a band play," she said, brushing at a grasshopper that had ventured onto the cloth.

"I feel that way too. I've never gotten to play in a band, because I play the violin."

"The violin? You do?" She looked at him with admiration. "What is that they're playing? I mix up one tune with another, but I can hum them all. I think it's 'Liberty Bell.' "

"I'm the same way. But I think that may be 'King Cotton.' It's so popular." Chad jumped up and ran to herd some ducks which were waddling awkwardly from the water down by the canal.

Mack craned his neck to be sure Chad wasn't too close to the edge of the canal, then helped Alice fold the cloth. "What is it about Sousa?" he asked, picking up the satchel. "His music just makes you want to get off the chair and wave a flag or bang on the table."

"I know. It's as if he gets into your bloodstream and pounds with the beat of your heart. Something palpitates inside when you hear some music. Other songs or musicians just leave you blank."

"Do you feel that way too? When I play Mozart, or better, listen to it played by an orchestra, it seems to set strings inside me resonating!"

"You've said it exactly right, Mr. Scott. I've felt it but never thought of it just that way." Alice smiled at him.

"There! Now I do know that one. It's 'High School Cadet.' It's my very favorite!" she cried. They both went to go separate Chad from the squawking ducks.

As Mack scrambled down a little incline, he offered his arm to Alice, so she wouldn't slip in the thin leather slippers she wore. "I saw Sousa last year at the English Theatre," she said, as she took her arm from his at the bottom of the hill. "I was chaperon for a Methodist Epworth League young people's party. It was so marvelous, there in that beautiful auditorium, with the band in their bright new suits playing song after song."

They found the ducks happier than they had sounded a minute before. Chad had dropped the stick and was throwing bread left over from the tea snack lunch at them, and they were clustered around him, rushing for the next crumb. "English's had the Divine Bernhardt," Alice continued. "But I don't get to go often. Walter doesn't like serious theatricals." Her tone was resigned.

"There's nothing I like better," Mack said boldly. This luscious woman! Fanning obviously didn't appreciate the wildflower he'd collected from that little town.

She looked up at him again with a "kindred spirit" look. "Oh, Mr. Scott, I know we're going to get along splendidly."

As they left the park, they discussed his duties. He was to tutor the bright but fragile little boy in reading and writing, because Chad had missed most of the first grade. They were also to do sums during the three afternoons a week Mack wouldn't be working for Fanning. He was to take Chad on walks, because walks in the fresh air would invigorate his appetite and strengthen his weak heart. And sometimes, since Walter didn't enjoy it, she said, Mack would drive for her, or they would go on shopping trips or picnics together.

They rushed to catch the streetcar home as the afternoon cooled and the shadows of the huge beech trees lengthened over the paths. "Do you think you will like the job I've described?" she asked him.

"Oh yes, absolutely," he said. What he was really referring to was the last part—that he would sometimes drive her and that sometimes she would accompany him and the boy. That truly would give him pleasure, he knew.

And so on the next day, Saturday, he took up his tutoring duties, and he and the boy sat going over the McGuffey Level One in the family parlor. "The cat is on the mat." Chad was quick but unable to concentrate. Was his short attention span the result of distraction? He'd seen boys in his home town nervous because of problems at home. Was Chad like that? He sat uncomfortably forward on the settee as if the plush was irritating his legs, kept asking questions, jumping up, pointing at birds out the window or otherwise changing the subject from studies. It was going to be a challenge to teach him.

Finally, near the end of the hour they'd set aside for reading and writing, Mack said, "Look, Chad, we need to make a deal. How about it? For each hour of book work we get done, we'll take an explorers' walk. That's it. We'll discover something new, try to find some secrets or adventures, maybe build a fort of our own. Just you and I, as part of school."

"That could be good. If it happens." The boy looked suspicious. Was he often promised things and then un-promised them?

Later that evening there was to be a formal supper party. The cook, Mrs. Bascomb, whose sleek black hair, bound tightly in a bun, and large nose made her look more than anything else like a crow, officiated. She was to cook and serve seven courses with the aid of the young, fluttery red-headed scullery maid (sister of the hugely freckled carriage attendant) who was now chopping beef tenderloin under strict supervision in the kitchen.

Mack and Chad ate chicken pie and fruit salad in the kitchen before the party. "The Lillys and Marmons and Mr. Fletcher—only tony, elegant folks are coming. Everything has to be just so," Mrs. Bascomb said. She pulled out the menu, carefully written in what Mack thought must be Alice's hand. First course, turtle soup, second course, planked pike, then the serving of the sorbet, then squab (of course, he thought) and a beef with burgundy, vegetables, and a Spanish sweet called *flan*. This last, Mrs. Bastion told him, was nothing more than a carmel custard upside down in little cups.

"Nuts and chocolates served last in the epergne on the table," she said, and with a flourish whisked the menu away, and handed it to the scullery girl to stand up in a napkin holder on the kitchen table. Epergne. That must be the footed, two-tiered silver thing in the middle of the table. He was learning a lot.

"Sounds delicious. Doesn't all the food get cold waiting?"

"It had better not. Mr. Fanning is very fussy about that."

"Mr.?"

"Of course. He's the one who sets the pace in the suppers here. Lets her choose the menu and supervise the shopping and cooking, but all had better be just so or he lets us know."

Apparently everything was not "just so" in some way or another, because there were angry voices late at night after the guests left, and weeping echoed through the halls before this husband and wife retired to their separate bedrooms, separate floors. Muffled weeping continued down the hall on his own floor for over an hour, until it ceased, and all was still, except for the splashing of the fountains in the balmy night air of Woodruff Place.

The next day, Mack sat down at the small desk in his room to report on his new situation.

Dear Mother,
I know its inexcusable that I haven't written, not that you are the sort of person that would complain, good mother that you are. I am well set here with a fine family in a fashionable addition to town. I met a man in a gathering the first night I arrived and he hired me on the spot to be his secretary. I type letters and file at his company, which is known as Indiana Poultry Purveyors. When I am not active in secretarial duties I tutor his son Chad. I have a fine room on the third floor. I am attempting to keep my health habits regular. There, I knew you would want to know that. Is Pa doing any tutoring? I hope he is able to keep up the mortgage payments; it is a worry to me as I know it is to you. I have been invited to church with the family tomorrow, a Methodist church, supposedly quite prestigious where all the best families go, so they say. You know I do not take much stock in such things. Well, I must see to my laundry.

Your son, McClure

He stuck the letter into an envelope, then straightened the heap of dirty socks, linen and shirts in a wicker baby basket the cook had provided for him and which he had shoved into the closet behind the curtain. He would have to find a way to get it done.

Husband and wife were yoo-hooing up the stairs to him, as Chad began clumping down the stairs in his best brogans. Certainly it was time to go. He descended the staircase, stopping to fix his tie in the front central hall. In the mirror he could see Walter Fanning, cool and hand-some in the morning sunlight which streamed in through the front window. Alice was flushed and expectant and in her best church-go-ing mood as she stood before the family parlor looking glass patting the small hat on her chignon. If there had been anger and discontent be-tween the two of them last night after the elaborate dinner party, it was not obvious on this calm Sabbath. Surely this was the ideal family of *Godey's Ladies' Book*. Anything else must be imagination, he told him-self, or only the normal strain of conjugal life.

They walked up Tenth Street, the husband and wife strolling along arm-in-arm ahead, he behind with Chad. Their forms cast elongated shadows on the new sidewalks, shadows which disappeared only when they walked under maple trees whose branches loomed above them every fifty feet or so.

"Step on a crack, break your mother's back," Chad said, capering around a little and pointing impishly at his mother. Mack wondered at the odd little smile Alice shot back at him, half amused, half reproach-ful.

"There's the church spire," she said, as they came to College Ave-nue.

"Real landmark of the town now," Fanning said between puffs of his cigar. "They can thank some of us for that!"

Goal in sight, they hurried on to Central, where the faithful were gathering for the rituals of Sunday morning in Indianapolis. Mack felt a sense of wonder that nine out of ten citizens in the city were partici-pating in that same ritual in the many stone temples scattered on al-most every block at this hour. So the *Indianapolis Journal* had recently said. America was, indeed, a "churched" nation and Indianapolis a "re-ligious" town.

Chapter Three

The tower of the church, growing larger every minute, struck Mack as singularly odd as they approached that Sunday morning. He was used to tall-towered Gothic cathedral replicas or the belfry towers of country churches, peaked with dainty spires, but this was so different as to be unique. He asked Fanning what the style of architecture was.

"I've heard it called Romanesque, but the paper called it Moorish when it was dedicated in '92," Fanning answered, tossing the stub of his cigar into the gutter. He helped Alice down off a curb as they walked north on Central.

Moorish. Well, maybe. There was a primitive, almost barbaric look to the tower, as if it had been put up by some potentate in an Arabian city of the Middle Ages. There were holes, like defensive slits, in the stonework all the way up the tower and what must be two dozen small square holes at the top, as if to provide a place for bowmen to stand in the belfry and fire on those below. And the pinnacle was very tall and pointed.

As they drew nearer, Mack could see a second tower, even more like a minaret, behind the first. Then, as they came within a block of the church, he saw wide arches over low doorways and still more "harem" towers clustering around the first two.

"The church wanted to build something the town had never seen before, a departure, they called it. They wanted to emblazon forth in stone and glass the new age of religious worship in the city, something like that, I think the architect said." Fanning took off the straw hat he wore and held it by the brim. They climbed the steps and Fanning and Mack entered the foyer. Alice went into in an older frame building, where she was to drop Chad off for Sunday School.

"Is that a fireplace?" Mack wondered, glancing at the back wall of the foyer. "One of five," Fanning said, leaning his head confidingly towards Mack. "There's one in the pastor's study, one in the Epworth League Library and two more." Mack shook his head in wonder. The ornamental brick background with a butternut wood carved mantel was truly a work of art. His sense of wonder grew in the next hour. The sanctuary would seat five hundred. And, Alice Fanning whispered as she slid beside them in the polished hardwood pew, "this auditorium contains eight thousand square feet of space. There's a three-part pulpit, made of brass and oak, with scrolls and crosses." He himself could hear the prelude being played on a pipe organ that thundered like a storm in July.

Women with ruffles on their bustles, wearing large hats, and men in three-button suits filed into the pews in front and back of them. Their muted chatter hung in the air like bird noise in a sunset forest.

Alice pointed to the stained glass windows and told him the symbolism. "That one has an open Bible, the other a cross and that one a heart," she said.

"That kind of cross, along with a crown, is the symbol of Christian Science" he told her.

"Oh yes," she answered with a trace of embarrassment. That was the way most people in his hometown reacted to the religion he'd known for the last ten years. They thought he and the other fifty people in the Traverse City church were breakaway religious freaks who worshipped Mary Baker Eddy. Maybe a few of them did. He hadn't found many that deified the old lady-prophet, though she seemed to him through her writings to be an inspired, practical religious teacher. But then that was the fate of denominations while their founders were still alive—to be considered fanatics, followers of insane heretics. So had it been in John Calvin and John Wesley's times. Although in all honesty you had to admit Mrs. Eddy was a little odder than John Wesley or Calvin. She had been raised from imminent death by reading the book of Matthew and founded a religion which would demonstrate that healing was a part of Christianity. And she lived in a big, fancy house and spent a lot of time defending her discovery with million-dollar lawsuits against those who would imitate it.

"My favorite is the stained glass window representing the Holy Spirit as a dove. I love that passage, where the Holy Spirit descends as a dove to Jesus." Alice's eyes were dreamy for a minute, then she went back to pointing. "There's a seven-branched candlestick and the triquetra chalice."

Mack wondered what that was. Some kind of cup, maybe. His little store-front church above the theater didn't go much for symbolism. When they sang hymns, it was to a rickety piano. They even got rid of the choir in the name of purity, opting for one soloist. Lay people read the Bible and readings from Mrs. Eddy, based on scripture too. Responsive readings and hymns, that was it. Then go out and do what was read about all week long; by their fruits ye shall know them. Simplicity itself, even though by the time he'd left home, he felt smothered by it all—too much of a good thing, perhaps, like cotton candy after the first ten bites.

The seat seemed hard, without a cushion. Walter Fanning was restless already, pulling pencils out of the offering boxes on the backs of the pews and thumbing through the hymnal. Promptly at 11:15 the minister and the large choir, all suitably robed in black, came in from the sides, not the back of the church in usual Protestant fashion, and the service began.

"Dr. Brockelhurst is preaching today. He's the assistant minister. Dr. Clayborne is away at General Conference," Alice whispered.

"Two ministers?"

"There are over twenty programs going here," she said, shrugging a little. "Our congregation believes in the social gospel."

The choir sang a ringing welcoming anthem, and as the scriptural lesson, the stating of the Apostle's Creed, the pastoral prayer, and the responsive reading unfolded, he stared at the ceiling. Bulbs—there were scores of them—brand new electric light bulbs set in circular patterns. Only a few were turned on this morning, but what a light they must make at night. The starry firmament on high?

At the end of the service, as they filed out past the ornamental brick fireplace, Chad having joined them at the front steps, Mack picked up a pamphlet from a wooden box in the foyer. "The holy service at the laying of the Cornerstone of Central Avenue Church," it said. "Saturday, September 12, 1891." He read the hymn sung by whoever it was that gathered around there at Twelfth and Central to put documents in a box to commemorate this magnificent temple:

> *Let the holy Child, who came*
> *Man from error to reclaim*
> *And for sinner to atone*
> *Bless with Thee this cornerstone.*

Well, would that He would. Any church would pray for that.

He read on as they sauntered down the street, ready to turn east for home.

Open wide, O God, thy door
For the outcast and the poor
Who can call no house their own
Where we lay this cornerstone.

The outcast and the poor? These people in their dressmaker gowns and expensive, silk-lined coats didn't seem very outcast to him. And the poor? Well, as far as he could see, they were—what was it Fanning had said—far away, closer to "Niggertown." And the Chinese, mourning one of their number killed in that awful way—with his head cut off—they certainly weren't looking at the sixty-six lights over the altar which symbolized the sixty-six books of the Bible. Not at all. It was interesting to him that he was noting it; he wasn't used to the outcasts and the poor, either, in his little town. If truth were told, it was odd to him to have so many colored and oriental people around him in this city. Still, a church should welcome them, shouldn't it? Well, for those who came it was a rich and opulent feast, a religious feast for ear and eye and heart.

"That church is the most magnificent I've ever been in," he said to Alice as they strolled back beneath the maple trees.

She smiled faintly for a long moment and then, in a low voice so Fanning who walked ahead of them wouldn't hear, she said, "I don't always like it very well."

"Why?" he asked, surprised.

"It frightens me," she said quietly.

He had lunch with Abby Nessing most of the days he was in the office during the next week. On Thursday the drayman took him over to the shade of a grove of trees for lunch. "After work today, come see my family," he said. "We live over on East Street."

"I'd like to, but there's something I have to do. My laundry—" he pointed to a sheet tied into a bag in the corner of the stable.

"You have to do your own linen?" Abby asked.

"Mr. Fanning made that clear in the beginning. 'You're not to consider the servants your personal lackeys,' I think was the way he so graciously put it. I think after work I'll stop by the Chinese laundry over across the street and leave my bag of clothes."

Abby smiled.

"What's the matter. Don't you think I can afford it?"

"No. It's that there's someone I want you to meet. I'll be at the back door at three o'clock when I finish with the runs."

Later that afternoon, as planned, they walked to the laundry, and Mack paused to stare through the plate glass window. There was the face of the man who had scrutinized Fanning as he crossed the street. Yes, the same one, the leader of the funeral procession, staring out from behind a counter as he folded shirts.

A bell rang when they entered. "Hello, Lee Huang," Abby said, and the man nodded and bowed. He gave no sign that he recognized Mack or that they had stared at each other through the window on the day of the cafe visit.

"Where is Chiang?" Abby wanted to know, and Lee Huang gestured towards steps in the corner of the room that Mack supposed led to the basement.

They went downstairs towards the sound of singing, not the jangling dissonance of Chinese music but "A Bicycle Built for Two." The young Chinese man about the age of Abby, whom Mack had seen ironing before was now doing the same task in the corner of the basement. He did not see them but stopped, picked up a bottle of water and raised it to his mouth, then spit the water out methodically and in a fine spray on the shirt he was ironing. Abby laughed.

"This is my classmate, Chiang Chung," he said to Mack and Chiang put down his iron and came over to shake hands. He did not bow in the Chinese way, and he wore western trousers, although the shirt over them was a blue-green Chinese smock.

"How now, brown cow," Chiang said then smiling broadly at Abby.

"Why do you frown down on me," Abby retorted. "I'm giving him elocution lessons," he said to Mack, "to improve his pronunciation of English, and we use tongue twisters. He's in the Debate Club with me at the High School, and he knows a million words in English. He just says them in a funny way."

Mack was still carrying his sheet full of dirty laundry, and he gave it to Chiang, who took pencil and paper out of his pocket to note the items in the sheet. Then he went to an old table and picked up a pen and black ink and made a character on the inside back of each shirt.

"Won't that show through?" Mack wanted asked Chiang.

"I think not. We do letters lightly. It's our own identification system." Abby smiled at Chiang. "Can you take time off to come with us on the route? And then to my house? Let's chew the fat."

"Well—we'll just see if fat can be chewed," Chiang said, neatly putting away the shirts and stowing the flatiron on the stove where it belonged. He took the stairs two at a time and as Abby and Mack emerged from the basement steps, an animated conversation in Chinese between Chiang and his uncle Lee Huang was going on.

Finally Chiang returned to them. "Uncle says I may masticate the suet, so to speak, one-and-a-half hours, no more. Do you think we can be back by then?"

Abby nodded, smiling. "If my mother and Aunt Sophie don't talk us into the next day," he said.

They drove into the downtown to pick up the hotel chickens, heading towards the canal/railroad district where the plant was located. They trotted the horse as much as possible to gain time. Mack thought about the oddness of sitting next to a Chinaman, on the same seat, and chided himself for feeling odd.

About a block from the plant, right on the canal, was a street of tumble-down slab lumber houses from an earlier day. A black man came out of one of the sloping cabins with two bags full of chickens which Abby weighed on a scale. He paid for the fowls, which they quickly delivered to the plant refrigerators.

"The smell here is really terrible," Mack noted as they drove into the freight yard.

"Well, it's summer, and these are poultry. The jobbers are to supply only fresh chickens or wildfowl with only partial shipment of giblets. But sometimes they forget and put in innards. Or—" he gestured towards big furnaces at the back of the lot—"the chickens are too far over the hill in this hot weather."

"Over what hill?" Chiang asked, looking around the terrain.

"It means gone, rotten," Abby told him. "They have to be burnt."

A man was emptying the ashes from a huge trash kiln with a wheelbarrow.

"What happens to the ashes?" Mack wondered.

"They're dumped into the canal." Abby lowered his voice. "Sometimes the men at the plant here don't bother with burning the cast-off parts. They just dump the offal into the canal."

"And the outhouses from the plant—they go right into the canal too?" Chiang mused. "They call us Chinese filthy, but people drink that water downstream."

"Indiana Poultry Purveyors isn't the only one dumping," Abby maintained. "The packing houses further down have giant incinerators and also dump raw offal into White River."

"Anyway, let's do something else. Aren't we going to Abby's? This was supposed to be something of a joy ride," Mack suggested. He was suddenly aware that the only people he had to go joyriding with, the only friends he had made—were almost eight years younger than he. He knew none of his contemporaries. Well, unless you counted Fanning and Alice. Alice seemed to be about his age, perhaps a little older.

"Five o'clock, day's over," Abby said, listening to the chiming of one of the church clocks.

They rode across town to East Street, a proper residential street which formed the east side of a mile-wide square around the Circle, the crowded central turnabout which formed the center of the city. The wagon pulled up in front of a small, stretched-out clapboard house. It was painted lavender, and the entire front yard was a flower garden, with pinks and lobelia and cosmos and lupines, beautifully tended. Soon they were being welcomed into the parlor by two middle-aged women in black afternoon dresses, with their hair in braids. "Mother, Aunt Sophie, you know Chiang. I'd like you to meet my new friend," Abby said, as McClure came forward to take the hand of each. When the two women smiled, they showed large teeth, whiter than any Mack had seen in a long time.

"And how is the Debate Club this summer?" Mrs. Nessing asked Chiang. "Are you studying Burke?"

"No, since last time I saw you we been practicing Pericles' funeral oration and Daniel Webster." He pronounced it Wes-ter. "We expect to take the championship in the competition next year." They spoke for a while of the Indianapolis High School, not far up the street and around the corner from the Nessing home, which both of the boys attended: of its democratic student government, of the accomplishments of young ladies in all the activities of the school, of the fine teachers of science and the classics.

Then they seated themselves in red plush chairs. Family pictures, surrounded by huge Rococo frames, covered an entire wall of the house. "The school's having an art exposition," Sophie Stern, Abby's aunt, said. "I'm helping the art teacher gather works of the new styles for display in the salon. There'll be sculpture and Tiffany glass work and painting."

Then Mrs. Nessing and her sister threw questions at Mack, who told of his family, his sister, even his aunt Delia and Uncle Zach. He found that he was even telling them that his uncle and aunt had lost the family fortune in the space of a year. Mrs. Nessing smiled sympathetically and patted his knee.

"Sounds like something the Nessings would do. And some people think Jews are acquisitive. My husband never could keep a coin in his pocket for over an hour." She sighed. He had been gone just a year.

Mack felt as if he had known these people all his life.

He watched the ladies' expressive hands as they made points in the coversation, beautiful long-fingered hands emerging from sleeves with fine-worked lace at the cuffs. Seder glasses stood on the highly-polished mahogany table, beside a seven-branched menorah. And in the corner near the horsehair sofa, stood a table with a hundred stereopticon slides and a slide viewer.

"And so, Aunt Sophie, the ladies' club is taking up the study of Free Masonry in the United States, I see." Abby had picked up a pamphlet from the table in the hall. "This thing says that the Catholics and Jews are trying to take over the United States and we must beware. It's from the Masons for Freedom committee."

"Well, some of these broadsides are being passed around Indianapolis. The ladies' club took a little trouble to investigate," his aunt said.

"But here's another one," Abby said, thumbing through the pile he had picked up, "that says the Free Masons are trying to take over America and we should beware. It's from a Roman Catholic Community—the Servants of Jesus and Mary at Constable, New York. I think you better not go outside because you might be caught in the religious crossfire."

Abby went on to joke and laugh with his aunt in an elaborate way that Mack had never seen. Lemonade was offered, along with delicate little pastry puff horns filled with chilled whipped cream. Then they had to be on their way. Chiang kept looking at a watch in the pocket of his trousers.

"What about the murder of Li Ting a couple of weeks ago?" Abby said suddenly, turning to look Chiang full in the face as they walked along the board sidewalk towards the wagon. "How is the Chinese community dealing with it?"

"Ah, well, the Chinese Association has no clue."

"If that were true, it would be the first time," Abby muttered.

"I haven't heard much more about it. Wasn't it a murder?" Mack asked. "There was one long, lurid article in the paper—then, nothing more. An ax murder like that—aren't the police investigating it?"

"They are investigating," Abby said as he climbed onto the wagon seat and raised the reins. "But not thoroughly. The victim, after all, was Chinese. Still," he added thoughtfully as the wagon lurched off down the street, "I think they'll do their duty. It is a strange case."

"How do you know what kind of case it is?" Mack demanded.

"My brother Nate is clerk in the police chief's office. He tells me things." Chiang was silent.

"The man, Li Ting," Abby went on, "was decapitated and Chinese characters scrawled in blood beside the corpse. It happened at night, actually right here on upper Lockerbie Street, where he was a servant. He was apparently sitting in his lamplit little shack at the back of the Pollock family property on this very street—over there—I'll show you." He gestured with the whip from the bottom of the wagon—"someone came up from behind and actually cut off his head with one slice."

"But why?" Mack wanted to know.

"Probably it was connected with the opium den at the back edge of the property," Abby said.

"In this neighborhood?" Mack could not tie the information to-gether. The houses looked so imposing, comfortable, as if nothing but fashionably nice things ever happened in them.

"It appears that the old man that Li worked for, who was a former baking company magnate in town, was senile; he did not know that in the large cyclone cellar near the back fence people were coming and going—with a lot of frequency."

"My friend," Chiang broke in, "I do not wish to speak of this any more. You work on second-hand information. There are no opium dens in this city, you know we have discussed this fact before. Such a view throws bad light on the Chinese people."

"Of course," Abby smiled slightly. "No opium dens. As rare as aardvarks in Asia."

They swung around, towards one of the last houses on the street, and Abby pointed to a huge old mansion. "That's where Mrs. Teitel-baum lives. She runs the spiritualist sessions Mrs. Fanning attends."

"And I'm supposed to believe that claptrap?" Mack demanded. "You told me Alice Fanning visited spiritualists at night, and she hasn't even been out since I came. Not once."

"She will. Just give her time. Once Mrs. Teitelbaum summons them into the world of the spirits, they go and go again. I should know. She's my aunt."

Turning eventually onto Tenth Street, heading east back to the company, Abby pointed out O'Shaughnessy's Gymnasium and Pugilis-tic Parlor up one of the side streets. Mack nodded. He might just walk over there some day soon. He was surrounded by high school boys and women and children. While he didn't exactly miss the lumberjacks of his former occupation, he needed something physical and rough in his life. He was beginning to feel like one of the cream horns served at Mrs. Nessing's house.

"Tell me about Mrs. Fanning—Alice," he said as he and Abby were brushing the horse back in the company's livery stable. "What do you know about her?"

Abby seemed a little cautious. "Only what McCloskey says, and he's been at the company since the days before Fanning took it over. Fanning came to Indianapolis from a little town in the East, evidently from an uneducated family. He made his own way selling Bibles." Mac nodded. Just what Fanning had told him at the cafe.

"He bought Purveyors from his cousin, an old man, when it served only the needs of Indianapolis restaurants and hotels. He's built it fast—some say too fast." His eyes were evasive.

"And?"

"The old timers say he married Alice to be his hostess, his social partner."

Mack nodded. "She seems to know the right courses to serve at the dinner parties he seems to feel it's important to have, the proper way to receive guests. There's a definite art to all that." He had seen the delicately engraved cards in the cardholder in the hall, had retired upstairs with Chad when the ladies of Over the Teacups Club came to call of an afternoon.

"Yes, and there are many proper guests to be received when you're up-and-coming in this town. How she got that way in a small town in Indiana I don't know. I only know she was married with a purpose." They began bedding down the horse for the night. "She is like, well, like the beauteous lady in her little tights who holds the ladder for the man on the flying trapeze in the circus. She steadies his climb, smiles all the time and watches to be sure he has no misstep."

"While he takes all the dangerous risks high above the tent."

"I suppose so," Abby said. Leaving the horse comfortable, they closed the stable door, bolted and locked it and headed towards the street. "Speaking of risks, are you going to French Lick? To the meeting of the Elite Poultry Purveyors Association? It's coming up in about three weeks, and it's the big event of the year."

"What does that meeting have to do with dangerous risks?"

"Some things it's better if an employee doesn't know," Abby said, and rolled his eyes. "Miss Farquharson isn't the only one who has big ears around here. The walls have 'em too. And if they could talk, especially about the Elite Poultry Purveyors Association—the paint would peel off 'em. You'll find out." He rolled his eyes comically, slapped Mack on the back, belched, and then sprinted for the streetcar stop.

"You are one hell of a smart-aleck seventeen-year-old kid," Mack yelled after him." They teach you that sort of stuff in the Debate Club?'

The next work week passed in a blur of letters dictated and mailed and carbon copies kept in the locked filing cabinet behind Miss Farquharson's desk. Mack left work early on Friday afternoon to catch up on some of the tutoring chores he'd missed during the week; Chad had been in bed with a slight cold, which his mother felt was always dangerous with his rheumatic heart. The boy seemed bored as Mack tried to take him through his sums, flashing cards with addition facts on them.

"I know," Mack finally said. "Let's take our adventure walk early. We'll go out and try to measure some things and maybe you can get excited about all this two-plus-two stuff that way."

Chad jumped down off the couch. "Yes, let's! Where shall we go?"He was already in the hall.

Mack stood up. "How about the Arsenal?" Chad shouted his affirmation and headed towards the door. "You can't get into it from our back yard and the Tenth Street gate is permanently locked, they say, these days, so we have to walk up to Michigan Street," Mack called.

"I know that, McClure," Chad said impatiently. "I live here." He was soon leading the way, walking rapidly up the street.

Well, it would be interesting to see, a place that piqued Mack's own curiosity. What would an Arsenal do in such peaceful times? Someone had told him it was really a fort, with a small garrison of soldiers. Were the soldiers bored being in a backwater of America guarding a bunch of old Civil War guns and documents?

They walked up West Drive to Michigan Street and turned west to stroll along the south edge of the grounds of the Arsenal. The stretch of lawn was idyllic, no doubt about that, with a small bandbox of a guardhouse set at the front gate. A guard patrolling the grounds out of the guardhouse was wearing one of the spiffy new khaki, choke collar five-button summer uniforms the U.S. Army had adopted lately. Some way these new soldiers didn't look right. Soldiers should wear either cross chest bands and tall dragoon hats or Civil War jackets and trousers of Federal blue with fatigue hats.

The guard, just turning on his heel, looked at them sideways as he passed. His eyes were slits of official decorum.

"He can't talk to us," Mack whispered. "I wonder if there are tours. We'll go up to that big armament storehouse to see." They walked past the guard toward a long building with a clock tower fronting it. It had a handsome drive-up porch in front where ammunition and armaments could be unloaded. But instead of following Mack into the building, formerly the Arsenal and now the administration building, so they could inquire about tours of the facility, Chad took off and then called him around to the far east side of the building.

"Nobody's around here," he said. "I've got an adventure idea. Let's take a tour on our own. Prowl around the grounds and see if the sentry will notice us."

"But we can't do that. This is a Federal facility, and even though it's kind of run down, still they don't allow—"

"Come on, McClure. You said adventure. I want to see if they'll catch us. Let's explore on our own. There are kids walking down the way anyway." It was true. On the far side of the field, groups of children were crossing the grounds, walking toward some little houses which he thought might be homes for married officers.

"Well, I guess we could walk a little." They walked past the commander's house through a grove of trees on the eastern, Woodruff Place side of the Arsenal, looking at the bright new fence with its black-painted pipe pickets surmounted by iron spikes. Mack held Chad up to measure one of the pikes.

"Seven feet tall," Chad said.

"Nobody's going to get through there," Mack murmured, setting him down. "Now why don't you tell me how much taller the fence is than you are—and than I am, too."

Chad figured on his fingers, then came up with the right sums. Mack tousled his hair and congratulated him.

"I watched them put the fence up last year," Chad said, as they walked further through the trees. "They tore the old boards down and burnt them up. It was the biggest bonfire."

"I bet," Mack said. He himself felt excitement at taking the chance of confronting the guards. It was an old familiar impulse to mischief, one left over from childhood. He couldn't remember when he hadn't felt it, the physical frustration at too-long lyceum meetings or Sunday School classes which combined with a pent-up anger at being confined. It resulted in things he'd gotten smacked for—the fat lady turned her back and Mack leaned out from behind her to make a face. The teacher went out for a minute; Mack put a toad in her lunch sack and then sat down looking innocent. And sister-teasing—he had refined that skill to an art which would do the Spanish torturers proud. So he understood Chad's impulses.

The grounds were a wide rectangle. Chad and Mack advanced from that large, dignified "arsenal" ammunition storage building which stood at the very south end of the grounds, sneaking through bushes as they walked about half its length. So far so good, but the dangerous part of the adventure had just begun. They had to cross the grounds in the open.

The guard had just started back south after having turned at the midpoint in the patrol grounds. The only other guard, who had begun from the opposite end of the grounds by Tenth Street, would soon march to that midpoint and turn, and Mack would have both of the guards' backs in sight. Mack and Chad could hurry, trot really, crosswise across the grounds and miss being seen if they chose just the right moment. "Hurry, follow me," Mack said.

They passed through trees behind a couple of frame buildings and then, before the sentries turned at the far ends of the grounds and began their walk back, streaked to the powder storage building.

Panting and laughing, they struggled to climb the tall mound which surrounded the old powder storage shed.

"You are trespassing on government property," said a cool voice. They paused on top of the containment mound, then looked down at an officer, a captain if Mack knew his military rank correctly, who had come out of the door of the shed just as they mounted it.

"We're sorry, sir," Mack said contritely. He meant it; he shouldn't have allowed Chad to be involved in this damned exercise in bravado.

The captain scrambled up the steps of the bunker and walked over to them, brushing his hands together to get off the dust of the shed. "I should put you in handcuffs and take you to the guardhouse," he said. He glared at Chad, whose eyes were as round as pie plates. "In fact," he said, putting his arm around Chad's shoulder and leading him down off the mound, "I'm going to do just that with you, young man. We've had too many of you youngsters walking around the grounds. This is a real armory, you know, even if we sometimes don't look like it." He turned to Mack and winked.

"Let's get going," he said with mock sternness. "I'm going to walk you right to the Tenth Street Gate." He snapped handcuffs on Chad's thin wrist and walked him towards the gate, albeit with a fatherly arm around his shoulder. The north guard, who had made one more pass and was returning to the middle of the armory lawn, met them on the path, gun over his shoulder.

"I saw children walking across, some with jump-ropes," Chad ventured in his own defense, looking up at the officer with more respect than fright.

"Yes, and two of them are mine. They're allowed to walk to and from school only." Mack looked up, at the row of houses across the street from the Arsenal, where the officer's family must have been quartered.

"Now here we are, and I'm going to unlock those cuffs," said the captain as they reached the ornate iron north gate which ran perpendicular to Pogue's Run Creek as it went out of the grounds. He took a key out and, picking up Chad's wrist, unlocked the cuffs. "Don't try any more funny stuff, all right?" This time he was looking seriously at Mack.

Mack saluted and, seeing the act, so did Chad. "I'll unlock the gate and let you out. Everyhing has to be locked up by sunset," the officer said, a little less gruffly.

"We always hear the boom when the sun sets," Chad said as they went through the gates. "And the clock tower chiming too."

"Try to respect the United States Army," the captain said, shutting the gate. "Remember what happened to Benedict Arnold."

"Who's Benedict Arnold?" Chad wanted to know as they rounded the corner into Woodruff Place.

"We'll talk about that another time," Mack told him ruefully.

But it was a week or two before he even ventured to mention the Arsenal. He was probably a little too old to play make-a-face-behind-the-fat-lady, he told himself, and besides there was plenty to do getting the business caught up for the anticipated meeting of the poultry association at French Lick. Miss Farquharson and McCloskey had been talking about it. They made it sound like the Chicago Exposition, complete with serious exhibits, honky-tonk entertainments and its own particular kind of freaks. If that were so, it was something to be looked forward to.

Chapter Four

Mack lay on his bed in the dark, listening to Mrs. Bascomb snore in small, grunt-like snorts. Her bedroom was on the third floor next to Mack's. It was a small room with a dormer, fixed up with bookshelves holding the dime novels she loved to read. Chad slept next to her, and their rooms connected through a little "stooping-down" door. Chad's bedroom had originally been intended as a clothes press for out-of-season woolens and furs, but it had a large window and served him well as a cozy bedroom, with the pictures of Sir Galahad and Captain Blood that he liked so well near his bed.

It half surprised him that Mrs. Bascomb could sleep so well on a night as hot as this. None of the rooms were unbearably hot after about eight o'clock at night, even in this midsummer heatwave, perhaps because of the huge tulip trees out back which shaded it from the hot afternoon sun. Still, it was smotheringly close tonight.

Mack lay on his bed in the dark, thinking about the week at work. After five weeks on the job, he felt as if he were finally gaining some sureness in the job, and Miss Farquharson had quit acting pained in his presence and taken him under her wing instead.

Mack was learning a good deal about the city from Mr. McCloskey's constant comments about the "leading families" and their doings. How the old bachelor picked up so much gossip about the personal and political doings of the city was not obvious—some of it was in the *Indianapolis Journal* but the juiciest tidbits weren't. The man chattered on to Miss Farquharson by the minute when Fanning wasn't around about the latest sensational divorce case or whose upstairs maid in Woodruff Place had quit because the Old Man had chased her around the bedroom. When Fanning was ensconced in the inner office with the door open, McCloskey sat in silence on his stool at the high order counter, shuffling and filing invoices for squab or capons. He treated Mack as if he were a coatrack, gesturing without looking up if he had something to say to him, but at least he wasn't hostile now.

Mack had been kept busy writing letters inviting members of the Elite Poultry Purveyors Association to the meeting next week in French

Lick. Each of these Midwesterners in the association, he found out, had his own territory. Elgin Whistel, who sent letters couched in Southern gentleman euphemisms, controlled the Southern Kentucky territory as far north as Columbus, Indiana; Bob Bertrand, who seemed to do whatever anyone wanted and came when they called like a dog, controlled an area east from Richmond, Indiana to Columbus, Ohio and encompassing all of western Ohio south to the river. B.J. McGonigal, whom he'd written to earlier, was "the Detroit area" and central Michigan.

When another member of the association, J. S. Sidlow was mentioned, Fanning's face grew dark and he dictated strong sentences, clearing his throat. Sidlow was the young man who had recently joined the association and had all of Illinois as a territory. He didn't seem to know his place. Fanning, of course, controlled by tradition some of the Chicago trade and all of northern Indiana and the rich resort area of southern Michigan.

He reviewed in his mind the lessons with Chad. They had gone well in the three weeks since they had explored the Arsenal. The three afternoons a week spent tutoring raced by, with Chad moving quickly through his sums, mostly successfully, so they could go to the oldest house in Woodruff Place, or the last section of the "Dark Woods" which preceded it, or a new and interesting notions shop on Michigan Street which featured handmade marionettes. Sometimes they just walked, going to buy chewing gum near the downtown and noting the animals they saw in a nature book they were keeping together.

Mack had eaten most of his lunches with Abby. He had grown to know the young man, and through him and his rambling stories, his family the Nessings. He hadn't had time to cross the street to see how Chiang was faring and, if truth be known, to satisfy his curiosity as to whether any suspects had been found in the Chinese murder. He searched the papers every couple of days, but the murder of a Chinaman seemed not to be of interest to the newspapers in the town.

Tonight he had read later than he'd expected to in the library and now he was ready for sleep. He sighed and rose to go down the back path one last time before he put on his pajamas. Quietly he slipped down the back stairs; Fanning was out as usual on whatever downtown night pursuits he sought. With exhaustion fraying the edges of his consciousness tonight, Mack did not particularly want to think about his employer's night life. It must have been almost midnight; Mrs. Bascomb's snorting snores had eased to gentle breathing.

After he finished in the outhouse, he walked about a little in the buzzing, heavy darkness, into a grove of trees. The stars looked muffled, far away tonight, as they did in winter. A sweet, exotic odor floated from bushes under one of the huge poplars. What was it? He walked closer, trying to identify the smell. Then, as he turned and looked back towards the path, he saw her. Alice. She was walking, almost gliding, in the light of the moon which had just slipped from behind shredded clouds. He retreated quickly into the shadows; for some silly reason he didn't want her to know he had been taking a privy trip. He would just wait here a moment until she stepped into the outhouse, then go back.

But no, she was turning in the opposite direction, over towards the south side of the garden, to a little gazebo nestled among bushes. She stooped, looking at the huge moonflower bushes which were unfolding shadowy trumpets to the sky. How beautiful she looked in the flowing gown—a black nightgown, with a peignoir over it. He felt ashamed, observing her in a private walk—she was leaving the garden, walking not back towards the house but towards him. She would pass within a few feet; he stepped back silently, further into the shadows.

Strange! He could see her face clearly in the dim light of the fading moon. Her eyes—they were vacant, except for some dimly automatic function that kept her from stumbling.

She was sleepwalking. It chilled him to see her so, draped in black, passing under trees and to the garden gate at the back of the property. She stood with her hand on the gate. For just a moment, she moved her hand slowly over the pickets, as if feeling their sharp shapes, then she slowly turned about and moved back up the path to the house with that gliding walk, like someone ice skating.

Then the back door swallowed her slim, darkened form, and he was left to enter and creep up the stairs alone. It was difficult to sleep the rest of the night, but at about four o'clock he fell into troubled dreams.

"Last night I was out for a trip to the comfort house and saw Mrs. Fanning. I believe she was sleepwalking," he muttered, stirring coffee at the breakfast table the next morning.

Mrs. Bascomb was dishing up eggs and ham for him.

"Y' don't say."

"Yes. She took a stroll around the garden, went to the gate, then returned into the house, all without seeming to see a thing. I—I watched from the shade of the trees."

"You like to watch the ladies runnin' around in their nightgowns?" Mrs. Bascomb asked dryly, then when she had let him suffer discomfort long enough, put her hands on her hips and lowered her voice.

"She sleepwalks every week or so. Slips out of bed when everybody's asleep and goes down those back stairs. Never falls, usually doesn't stay long. But sometimes she's out there for a couple of hours or so. At least she was about a month ago." She frowned. "That's the reason—one of the reasons—she sleeps on the third floor and he sleeps on the second, I guess."

He had put down his fork. "How so?"

"Mr. Fanning has to get a good night's sleep. He says a business-man must face the day refreshed and clear o' mind."

"So he never follows her or tries to wake her up or makes sure she isn't in danger?"

"They say 'tisn't good for sleepwalkers. I think he hopes it's just a phase. That if he lets her alone, she'll quit doin' it. Anyway, she's be-yond his control nowadays."

"How long has it been going on?"

"Ever since she had her lying-in with Chad. Or so the cleaning girl before this one told me. I just came two years ago."

He began to eat again, pouring syrup on his panfried cornmeal mush. Then he thought he'd change the subject. "Do you know any-thing about O'Shaughnessey's Gymnasium?"

"Well, that's where the young sports from Irish Hill hang out. They're impressed with Gentleman Jim Corbett and like to pretend they can fight like he does. Anyway, I do know O'Shaughnessey. I'm Catholic and he's in my parish. As honest a man as ever strode the streets." She took a few more slices of the crisp, sliced mush out of the pan and slipped them on his plate with a spatula. "What's it to you?"

"Well, I feel a little lethargic, and I thought I might drop over to the gym to try the manly sport." He smiled up at her engagingly. The mush was good, lacy with lots of butter, the way he liked it.

"Well, you could do worse than get to know the men of Irish Hill. They're buildin' this town, though small credit they get for it, I s'pose."

"Building it?"

"Sure they are! They furnish the bricks and set them, provide the tradesmen who do the plumbing for all the downtown hotels and even the new Monument. But to almost everybody, they're 'Micks.'"

"You have Irish blood?" he asked, smiling.

She sat down beside him. "That I do. But I have every kind of blood, includin' Indian. My pa and ma came up here from Nashville. Grandpa was a full-blooded Chickasaw and one of my other grandpas was black." She looked at him quickly, then away. "Mr. Fanning doesn't know it. Don't know what he'd do if he did. He isn't a bit broad minded."

He pushed the last piece of mush into the syrup and popped it into his mouth. "So I've noticed," he said, putting down his fork.

She stood and picked up his plate. "But then that's not much different from half the people in this town, the whole state, I mean. White Methodists or Presbyterians are the only true kind of folks. Not that I fault any of 'em. Just tryin' to get by, all of us, doin' whatever we can. Like Phil the Fiddler, or the hero in *Strive and Succeed*."

"Horatio Alger? I thought only boys read those."

"I read 'em. And what's more, I swear by 'em."

He stood up, brushed himself off, but did not make any attempt to leave the kitchen. "How did you get to be such a reader? Collect all those shelves of books? Must be a hundred up there." She looked at him with shrewd eyes. "Well," he apologized, I walked past your room when the door was open."

"Hey! I didn't learn to read in school, m'dear. Pa and Ma could never afford to send me to the subscription school and I had to make my start as a kitchen girl in one of those lovely old places on Meridian Street when I was ten. One of the first mansions built. 'Twas a different town then, I tell you. Cows on the Circle and a wheatfield not far away. Now all the big theaters and the newspaper buildin' and that Monument reaching up for all the world into the sky! When I see that big statue they got to put on the top of the monument and think about the cows and pigs that usta be—I think some fairy fae's come down and charmed us all. Progress! Whew!"

Mack smiled and poured himself a glass of water from a cut glass pitcher on the table.

A knock at the back door took Mrs. Bascomb away for a moment. Mack looked through the open back door into the beautiful early morning of the summer day. A girl of about ten with shining black ringlets stood nervously balancing on first one foot and then the other. Mrs. Bascomb seemed to be giving her instructions, then bent to kiss her on the top of the head.

"A beautiful little girl," Mack commented when the housekeeper returned to the kitchen.

"Elsbeth is my oldest. Margaret—Meggy is eight. My old man was killed when a brick wall fell on him. Sometimes I think he had the better lot." Her eyes clouded with sadness. "They have to stay with my sister. I see 'em on the weekends, when I can."

"The times seem to take women out of the home," he said sympathetically. "But—go on. Tell me how you came to be such an avid reader when you never went to school."

"I taught m'self to read when I was four. A woman Ma worked for had given her a basket of old books, and Ma was quite a reader herself. 'Twas was a book titled, *A Child's Guide to Courtesy* that caught my eye. I memorized it. It's served me well, sure enough, in the etiquette for all these fancy dinner parties." She stood at the big metal dishpan in the sink, staring into the distance, absently washing a plate.

He sipped coffee, then said, "Well, my study bribes have been a little tame lately. I think I'll take Chad for a special adventure today," he said.

"Livin' in this house is adventure enough for me," Mrs. Bascomb said.

"What do you mean?"

"Just life in general in the average American up-and-coming mansion. Wife sleepwalks and calls up the spirits from their graves. Child is often left by his mother while she goes to call up the spirits. And the father, the father, well enough said. When you're three sheets to the wind all the time the ship don't sail too well. And that don't even touch what goes on over there at the business. But I don't really see any of it. I don't want my eyes gettin' me fired."

Mack looked at her, questions framed in his own eyes that he didn't really want answered.

Mack had travelled to the downtown library the day before, so after he and Chad had done their sums, he brought out a children's book on China. It had words in large type and drawings of men wearing coolie hats planting rice shoots in a paddy. Chad was fascinated and spelled out the words with one finger, looking at the pictures of cormorants on ropes and the odd, tall boats.

"McClure, did you know any Chinese children when you were growing up?"

"Well, no. There were Indian children near us, but we didn't play with them." Actually, his parents had told him not to get too close to people who "weren't his kind."

"I'd like to know a real Chinaman."

"I have an idea," Mack told him. "Let's go meet a real family from China. I have a new friend up by your father's business. We'll do it to-morrow afternoon."

The next day, after Mack had finished work, they walked quickly the three-quarters of a mile to the small commercial district. Chiang had not been in the shop when Mack had dropped by in the morning, but he hoped he might have returned now.

Chiang's grandmother Mrs. Toy Gum was behind the counter sort-ing clothing, and he thought of her carrying the food offerings for the dead at the Chinese funeral. The death! What an odd town it was— only a month or so ago and people ignored the death. Even McCloskey wasn't talking about it. A Chinese murder. "We can't be expected to find out who shoots every dog in town," the people in town seemed to say.

Chiang, Mrs. Toy Gum said, in soft, broken English, was down-stairs. Then she yelled down the stairs in unexpectedly loud Chinese, and her grandson appeared in a minute bounding up the steps. Chad solemnly shook hands, his eyes wide at the strangeness of the place, the odd scents, the woman's slick, black hair and the look of clean, fine silk she wore.

Chiang walked with them up the block to Ashby's cafe, where they sat at one of the checkered-tablecloth tables with Chad, looking at the book about China.

"I came to America when I was five, but I remember these junks in the harbor at Canton," he said, pointing to one of the drawings. "They go up the river. Some have families on them, children, dogs, ducks," he told Chad, then to Mack, softly, "and other, not-so-good articles of trade—pipes and drugs to smoke."

Well, so he did admit they had opium pipes in China even if the Chinese never, ever, had them in Indianapolis. Mack turned the page and Chiang smiled softly. "Somehow these books all seem to make us cartoons," he said. "Rice, pointed hats, ducks. I keep trying to get my high school to teach Chinese history. In the T'ang Dynasty in the six hundreds, scholars travelled to Byzantium and scientists invented complicated clocks. Everyone in Rome, including the common people, wore the silk of Chinese merchants three hundred years after Christ. Mack, what is your cultural background?" He pronounced the words "coe-chrul background." But his English was very sharp, indeed. Abby's lessons were working.

Mack looked for the waitress with the bangs and hairbow who had waited on them when he was in the cafe before with Fanning. Mack, Chiang and Chad were the only ones in the cafe; she was cutting pie in the corner." I'm Scotch-Irish," Mack said.

"Your kings were living with cows in cold, drafty castles of stone in Scotland. Most of them couldn't read," Chiang told him, nodding seriously.

"Indianapolis High School must be a very good one," Mack said, the corners of his mouth turning down.

"It is, surely. But my education has come from the Old Grandmother, the woman you saw upstairs. She is my grandmother, mother of my uncle. And, of course, my father, who is dead."

Chad had gotten up and was looking at the pieces of pie in a glass counter case, eyeing them one by one. Mack had told him he could select a piece.

"And your uncle? What's he like?"

"Lee Huang is very smart. More than that I do not say." His eyes were veiled.

"I saw him march in the funeral parade, the night I came in," Mack ventured.

"He is the leader of the Chinese Association in town," Chiang said, then was silent.

After Chad had eaten half of a piece of pineapple pie, they returned to the laundry. Mack picked up his laundry, now spotless, starched and neatly boxed. He had come here twice with his pillowcase of clothing, and was pleased with the results. The Old Grandmother, Toy Gum, was nowhere to be seen.

Through the doorway, he saw the uncle Lee Huang, intently talking to two men at the rear of the laundry. One was a short tub of a man with greasy locks that fell in his face, while the other was taller, with thick spectacles. There was much gesturing, and Mack felt anger in the voices, though they were in a salty, foreign tongue. It seemed to be something Chiang did not wish Mack to see, because he ushered him and the boy out the front door and saw them half a block down the street before he turned to go to the laundry.

Later, Alice was upset. "You took Chad there? You took him to that place?"

"It was interesting. Chiang is a fine young man. He is an honor student at the high school and—" She stood before him, fire in her eyes.

"Mr. Scott. My husband believes you have made a fine start in the business. Your work with Chad is nothing short of miraculous, so far. He is a new boy, as far as his studies go. But you cannot take him to a Chinese place—" Her voice paused over the word Chinese with loathing.

"Of course I will obey your wishes," Mack said. "But I myself have no reason to shun it. It is a very good laundry." Something in him that he hadn't suspected existed rose at the hatred in her voice at the Chinese, the intolerance behind it. At least he thought it was intolerance. Perhaps he might have said something equally vehement against them once if they'd crossed him. But since knowing Chiang, liking him as a person and caring about his family, he couldn't shout out invective against Chiang's race. It would be too much like betrayal, the sort of thing a person doesn't allow to be said against a friend.

"I will do your laundry myself," she said through clenched teeth. "You don't know what they are like. Liars—they don't have any knowledge of what's right and wrong. Not a shred of an idea. Killers, sneaks—I hate them. No, never, never take my son over there again." And then she turned on her heel and was gone.

The ferocity obvious in the face of this usually gracious woman surprised and troubled him. Clearly it went beyond even the normal bigotry in this town.

Alice was herself again as the family shared an early evening ham and bean supper on trays in the family parlor. Fanning chit-chatted with Alice about the doings of the up-and-coming families in Indianapolis. William and May Fortune were visiting the Eli Lillys at Lake Wawasee, she said.

"Look, here in *The News*," she went on, pointing a finger at the folded paper on a table beside her. "A lawsuit's being brought against our neighbor Mr. Fortune. For receiving too much money raised from the public when he was in charge of the G.A.R. convention last year!"

"Fine state of things," Fanning harumphed, gesturing with a hand that contained a piece of cornbread. "Five thousand dollars was little enough for all that organizing of hotel rooms and parades, arranging meetings in Tomlinson Hall and putting up bunting for the old geezers. Put Indianapolis on the map, I tell you! But that editorial's no surprise! *The News* hates our Commercial Club and Fortune was one of the founders."

Mack looked up inquiringly at Fanning, hoping he'd say why.

Fanning obliged. "Says we're a bunch of snobs and elitists who scratch each other's backs. That Mr. Lilly controls the town and milks it like a cow. It isn't fair. The Commercial Club organized the food and rent distribution for all those Micks and colored folks out of work last year."

"Walter visited some of the homes of the poor in the colored district for the Commercial Club," Alice said evenly, as she took up her fork.

"Bunch of little nigger pickaninnies standing around in a room the size of a closet with bare feet in the middle of November," Fanning grunted. "Eating parched corn out of a pot."

Mrs. Bascomb came to take the trays and Fanning searched his cigar box for the proper smoke. Chad watched bicycles and buggies go by outside the window, and Mack observed children with poles pushing hoops down the street through the gathering twilight.

Privileged youngsters these indeed! Fine cotton blouses, sailor hats on the boys' heads, satin ribbons in the girls' hair which flew behind them as they ran. And not a care in the world as the flowers bloomed and birds sang in the pecan and copper beech trees along the esplanade. He could not help thinking of the people in that box-shack that Fanning had described. Yes, and of long hours the people at the Chinese laundry worked, and of the relatives of the man who had been murdered across town from them in some sort of gang murder nobody seemed to care about.

Fanning intruded on his thoughts. "Scott, will you drive the rig for Mrs. Fanning? She is going to her meeting in Lockerbie neighborhood tonight."

Mack nodded affirmation. This is what everyone had been telling him. Finally, they were to test the spirits and see if they were receptive.

"Do you believe in contact with those who have gone to the world beyond, Mr. Scott?" The last rays of the August skies had faded to deep purple and orange in the west, and they drove along, watching the sunset through tattered shreds of clouds.

"No, I guess I don't," Mack said. "I was brought up to believe that Jesus taught we go on to live beyond this plane of experience in his many mansions. He doesn't say anything about coming back to haunt the people left behind in the miserable shacks on earth."

"Haunt—it's not like that. The Bible also talks about the reappearance of Samuel to Saul. And Moses and Esaias appeared to the Lord on the Mount of Transfiguration."

"So they did. I've never figured that out. Maybe it was a special appearance for that night only." He didn't mean to be flippant, but really, all this hoot and holler about ectoplasmic manifestations, and mediums who can hear on clear channels to the other world wore on him. When he thought about it, it made the other side sound like a true bore. Evidently the only kick anybody in the Great Beyond ever got was standing in line to send a message to Grandson Harry about where the keys to the strongbox were. Didn't they have anything better to do on the streets of gold near the Heavenly Throne than peek through the clouds at the bumbling mortals in the "lower plane?" Stupid, that's what it was. But he said, "Well, I'm always open to changing my mind if the facts warrant it."

The knocker on the door of the newly-painted, three-story house was an angel. Bad choice: angels didn't talk through mediums, they shouted news with trumpets. There he was again, being flip.

The woman who answered the door was tall and svelte, with a wide-toothed smile. She did not wear a turban like mediums in the newspaper cartoons, but a fashionable sea green gown with pearls sewn into the skirt.

"Mrs. Teitelbaum, this is Mr. Scott. He is accompanying me tonight," Alice said, nodding her head towards Mack.

They moved down the hall over an expensive oriental rug. Lining the hall were small tables loaded with sculptures from abroad: Mercury wearing a little hat with wings, women of alabaster dancing on one foot and pointing at unseen birds, naked slaves from Africa. "Is Mr. Scott a believer in the power of our friends beyond?" she asked.

"I'm not a believer, but not a denier either. I suspend judgment and have come with my mind open. After all, I'm a guest," Mack said.

"Well, that's all we need, my dear," Mrs. Teitelbaum said. The fingers on her hand, resting on his shoulder as they entered the parlor, were covered with ruby and emerald rings.

An odd little assemblage sat around in the drawing room: an old Civil War veteran wearing a tight blue uniform, two or three wide-eyed young matrons, a striking, fashionable woman of about forty with her hair piled high and a veil pulled over part of her face, and a dwarf in a perfectly tailored little herringbone suit and smoking a cigar. Mrs. Teitelbaum introduced Mack, touching everyone on the arm in a rather grand way.

"Shall we get down to our evening's session, my friends?" she asked, and all nodded eagerly. A man servant appeared at the door, and she nodded to him. In a moment the gaslights dimmed, fading to a dim aura. Mrs. Teitelbaum stood before one of the lights, her eyes glowing. "Mr. Svenson," she said, addressing the dwarf, "as always, we will have to ask you to put out your cigar. The atmosphere must be pure." The servant, a nervous, effeminate young man with flowing mustachios and hair parted in the middle, opened a window and went about with a peacock fan, ventilating.

"Now a few words of explanation for the two of you who are new." She nodded to Mack and the Civil War vet. "This is not a public entertainment. It is what I think of as a religious experience. We are contacting those who have gone on to the Fields of Summer. Some of you here are Christian; I am Jewish. The Fields of Summer or the eternal side of our endless life, we are told by our contacts, is a blissful place, filled with love and governed by the religious leaders of each faith. Thus Jesus is there for Christians and Abraham for Jews, Buddha and Mohammed for their followers. You have probably read a good deal about spiritualism, and not all of what you read is favorable."

Here she stopped and looked at Mack. How did she know? He had read newspaper exposés for four or five years now; it was, in fact, a favorite subject of his. Reporters who went to the spiritualist meetings and found hidden devices which talked or secret doors or platforms through which hired "spirits" could appear—detectives who discovered that the spirit was really the medium disguised—all of these interested him. Still—there were the stories about how a lady named Florence Cook had actually "materialized" a pirate's daughter over and over again in England. Mrs. Cook was found to be present and asleep herself when the spirit was there, many times, so she couldn't have been acting the part. These happenings weren't explained, but he was sure they could be. Still, he had promised to be open-minded.

"I do not materialize those on the other side. Neither do I go into the cabinet which others use. My medium's gift is the use of the spirit voice. Everything is open and above board. I'll ask you to sit around the dining room table. I will sit at the end of the room in an armchair, alone, and we will dim the lights almost off. Then we will see what we will see tonight."

"It wasn't as I thought at all," Mack said to Abby the next day. "There was something appealing about it, almost sad, and I felt sorry for the people reaching out to find out if their relatives had survived, if there could be hope beyond the grave."

"Well, Aunt Erna has a tender heart. No doubt about that," Abby replied. Mrs. Teitelbaum was not really his aunt, but a dear friend of his mother's, who discovered she had the gift about ten years before. "What were the manifestations—isn't that what you call 'em?"

They were sitting in back of the livery barn after work, eating a second lunch.

"The dwarf had a brief message from the prioress of some convent in Bohemia, seems to be his guardian spirit and has spoken to him before. Told him to be brave, that his troubles were known on the other side. I had the feeling he was there to try to get some meaning, acceptance of his lot in life. But there were just two real manifestations of any length on this evening," Mack went on, crumpling the paper his sandwiches had been packed in. "They said that was pretty good. Anyway, there was a young woman with a high pompadour, veiled up so people wouldn't know who she was, and I guess she wanted to reach her dead child."

"Yes, they often come for that. It's sad. I wish so many children didn't die so young. Doctors ought to do something about that."

"It's better than it used to be. Smallpox vaccinations and all that. Anyway, this child died last year, at the age of eight, and the mother has never been at peace. So we were all quiet for quite a while and Mrs. Teitelbaum seemed to be asleep there in her chair but finally her voice spoke up, sounding odd, like a child's I must say, and said 'Mummy, don't grieve because you let me out to play in the creek at Grandpap's farm when Pa didn't want me to. I didn't catch pneumonia because of that, but I had inherited lung weakness and tubercles had invaded my lungs, though you didn't know of it. I'm happy here and will meet you someday.'"

"Hmm. Well, she could have found all that stuff about the little boy's death out from anyone."

"Girl's. It was a girl. Well, no, the woman said later that they didn't know the cause of the child's death, though she had been a little poorly over the winter. A sudden chill."

"Anybody else?" Abby wanted to know. The day was cloudy; they were both scanning the dark gray skies for signs of rain.

"The Civil War veteran thing was interesting. This man said he hadn't told Mrs. Teitelbaum one thing about why he was there. But after a while she spoke again. 'Someone who used to live in Illinois is here,' she said. 'Wishes to speak to an old war comrade.' And the old man in a shaky voice spoke up. 'Could be me,' he said. 'Ask the name.'

"The voice said he was Lemuel, something like that. 'Lemcool?' the vet asked. Then he got excited."

Abby took out two new early blush apples and offered one to Mack, urging him to go on with the story. A Chinese family was going into the laundry across the way; it reminded Mack he needed to take over more laundry he'd brought in a pillowcase to the office. He wasn't going to take Alice's suggestion that he stay away from the laundry. It would make him feel even more like he was betraying a friend. And anyway, it was his own business what he did with his dirty undershirts.

Abby was looking at him, expecting more of the story. "The voice told the oddest story, but it sounded realistic, actually," he went on. "This Lemcool manifestation—I guess you call it—said he remembered they had been in Tennessee, couldn't name the regiment, something about lead—and the old man intruded, saying he had been in a regiment from Galena, Illinois, mostly lead miners. The others told him to be quiet. Anyway, the voice kept saying 'lost dispatch, lost dispatch, as you thought.' The veteran was rather agitated, until the voice told his comrade to be at peace, that he was at peace about the war, that they had an organization of Confederate and Union veterans on the other side."

"Oh, of a certainty. We're tenting tonight near the Throne of Grace," Abby said, walking to the oil drum that served as a trash container in back of the office building.

Mack walked with him. "I know, that sounded really silly. But after the séance, the veteran told us that they were fighting in the Ft. Donelson campaign at someplace called Erin's Hollow, a really obscure little battle. They had been ordered to advance and take a position. Meanwhile, in the time since the orders had been issued, an enemy Confederate Irish regiment from Tennessee rushed in to occupy the rifle pits above them. The Northern colonel was in a quandary; should he obey the order now that the enemy was firmly entrenched? It would be suicide, so the old man said. The colonel sent his adjutant asking the general to rescind the order to attack—but no new orders came back. He waited fifteen minutes, then sent the men in. The old man's cousin and best friend, Lemcool was his name, was killed in the useless attack."

"You're saying that in some way the spirits were confirming that the adjutant got lost."

"Yes, thus being responsible for the loss of about twenty men, including the spirit who spoke. So it seemed."

"But Mrs. Teitelbaum could have gotten that information from someone who knew the old veteran was coming to the séance."

"You're right as rain, and I thought the same thing, though it seems a little specific for anyone to talk about much," Mack said, finally tossing the apple core away into the bushes. Then, again, he spoke. "The oddest thing of all was the way Mrs. Fanning behaved herself." Abby looked at him with one eyebrow raised.

"Yes, she sat silent through the three visitations, and when Mrs. Teitelbaum sank deeper in her sleep, speaking no more and those around the table seemed to sense that the séance was about to end, Mrs. Fanning gave a little cry. 'Nothing for me tonight? Nothing from the spirits? Shall I never have my answer?' And then she regained her composure. And all the way home she did not speak, seemingly sunk in despair."

Abby looked at him with wonder.

"What kind of place have I come to?" Mack asked. "All sorts of weird things go on in that house—with both husband and wife," but Abby had no answer.

What Mack did not tell Abby, because he didn't think it was his business, was that after taking Alice Fanning last night to the séance, after sitting near enough to her that her elbow touched his and feeling himself shiver, he had gone on his noon-hour to O'Shaughnessey's gymnasium. There he took up boxing gloves and went into the ring to spar, hugging and sweating and pounding his partner until the owner, Ray O'Shaughnessey came over and quietly told him to take it easy, this was not a blood feud or a fight to the finish. Still, he had come to work in the afternoon feeling eased, as if he had dropped a burden of contending emotions.

The next day as Mack came to work early, at about seven o'clock, and approached the office building, policemen came around the corner from Tenth Street, and a hearse approached the building from the other direction. Following them, Mack proceeded quickly across the street. There he found Chiang and his grandmother wringing their hands and weeping on the step of the Chinese laundry. Chiang's uncle Lee Huang had been killed, stabbed sometime in the night, apparently, in the shack where he slept in the back alley, and the unknown assailants had gotten away clean. Mack stood watching the covered body being taken into the hearse, the investigators for the police department, and the sad family. He soon was aware that Fanning had come up behind them.

"And so the tongs are at work again," Fanning said, in the same soft voice he had used the day Mack had come to Indianapolis.

Chapter Five

"It took two Chinamen dead for the police to know that the tongs are active in Indian-no place," Abby said, leaning his head back against a crocheted doily in the Nessing home. He and Mack were drinking cold tea and eating oatmeal cookies.

"Their view is that it takes two Chinamen to equal one white man, so that's why they finally noticed," Nate Nessing told them scornfully.

This police clerk brother of Abby had come in excitedly in the midst of Mack's Sunday afternoon visit to the Nessing house with the news that he was going to be allowed to work on the Chinese murders. He'd begged for a chance to do a real police investigation instead of typing and filing and working with the payroll.

"Rossi is going to be the investigator-in-charge, but I'm to do the field work."

Mack put down his tea glass. "Rossi?"

"Sergeant Eduardo Rossi. He's a huge lump of a cop who lives and breathes police work. His parents were among the first to come over from Italy. They came from New York to the south side of Indianapolis. He was born here. He likes me, says I remind him of his dead younger brother. He's letting me develop the portfolio of evidence for him." Nate's mother and Aunt Sophie nodded with satisfaction. Jews in the city had to work harder than others to get equal job opportunities, but those opportunities usually came eventually. Maybe Rossi felt kinship with Nate, too, because they both came from the "outsiders" groups.

"And I—we—" Abby looked questioningly at Mack—"will be your assistants." Mack gave a confirming nod. "Sherlock Holmes needs Doctor Watson—and his friend in this case." Abby sat up a little straighter, pointing a finger at his brother. "What evidence do we have in the first murder, that of Li Ting?"

Nate flipped through the pages of a little brown notebook, bound in lightweight leather. "I went down last week, to the area around—well, actually around the Indiana Poultry Purveyors' plant over by the river, before the second murder. Interviewing four Chinese families and one Negro neighbor who knew Li Ting, I found out that he and his wife had come to Indianapolis from San Francisco by way of Chicago about three years ago. They were brought as children from China to the Golden Gate city." He was looking at a notation. "Both the husband and wife worked for the old man, Mr. Pollock, in Lockerbie neighborhood. She was the cook, he the grounds keeper and liveryman. They were friends of the old woman Toy Gum at the laundry; she was the food bearer at the funeral and her son Lee Huang was the chief mourner."

"Did Li Ting have any enemies?" Mack asked, caught up in the excitement of the investigation. He could well recall the stolid, grim look on the mourners' faces that night. What secret knowledge did they have as they marched in that parade? "And what in the world are the tongs that everybody keeps talking about?" he asked.

Nate pursed his lips and moved forward a little in his chair. "Tong is a word that really just means association, or grouping."

"Chiang said his uncle Lee Huang was head of the Chinese Association here. Is that a tong?"

"Well, he was head of the benevolent association which provides funeral money for burying here in America or China, helps indigent Chinese and so forth. That kind of association is still around, but it's an old-fashioned form of the groups they had in China. Today's tongs or gangs actually grew out of old benevolent associations of thirty years ago. The Chinese had good reasons for getting together to take care of each other in San Francisco, and the association did important things for them, including bringing in wives. The word tong wasn't used then."

"So these tongs are an American-Chinese innovation?" Mack wanted to know.

Nate was a nervous, intense man. He smoked, against his mother's wishes. He took out a cigarette case made of wood and extricated a ready-made cigarette. "Tongs are an American product in their present form. But they did exist in China as secret societies. The Chinese have had brotherhoods of various sorts through many dynasties."

"Well, who hasn't?" Abby said, rising with an empty cookie plate. He headed for the kitchen and his voice trailed behind him. "Jews in Germany formed their own groups and here Germans get together in the Turner gymnasium classes, and ladies form things like the Irvington Literary Club."

"Well, but the difference is that in China these groups had philosophical and religious and strong political ties behind them. And, they were secret and sometimes dangerous," Nate said.

"How so?" Mack wondered.

"Well, take the Society of Heaven and Earth, a famous one, for instance. It was a part of the movement which led to the Taiping Rebellion of the 1850s. It rose at the height of the opium wars, when the Manchu Dynasty was selling Chinese society down the river to the English and other Europeans who wanted to practice the opium trade."

"I remember studying it in World History class," Abby said, returning to sit cross-legged on the floor. "And—didn't it almost succeed? The Taiping Rebellion, I mean?"

"Yes. The Taipings were a religious horde—even had some Christian influence—marching against injustice and the evils of the Manchus. You could call them a tong if you really stretched the word. They took over the city of Nanking and then, like lots of fanatical movements, their efforts turned into a bloodbath against anyone they thought was impure, a tool of the evil emperors."

"Sounds like the French Revolution," Mack said. He recalled that from his high school classes, though he had never heard of any of this Chinese history. Whoever studied Asians? The sound of a piano tinkling came from the other room. Aunt Sophie was playing "Jeannie with the Light Brown Hair," and Mrs. Nessing was humming along.

"Well, it was a good deal like that. At any rate there were mass executions and anger that lasted well beyond the revolt, when it was finally over."

Abby was back and squatted on the floor with the cookie plate in front of him. "Some of the people of the revolt time came to America."

His brother nodded. "Bringing their old hostilities and hatreds with them. And their experience with associations. And eventually these benevolent associations became vicious and self-serving tongs—more like the secret societies they'd left behind in China. And in some ways the tongs preserve the old splits in the China left behind."

"The Chinese are treated like doormats here," Mack said. As were the Indians in Traverse City. The Chippewa were somebody to hate for many people whose jobs and images of themselves were threatened. Why had he never thought about it when he was growing up? Probably because it was accepted. "Stay away from those who aren't your own kind."

"Yes," Nate told him, "but it wasn't always so when this country was newer. When the Chinese first came to America, they were welcomed. California was a raw place then which needed laborers to mine the gold fields and build railroads to join the west coast with the east. You remember the Golden Spike which sealed the joining of the east and west branches of the transcontinental railroad. The Chinamen built both branches. There were lots of strange people out there anyway, so the Chinese didn't stand out. But soon the situation changed. So they tell me."

"You're in their confidence, over in the Chinese neighborhood?"

"Well, I saved twin sons of one of the families from going to jail under false charges. And I've made a study of the Chinese here, even before the first murder. Abby has become well acquainted with the family of Lee Huang, and Chiang's often at Mother's house. I like Chiang and he's got a bright future. Or did—" His face clouded.

"This murder puts him in a bad light?"

"Well, being caught up in a tong war—if that's what's happening—is not something that you want your friend to be involved in."

"How would Lee Huang—or the first man, Li Ting, be caught up in these tongs?" Abby wanted to know.

"Almost all of the Chinese have found themselves involved with tongs in the last twenty years. The newspapers are full of all the intrigues. In San Francisco, when the citizens became more suspicious of the tongs, about twenty years ago, the Chinese really began to withdraw from society. They pressured all their own Chinese brothers to join one tong or another, demanding that they pay protection money if they didn't come along."

Mack looked out the window at the rain, which had begun early this morning, when he had driven the carriage for the Fannings to Central Avenue Church. "But—don't the old benevolent associations still exist? Lee Huang was known as head of one."

"I think the word 'association' is just a convenient word for tong in Lee Huang's case. The tongs have taken over the old associations' work of fixing up marriages and arranging for funerals and the like. So that part of the picture is true. But mostly they are an underground police force and just as rotten as they can be. Extortion is their game. They go around to businesses and demand that shopkeepers pay money to further good relations with the Chinese community. They import slave girls—there aren't enough marriageable girls in Chinatown to go around—and imprison them in brothels, which dooms them for life. The tongs' occupation is the ruining of lives, and we—the police department—can't get them. Not many in the department even try." His two hands, the small, delicate hands of an artist, were slightly clenched.

The brothers' mother, Mrs. Nessing, had come back to the door and was listening. "How terrible," she murmured.

"There are terrible vendetta wars among the several tongs in San Francisco, wars over territory, the slave-girl trade and, most of all—" he stopped what he was saying to pantomime the smoking of a pipe.

"Opium," Abby said.

"Yes. It's a rampant addiction among Chinamen, both in China and now here."

"Western society has to take the credit for most of that, I think," Mrs. Nessing said. "Didn't it say in *Harper's Weekly*—the last issue I think—that the English encouraged the opium trade so their wealthy entrepreneurs could build English businesses?"

"The evils of it are awful, and the tong involves itself in every aspect of the opium trade."

"Here in Indianapolis, too?" Mack continued to watch Nate's hands. Everything he said was accompanied by graceful gesturing as if he were drawing a picture. He seemed to be a passionate man, intensely affected by injustices. Would that serve him well in police work?

"We have tongs—in a limited form. They've spread from the West Coast to New York, Chicago and smaller towns in the last few years. They fight each other, sending hatchet men around to get even with whoever they think has insulted them or broken the unwritten laws."

"Hatchet. They could have caused the death of the first Chinaman here, Li Ting, couldn't they?" Abby asked.

"Some of the Chinamen here may have been involved in battles over terrain in the opium trade or vendetta murders. That's what I'm trying to find out," his brother answered. "I need to get information from inside. The one man I know, from the family whose sons were unjustly accused, is afraid. Probably he should be if the tongs are involved. He tells me he won't say more."

"Chiang could help," Abby said, rising from the floor to stretch his cramped muscles.

"Yes, I think he could. But I can't just go over there and burst in on a family in mourning. The old grandmother must be grieving terribly. Someone told me this is her last son."

"What happened to the others?" Mrs. Nessing asked from the doorway.

"Lee Huang was the youngest," Nate said. "The oldest was killed as a young man, thirty years ago, in the last phases of the Taiping Revolt. And the second one, Chiang's father, died of typhoid in California, along with his wife, Chiang's mother."

"Nate," Abby said suddenly, "I need to talk to Chiang about the Debate Club. You could come with me. You've met him a couple of times anyway."

"Abby and I should pay our condolences," Mack added. "Perhaps take him out for a luncheon, get his mind off the trouble."

Then he excused himself; he needed to get back to give Chad a makeup lesson and prepare to be part of the Fanning family group again at Sunday evening supper.

Mrs. Nessing accompanied him to the door. "And how was your church service this morning, Mr. Scott?" she asked with her wide smile.

"Being at the Central Avenue Methodist Church is like being in a Catholic cathedral in Europe—or possibly in the midst of the setting of a Medieval drama. Everything is so opulent, rich."

They stood at the door a moment. Mrs. Nessing held it open and leaned against the edge. "And the message?"

"Today the senior minister, Dr. Clayborne, gave the sermon. It was on acquisitiveness."

"And was Mr. Fanning listening?" The smile grew even broader. Fanning's ambitious nature, and probably his late-night dissipations, were well known around town.

"He was asleep, as he usually is. Or at least dozing. But he had been out late at the Pleasure Palace last night. Anyway, I was dozing too. Clayborne's not nearly as interesting or intense as the associate minister, Brockelhurst. He's the one who fascinates me. Anyway, it was a long hour."

"Well, you can always go to temple with us."

"I couldn't give up my Saturday," he answered with a frank smile. "Sunday—the day we have to go worship—isn't nearly as good a day to have free as Saturday, when you're visiting the temple. So—" He shook her hand and started out the door smiling and singing the popular tune, 'You go to your church and I'll go to mine.' "

She completed it " 'But let's walk along together.' Come back soon, Mr. Scott. How about next Sunday? Since it's a lost day anyway?"

He laughed and put on his straw boater. "Well, business before pleasure. I'm going to the meeting of the Elite Poultry Purveyors' Association in French Lick. Abby too. Hasn't he told you? Mr. Fanning, Abby and I are taking the train down, and then Abby'll drive and run errands at the convention."

"But registration for school is the end of this next week."

"He'll tell you—I understand he's already asked his principal if he could register early."

"It's important for him to make a good start to the school year," she complained, shaking her head a little. And, as he turned to go down the walk, "Do I understand that you have been communing with the spirits? My dear friend Erna Teitelbaum tells me you were a respectful sitter at the last séance."

"Yes, but there were no messages for me," he called back to her.

"Just wait. It's my understanding that if you go enough eventually there will be one for you."

As he rode the streetcar home, he wondered how long Alice Fanning had been waiting for her message. And just what it was that she wanted so desperately from the spirits.

Chad was listless, even felt a little feverish later that evening. He sat in the library in a chair wrapped in a light quilt and being fretted over by the Fannings during the Sunday night supper. After Mrs. Bascomb came in from her weekend with her children, they sent her upstairs to put Chad to bed. Alice followed to read a story, then turned out the light. The boy could be heard all the way downstairs coughing and gasping for breath until finally he fell asleep.

That night Alice Fanning walked again, this time through the dark night down the back path as he watched, sleepless, from the hall dormer window at the back of the third floor. To his surprise she did not pause near the bushes and turn into the garden area, as she had done before, but went instead to the garden gate and unlatched it, passing through and into the abandoned alley. He crept downstairs and softly opened the screen door and went to the gazebo. Where had she gone? He and Chad had seen the new pike fence at the Arsenal. She couldn't have passed through that; there was no gate. Was she walking along the alleyway? He did not think he should go to the back garden gate— what if she should appear and awaken suddenly and see him there? He sat on the dewy garden seat, staring apprehensively through the trees into the murky grounds of the Arsenal.

Finally about a half an hour later, she came to the gate. Still walking with that strange, gliding step, she unlatched the gate and passed through, up the garden path and into the house. Quickly he returned to his bedroom. Where had she been? Had anyone along the alleyway or in one of the houses seen her?

When he still could not sleep he went to the comfort house, carrying a small lamp. As he returned, something in the flickering light caught his eye. He stooped to pick up a bright, enameled flower button. It was from that beautiful black peignoir she had been wearing. He supposed from the sleeping arrangements in the house no man had admired it for many months, if not years. How he envied the opportunity this stupid man who was her husband had, and was too dense, or coarse, or dissolute, to appreciate.

He put the button in his pocket and did not return it to the ironing room, but instead put it in his own small chest of drawers.

The next morning Mrs. Bascomb was dusting the family parlor early. She had set cold breakfast on the sideboard for the family.

"How did the weekend go with Maggie and Elsbeth?" Mack asked, while she feather-dusted a piece of French porcelain, a courtier dallying with a lady in a swing.

"Ah, affairs are a pretty mess at the cottage," she said. "I came in early last night to avoid all the hullabaloo there. M' sister's on the nest again and cryin' about it all the time. And Michael her husband was drinkin'."

"Does he get wild?" Mack wondered about the two children Mrs. Bascomb had to leave there.

"Just sits and nurses a bottle in the back room until he falls off the chair. He was released from the boiler plant last week. Times are bad."

She left the room and he followed her. "They depend on m' salary. But," she turned to him, "Father at Our Lady of Lourdes says that the girls can be enrolled in the new school this fall." Mack nodded encouragingly.

"There's better times a-comin" she said cheerily. "The young ones must learn to read and do sums. Maybe type like you. There's an old Irish saying, 'Give the child a shovel, you have set him on the path to daily bread. Give the child a book, you have set him on the path to power.' "

They walked into the kitchen, where soup for noon dinner was cooking. "Last night Mrs. Fanning walked again, for about a half hour. Now that's the second time," Mack said.

Mrs. Bascomb went to the pot, stirred it slowly. "Not the second—since you've been here. She walked last Friday night too. I was wakeful, came down the stairs behind her, slow, so she didn't see. She was out a good hour and a half—till just before dawn. I saw her disappear behind the coach house, up that alley."

Mack walked to the stove, looked her full in the face.

"You didn't hear her this time?" he asked.

"No, nothing at all. A half an hour this time did you say? Up the alley?" she asked. He nodded affirmation.

"What'll it all come to?" Mrs. Bascomb asked. He shook his head silently, not knowing the answer to her question.

Abby came into the office on Tuesday as Mack was sending out telegrams explaining the schedule to the members of the association for the meeting beginning Friday.

"Join us after work to go the laundry," Abby said. "Nate wants us both to come with him to talk to Chiang and especially to Mrs. Toy Gum, the Old Grandmother about the murder. They've invited us all to take tea together this afternoon, a little more like a social hour. Oh—and I'm ready to go on the trip to French Lick. I'm missing all of the registration meetings at school. Mother had a cat fit over it, but finally she's come round and even thinks it will be interesting for me."

"Four o'clock all right for our meeting with Chiang? I get off then."

"More like four-thirty. That's when they thought they could break from the laundry for a while." Abby shot a pencil stub from a rubber band toward the broad posterior of McCloskey, who sat on his high stool, with his head down over a drawer of files. When McCloskey turned around to see what the irritant had been, Abby was already halfway out the door.

"When do we have to be at French Lick on Friday?" Abby asked as they stood outside on the stoop.

"We board the Monon train in the morning early. Fanning has some private meetings and you have to hire a rig."

"Do you know what it's like at a spa? Will we take the waters?" Abby was watching McCloskey through the window. He admitted to being fascinated by the old bachelor, who seemed to be devoid of all human graces. It was a game with him to try to engage McCloskey in some sort of conversation, to prove that he was not a windup doll, as he seemed to be. But to no avail.

Mack pulled him back from the window. "I don't know about you, but I'll probably be too busy to dip myself in a bunch of smelly sulfuric water."

"It's good for what ails you, so they say. And the place is pretty, down near the knob hills in Southern Indiana. Here—Mother got this advertisement in the mail." Mack scanned the slick-paper brochure which Abby handed to him and read:

> *Nestled in the Hoosier hills, carpeted with green velvet*
> *grass, robed in the emerald of historic oaks and beeches and*
> *maples, domed with the azure of a semi tropical sky, this*
> *notable virgin spot like a bride in her wedding splendor,*
> *stands kissing her hands in welcome.*

"Actually sounds pretty attractive, with all those virgins kissing their hands to us," Mack said.

"I like the part about semitropical. It has turned awfully chilly for the first of September."

"It'll be better by the end of the week. Maybe the hand-kissing virgins will warm it up anyway." He leered meaningfully at Abby.

"You've been spending too much time looking at the girlie calendars at O'Shaughnessey's gymnasium."

How'd he know? Mack had only been there twice, but there *were* more types of girlie calendars and more pink flesh on one table in the corner than Mack ever knew existed. Abby waved as he headed for the barn, waddling delicately in an exact imitation of McCloskey.

Cold, sleeting rain began as they entered the dark gloom of the Chinese laundry. It was quiet, tomb-like, with only the ghosts of soap smells and starch behind the counter. Chinese mourning custom was that no work would be observed for a week.

"I've never been in their living quarters," Abby murmured as they climbed the stairs behind Chiang. The laundry was a false-front building one-room wide: the family quarters had a kitchen on the back end with windows facing the alley, bedrooms in front of the kitchen, and dining room and parlor beyond them overlooking the street.

The grandmother, Mrs. Toy Gum, met them at the top of the steps, bowed from the waist, then shuffled sideways, pointing towards the living room. They sat on ornate Chinese chairs with winged dragons and fish carved into the dark woodwork of their backs. China vases as big as a man decorated the corners.

"Where did they get those?" Mack wondered, nodding at the vases as Mrs. Toy Gum and Chiang went to the kitchen to get the tea.

"There are shops in Chicago which sell nothing but Chinese things," Nate whispered. "They must have ordered these down on the train, or perhaps they brought them from Chicago."

The grandmother reappeared, carrying a dark wood tray, Chiang behind her with store tea cookies on a saucer. They drank small cups of steaming green tea, served by the much-bowing old woman, who nodded her head frequently, like a bird.

"Mrs. Toy Gum," Nate said to the old woman, "we regret having to intrude on your life at this time of sadness. To have your son killed and be the one to find him is a good deal to bear."

The old woman, seeming to demur, looked up at them animatedly and spoke rapidly, waving her hands, and Chiang translated. "She says you are indeed courteous to mention it, but the mourning period will soon come to an end. It is fitting to proceed to life's duties with a spirit of acceptance." The guests nodded. She went on in a sharp, strong voice, in Chinese, Chiang trying to keep up. "It is also fitting that the killers of her son be found, because justice must be served. Justice is a solemn god, she says, and yet he balances right and wrong as two balls in the air, like a palace juggler. Her son must pay the price after this life if he has done wrong, if the black ball comes to the hand of the juggler of justice. But those who took his life must also pay their price. That is the Eternal Way."

Mrs. Toy Gum sat on the edge of her chair, in the way of an extremely energetic person who had only a few minutes to waste on conversation. Abby had told them earlier that it was she who had really run the affairs of the laundry.

"Now let me see if I have the facts straight as you recall them, Ma'am," Nate said, nodding deferentially. "To do that we will need to go to the rear of the apartment. Can we walk back?"

They all went to the kitchen and looked out the one tall window into the back lot.

"Two dependency buildings," Mack murmured, looking out at an old, two-story wooden barn and a rectangular shed with a crooked chimney crawling out of the upper side.

"Yes. According to the first investigators' reports made when they were called to the scene, those are the old summer kitchens for this building, used so primarily when it was a restaurant and now serving as a washhouse, and the storage building, an old livery barn built to accommodate one horse. Is that right, Chiang?"

"Yes. My uncle was found in the washhouse building. The Old One woke me up before dawn; the police didn't get here until about seven o'clock. Well, you know. I saw you watching us."

Mack nodded, embarrassed. He had intruded that morning into a moment of private grief by staring like a spectator at a baseball game.

"Grandmother was up about five-thirty to draw water and make the fires for the day's work, and she went to the building, where Uncle was found stabbed," Chiang said.

Nate wrote in his book, "He was lying on a cot, I believe."

Chiang translated for his grandmother. "Yes, she says, he often took dream repose in the washhouse. But he was still warm when she found him. Poor, poor son, she says. As if the spirit had just fled, and she had just missed it to say goodbye." Here Mack saw she had a tear in the corner of her eye.

Nate cleared his throat, consulting his notebook. "So someone must have come into the alley about four o'clock, the report says, since the body signs showed he was recently dead, and entered the building while Lee Huang was asleep and stabbed him before he was aware of them. There are, let's see, three more buildings beyond yours until we get to Fourteenth Street, then in the opposite direction, two long blocks to Tenth Street, a major thoroughfare. Just before dawn the killer came from some direction—which is unknown. All the streets are patrolled heavily these days east, south and west of the area where the murder occurred."

"Is that unusual?" Mack wanted to know.

"There have been cat burglars out committing robberies for several months in the elegant residential areas, College Corners, Woodruff Place—well, all the way out to Irvington. The citizens have demanded increased police protection and five officers have been added to the night beat."

Mack and Abby both nodded. "And nothing unusual was seen, according to Sergeant Rossi. The only real thoroughfares beside Tenth Street, are Massachusetts Avenue on the north and Michigan on the south side of this neighborhood. The murderer would have to have been on foot or in a buggy because the first streetcars don't even start up until six. And no buggy, not one, was seen from three until after dawn. Baskerville, the patrolling officer is sure of that."

"Couldn't someone in the neighborhood have done this? Does it have to be a suspicious—a suspect I mean—coming in? Or how about the train?" Chiang wanted to know.

"Very few people actually live in this business district," Nate said. "It's like a little island of commerce cut off by the streets and Pogue's Run Creek. I've checked train schedules and there was no train from midnight until six o'clock that night. No, the killer came on foot but not down one of the thoroughfares."

"It's like a Chinese maze on paper, with all escape routes blocked off," Chiang said, shaking his head.

They returned to the parlor of the upstairs living quarters.

"What do you know about the Chee Kong tong, Mrs. Toy Gum?" Nate asked as they settled themselves again on the dark wooden chairs.

Chiang looked intently at Nate for a minute, as if he didn't wish to translate this, but, sighing, he did. A vigorous conversation, with a lot of hand waving and exclamations, followed.

Chiang sighed again, then began to try to translate what she had said. "She say her boy had nothing to do with tong. Tong is bad demons come to earth. They swoop down on innocent people like hawks taking chickens from the pen. They live on other side of town, come to shop sometimes and she shoo them away. No, Uncle was not a tong member, she say, she cannot believe that. He was victim of his dream-pipe repose, made less than a man by it." She went on for a sentence or two, then shut her mouth with finality and Chiang, too, stopped.

"If we look to find that connection—of the dream repose, she insists," he said with obvious reluctance, "we will find who killed my uncle. That is all she wish to say."

She stood, politely bowing to each, and left the room. They also stood, then set the tea things on the tray and descended the steps, without Chiang.

Nate excused himself to walk around to the back washhouse. Mack and Abby stood in front of the shop on the board sidewalk, waiting for him. They watched Miss Farquharson exit the Indiana Purveyors' office, followed by McCloskey, who carefully locked the door before following the lady down the street.

When Nate joined Mack and Abby, they walked up Newman towards Tenth Street, Mack to go the Fanning lodgings in Woodruff Place, the two brothers to catch a car home.

"Dream repose—how could his sleep get him into trouble?" Mack asked.

Abby kicked sycamore leaves shaped like large, green hands as they walked. "They're falling early this year," he muttered, then in a louder voice, "Dream repose is an opium trance. That's their way of saying he was an opium eater. That's why Chiang was so reluctant to translate some of that stuff. He hates to admit his uncle was an opium addict."

"Slept on that couch, the neighbors say, almost every night. The heat from the washing pots kept him warm in winter," Nate added.

"He had a five-pipe-a-day habit," Abby went on. "That's the word around the police department, isn't it?" He looked at Nate, who nodded confirmation.

"Is she right about the tongs? That he had no connection with them?" Mack wanted to know.

Nate took a cigarette out of his vest pocket and searched for a match. "She is a mother. Like all of them she refuses to face the truth," he said. "My contact in the Chinese community on the other side of town—the one whose sons I helped—"

"How'd you meet him anyway?" Mack interrupted.

"In the workingman's library downtown. Anyway, I spoke to him yesterday, and he was a little more willing to answer questions—a few of them. He laughs when I called them a benevolent association. Yes, he says, Lee Huang was a tong member, nobody's denying that. But not of the Chee Kongs. Lee Huang was a leader of the Progressive, Pure-hearted Brotherhood—the Hip Sings—the rival group, strong in this city. Had been for many years, since he lived in San Francisco."

"Rival tong? Everybody's heard of the Chee Kong. I had even heard of them in my little town in Michigan. But Hip Sings?"

"There are two tongs here. Chee Kong is the older, more traditional, Hip Sing the upstart, younger group. The Hip Sings are strong in Chicago, too," Nate said.

"Are there other Hip Sing members here in town?" Mack wanted to know. "It seems so odd, Chinese secret societies here among these cornfields in Indiana."

"Several members. The tongs spread like poison plants, laterally. They establish a dirty little clump in a big city, and that clump takes root, then spreads, sending out a side runner in a smaller town. And a runner from that plant goes into another, nearby town. They don't have to be big groups to do damage."

They reached the little bridge over the creek, Pogue's Run, where Mack stood each day to watch the water ripples as he passed to and from work; Nate tossed a used cigarette butt into the water, then lit another smoke.

"What did you find in the washhouse?" Mack wanted to know. Nate had wanted to go it alone back there; after all, he was part of an official investigation, and they were just guests of the Chinese family, brought along to smooth the call of the arm of the law.

"I found cold boilers, empty wash pots and cots, three of them along the wall."

"Three?" Abby sounded surprised.

"And a well beaten-down path from the back door. There was no opium paraphernalia in the shed, no, that had obviously been removed or locked up by Mrs. Toy Gum or whoever wanted to take away the signs of a dope den."

Nate's cigarette smoke stood on the heavy air like cow's breath on a cold morning. "But in the weeds to the side of the shed were over twenty vials and the oozy black plug of opium they burn to get the smoke going. And three rubber pallets. No, this was not a solitary dreamer. Far from it. Lee Huang was running an opium den, and if the Chee Kong tong was on the other, rival, side of the fence, the killing was about opium, surely. That has to be it."

They started walking and reached Tenth Street. Mack paused at the streetcar stop, still talking. "How will you find out about the tong opium trade here in the city? It's all so secret."

"Yes," Nate said soberly. "Not even the best investigators in the department can crack that nut, assuming, of course, that they really want to. Well, that'll be my job this week. The autopsy is due in at the end of the week, and we'll know the hour of death. He was stabbed, but we need to confirm if opium was in the body. Then we'll put out feelers. My friend from the reading room has told me all he knows, or cares to. I need to dig to find out a little more about the Hip Sings—the Progressive Pure-hearted Brotherhood."

"Which seems in this case to be about as far from progressive and pure-hearted as you can get," Abby said. The street car lumbered up and they lurched onto its side steps, then jolted off, Mack waving goodbye.

Chad was shuffling schoolbooks and papers by the light of the electric lamp in the family parlor before supper, trying to get in the mood to study. "We need to get ahead in your studies, since I'll be gone for the weekend," Mack told his young student firmly. He would be tutoring only twice a week once school started. Chad was going to be part of his second grade class this year; every day Mrs. Bascomb would deposit him at the school door and pick him up at one o'clock because he would still need to sleep in the afternoon. The extra tutoring would help him keep up.

"We haven't had our adventure this week," Chad complained, scribbling in his penmanship tablet. He seemed better, though he was still coughing. "I liked the one outdoors at the Arsenal."

"So did I. But—we might have gotten into real trouble. They could have shot us, you know."

"That's what made it a good adventure," Chad said, looking up with a little smile on his face. Mack looked at him as he returned to making the round O's on the page, the long shock of blond hair in his eyes and the light of the new lamp, with its shade, casting shadows on his face. What would his future be in this dark house with troubled parents?

"Always adventure. Sounds like someone I know," he said.

"What do you mean?" Chad asked, searching Mack's face. This was a child who always wanted to know people's motivations.

"Well, I always felt itchy as a child and young man. Just couldn't sit still and couldn't stand the long hours in school."

"I'm that way too. That's why I hate being sick sometimes. All those covers and flannel poultices on your chest."

"After my second year in high school I just left my home and went out to the lumber camps in the woods to cut trees."

"Wow! Those huge trees. We have stereopticon slides of them. Did you stand on log piles six feet tall by the river like in my picture?"

"That I did. Almost got killed when the logs shifted. My mother and father hated it, forbade me to go in the first place. But I went anyway. Something in me would have exploded if I'd stayed." Why was he telling the boy? Perhaps he felt some identification, at least with the restless part of Chad.

It had been a life of the strongest physical work in the world. He was a meringue puff now, compared to the shape he'd been in then. The physical inertness of the days at the office told; his muscles were soft, and his stomach was getting flabby. Well, he could walk a lot at French Lick, beneath the "emerald oaks" and across the velvet grass. He could also go work out at O'Shaughnessey's. Yes, that would be good. He felt like a steam engine building a head a lot these days. Being in the same house with a radiantly beautiful woman who attracted him without meaning to every time she rustled through a room was driving him berserk.

Sending Chad out to see the livery boy groom the horse, he sat reading a magazine and looking through the door to the kitchen where he could catch glimpses of Alice, listen to the cadences of her voice.

That night, supper was jolly, with Fanning livelier than usual, joshing with Chad and Mack. "You can see that business is not all of my life," he said to Alice, after telling a funny story about dogs in the circus, and she nodded almost imperceptibly. Fanning's smile faded. Had he expected a response? Alice usually seemed to tolerate him in the house as the father of the child and her lawful spouse, playing an expected role as if she were on the stage of the English theatre. And obviously they argued a lot; that was probably why she cried at night. She often had a distracted quality about her; was she thinking of the spiritualist meetings? Fanning rose abruptly, and as he looked for his driving gloves to go out for the evening, he asked Mack if the telegrams had been sent to all the members of the association and was glad for confirmation that they had been. His brisk spirits returned, obviously stimulated by the thought of the weekend to come; a horse at the starting gate, leaning into the wind and ready to start the race in the Age of Progress. Ever more progress!

At a little past midnight Mack awoke to the sound of voices, unusual in this third-floor retreat under the eaves. There was a slurry, animated man's voice down the hall—surely it was Fanning's. The tones were beguiling, wheedling, pleading, chillingly so. He couldn't quite make out the words. Then, a sharp "No, no! I won't! We've been through all this!" and a sort of scuffling sound, a creaking of the bed, muffled woman's cries and grunting of a man—it made his hair stand on end. What in the name of God was going on in there? And, finally, a huge thump as someone seemed to crash to the floor, light feet running in the hall, then down the steps and the turning of a lock somewhere on the first floor, slamming of a door and the lock again.

And, at last, as he lay there, sheet up to his chin in absolute fixated fascination, he heard the slow lumbering of a man's footsteps along the hall and down the steps. Then, again, the odd pregnant silence which seemed to possess this house during the dark hours of the night. God! At least he didn't seem to be pursuing her! For an instant he wanted to rise from the bed, follow that drunk reprobate and beat the absolute hell out of him. Leave the house. No, he couldn't do that. Not at all. These strange sad people had tied him into the cat's cradle that was their lives. There was Chad. Chad, depending on him, for attention, for help in making his life normal. And downstairs locked away from her husband in the butler's pantry, Alice. Alice. Her name sounded in his mind like a bell clapper against porcelain. He sighed and spent the next few moments listening for more frightening sounds, which never came.

What he heard, sharp and poignant in the still night, was the cry of the boy who had been awakened by it all, dry coughing echoing through the halls like small shotgun reports, and the cooing sound of Mrs. Bascomb comforting Chad, waiting with him until the half-asleep coughing eased. Mack could hear her at last padding down the hall to her own bedroom.

A few moments afterwards, as he tried to relax his mind enough so it would lose its hold on troubled consciousness, he was startled by a shape standing by the bed. It was Chad.

"McClure, could I sleep in your bed for a while? I'm afraid."

"Crawl in, pal o'mine," Mack whispered, pushing himself against the wall so there would be room.

"There were awful noises in Mama's room. I thought someone was trying to kill her."

"No, not kill her. It was your father. Maybe he had too much to drink."

"Oh." There was silence for a moment, broken by the creak of the bedsprings as the boy shifted, trying to get comfortable in his little space. Mack could feel his bony legs against his own.

"I hate it when he does that. At times like that I wish he wasn't my father."

Mack patted his shoulder. Some truths, he told himself, could be said in the dark that couldn't be voiced in the daylight.

The group from Indiana Poultry Purveyors walked to the livery stable from the railroad station at French Lick, and soon had a rig hired. It was Friday at about noon, and Fanning was again his animated self, after several nights of being gone until almost dawn and days of listless, distant behavior after the third-floor incident. But this morning he had seemed fully recovered; he pointed out things along the road towards the French Lick Resort for his two apprentices. "There, is the big plea-sure palace—Brown's. You can take up a hand of cards, play the wheel, whatever strikes your fancy." The way his eyes lit up, it was plain many of the pleasures would strike his.

They came to French Lick Springs resort in the heart of town, nestled, as the brochure had said, among hills that rose around it. They saw a park of newly planted trees, round beds of freshly bright yellow chrysanthemums and Dusty Miller. "What's it remind me of, I wonder?" Mack said aloud as he watched the large winged hotel come into view at the end of a winding drive.

"Sort of like the Prince of Wales Brighton Palace in England," Abby said. "Round turrets, little dormers and cupolas—looks like a se-raglio." Fanning surprised them with a loud, hee-hawing kind of laugh at the comment.

Mack, Abby and Fanning put their grips in two rooms upstairs, walking through long, winding halls that never seemed to end. They settled into clean, carpeted bedrooms taller than they were wide but neatly furnished.

Fanning emerged from his room soon, straightening his tie for the preliminary meeting with B.J. McGonigal of the Detroit District.

"Get your notebook, Scott," he said. Abby was to unpack the bags in Fanning's room and stand by to take both men for a drive after lunch. Mack and Abby were to eat in the servants' lodgings, though Fanning had not insisted they sleep out there.

The day was a perfect early September day. The rain and cold of the last few days had passed through, replaced by fresh-washed air with cotton clouds against a deep blue sky. McGonigal, Fanning and Mack strolled towards a gazebo near the Persephone spring. "This is one of the biggest health spas in North America. They call the big spring Pluto—Pluto water comes from it. It's a real purgative," McGonigal said. He was a balding man with what had once been a slim physique, still small hips and legs but rolls of fat coming over his belt, the sign of a good life with plenty of his own fowls, Mack thought. Beads of sweat stood on McGonigal's temples from the bright sun.

They sat in the gazebo covering the Pluto Water spring, watching couples strolling on pea gravel paths through the grounds. Behind them, forest-clad hills were etched beneath banks of rolling clouds and a cobalt-blue sky.

"Wasn't this place built by a Copperhead?" McGonigal wanted to know.

"Call him a Southern sympathizer," Fanning said. "Bowles, the founder of the Knights of the Golden Circle. He was persecuted by Lincoln during the treason trials at the end of the Civil War and thrown into prison, but he got out." Southern sympathizer—that wasn't the way his dad, the Civil War veteran, talked about the Knights. They were a bunch of draft evaders and traitors, Mack thought. Anyhow the place was pretty enough.

"After Bowles' death, investors bought the place." Fanning said. He was pulling off his tie, mopping his handsome face. "Don't know what the investors sank into it, but I don't see how it'll return anything."

"The concierge said they were planning a hall for bowling and billiards," McGonigal commented.

"Good, good," Fanning said, distractedly. He had a small valise with papers in it; the ones Mack had prepared for the meeting. "Now I want complete notes of this conversation, Scott," he said, pointing a pencil at Mack. "Typed up and put in the locked file. But there are to be no carbons. Understand me?"

"Perfectly, Mr. Fanning," Mack said. He sat on the far side of the gazebo. Across from him Fanning and McGonigal leaned over their knees, talking in low tones to each other, as if someone might be listening in the yew bushes beyond the gazebo. Notes had to be taken quickly in shorthand, and as his pencil raced, Mack's mind was trying to sort out the gist of it all: Sidlow in Chicago was extending his territory too much, even after the warning. The exact nature of his transgressions in the poultry area were stipulated and the geographic area he was involved in.

It was the Illinois River valley around the river town of Henry where he was practising duplicity; he had lined up two fine duck hunters to get the best of canvasbacks from Lake Senechwine and the river by Henry and they were supplying scores, hundreds of ducks to—no, not the Palmer House, but to three other first-class hotels.

McGonigal's words, though whispered, were precisely enunicated. "Now tell us exactly how you know this, Walt. We must document everything, because he is breaking the agreement clearly." Heat rose from the bushes, steaming up from the loamy soil wetted by recent rains.

"This could be unpleasant," McGongal went on, pulling at the stiff collar around his neck. He picked up a fan left in the gazebo and inscribed, "Bead's Funeral Home, French Lick. In your hour of need, think of Bead," and began fanning himself.

"I have my spies over in Chicago. The night has eyes, if you're willing to pay to open them," Fanning said. "And I am. There's over $5,000 a year in sales in that Chicago area. It's mine!"

The sweat on McGonigal's forehead was dripping down the end of his nose. He slid his rear end into the filtered shade of one of the "emerald robed" historic oaks near the gazebo. "Walter, this really affects you, so to speak, more than it does me or say, Whistel or Bertrand. After all Chicago is your territory. Now why don't we just talk to Elgin Bertrand."

"Bertrand is a nincompoop. He has the spine of an amoeba."

"Amoeba," wrote Mack, then turned the pencil upside down and erased it out carefully, marvelling at the crassness of the conversation. It was absurd; he was involving himself in the operations of a shady cartel. But he was an employee and needed to stay one for a while.

Fanning was scratching his mustache, studying the situation. "It's the principle of the thing, B.J. You know that. If we are going to have an agreement, an association, nobody can get greedy. We need to plan each area, take just what the traffic will bear, set the prices—"

"Well, yes. And that presents a small problem of course, nothing to really worry about, I suppose." McGonigal's voice had taken on a nervous edge.

"Now, B.J. you aren't worried about restraint of trade, are you? Don't ride that dead horse. The Sherman Anti-trust Act isn't being enforced, you know that. They've buried it with all the talk about the robber barons."

"Well, they had buried it," he responded. "But this is a Democrat administration. Restraint of trade is against the law, you know."

Mack watched McGonigal diffidently shifting his weight on the wooden seat. There certainly was more intensity in this discussion than he'd expected.

"It's just that I sometimes feel like I'm sneaking around," Mc-Gonigal said. "My wife's a member of the Christian Daily Life Committee at our church and—"

Fanning exploded. "What in the hell do you think this has to do with Christianity, B.J.? I guess I'm as good a Christian as any other man's son." He pointed a cigar he'd just taken out of his pocket. "Free trade is a Christian principle. And just what the hell does the Christian Daily Life Committee have to say?"

McGonigal turned and spoke in a hushed voice, though there was nobody to hear except a few squirrels. They both seemed to have forgotten Mack. "Well, just that when we get together this way and set the prices, then the customers have to pay a lot more for the produce we distribute. Sometimes prices are a lot higher."

"Oh—I—see," Fanning said, lighting and puffing the cigar into life at the same time he spoke. "We are cheating the fancy dining room at the English Hotel in Indianapolis. I regret Mr. English's loss, poor old millionaire. We are denying the McCormicks and Swifts in Chicago the right to less expensive pheasant." Fanning quickly flicked away a large ash. "McGonigal, you must see how silly this argument is."

"It's the principle of the thing, as you just said. Somebody has to suffer when the prices are set and secret trade agreements organized. Usually it's the merchant in between or the poor laborer. That's what Eloise says."

Fanning looked at his cigar and then stubbed it out. "What kind of a man are you anyway, letting your wife push you around like a worm on the sidewalk? A man has to be a man, and believe you me it's that way around my household. The new women may be emerging but there are ways to keep 'em in line. Now get this straight, B.J. I'm expecting you to back me up on this. We hold our position firmly. Nobody deviates or breaks. And church is for Sunday. All right?"

McGonigal sighed, and they both began walking back towards the hotel. Mack picked up his pencil and pad and followed behind. Finally Fanning thought of him and turned around. "Scott, you didn't need to get all of that down. Just brotherly talk, you understand. I trust you to stick to business."

"Of course, Mr. Fanning. I wouldn't—well, yes."

The Bertrand who had been described as a mealymouthed amoeba came in, rolling his head back to look in an impressed way at the cavernous ceiling of the lobby.

Whistel, from the Louisville District, had arrived by the time they had all finished a cold beef and salad lunch on the porch of the hotel. He was a florid, white-haired man with a sun-wrinkled face. They had a sandwich made for him, then Abby drove them around while they talked about the business. By three that afternoon the others had arrived, and they all—Fanning, McGonigal, Bertrand and Whistel—decided to take the waters.

"Scott, I want you with us," Fanning boomed at him in the hall outside the hotel room door. "Business occurs in the bath as well as at the desk."

"Do we—Mr. Fanning—that is, do we wear our bathing attire?"

Fanning whooped again, sounding like a bird heard across the water. "Well, you don't think we're going in stark naked do you?"

"Well, the bellboy said they sometimes do." He did have a bathhouse suit, made of wool. He had worn it in Lake Michigan, where the wool felt good. As he wrapped it in a towel and headed for the bathhouse, he thought angrily that this was the stupidest situation he had ever been in, bathing in stinking sulfur water with a bunch of people who had created an illegal monopoly and who justified it as the height of the American way, who treated him like a rag rug under their feet. He had to make mealymouthed replies when they said absolutely ridiculous things that made him want to shout out, calling them orifices of the posterior of the body for the stupidities they were uttering.

He wished he had Fanning and McGonigal and even Whistel in the gym at O'Shaughnessey's where he could paste them. He felt the steam engine firing up again, an overwhelming urge to bloody Fanning's nose. Then he looked at the cobalt sky. If only he were out in the woods, skidding logs where everything was simple. He pounded one fist against the other. It struck him that the head of steam he was generating was connected with Alice Fanning and what had happened in the third floor maiden lady quarters the other night. "Keepin' them in line" apparently had few limits, just as in the case of this cartel. When you were behind closed doors, on the third floor in Woodruff Place, it could include forced marital relations and who knew what else.

Colored men in white coats passed out glasses of Pluto Water. "Now suh, you're s'posed to take the waters on the inside while you soak in 'em on the outside," a smiling server told the group from the associaiton.

"But Rastus," Bertrand said, looking out of the pool as he stood in the water up to his shoulders, "what are we going to do if the waters we're putting *inside* us agitate and want to get *outside* us all at once? That's the name of the game, ain't it?"

He was evidently trying to make a little joke. Maybe he knew they thought of him as a one-celled microscopic animal.

"Well, suh, you just come to the side of the pool as fast as you can, and I'll help you to the room where you can get what's *inside* you *outside*. It ain't far!"

They floated in the water, whose sulfurous depths sent clouds of hot, reeking steam into the air; talking in soft murmurs. Mack caught snatches—"Brown's gaming tables," "women whose charms are displayed for all to see," "trade growing at a 20% rate each year." There seemed to be nothing for him to take down in the way of secretarial notes, and when he emerged after an hour, he felt like a bored, simmered prune.

Dinner was formal; he was not invited, but that was fine with him. It was to be ceremonial anyway; the group was gathered by the mahogany doors in cutaways at seven o'clock to enter the candle-lit dining room, where the strains of an orchestra could be heard. He saw them as he passed to the help's dining room, where he ate overcooked cabbage and beef with Abby.

"They're meeting tonight in the Rose Room to discuss this year's fortunes and the allocation of territory," Mack told him.

"Then tomorrow I take the ones who want to go on a morning ride around town," Abby said "and then they finish with the big, future planning meeting at one o'clock."

Mack nodded, trying to ignore the rumblings in his stomach, which was overtaxed by Pluto water and cabbage. He had been told to be on tap in a timely fashion in the Rose Room off the grand salon after the group took supper. Actually, he was looking forward to it. How would this odd agglomeration of personalities who had taken on the monumental task of controlling the destinies of the fancy fowl of the Midwest act when they got together? It could shake the world, at least as it was known in Hoosierdom.

And later, there they were at nine o'clock, stoop-shouldered men who had eaten too much rich food and drunk too much brandy in the dining room, hovering over a huge map on the richly carved table. The brass electric chandelier with its bulbs in imitation candle holders glared above them. Mack stood in the corner of the room, ready with his notebook. He was avoiding the brightness of these bare incandescent bulbs which seemed to scream, "Wake up. This is the Age of Progress." Well, it was almost too much of a good thing. Gaslight was really more flattering and pleasant.

Anyway, B.J. McGonigal was pointing at Michigan with a fat, ringed finger and looking at Fanning. "It's the Grand Rapids area I'm talking about. There are four new hotels there built by the lumber barons. Bifflo & Shields and the Petoskey Hunters Association have bought the land and begun construction on summer resorts and you aren't even aware of it, Walt. They pick up people from the train lines, take them to these elegant resorts in the northwoods. They should be eating our fowl up there." His eyes glinted with greed; he seemed to have forgotten his wife's admonitions.

"I know about it," Fanning told him loftily. "It's just that my territory is a little far-flung. And anyway, they seem to be able to get local fowl."

"They'll go with us because we're bonded and reliable. Some of those local pigeons make people sick. Now— this is what I've been talking about all evening. We need to redraw the lines there. Let me pick up G.R. and you, Walt, stop at Saginaw. After all, we let Whistel get the Ohio River hotels from Bertrand."

"Grand Rapids has been one of my prime areas," Fanning said, shaking his head uncertainly, unwilling to let such a rich plum go. After some low, bargaining talk he demurred, calling Mack over to record the changes in the map.

There was other discussion about prime selling towns, a good deal of jockeying around. The meeting, Mack observed, had the restrained, male competitiveness, bravado and mock hostility of a lumber camp poker match, which Mack had learned to keep away from when he'd had his stint in the camps. Finishing his draft of the new territorial arrangements, Mack drew some lines north of Saginaw, Michigan, and across the bottom of the page near Cincinnati and began to take the sheet around to the members of the cartel. Then as he presented it to McGonigal, he noticed something. Someone was missing.

"Where is Sidlow?" Mack asked McGonigal. "From the Chicago district? He came in late I know but where—"

"He was at dinner," McGonigal said coolly, "but he left. I assumed he would be joining us." He took a plug of tobacco out of his cutaway pocket and bit off a chew, pulling a cuspidor to him with his foot. "There was, actually, a bit of a disagreement between him and Mr. Fanning."

At that moment, the double French doors at the entrance to the room burst open. A tall man, handsomely dressed in a black cutaway with a scarlet red cravat came through the doors. He took white gloves off and threw them on the table.

"Well, I'm here, gentlemen, to represent my Illinois interests," he said, with irony in his voice.

"Very well, sir, very well," Whistel said, approaching him with a nervous smile. "Business is business after all."

"Yes it is indeed," Sidlow said, coming to the map of "territories" that Mack had put on the table. "Now let me see, we'll just write the name Jesse Sidlow right here across Chicago. All fine poultry sales to Sidlow and Company, suppliers to all fine hotels and no exceptions." He looked at Mack. "Will you write that, please, mister secretary?"

Fanning cleared his throat, a deep guttural growl that seemed as much a warning as a prelude to speech. "Now Sid, we fought this all through at supper and you know I have absolutely no intention of surrendering my part of the territory I have worked six years to build up"—he looked disdainfully at the gloves on the table—"to someone as new as you to the business."

Sidlow looked around at all of them. "New I am, but in the year I've been there I have made my way by day and night labor. I supply all the secondary hotels in Chicago because my product is good, unfailingly, and I have built my contacts personally with the hunting clubs in the Illinois valley. They prefer to deal with me." There was a stolid, unyielding silence. Every man around the table stared straight ahead.

"It cannot be, Sid. We have a gentleman's agreement here," Fanning said, looking him straight in the eye.

Sidlow stared at him. "Gentlemen! A bunch of small-time monopolists in a stinking waterhole in the midst of cornfields acting as if they are John D. Rockefeller and Andrew Carnegie! I went to school with the poor children of Chicago, sirs! I cut my teeth in the steel mills, gentlemen! And I am tired of the duplicity, the fear of the government, the buying off, or cutting off of enemies—"

Fanning strode away from the table and came to stand directly in front of him. He was almost as tall as Sidlow and every bit as angry. "Now you listen to me. You were taken into this association knowing that we operate to control trade. You signed a document of trade appropriation. Our lawyers believe the government will not punish us for restraint of commerce."

"Not yet—" Sidlow said scornfully.

"It will not occur. We have cultivated our political friends too carefully to let that happen."

Whistel attempted to put a hand on Sidlow's exquisitely cut coat. "It's an efficient system, sir, bringing good products to everybody without the cutthroat—"

"Cutthroat competition that reduces prices and lets the public buy things fairly," Sidlow angrily interrupted.

Fanning's face had grown dark. The guttural growl was now as sharp as the rasping of a saw. "Listen to me. You will not do this. Stay within the bounds of the cartel and honor your agreement or—"

Sidlow gave Fanning the slightest of pushes and drew himself up in confrontation. "Or you will have your Chinese hatchetmen come after me in Chicago the way they did the last man to fight you?"

The group in the room stood absolutely transfixed. Sidlow took up the gloves and slapped Fanning across the face, then purposefully strode out of the room, his long legs covering the space over the rose rug in less than ten seconds.

Chapter Six

"Chinese hatchetmen," Abby repeated, as they sat watching the countryside go by on the Monon line just outside French Lick. He repeated it again, staring at Fanning's back bouncing along ahead of them. Fanning was reading a copy of the *Police Gazette* and nursing a headache gained at late-night gambling at Brown's casino which had followed the Saturday association future planning session. Sidlow, of course, had not been present.

"It might explain the mysterious connections with the laundry," Mack said. "But I don't see how."

"As long as I've been there—about a year—Fanning hurries by on the other side of the street when he passes the laundry," Abby told him.

"And I saw Lee Huang's expression when he caught sight of Fanning—midway between fear and hatred. Could the hatchetman Fanning's supposed to have hired be Lee Huang? If somebody did end up killed as a result of what Fanning ordered, do we have a murder in Chicago too last year? Maybe Fanning and Lee Huang have both been suspicious the other would talk. Evidently the police don't know about this. I can't believe Alice Fanning does either."

"Well, Sidlow might have invented the whole thing in his anger, for effect. How did the others react?"

"With what I'd call dismay. Not because Fanning was being accused of having stopped the competition with hatchetmen, but that Sidlow knew and broadcast it. Nobody was really denying that Fanning went after the competition in Chicago. They probably accepted it as part of protecting free trade. John D. Rockefeller has been doing as much or worse every month of the year, after all. The meeting broke up soon after that."

They were silent, looking at the people in front of them, a mother and two children with a picnic hamper. The mother seemed tired, pushing toys at the children.

"I can't make heads or tails of it all, "Abby said, "but Fanning's clearly in trouble with the Chinese community, more than knee-deep."

He fell silent for a moment, then said, "I keep wondering if Nate's nosed onto something by now on Li Ting and Lee Huang's killings."

Up ahead Fanning slumped down into his seat, the newspaper over his head like a pup tent. For the moment, at least, he looked defeated, but Mack thought it was only an illusion. "The first thing I want to do the minute we get back is talk to your brother. See how that police investigation is going," Mack said.

They were silent a minute. The boy and girl in front of them had spilled marbles under the seat and were crawling around, laughing and pinching each other. Mack began speaking again.

"What did you say?" Abby wanted to know over the noise.

Mack put his hand rather severely on the boy's wide collar and told both of the children to return to their own seats. "I said I had somehow hoped I'd get to visit my relatives a couple of counties over in Southern Indiana. Shouldn't have pinned hopes on it. We were busy all the time."

"It was a time of frustration for several of us," Abby said, looking ahead at Fanning. "He didn't get his way this time."

"Frustration? Will Sidlow really leave the cartel for good? Fanning will surely do something strong to stop that."

"I don't think slapping a man's face with gloves 'll result in a duel in 1895 do you? Especially for that group of pot-bellies. Brandies at fifty paces?" Abby raised his imaginary glass to the cows in the countryside.

"I don't know," Mack said. "If Sidlow preempts the territory and leaves the cartel, there could be trouble." A long minute passed before he said, "And if there's any truth to what Sidlow said about Chicago last night, it obviously isn't the first time."

The day after their return, Chad became seriously ill. The cough worsened, and he was pale and wrung out.

"It looks like pneumonia," Alice said, cradling the child against her in the library. Mack thought, against his will, how exquisitely beautiful she looked there, in the lamplight, with a couple of soft curls down on her forehead and with her large, concerned eyes meeting his.

"The doctor was over, but he said the crisis won't come till tomorrow. Nothing he can do 'till then." She shrugged one shoulder weakly, and kissed Chad's hot head. His breathing jerked, in an extremely labored way, as if his lungs were a small bellows expanding up and letting loose. Obviously his lungs were filling up. And with the weakness of his constitution—Mack did not like it at all. The boy had become important to him.

Mrs. Bascomb brought them supper in the library and quietly withdrew. Fanning too sat in there, doing paper work at the table without saying a word. Both he and Mack had gone to the office to do catch-up work that had accumulated the week before the conference. Fanning had said nothing about the incident in the drawing room at French Lick; no angry telegram had come from Sidlow in Chicago.

The boy was still struggling for breath as Mack went to bed about ten o'clock, and as he finished his wash at the commode in his room and stepped into the hall to turn off the light, he saw Fanning carrying the boy in his arms up the third floor stairs. Alice was behind him. "I'll sit up, Walter, and call you if there's a change."

Mack lay on the bed, listening to that awful gasping for breath. Alice had made a tent of sheets and was boiling water and menthol in a pot on a gas plate to make steam.

He awoke with a start, was it an hour or two later? The boy had cried out. He rose and went to Chad's bedside. The shadows from the street lamps outside the window sent ghastly shadows across the bed. The child was tossing his head and shoulders about, murmuring about pirates and characters from his storybooks.

"He is out of his head," Alice said coming up beside him. Tears stood in the corners of her eyes. Mrs. Bascomb, in a long flowered robe, stood in the shadows behind them.

"The doctors know nothing," Alice said scornfully, watching Chad's flushed face, a contrast to the stark white of the pillow. "They can do nothing."

"Well, of course that's why no one trusts them and people turn to the phrenologists and quacks," Mack said, not knowing what else to offer.

They sat, listening to the wooden clicking of a small Swiss cuckoo clock. Chad caught his breath now only in gasps, with split second intervals in between.

"Shall I call the doctor again, Mrs. Fanning?" Mrs. Bascomb wanted to know, waving her hands like a frightened animal by what seemed to be an early crisis in the illness. It boded ill.

"No," Alice said firmly. She seemed to have decided something. "I have been thinking. No doctor can help; they have admitted it. I won't let him die this way without trying—something else."

Mack rose from the bed. "What do you want to do?"

"Get the horse ready at once. We are going to try spiritual healing."

"What? Christian Science?" Mack wanted to know. He was willing enough to give it a try, though it had been his mother who had always practiced it at home.

"No, though you can start praying for him too. We are taking him to Mrs. Teitelbaum's. Mediums can bring healing. I have seen it done."

"Are you sure—"

"Go, please, Mr. Scott. It is a mild night. I'll wrap him in his blanket and Mrs. Bascomb and I will carry him down the steps. We'll not tell Walter. I don't want him to go. He doesn't understand and will only thwart whatever good may be done. And it can't get any worse." She pushed the damp tendrils of hair out of her eyes.

And so, within minutes the mother and child were dashing with Mack through the night at breakneck speed, Mack whipping up the horse, she huddling in the corner of the buggy, protecting her desperately ill son from the night vapors—heading to what? This is insane, he thought, rank, stupid insanity. And yet what could be hurt by it? He too knew the inability of the medical profession to help so many conditions. Surgery, perhaps, they could often perform, but then half the time the patients died of shock. Bitterly he counted over the common ailments that doctors could not cure or even aid, whose cases they must give up: stroke, heart trouble, diabetes, cancer of any sort, peritonitis, gangrene, typhoid, even the grippe. He had seen spiritual healing work, had grown up praying for help in sickness and staying well that way— it was the way he had been raised. Some people in every town trusted phrenology, knowing which parts of the brain controlled certain parts of the body. Others he knew relied on homeopathic medicine, where watered-down doses of mineral salts seemed to restore the balance in the body. But healing through asking help of the spirits in the next world? Now that was something beyond all the rest of the panaceas he knew.

He helped Alice down from the buggy, then saw to the horse while she carried her light burden to the doorstep. It was late—almost midnight—and the mist rose from the paving bricks and curled around the street lights of Lockerbie. The silent houses loomed like witnesses to the frantic, desperate need of the human beings for aid. The bell jangled; a maid in a bathrobe appeared to open the door a crack.

"Please—call Mrs. Teitelbaum. I need her assistance," Alice breathed. The face disappeared and soon the wide, serene face of the medium appeared in its place, her body clad in a voluminous dressing gown. Hearing their mission, she ushered them in.

Sitting Alice and Chad on the couch, she turned on a small gas jet on the wall of the sitting room and began to speak softly, her words coming out of the gloom to Mack huddled in the corner in a chair.

"We can channel the powers of good that flow through the universe. They exist in the world beyond this one and here in this room. Our friends beyond are available; I can feel them near. Their energy can come to Chad, to surround him with care and love and healing power. Let me reach out to them."

She sat on the end of the huge couch, her hands clasped firmly on its serpent-head mahogany arm. The only sound in the room was the still-labored, stop-and-start breathing, now slightly worse. How much longer can he find his breath? Mack thought, listening to the wracking, painful breaths, peering at the mother and child through the darkness. It's as if he's reaching down into his lungs to grab his breath and one of these times he's going to pull and there will be nothing. And we will remember for the rest of our lives the most god-awful, horrible silence as he strangles to death.

Mrs. Teitelbaum's form jerked slightly. "Yes, yes, I can feel your power, friends from the next plane. Bring us the energy of the healing you know there, where there is no pain. Send it coursing through us." She turned and began to talk in a very low voice, so low Mack could not understand her words. She touched Chad's head, arms, hair, still murmuring in a comforting, uplifting tone.

The oddness of the situation struck him, and he was disgusted at himself. Mumbo jumbo! Desecration! Why had they done this, Christians that they were—with that fancy new church only blocks away—they were involved in sacrilegious folly. And while this woman was in her trance, the boy might die, here in this odd place they should never have come to, without his father. No, he would not stand by. He would pray; he had been taught; he would say his own prayer and stay at it.

Minutes passed, the cooing stroking and also the gasping breathing continued . Mack felt he must rise, go to the couch; he could see only their backs. He went towards the group in the dim light; Chad, with his head thrown back, fighting to bring air into his failing lungs, Mrs. Teitelbaum oblivious of all but her trance-like massage. Mack knelt, took Alice's hand. She looked into his eyes, reading all the sympathy and anxiety he felt to the core of his being. "Pray, too," she said.

"I am," he said simply. There they stayed, he on his knees beside her and the boy, the unknowing Mrs. Teitelbaum, Alice with her head bowed, her hand in his.

And, against all chances, Chad's breathing began to ease. Not much, just a little. The gasping gave way to shallow inhaling. Mrs. Teitelbaum took her hands off his arms. Then she opened her eyes. "I think our friends have answered us," she said simply.

As they drove home through the night, Alice smoothing the boy's hair, Chad sleeping more soundly than he'd done in two days, Mack was filled with a sense of wonder. What had happened there, to make the boy better? Was it chance that the crisis of the illness came at the hour they were in the spiritualist's house, and the boy, fated not to die, turned the corner? Or did mesmeric electrical forces from the spirit realm bridge the gap of matter and spirit with an infusion of healing? He turned into the back alley of West Drive of Woodruff Place. More likely, if anything, it was the simple prayers—of Alice the communicant of the fancy temple of the thousand lights which stood near this very street, and of himself, who could only mouth the Lord's Prayer at that moment of crisis with more fervor than he'd ever felt.

They would never know. And it didn't matter at this moment. There was Mrs. Bascomb waiting at the front door, ready to bustle the boy inside and hear all about the miracle of recovery. Fanning, roused by the commotion, was behind her, his face worried. But there was more to wonder at, he thought as he unhitched the horse in the carriage house.

When he was finished, he stood by the back gate next to the carriage house and raised his eyes. Stars were showing mistily through the tops of trees that stood beyond the gate on the Arsenal grounds. The last of the closed morning glory trumpets of the season twined around the finial on the gate.

What really confounded him was what he felt now, at this moment, had felt ever since that instant when his eyes had fixed on hers as he knelt beside the boy in the darkened room. In his anxiety he had opened himself up to her, had reached for her soul with his and had felt her unguarded and inmost being. He loved her totally, passionately and with a devotion that would never change. They had looked death in the eye, with deepest trepidation, and they had held it off together, and that shared experience bound them in a way that few would ever know. Sighing deeply at the implications of what he had just admitted to himself, considering guiltily the interrelationship of anxiety, religion, death and love, Mack turned from the gate and walked to the house, carrying a closed-up morning glory in the palm of his hand.

The next morning both Fanning and the child slept in. Alice sat in the grape arbor in the side yard, dreamily looking at the sky and reading a book. As Mack was galloping down the stair, tying his tie to go in to work, the doorbell rang. Mrs. Bascomb, with her own eyes sleepy and her step a little slow, answered the door. Mack stopped and stepped into a closet alcove on the second floor to stick his tiepin in the tie to complete his dressing.

A deep, resonant male voice cut through the dullness of the morning. "I should like to leave my card, please. Pardon the early morning call, but I was deeply concerned about Chad's health." Brockelhurst, the minister from the Methodist Palace, Mack told himself. How was he going to sneak by him? He didn't want to confront any ministers today.

He tried to bypass the visitor by stepping into the kitchen, but by the time he had picked up his lunch in a bag from Mrs. Bascomb and tried to exit by the back door, Alice was coming in and caught him by the arm.

"Mr. Scott! Please join us for a cup of tea in the parlor. Dr. Brockelhurst is here."

"Oh, I'd like that, but of course I'm going to work. I'm late as it is. What with Mr. Fanning not there I think—"

"Nonsense! You can visit for ten minutes. The pheasants and quail will do very well without you." She smiled, her head tilted a little to the side. His heart jumped. Damn! It was so awful feeling this way towards her. Maybe it would go away.

But it didn't. And so he chatted politely, as Mrs. Bascomb brought the tea in Haviland cups with pink roses on them, and the reverend received the good news about the illness, though of course the circumstances of the miraculous turnaround were not alluded to.

"I am so happy," Dr. Brockelhurst said. There was a rattling of teacup against saucer. His hand was shaking slightly. Mack looked at him carefully; it was the first time he had seen him close up. He was small, almost tiny for a man. That Mack had fleetingly noticed as the minister had stood in the pulpit at church. Receding hairline, strong, aquiline nose almost like a hawk's beak. Translucent, pasty complexion. Something about him seemed almost sensual. Perhaps it was that open mouthed-breathing. "God did not want him," he said piously.

Alice put her teacup on the table. She looked straight at the minister. "I have never thought God killed people, you know."

He too put down his teacup, perhaps to stop the slight shaking. "Perhaps I was giving a conventional truism. Tell me what you mean."

"God is the source of life. He maintains us that way, I think. When we die we do not die because he wills it, but because our health or morals have failed." Mack studied her intently. Alice's strength of character and independence of spirit always surprised him in one so slight and gentle.

"That is not exactly conventional Methodism."

"No, but it may be conventional Wesleyanism. I have been reading the autobiography of John Wesley, and I find that he practiced spiritual healing on the hillsides in England. And he tried to raise the dead. He did not believe God willed bad things." Her voice was firm, her mouth determined.

Dr. Brockelhurst gave an odd little, half exasperated laugh, and then ran his fingers through his thinning hair. "You are an independent Methodist, Mrs. Fanning," he said. He reached for a tea cookie, his hand hanging for an instant above the china plate before seizing it.

"Independent, yes! I take that as a compliment, Dr. Brockelhurst. There is a lot I disagree with. I suppose I would call myself an uncomfortable Methodist."

"I believe I have sensed that in services. Does the uncomfortableness extend to Central Avenue Church itself?"

She turned towards Mack, who was not eating, but sitting leaning over, with his hands clasped between his long legs. Speaking of uncomfortableness, he was experiencing it here, with them, with her.

"Mr. Scott—you have visited the church," she said. "What strikes you about it?"

"Well, its beauty. It is impressive above all else. The domed ceiling, the electric lights to symbolize the stars of heaven, the fireplaces and stained glass. It's resplendent!" Was that what Alice wanted? Well, it was what he felt.

Alice pointed a finger, gently. "Do you notice, Dr. Brockelhurst, that he spoke of the building's physical beauty. He did not speak of the spiritual witness of the congregation, the uplifting aspects of the service."

"No, he did not, but he could have."

Alice smoothed a couple of crumbs from her morning dress. "Here is what I think, since you have asked about, have sensed my discomfort. I felt it most strongly last night, when I was—praying for Chad's healing." She shot just the slightest oblique glance towards Mack. "I think there are more things on heaven and earth than this world dreams of. We Methodists, and—the Baptists and Presbyterians too, have boxed ourselves into nice, predictable, tight little religious islands. All is pretty, and impressive, with new church edifices replacing the simple little frame buildings, and huge pipe organs with hundreds of stops, and expensive fixtures. And a hundred committees to run everything."

"And?" he said, eyeing her thoughtfully.

"And we do not listen to simple ideas anymore, to prophets who come among us."

Spiritualism? Mrs. Teitelbaum? Mack wondered.

She went on. "Those little frame churches had the better answers,

Dr. Brockelhurst. At my own little church in Delphi, Indiana, you could hear the redbirds sing and look out and see the Queen Anne's Lace in the fields, and the graves of the people who had founded the church, and your own loved ones who had gone on, and know that they slept in peace. There were no organs, and the ministers read out the lines of the hymns for the congregation to follow, and people testified at prayer meetings. And Methodists where I grew up, and in the first little Central Avenue church, too, in pioneer times, weren't afraid of laughter in church, or tears."

"And we are?"

"No one would dare to show such emotion in Central Avenue church—or First Presbyterian either. It wouldn't be decorous in such fine places." There was a silence as Reverend Brockelhurst smiled faintly, not looking at her.

"We are ashamed to talk of Christ as our friend, Reverend Brockelhurst. And God is only mentioned in the sermon. Such revivalism is beneath us! We're too well mannered. These new churches give their members very weak milk instead of spiritual meat."

The minister looked her squarely in the eye. "Do not speak for all members, Mrs. Fanning." There was an unexpected edge of brittleness in his voice. "You will be mistaken if you think some, or most, do not feel comforted and uplifted in the new cathedrals we build. After all, religion is an individual thing. There is an old Chinese proverb—'the stairs that lead to Divinity are only wide enough for one.' Why should a person not find God in the large new churches? He is everywhere, after all. There is no Queen Ann's Lace outside the window because there are no fields left in the city. We bury our dead in city cemeteries, not in little churchyards, because of health laws. This is a grander age. We are in the nineties and most people say the church must change to enter the Age of Progress."

Alice looked at him thoughtfully, considering, Mack thought, not so much what he had said, but the statement "most people." It was often used when the speaker did not agree with the point of view expressed.

"And you, Dr. Brockelhurst," Alice went on earnestly, "tell me about your own personal witness, your own view of how we should live scripture in our lives. What's your faith?" It was an unusual question to put to a minister; usually they were the askers.

Brockelhurst pursed his lips and frowned. Then he sniffed and began to speak with relish, as if he were glad someone had finally asked. "Well, I have no quarrel with the grand new church buildings. It doesn't matter where the gospel is preached, and we must keep up with the times. What suited the log cabin folks won't suit an up-and-coming town like Indianapolis." His eyes were far away. "But as to what I preach—I suppose you could call me an Old-Testament preacher. A little of the fire of the prophets is in me. There are lots of new experiments and religions"—he glanced at Mack—"the Mormons and the Christian Scientists and the Spiritualists"—just the flick of an eyelash at Alice. He seemed to know many things. "All of them and most of the mainline churches today just talk about love and good feeling. They're forgetting about the strength of sin."

Mack nodded. No one could deny that it was strong and that most people were too refined to want to hear about it these days, even in church.

"I'm an Elijah-type of minister, who believes most in a God of justice. If you sin, you will face retribution!" The minister smiled, as if to soften the strong tones in his voice. "We've grown too mealy-mouthed. All of this, and even the sort of rapture you're talking about, Mrs. Fanning, in the little country churches, goes back to the time about ninety years ago when New Light took over America. Go to revivals, make your peace face-to-face with Jesus and love from then on in. It was all so sweet, like a stick of sugar candy."

Both Mack and Alice were looking at him earnestly.

"I would have been more at home in the America of Jonathan Edwards, I guess. I believe in hell and its torments, and I think our parishioners ought to live to avoid them. I should have been a Calvinist." He smiled and picked up one last cookie. "So that's why you'll hear me quote from the Old Testament as the scriptural lesson most often," he said. "I believe in a God of justice."

Alice nodded politely, without conceding anything.

After a slight, awkward silence the subject shifted comfortably to church members in the neighborhood. At last Mack felt he could excuse himself and hurry out the door and down the street to work. His emotions were still churning: Chad's salvation from the jaws of death;

his own tumbling into love in a few moments as he watched the boy with Alice, the minister's thundering about hell and retribution; he must consciously put all the turmoil aside. He wanted to look ahead, really welcomed with relief the opportunity to concentrate on the aftermath of the meeting of the fragmented association of poultry purveyors that Fanning had given him responsibilities for. As he strode along he felt glad Fanning would not be present for a while; he wanted to organize the minutes of the weekend meetings (or blowups) without him looking over his shoulder. Yesterday they had done nothing but catch up on office details. Now the company and association must face what Sidlow had done to them at French Lick. Distasteful as many of the doings were, he was still working for the company and the association. And in all honesty, he didn't know whether Sidlow was right or just a crazy, overwrought free market individualist who would resort to any tactic to get ahead.

And there was the matter of the murders. The Chinese killings lurked in the back of his mind, niggling around the edges of his consciousness. Who could have killed these men so near the neighborhood where he lived? It wasn't really his mystery to solve—nobody cared much, sadly. Nate was at work and would report later, but for some reason he didn't think he'd get very far. Suspicion and fear in this town would hide the answers, and the police would give up again, too easily.

But it wasn't right to just forget about the murders. In some way what Mrs. Toy Gum said kept ringing in his mind. "Poor, poor son, his soul had fled his body before I could even say goodbye." Lee Huang was still her boy, even though he was probably killed in an opium war retribution slaying. The men who died, everyone who died for that matter, was somebody's child, probably loved as a baby, fretted over when sick, cherished at some point by someone of the opposite sex. The Chinese victims had met their ends as human beings. At the funerals of those from upper class neighborhoods, the fashionable communicants at Central Avenue, for instance, loved ones whispered the details of death, mentioned what had happened during the last hours, reciting it almost as a litany when that final page was closed. The circumstances of the two Chinamen's deaths should be known, too, the murderer dealt with. It was, as the minister had said, a matter of simple justice for human beings.

But the question remained—why should he stick his nose into something no one else seemed to care a hill of beans about, in a town he'd just come to? Stay with your own kind—the eleventh commandment, and he was breaking it all the time. He should get out of this intrigue, leave the company and the town. And the house. Leave Alice and Chad.

That he could not do, not now.

Besides it was interesting—the old curiosity, search for adventure. He was as bad as Chad. Puzzles are made for solving. His maternal grandmother Addie Lavenham was obsessed with jigsaw puzzles, worked at them constantly. When he visited her, he used to see scores of jigsaws in their boxes on their shelves. Sometimes he had been allowed to take them down and put the pieces together. This Chinese mystery was like that, many pieces, all distributed around, though why he was the one seeming to put them all together, he really did not know.

"Tell me about your conversation with the family of the first murdered man, Li Ting," Chiang said. He, Abby, Nate Nessing and Mack were sitting around the corner from the office at Ashby's Cafe, having a bowl of soup later that day. "Does his killing have any connection with my uncle's that they know of?"

"They kept saying 'Hip Sing,' 'Hip Sing' and 'Chee Kong,'" Nate said, "but when you ask them what they mean, they won't say. We need a definite connection to bring anybody in for questioning." He sighed. "I think I've exhausted my leads in the Chinese community. Everybody knows me, and they've said all they're going to say. Whenever I come near, they say to each other with a smile, 'Here comes the Jewish policeman.' And Sgt. Rossi has even less touch with them. We're too well known in the town to find anything out."

Mack remembered something. "What about those two that were arguing, pushing your uncle around in the back alley that day? Could they have any connection with his murder the next night?"

Chiang looked mystified and even Abby didn't react. "You know,"

Mack persisted. "We were here in the laundry before school even opened, meeting Chiang, and the two Chinese men, one with thick glasses, scuffled around with your uncle outside the window."

Chiang thought about it. "Oh. You mean my cousins from the other side of town. They argue like that from time to time."

Nate leaned towards him. "About what?"

"About—debt and sometimes the family," Chiang said evasively.

Nate lowered his voice. "Now listen, Chiang. It's all well and good to defend your family's honor. But you know very well your uncle was in the opium trade. Opium was found in his body. And that shed out back isn't a kindergarten classroom!" Chiang said nothing, staring at the table.

Nate went on. "You have to understand. We will never find the truth in this matter if you don't help. You can't want your family honor to be based on covering up a lie."

"My grandmother—"

"An investigation may find your uncle guilty only of opium eating and selling, not much else. And if that's the case, everybody already knew it and he's not much worse than thousands of other victims—Chinese and otherwise—out there. Let us get at what really happened."

Chiang folded his napkin carefully. When it was in a small square, and he had laid his soup spoon on it, he said, "There is truth in what you say. I didn't think Grandmother was right, wanting to get to the truth. I've never wanted to know—just go to the high school and be in the Debate Club and act like all the rest. But I'm not like all of you. And deep down I know anyway that I can't rest until I find out who I am myself. And I must start with my family, so I will help."

"Then you don't know—don't have any idea—who killed your uncle."

"No, but we will look at the tongs. Everybody says Chee Kong may have hated him. And yes, we will start" (he looked at Mack) "with my cousins, Fook Soy, the one with the glasses, and Bee Chee, the round one who looks like a girl. They are the ones you saw arguing, and we will scrutinize to see if they belong to Chee Kong."

"How can you find that out?" Nate demanded.

"There is a record—somewhere in my house."

"But I have heard that your uncle was a member of the enemy

tong—the Progressive Society—the Hip Sings for short." There. It was on the table. Could Chiang face it?

He sighed. "Yes, he was. But there are records, I tell you, of the rival tong, the Chee Kong. Let us look, now, today."

They raced down the stairs into the ironing cellar, pausing to bow to Mrs. Toy Gum, the Old Grandmother, who stood counting change behind the counter of the shop.

In the basement sitting on the floor were baskets of ironing, carelessly sorted, no doubt reflecting the confusion still in the laundry over the uncle's death. Back against the wall was an odd, framed window opening, beyond which was a higher dirt floor.

"The unexcavated part of this house. My uncle kept the records of the business back in there with the pipes."

Abby and Mack walked to the musty opening and peered inside, awaiting the outcome of the search. Chiang crawled into the dark interior of the opening. "Receipts for 1894, running accounts, paid, overdue—now it must be here somewhere. I saw a list once, when he did not know I was snooping and he had the record book out. "Let's see, yellow tablet sheets, written over in Chinese." He climbed down out of the pipe access space and put the papers on the nearest ironing board, smoothing them out. "Yes, here it is! It seems to be a poem." For a moment there was silence. Then he said, "It's in Chinese and then in English." He read:

By this red drop of blood on finger tip, I swear
The secrets of this tong I never will declare.
Seven gaping wounds shall drain my blood away
Should I to alien ears my sacred trust betray.

Then the initiate is to crawl under the chair of the Ah Mah to symbolize being born from the womb of high heaven.

"It is the sacred swearing-in ceremony of Chee Kong."
Abby whistled.

"Then there are a lot of hateful imprecations against the Manchu emperor."

"Why would those be there?" Mack asked.

"The Chee Kongs were founded in China, as part of the Triad Society, to fight against the Manchus. They hate the emperor, well, used to, before they forgot politics and got involved with opium and prostitutes. Some of them talk about the emperor now and then but mostly the members line up on the opposite side of some other tong in an alley and get ready to knife the enemy."

"Aren't there any names?" Mack asked.

"Yes, I think this is it," he said turning the poem over. "Fook Soy is here. But not Bee Chee. Odd. One is Chee Kong, one isn't. And here is the name of Wong Woon."

"Who is he?" Nate asked, looking intently at Chiang.

"He lives in Chicago. He was my father's best friend. See this mark here? It is the mark of the Ming emperor."

"What does it mean?" Abby asked.

Chiang studied it a minute. "I do not know. But I can find out." He turned and strode quickly up the stairs, his feet, clad in soft leather, making padding noises on each step.

After what seemed like a long time Mrs. Toy Gum came slowly down the stairs and hobbled her way to the ironing board. Her look was impassive.

"I have told my grandmother that I too now believe we should find out the truth," Chiang said. "We must be courageous for the honor of our family. She will have to accept that Uncle was a tong member. And," he said, looking straight at her, "if there was a thing not honorable, perhaps the father of the family, in our case Lee Huang did what he did to preserve the ones he cared for—the family. Confucius says we must honor the head of the family at all costs. For us that is true even in death by knowing the truth about Lee Huang's killer." He said it again in Chinese, so that she would fully understand.

Toy Gum nodded, then looked at the characters on the yellow page. "Ming is the house the Chee Kong support in early days. In China. Now the sign mean—Wong Woon the head of the Chee Kong." These things she said hesitantly but definitely in English, evidently trustful enough of them to use the less familiar tongue now.

"In Chicago?" Nate asked quietly.

"No. It mean in all America outside the Golden Gate."

"Do you read that in the Chinese characters, Mrs. Toy Gum?"

"No, but it is true."

She turned and began to walk towards the stairs, and Mack spoke in a low tone to Chiang so she would not hear, "If Lee Huang, your uncle, was a Hip Sing, why does he have the records of the rival tong, the Chee Kongs?"

Chiang considered a moment, then spoke. "Chee Kong in this town, oldest but now smallest of the two tongs, was trying to gain power over Hip Sing, the new big shots here. It is wise to know your enemy. Perhaps that is why Hip Sing leader here, my uncle, has these documents, to know his enemies. But to have documents naming secret members—there are a few others here at the bottom—was to put his life in grave danger if they found out."

"Was that the reason your uncle was killed?" Mack asked.

"Maybe yes, maybe no," Chiang said, tiredly.

Nate said he had to take the documents as evidence for the police and began to fold them.

"No, do not do that. Chee Kong papers turned over to police could be very dangerous, even for those of us in this room. Let us get rid of them in our own way. These are my property." Nate, looking unwilling, put down the papers.

"Toy Gum said Wong Woon in Chicago was your father's best friend," Abby said, trying to understand. "Lee Huang, your uncle, was ambushed by his brother's best friend?"

"We do not know," Chiang said. "But someone does. Li Ting, killed first, was a member of the Hip Sing too. The first murder is surely connected to my uncle's. Maybe somebody is trying to get Hip Sings."

"It says on this sheet that only your one cousin, Fook Soy, is in the Chee Kong. So the other cousin must be in the Hip Sing tong."

Chiang shook his head. "Maybe not. The list show only that Bee Chee is not listed as Chee Kong. Or perhaps he is a new initiate and not on that list."

Abby said. "I'm assuming these two cousins have to be involved. Otherwise, why the arguing?"

"You can assume nothing, Dr. Watson," Nate said dryly. He put up his hand as if swearing an oath and gestured for the others to follow his example. "Nothing goes out of this room. By this red drop of blood on your fingertip and may seven gaping wounds drain all your blood away if you talk."

They all laughed a little uneasily and swore. But Mack, walking out the door of the laundry, wondered if they were all biting off quite a bit more than they were going to be able to chew very well.

Dark rain clouds promised an early dusk as they separated. Abby and Nate raced to the streetcar, waving Mack goodbye as they ran. But Mack heard a voice behind him. "Stay, my friend." He turned to see Chiang, standing at the door of the laundry.

"Mack Scott, I notice that you see things that the others do not see," Chiang said impassively.

"Do you think so? Perhaps it is because I am an outsider. Different perspective, probably."

"Or your mind is wiser from having lived longer and worked harder than the rest of us. Being in Indianapolis High School is not everything when it comes to understanding the realities of the streets."

"And so?"

"Help me, McClure Scott. Help my family. If we are going to start again, we must find the murderer of my uncle. I did not wish to face the truth before, but now I do."

"But the police—Nate and Rossi. They'll do their job."

"As best they can. But the town is closed up tight as a tin of salt fish to them. And they do not have the key to open it. You as an outsider can go anywhere, learn from all sides of the town. I have seen you doing it."

"Well, I'm curious. I have been interested in the murders. I don't like to see the death of these men shoved aside like debris for the ash can. Like the rotten chickens at Fanning's plant."

"Will you help me? Will you act as first friend? It is a Chinese custom, someone to help the young man of the family when there is a death."

"Mack breathed deeply. "Of course I will." Briefly it crossed his mind that his town would think it odd he was "first friend" to a Chinese boy.

Chiang had moved during the conversation and was standing in the street. His eyes darted around and, suddenly, he pushed Mack back into the doorway. "There is more," he whispered. "You live in the heart of the mystery."

"What do you mean?"

Chiang walked cautiously to the side of the building. "Look around here, just tilt your head towards the washhouse."

Mack slowly looked around the edge of the laundry building. Walter Fanning was at the door of the shed, peering in, umbrella in hand. He and the shed were outlined against the branches of elm trees beginning to be tossed in a sharply freshening wind, and against blue-black clouds promising a storm to come soon. In a moment he put the umbrella tip through the door, poking at whatever was on the floor.

"Why does he need to poke around anyway back there? He has hovered around our lives for a year now. Do you know why?" Chiang asked, looking anguished.

"No, but I'm trying to find out," Mack said. After saying goodbye, he walked quickly towards Tenth Street. Fanning sifting through the debris! It was ominous, taken with the story of the hatchetmen in Chicago. He must know what was in this man's past. And, as Chiang had said, he was in the best position to do so, because he lived right in the heart of the mystery.

Only one light twinkled in the windows of O' Shaughnessey's Gymnasium in the late afternoon twilight a couple of days later as Mack approached after work.

"Well, and I suppose you are here for the sparring. I dona' think there are partners about just now," O'Shaughnessey called out as Mack came through the door. The gloom was broken by just one light on a twisted cord; Mack could barely make out a couple of shapes bent over the newspaper in the office at the side of the gym.

"No, I just want to punch the bag," Mack said, tossing his jacket onto a chair. O'Shaughnessey came out of the office to catch the coin Mack flipped at him.

Mack went into the grimy little dressing room, with its gray water closet, spigot and sink in the back. He put on trunks and a cotton shirt, then soon was grappling with the hanging bag. "Thump, thump, rat-tat-tat-tat-tat." Over and over with a ferocity that continued to surprise him, he thumped it, battling and grappling until sweat stood out on his forehead and his heart and head pounded.

The two men sitting in the office put down their newspapers and came out to watch. Finally, he sat down on a bench, panting and gasping for breath.

"You're attacking the bag like it was the devil from Hades," O'Shaughnessey said, his small form casting long shadows as the light bulb swung on its string.

"Maybe I'm trying to exorcise the Devil," Mack said. The image of Fanning poking around the murder scene had not left his mind. O'Shaughnessey looked at him for clarification. "Do you ever feel like you've been walking around in a maze with no way out?" Mack asked. Certainly that was true. Recent feelings that he didn't know himself, that he was a hick from the sticks still tied to home—hadn't had a drink since he'd been in the lumber camps, never had a woman—bothered him. And anguish over the woman, the woman who was in his dreams, who hovered in the back of his mind while he typed or talked at work, luminous and lovely, walking along a path in the night air, amidst the smell of flowers. He burned for her, with a fire that started at his loins and spread to his heart. It was all so complicated and hopeless, with the mess of the murders he'd promised to help solve, and the husband of the woman he loved so desperately involved in some real way. And that said nothing about what was troubling Alice. He couldn't sleep at nights wondering if she were going to walk that night, and what sent her to the spiritualists. He towelled his hair and walked back to the dummy. But O'Shaughnessey held it, refusing to let him punch. He looked at Mack steadily.

"I seem to recall from my readin' of the myth of Theseus and the labyrinth that there was only one way out of a maze." O'Shaughnessey was very literate, earning what must be the equivalent of a university English degree through his own reading of library books by the light of lamps in the living quarters of the gym. So Mrs. Bascomb had told Mack.

Mack tried to reach around him and touch the dummy, but O'Shaughnessey held it out of reach. He smiled enigmatically.

"The man's lady friend took string and helped lead him out," Mack said, exhaling resignedly.

"But to get out o' the mess he had to go right up to the door of the monster that was causin' all the trouble. Go right there and kill it. Confront it in the heart of its den." O'Shaughnessey swung the punching bag strongly right at Mack, who caught it almost in the face.

But he did not start punching again; carefully he let the bag right itself.

Well, perhaps O'Shaughnessey was right, he thought, as, a few minutes later he left through the back door. Perhaps he might get out of the maze by a little direct action. He might just find a way to go to where the answers were. First Fanning, then, just possibly, Alice. And somewhere along the line, the murderer he'd promised Chiang he'd find.

"Mr. Fanning, you know I feel a loyalty to the company," Mack said, standing before the man the next day. It was near noon, and Mack had watched Fanning write letters all morning, letters which he tore up in disgust after he'd written a couple of paragraphs. "I know very well your frustration with Sidlow. He hasn't telegraphed his intentions, hasn't written. It's his way of freezing you out."

"I need to know what he's going to do," Fanning admitted. "If he breaks the cartel—spills the beans—it could upset the whole price structure, ruin the business. Maybe get us in trouble with the law."

Mack did not lower his gaze. "Let me go to Chicago for you."

Fanning took a cigar out of a Cuban cigar box. "Chicago?"

"Yes. Put nothing on paper. Let me confront him, demand to know his intentions and affirm the association's resolve. At the very least, we'll know."

Fanning looked up at him with gratitude. "Yes, yes, that isn't a bad idea. It's the indecision. Holding us all hostage like a bunch of Cuban bandits would. We can get you a train ticket to go this afternoon."

"I thought so too. Chad's still recuperating—he's too weak for lessons. I could stay through tomorrow, maybe, see some of the old sights." No need to be devious.

"Yes, of course. Well, let's go into my office and set up the details.

Miss Farquharson can get the tickets. Very good idea, I must say."

"Please have her reserve two tickets. I'll pay for the second. I want to take a friend—Chicago at night isn't always friendly."

And so within the hour he had completed the arrangements. Miss Farquharson had reserved tickets as Mack prepared to rush back to the house and pack his grip. But not before he had stopped at the Chinese laundry and confirmed with Chiang the arrangements they had made the night before: to be at Union Station at one o'clock for a trip to Chicago. Someone had killed two Indiana Hip Sing tong members. The Chee Kong looked like a good suspect in those killings. He and Chiang needed to go to the source and find out why.

Chapter Seven

"The Chinese here don't live in a certain section like they do in San Francisco," Chiang said as they walked from Chicago's downtown train station. "They try to be accepted into the general population. Still, you can't say their digs are the McCormicks' or Swifts' palaces on the lakeshore."

Not at all. The Chinese population in Chicago lived up dim streets, really narrow alleys near the downtown, in shabby little enclaves nobody else wanted. Although Mack had lived two months in Chicago, he had never gone into this area, though he knew where it was. And he didn't want to go now.

"We're crazy," Mack muttered, reconsidering his resolve to get to the bottom of things in the harsh reality of Chicago. "We need to be incarcerated in the Seven Steeples Hospital for the Insane." Chiang looked at him questioningly. "We are going to visit the head of the Chee Kong tong right in his own lair. He's connected with some pretty brutal murders in our town. Why don't we just let the police handle this? What're we going to learn? Maybe only that the tong is going to order an ax hit on us for shoving into their territory."

"I suppose I've exposed you to my own danger. Old Grandmother thought it was a bad idea, even though she trusts Wong Woon not to harm us." Chiang said.

"Never mind. I asked for it."

A little girl with a sculptured Chinese face passed them, carrying some sort of crockery pot with a good smell coming from it. Chiang turned toward the smell for a moment, then said, "Well, we should be afraid not of Wong but of his friends. The tongs—well, there's more to all this than you know. But Wong Woon is an honorable man."

"Honorable? How can he be, when his organization countenances highway robbery of merchants and extortion and assault and battery and murder."

"Some of that happens and who can approve? But—see that poster?" Chiang pointed. "It says, 'It is of the utmost importance to educate children; Do not care that your families are poor or rich. For those who can handle well the pen, go where they will, need never ask for favors.'"

"And?"

"Wong Woon is one of three men who established a Chinese School—actually, I think that is it over there—for boys. It was the first one in Chicago. To bring them out of the poverty they face because they can do only laundry work." There was a wistful look on Chiang's face.

"You go to Indianapolis High School."

"Yes, but I am a strange fish there. Some good principal let me in the grade school, and I sat through eight grades alone. Wong Woon wants a whole group of boys to escape from this small pond into the big waters of Chicago."

They turned down a narrow street, evil-smelling and crowded to the very sidewalk with shops and eating places. "My father's friend runs the Crying Loon Restaurant," Chiang said. Curtains were drawn at its windows; above the door were several Chinese good-luck signs.

They went into an interior lit only by lanterns; at this four o'clock hour only a few customers drank tea at the small tables. A huge man pulled himself out of a chair and lumbered out to greet them. Mack felt the feeling of craziness return. It was impossible he had purposely sought out the very personification of evil in the Midwest, at least according to the evening papers on respectable people's parlor tables.

Chiang bowed. "Friend of my father, I, his most humble son, honor you." The other man bowed to them both. Then Chiang said, "We have come to seek advice and wisdom and answers to our inquiries."

Wong Woon looked at Mack questioningly.

"McClure is my friend, the only one that will help our family. Thus, he is to be trusted. But he hesitates to talk before your most imposing self." That isn't the half of it, Mack thought.

Wong Woon eyed him through eyes that had narrowed to slits, but then he nodded and his lips curled up in a slight smile. "There is no need to hesitate. I will answer your questions. Come, let us sit and eat something." He seated them at a table, snapped his fingers, said a few words to a waiter in silk trousers, and himself sat down.

"So you are afraid to ask, young man. I am a student of Confucius,

McClure. Do you know the story of Hsiang Toy? No? Well, he was a boy who dared to ask the great sage many questions, some of which might be thought very impertinent, and Confucius praised the boy because he loved to seek and speak the truth. We should never fear to ask, or tell, truth."

McClure nodded respectfully. Soon three bowls of soup were set before them, hot from the kitchen. Mack tasted his, poking at a dumpling-like thing in the middle and small pieces of white, floating substance. "It's delicious. What is it?" he asked.

"Fish maw and cow udder," the older man said seriously. Mack put his spoon down, but took it up again in a minute to eat the odd but tasty stuff.

Then came a platter that reminded Mack of nothing so much as a clear stew, with tiny bits of what he thought was pork and celery chunks. When they had eaten their fill and drunk the sharply-flavored tea, talking of Chiang's high school and Mack's life in Northern Michigan, Wong Woon said, "Ask your questions, McClure."

But where should he start, Mack wondered. Perhaps, like the disciple of Confucius, with the truth. "I think you are a leader in the Chee Kong Tong," he said. "I have come with Chiang because he is my friend and because we want to find his uncle's killer."

"Go on," the man commanded, waving away the waiter who wished to pick up the dishes.

"Well, Lee Huang was a Hip Sing. We think Lee Huang's rivalry with the Chee Kong may have caused his death in some way."

"And how is that?"

This was getting touchy. Mack sat silently a moment, looking into the tea. Then Chiang took up the case. "My father's friend, we believe Uncle may have been killed because of warring factions in the tongs. Someone has killed two Hip Sings in our town and Chee Kong are bitter rivals to Hip Sing from earliest times."

"And so we are at the wars between the tongs again. That is all that anyone ever speaks of."

Somehow the honesty of the man encouraged Mack to be blunt. "And should we not do that? Aren't they constantly putting up posters on the walls and trees ordering this or that person beat up or killed? Because they crossed the other gang?"

"That does occur. I do not deny it," Wong Woon said placidly. "Yes, there are gang wars over women and territory and insults. I do not condone it—at least all of it. Sometimes some of the violence is just retribution, and necessary in an evil world." They paused while the waiter took the dishes, then brought small nuts sugared in ginger. Mack sampled one, then reached for the water pitcher. They were so spicy they burned his tongue.

Wong Woon went on. "I do think the Chee Kong in Chicago to be different from the one in, one would say, San Francisco. I should know, I lived there—too long." He frowned. "Here we must be truly a benevolent association, because we have not been here long. The Chinese came late to this place, maybe only twenty years ago, and they have lived in squalor. Nobody thinks of us Chinese except as coolies, cheap hired labor, and maybe that is what we think of ourselves, too."

Chiang nodded, staring into his water glass. "But your school, revered friend of my father's, is opening a new path."

"I hope so. And the women's aid and Chinese family group, the Association of Chinese Waiters and the Burial Return Club, are groups which are advancing our race in this city. But enough. I must not deny the truth. Chee Kong is going down a path of fog and darkness. The young men carry sharp knives and guns and look for trouble. When they find it—" he took his knife and drew it across his throat. "Perhaps I will not be in my place much longer."

The noise outside the window, of hard-shod feet moving over cobblestones, intruded into the room. Chinese people entered the cafe, picking up trays of food and tea. Gesturing towards them, Wong Woon said, "Those who live in one or two rooms with no kitchen must buy their food at restaurant kitchens."

"They must eat. But what if they cannot pay?" Chiang wanted to know.

"The old ones of us hold the debt and wait for them to pay the debt, or we lose the money when they cannot. The younger ones know how to make debtors pay." He shook his head ruefully.

Chiang looked at his father's old friend and paused, then bowed his head deferentially. "And so, revered uncle, you may have information which will help solve our family puzzle. We must know the truth. Who could have killed Lee Huang and for what cause?"

Wong Woon looked about the room furtively. Could he, too, be afraid? He poured himself a small bowl of tea from a hot pot in front of him. "There is information," he said evenly. "But I may not be the teapot from which you can pour out that information. Lee Huang, brother of my old friend, was a Hip Sing, not a Chee Kong."

"Yes, of course, revered one," Chaing said, "but we cannot help but think he was killed by his enemies, the Chee Kongs. He was snooping in Chee Kong business. I will show you." He rose, put his valise on the table, and, looking around cautiously, took forth the initiation scroll. Solemnly he presented it to Wong Woon.

The older man looked it over, then shook his head. "The loon laughs because he thinks he knows all things on his little lake. And yet beyond the hills are many things he does not know of. I do not know of everything outside this Chinatown world until I am told. Word had come to me that Hip Sing in the southern cities had our secrets. And yet, I do not think your uncle was killed for this. The cause goes deeper. Hip Sings and Chee Kong in both Chicago and your town have much to quarrel about among themselves. In the last days of the New Year here in Chicago they have fought their own Civil War."

"May we know what it is over?" Chiang asked.

"Yes. Two years ago two groups of young men began seriously contending for the territories of Chinese fortune houses."

"Gambling dens?" Mack wanted to know.

"Well, yes. I sense the accusation in your voice. You do not approve of gambling dens, as you call them. Again to know all is to understand a good deal. If you lived with twenty of your relatives in a house where even human decency cannot be practiced, let alone dignity, where everyone must eat and comb hair and do work on the same table and sleep four in a bed, you as a man might seek some peace outside the house. So it is. Anyway, there is money in the gambling tables and the two groups fought."

He sipped his tea, speaking low. "Hip Sings became particularly good at beatings and assassinations with—" he swung his hand around, as if throwing a lasso at a cow.

"Rope weighted with lead?" Chiang asked.

"Yes. They were specialists and brutal things happened. Other brutal things were done by Chee Kong to get even."

Non-Chinese people were being directed to tables. Some were women with beautiful boas around their necks, wearing exquisite clothing. This was a fashionable off-beat adventure spot, obviously. The older man leaned over. "Even people from other cities came here to Chicago to hire services they needed done. They went first to Hip Sing."

Wong Woon was going on as if eager to be finished with this conversation as the shadows fell outside. "One such contract came from your city. From the Indiana capital city, where they do not have such specialists."

Mack felt his apprehension grow. "Who—put out such a contract, sir?" he asked.

"That you may not know from me, for I do not know the person's name. But Hip Sing took it up and swung rope on the head of right man. Then, though, there was trouble, wrong people hurt. That I know."

"And my uncle?" Chiang asked in a whisper.

"The brother of my old friend was a fool in many ways. He did not know what birds to flock with, let alone fly with. Ever was it so," he said softly, "even when we were young in the land of China. He, as leader of the Hip Sings in your town, made the contract arrangement. And some way it was botched, they were betrayed in Chicago, and he has, I suppose, paid. Someone may be seeking revenge."

"Then it wasn't over—the opium dream pipe?" Chiang asked, mustering all the courage he had.

"That you may not know because I will not tell you," Wong Woon said sharply. "And now, you must go. I have said enough for an old man whose days are few as flowers in snow."

Chiang leaned close. "But if I wished to know, as nephew of the Hip Sing, if I wanted to pursue this Chicago Hip Sing matter, perhaps I should go to those in the Hip Sing here in the city of Chicago?"

"You have not done that as yet?" the older man asked calmly.

Chiang stared at the tablecloth. "No, I am afraid."

"And well you are. To do so would be folly. The young men control Hip Sing. They are like dogs, slavering for a kill where there is power and money in this city which grows so fast. Fragile women, innocent children, even the old will not stand in their way as they leap in blood lust."

The three sat as if in a trance. "But—if you must know—must go among the Hip Sings even knowing the risk—you should go to the curio shop of Whi Ting Lo." He scribbled a few characters on a piece of paper. "There you will find the teapot you need to pour out your answers." They rose. "And may the steam not come up into your face and burn you," they heard him say as they walked towards the door.

Chiang looked at the paper Wong Woon had given him; they walked through a brisk, biting wind which blew off the lake. Lights came on dimly in shop windows: groceries where strange-looking cabbages and condiments were displayed, two furniture shops where through the gloom they could see the heads of dragons and serpents on the arms of mahogany chairs, and brass pots stacked up one on top of the other.

Finally, at the end of a dark, smelly alley, a dim glow illuminated the dirty window of a small shop. Only a few people shuffled down the street; women carrying the eternal bring-in suppers from the food houses and men with the vacant eyes of opium addicts.

"This is the address he gave me. Sign of the growling dog," Chiang said. A man brushed by them, heading toward the back of the tumbledown building. Mack watched the man disappear into the back entrance. At almost the same moment, a very old woman emerged, swaying and stumbling in her walk. Slowly she went up the alley, coughing as she went.

"Suppose we go to the back door," Mack said. Chiang looked at him warily. "I want to see what's back there."

"Opium, that's what's back there," Chiang whispered. The setup was similar to Lee Huang's laundry shack—and to what Nate had described of Li Ting's gardener's shed in the rear of the property on Lockerbie Street.

With a beckoning gesture, Mack persuaded Chiang to follow him. Chiang came forward, shrugging his shoulders, smiling and shaking his head as if he didn't understand his own bravado. Then he snapped his fingers as if to say, "Who cares?" They had come so far in this quest, dared so much, that a sense of morose recklessness began to possess them. They started around the building. Through at least ten years' dirt on the side window, they viewed the meager contents of the store: counters with dusty-looking porcelain, god images on rickety tables, paper dragons and snakes for celebration—as well as chewing gum and cigarettes and liquor seen dimly in a case on the other side of the room.

They came to the back part of the store, which had a small-cross paned window in it. They stared into it cautiously, through a crack in the parting of a curtain.

"Yes, it is a den of the devil," Chiang murmured. "Come look."

Mack peeked. He saw a room almost completely littered with trash—tin cans, paper wads, even dog excrement—disgusting. And bunks, on the side of the room, like a ship's quarters. There were two customers, one a short man of perhaps forty, lying vacantly with the cloudy water opium pipe near his hand on the floor, another, a young boy hardly out of his teens twisted into the womb position, his eyes wide open and vacant.

Suddenly a hand grabbed their collars, spun them around and knocked their heads together. In the foul-smelling gloom, they faced two toughs about their age. "Look into the Chinese den, will you?" one rough, taunting voice said. "Whi Ting Lo does not like that!" the shorter one said, beginning to batter Mack's face with slaps and blows. Vaguely Mack could see Chiang kneeling, covering his head as the other man beat him with what looked like a billy club. Suddenly as pain bit into his consciousness, anger exploded in Mack, and he pulled the man to him like the punching bag in O'Shaughnessey's. Strength flowed into his muscles; his fists felt like iron. He pummeled the man as he tried to avoid the blows descending on his face and head.

"Tell—Whi—Ting Lo we do not like his reception," he said and a kaleidoscope of images flashed before him as his fists pelted—a fight in the lumber camp on a cold night when he seemed to go berserk after his initiation into whiskey drinking and pinned a man to the floor slapping him over and over again; a boxing tournament in a summer festival where he half-killed the opponent, his mother reading "turn the other cheek" from a worn family Bible. But he did not turn the other cheek, and as he knelt over his vanquished, moaning Chinese opponent, half-seeing Chiang prostrate a few yards away, he heard a whiz and felt the convulsive agony of stone against head bone and knew no more.

When he finally struggled reluctantly back into consciousness, a cat was licking his face. He was in an alley. It wasn't the curio shop back alley—that was for sure, and it was the dead of night. His whole head felt as if it were a throbbing boil, ready to be lanced, and there, over there doubled up like a discarded doll, was Chiang. Was he alive? Mack pushed the cat away and sat up on his elbows. Softly he called Chiang's name. Was that movement? Thank God. After all, he was the one who had convinced Chiang to come up here on this stupid trip. He struggled to his feet and staggered over to Chiang, shook him gently, then helped him up. Together they made their way out of the alley.

"Where can we clean up? It's too late to find the YMCA," Chiang murmured through swollen lips.

"There—there's a round ball, a light in front of a building up ahead. The police station, Chicago District 211. That's what it says."

"Won't they ask questions?"

"I don't care. The truth is a good enough story. And we can't be in more trouble than we're in," Mack told him.

The officer on duty's name was Keefe, so a sign on the tall night desk said. He looked at them warily. They told the story: they had come to Chicago on business for an Indianapolis company and Chiang had sought out an old friend to ask if he knew anything about his uncle's murder in Indianapolis. Following a lead, they had evidently stumbled on a hornet's nest.

"Involving yourselves in the tong wars is about as smart as picking a fight with Kid McCoy," the balding officer told them.

He came around from the desk and felt the huge bump on Mack's head. "Are you dizzy? Confused—any more than normal?" He smiled a little. "I don't believe you've cracked your dome. I think I can hold you for observation without charging you. You can clean up and sleep for a while in a clean cell."

Keefe led the way into the lockup, keys jangling. The valise Mack had carried with him was gone. "Thank the gods of fortune that we gave that list of Chee Kong secret ritual to Wong Woon," Chiang whispered. He was difficult to understand because his lips were so swollen his mouth was just a slit. "We might have those gorillas on our tails too."

Keefe nodded to them and left. The door clanged shut. Mack looked down at his business suit. Oddly, it was only slightly rumpled; smiling ruefully he recalled that his mother had always said natty tweed wore well. Certainly did.

Sheets and one army blanket were folded neatly on each bed. After washing his wounded face in the basin in the corner, Mack tucked sheets under the corners of the straw mattress and took off the business suit and smoothed it out on the floor. He covered himself with the blanket; the cold wind blew in through cracks in the isinglass window.

"What are you doing with that tweed—sloot—idiotic friend?" Chiang demanded, his English accent slurring with weariness. He climbed up into the bunk above him.

"I have an appointment tomorrow with Sidlow. I intend to keep my clothes neat. Maybe now more than ever," Mack said. It was a while before he fell asleep through spasms of pain, and when he did, he did not dream.

Mack stared up at the doors of the tall, thin building which looked like a box of saltines lying on its side decorated with stoneware and arches reminiscent of a Gothic cathedral. Chiang was waiting on a park bench, where he would sleep and nurse his wounds until their train left at three o'clock.

His limped over inlaid mosaic tiles. A glass register told him that "J.S. Sidlow Provisioners," was located on the third floor. Yes, ring for the elevator. He looked at himself in the reflection of the elevator doors. Suit a bit rumpled, but no blood, miraculously. His head hadn't bled much. But the face—well, he'd think up a good one to explain a black and blue face and a knot that hadn't gone down appreciably after fourteen hours.

Sidlow sat on the other side of a big desk in a tiny office. He was his own secretary, and apparently his own drayman too, if what the livery man in the barn across the street had told Mack was true.

"I don't believe you," Sidlow said. "Nobody gets hurt just on the face when a horse runs over him. You were beat up." He stood up, obviously feeling menaced by this young man whom he recognized as his hated arch rival's secretary demanding to see him and showing up beaten the color of slate.

"I'm not here to discuss my own personal misfortune in the streets. I feel fine. I have come to find out what you intend to do with your contract with the Elite Poultry Purveyors Association."

"Contract? A cartel arrangement I should never have allowed myself to sign. I'll tell you what I'm going to do; I'm going to ignore it and make as much money as I can, and you can tell Walter Fanning he can —" he stopped short. "Wait a minute. That lump is from a throw stick. You've been beaten up by the tongs. What in the name of God?"

All of a sudden Mack felt the room lurch. He reached for the desk and realized he was being helped to a leather settee. Sidlow was giving him a glass of water, and soon the room stopped revolving like the inside of a butter churn.

His voice croaked like a frog's when he spoke to Sidlow. "What did you mean at French Lick when you accused Fanning of doing something to his rival up here, the one before you who ran the business. I've got to know, not for Fanning, he doesn't—can't—know I'm asking. Does it have anything to do with opium?"

"Everything in Chinatown has something to do with opium, but no, not directly, I think."

"Tell me, please," Mack whispered. "What did Fanning do up here?"

Sidlow's dark, serious eyes scrutinized him carefully. Finally he said, "Why not? Fanning knows I know. Two years ago he decided to get ruthless with Mapeltharp, the man who owned this business before I did. Mapeltharp wanted to break the traces, refused to keep the cartel rules and took the big Chicago trade from Fanning. Fanning decided to play rough, hired some—well, some Chinese thugs." He got up and went to the window, looking at the tops of maple trees in the park.

"He went to a Chinese laundryman in his neighborhood in Indianapolis. Wanted him to arrange for a hatchet hit on Mapeltharp. Not enough to put him out of the way permanently, just to scare him badly, make him quit the business, show Fanning's strength." He turned, his look full of scorn.

"He's everything I hate about these barons. If they can't win fairly with their free market theories, they buy any sort of underhanded treachery that will serve them. Push anybody in their way into the sewers, ruin them if necessary. Then they go into church on Sunday morning and fill up the collection plates with their rotten money." The spires of Central Avenue Methodist Church loomed suddenly in Mack's mind.

"But to go on—" Sidlow said, sitting down at his desk and studying his hand. "The laundryman contact in your city, a Hip Sing I guess, hired two members of the Hip Sings up here in Chicago. And one Hip Sing came from Indianapolis to 'supervise.' They waylaid poor Mapeltharp. In addition to throwing the weighted rope, they almost killed him with a barrage of shots. And," he turned to look Mack straight in the eye, "the Indianapolis hatchetman shot too and killed a passerby, a sing-song girl prostitute named Shi-Chi. She was carrying food from a take-home shop and was on the other side of the street when the firing started."

"And?"

"She was the girlfriend of Whi Ting Lo."

"The head of the Hip Sing." Mack's head was hurting frightfully. It was getting difficult to concentrate. Why had he come? Why was he continuing to take this punishment? He'd said he'd help a friend, surely, but more—he had to know. And he had been right. All of this did involve Fanning—as deep as a fly caught in a pot of molasses. And beyond him, inevitably, Alice. "Do you know the name of the Indianapolis Hip Sing who came to oversee the murder?"

"I'd know it if I heard it."

"Li Ting was murdered in Indianapolis in July. Was that the name?"

"I think so. But why are you involving yourself in the Chinese tong wars? Even the police stay clear. They may put the case on the blotter, but they won't soil their trousers by investigating down on Harrison Street."

Mack thought that if he stood up, the pain might ease. He did and it was a little better. Something was bothering him, though.

"How do you know so much about the Chinese, Sidlow? They tend to be closed-mouthed, from everything I can see."

"My father taught in the first school set up for Chinese boys a few years ago."

"The first school? Then he must have known Wong Woon. He

was a friend of the man who was murdered."

"My father made many friends. He was one of the few white men to look at a man with slanting eyes and not see a cartoon joke. He was a captain in the Salvation Army—gave his life in the service of others. I don't share his fatal disease of altruism. But you haven't answered my question. Why—"

"I may have made a few friends myself among the Chinese," Mack muttered, yearning to go. But Sidlow stood up and grasped both his arms, earnestly.

"Listen to me. You seem to have sense. Stay out of this mess. It's a stinking stewpot, as the Chinese say. And the worst stink of all is that your master—boss—Fanning is the cause of it all. He hired these people to rough up his competitor in Chicago."

"He couldn't have intended murder, I know," Mack said lamely.

"He is now an accessory to murder. And you are working for the man." In disgust he dropped Mack's arms.

Chiang and Mack both slept the sleep of the dead all the train ride home, but woke near Indianapolis to look out at fields where the corn stood with dry, drooping ears and leaves, ready to harvest. Cows stood eating pumpkins between the corn rows in the glow of an orange sunset.

"So Uncle was the middle-man in the hatchet murders?" Chiang said. "And Li Ting was to supervise, but ended up shooting his own tong head's love by mistake. And both Li Ting and Lee Huang were killed in revenge?"

"So it would seem," Mack said.

"Nate Nessing will want to know right away."

Mack nodded. Still, he wondered what the police would do with the information once they had it. And, of course, how it would involve Fanning. Accessory to murder?

"We both need a good night's sleep," Mack said. "Tomorrow we'll tell Nate Nessing what we found out. To go over it once more: there was a tong incident up here in Chicago last year. Both Fanning and the Indianapolis tongs were involved. Your uncle evidently orchestrated a hatchet hit which went awry, and some Indianapolis Chinese were involved in it. Then your uncle was killed himself."

Chiang nodded. "But who exactly killed Uncle and Li Ting? Who *did* the revenge hits? That's the prize we should be taking home from the tea party in Chicago."

Mack rubbed his face gingerly. "All right. Suspects. Well, Bee Chee the Hip Sing and his brother Fook Soy the Chee Kong member were arguing behind the laundry the day before the murder of your uncle. If the murders are tong efforts to revenge the bad hit, they could be involved, too. Maybe they're hired avengers, reporting to Whi Ting Lo. They have shady connections in town, according to Nate. They're prime suspects."

"I don't know about that. Just because they were arguing with Uncle?"

"An odd coincidence the very day before he died. We need to find out why they were arguing." He considered a moment, then said, "Yes, we're going to bring Nate Nessing in on this now. But tell Nate the details of the Chicago hit on one condition. He doesn't have to inform the office downtown right away. I want to let this line spin itself out a little. Most of all, right now I've got to think of something to tell Fanning about how I got beat up." Dusk was falling, and the lights began to gather in clusters outside the train window. It was a black, breezy September night when they climbed down off the train at Union Station, nursing their bruised faces, to the stares of people waiting to board the train.

Chapter Eight

Fanning was not in the family parlor when Mack walked in. "What in the world—" Alice said, rushing up to him, putting her hand on his face. Chad stood behind her, mouth open.

"I was knocked down by a hansom cab. Just grazed me." That would do for a while. He went to the kitchen and found Mrs. Bascomb washing up dishes.

"Anything to eat?" he asked, sitting down.

"Cheese souffle, a little fallen but good, stewed apples, bacon and corn gems," she said, eyeing him. She went to the oven and opened the door to take out the leftovers.

He spoke to her back. "I was brushed by the horse of a hansom cab and—"

"Did you give the horse as good as you got?" Mrs. Bascomb demanded, facing him.

"Well—yes. Very much so. I gave better than I got, I think," he said, smiling boldly.

"O'Shaughnessey will be glad to hear that," Mrs. Bascomb said, spooning the creamy souffle and stewed apples onto the blue tulip crockery plate.

"How are Elsbeth and Margaret?" he asked. "And your sister's family?"

Mrs. Bascomb stood at the front of the stove readjusting a pin in the bun at the back of her neck. She was looking into a little mirror placed in the shining metal top of the new stove. "I live for the weekends, then I die on the weekends. Michael says he's goin' to leave m' sister when the new little one comes along. Says he can't stand the caterwaulin' in the house when the two little babes strike it up and he won't put up with it."

"But they're his children."

"Well, one is," Mrs. Bascomb said, avoiding his eyes. As Mack began eating his supper, she added, "He beat her twice this week."

"Beat a pregnant woman? Why, what kind of man—"

"He's not a good man. Sometimes people say things like so-and-so's a good man but when he's drinkin' he's a swine. But Michael is a son of destruction cold sober. He cut his mother with a butcher knife when he was thirteen."

"How do you stand it, with the girls there?"

"I worry m'self silly. There's no place else, now, is there? I wake up in the nights up there and ask, Will tonight be the night he forces himself on one of them in their beds? He's capable of it, sure. But I have to work, that's what puts food on m' children's table. So I wrap myself up in Chad, poor little fella, like he was my own and I read my novels. *Arabella's Revenge* is the one I'm readin' now."

She clucked around him then, examining his bruises and looking for the liniment and iodine to put on the ones which were breaking the skin. "Hansom cab accident," she whispered scornfully. "Not unless the cab horses were throwin' string weights."

When Mrs. Bascomb had finished, Mack went into the library, where Alice and Chad were playing dominoes. Chad came over to him and whispered, "Would you teach me to box? It could be our next adventure!" So—the hansom cab thing wasn't working with him either.

"Well, maybe it would be good for you to learn to box. Strengthen the muscles all around. I could take you to O'Shaughnessey's gymnasium." Alice looked up with a horror-stricken frown, which then eased into a gentle smile.

"Well, the heart's a muscle too. Maybe it would be something he'd benefit from. Anything that helps. . ." They both turned their heads, watching the boy for a moment, then she said, "By the way, Mr. Scott,"

"Isn't it time you called me by my name? McClure or Mack?" Or darling or sweetheart or love? My God, my mind gets off the track easily these days, he thought. What if his will followed and he lost control of himself and grabbed and kissed her?

"Of course. McClure, would you be able to take me yet this evening—I hate to ask, seeing your bruised face and that lump on your head—to Mrs. Teitelbaum's? There's a wonderful group meeting for voice manifestation tonight at nine. Walter is off in town." Her eyes grew evasive. "That's about two hours. Do you think—"

"I'm better. I slept on the train." What a lie, but all right. Anything to be with her.

Through the night again they went. The wind was brisk in his face as he handled the reins on the buggy seat, with the front side curtains pulled around to give him protection. Right out of the northwest, as it had been in Chicago. It was a real three-day blow, as they said in Michigan.

And then the eerie routine he had come to know: the dark, gas-lit front yard, the opening of huge doors and the woman behind them in the velvet blackness of the house, the trip into the lamplit parlor, nodded exchanges with the "guests," and the beginning of the séance.

The old Civil War veteran, who stood courteously and reminded them his name was Elijah Becker, was there, and the dwarf and the woman with a scarf around her head and face—two others. The lights dimmed, but the oil lamp sent its glow around the face of Mrs. Teitelbaum, who sat down at the head of a library table and gestured to them to join her.

"As you know," she told them, after they had settled themselves, "I am grieved when anyone accuses me of trickery at these séances. None of you do that—no, but I go to pains to be sure that everyone understands I am just a vessel for the conducting of the spirits' responses to you." She paused a moment. "Or—more rarely—when they attempt to contact you about something important for your lives. I shall leave the light on, dimly. Shall we proceed?" Mack didn't wonder she was nervous. There had been an article in the *Indianapolis Journal* during the week about a reporter who had attended a séance on Central Avenue. He wrote an article revealing "subterfuge and nefarious deception" when manifestations appearing in the medium's spirit closet were shown to be from a hidden magic lantern.

At Mrs. Teitelbaum's request the group held hands around the table, Alice not next to him, thankfully. The touch of her hand on his would—well, anyway, one of the newcomers, a large woman with a heaving breast, sat next to him. On the other side was the dwarf, Mr. Svenson, in the suit, hesitantly polite, placing his hand in Mack's diffidently, as if he, who often seemed to give offense, did not wish to do that with his séance neighbor.

Five minutes passed, with only a little throat clearing, a cough or two on the part of the veiled woman, some grumbling of Mr. Becker's stomach. It was warm enough in the room, Mack thought; he found himself drifting off into slumber. It was, then, a shock, when an odd voice began to speak. Mrs. Teitelbaum was the medium for a spirit communication, and the spirit communicating was a child. Was it the same voice that had been present at the séance before, talking of tubercles?

"Mummy, I am having fun here," the smug little voice said. "Someone is here to tell you I'm well taken care of."

"Who is it?" the veiled woman said in a whisper.

"He is—a cousin of yours," the child's voice enunciated.

"Which cousin?"

"Cousin—is the name Harsh? He says he was your playmate."

"Harsh? Archie? Archie?" The veiled woman began to excitedly talk to the Civil War veteran next to her. "My cousin Archie died when we were both twelve. This is proof—"

Then a man's voice. "Elise, do you remember the swing?" Then silence. Nothing more.

"Estella?" said the mother. "Come back and talk to Mummy. And where is Archie? Are you there?" But the spirits would impart nothing more. Silence again, for as long as five or six minutes, and Mack almost dropped the hand of the heaving-breast woman and dozed. Then, a rough voice,

"Arken, Arken here looking for the little miss. Sons and daughters, is the little miss here?" A sort of stirring as people sorted out that message.

"Bastards, they're all bastards. Almond eyes—" the rasping voice continued. Alice gave a little cry.

"Papa? Papa? Have you come at last?"

Humming, in a low voice that was definitely male-sounding, "Yes, the gandy man's here. The old railroad man."

"Speak to me, Papa. Why did you—why did you go?" Alice's voice was pitiful. Silence. Then, for the first time in the séance, the voice of Mrs. Teitelbaum herself.

"The spirit has a message he is unwilling to convey. Great emotion. He says—what is it? 'Shanghaied the Almond Eyes and he druv me to 't.'" Then in the voice of the man, almost sobbing, "Never gave me a moment's peace. Sorry for the little miss."

"Papa, Papa, don't go, please don't leave me. I need your comfort," Alice sobbed, but there was silence. In a moment or two Mrs. Teitelbaum opened her eyes. She smiled.

"Well, did anyone get a message tonight?" she asked brightly.

"Well of course that Elise woman, the veiled mother of the child could have talked about her cousin Archie to someone who knew Aunt Erna," Abby said the next day when Mack told him of the late-night escapade into the spirit world.

"But that the cousin's name was Archie? And what about the swing? Later she said that when they were little, he had swung out a rope swing and its seat hit her on the head. That's what the woman said."

Abby was standing by the wagon, ready to pick up fowl at the processing plant for a hotel delivery late in the day. "And so Mrs. Fanning finally got her message, too. That's interesting. Almond eyes. A Chinaman. And you say she was visibly upset."

"More than I've ever seen her. Even if it wasn't her father coming back, she seemed to think it was. Evidently she has waited a long time to hear from him."

Abby climbed up onto the buckboard and took up the reins. "Well, all this is a side dish to the main course. The murders. Come to our house tonight. Tell Nate all you told me about the Chinese escapade in Chicago. He wants to talk to Chiang, too. Come at eight."

"I can't," Mack said, "I have to give Chad his lesson. I'm trying to catch him up a bit. He's actually doing better in school. But I told you all I know. Nate needs to go see Bee Chee and Fook Soy. If this is a Hip Sing revenge killing from Chicago, and the Chicago tong has hired the rival gang—the Chee Kongs—to carry out their dirty work, Fook Soy and Bee Chee may be the two parties involved—and covering up something dire." The horses were starting down the yard. "Wish me well. I've been trying to get with Fanning all day. There are some things I have to say to him."

Fanning sat behind his desk the next day smoking his inevitable cigar through late afternoon shafts of sun.

"Sit down, Scott. I've been looking for time to see you all day, but then—busy time, busy time, thank God. More orders than we can handle locally. Your face looks bad enough."

"I guess Mrs. Fanning told you I got plastered in the street by a cab."

"Hmm. Unfortunate. Well, what did Sidlow say. Did you get to talk to him?"

"Quite a bit." So this was it. What was he going to do? Fanning, the employer, and he, the employee—they were so compromised, so involved in this, as if they were both walking a spider web with the black widows lurking in the shadows at the edge of the net. Well, in that kind of danger, it wouldn't hurt to bounce the web a little. Up and down. Besides, the son-of-a-bitch deserved it.

"Mr. Fanning, Sidlow said he was going to proceed to take whatever business he desired. He did not feel bound by something that was not fair to him, so he said."

The puffing made the air dense. "He did, did he? Well, he can wreck things if he chooses."

"Or maybe not. Suppose the group just goes ahead without him but cuts him out of all advantages through fair trade. I imagine you can outbid him with the Illinois River Valley hunters. He doesn't seem to have much money and you can offer benefits to them. Maybe five-year contracts for exclusive rights. That would keep it nice and clean."

"Maybe so, maybe so," Fanning said, nodding his head. It had not occurred to him that he could beat Sidlow honestly. "I've the skill to try that," he said, staring reflectively out the window.

"And—he said more. He intimated that he had you over a barrel." Fanning looked at him anxiously. Mack's heart knocked like a piston. Best plunge on. "Yes. It seems that, well, that the murders here among the Chinese are connected to your trying to get even with the last sales firm up there in Chicago. He's very blunt about discussing the situation, though I believe I'm the only one he's told." Fanning put his cigar down on the ashtray on the desk and stared at Mack open-mouthed.

"That because you ordered a hatchet hit that went too far, the girlfriend of the Hip Sings was killed by mistake, and they're out to seek revenge against the men you hired here."

Fanning's face turned to library paste. "Why—" he gasped. Mack took a step toward the desk. There was only one direction to go—forward. Jump out of the muck or go under.

"Mr. Fanning. I know you're shocked to see I have knowledge of this dangerous business. That I realize you're an accessory to murder. But I want you to know I think I can help you. Although it wasn't spoken, the gist of my conversation with Sidlow was that if you let him alone, he'll let sleeping dogs lie in Chinatown."

Fanning took up the cigar, carefully grinding out its charring end in the ashtray. "Well," he said ruefully. "Well, I'll be damned." Then finally, sighing acknowledgment, "How in the hell could Sidlow of all people know? The Chinese community has been completely closed-mouthed. I know the police could find nothing out—thank God."

"I know you trust me, Mr. Fanning, and in the short time I've been here I've shown myself to be a loyal employee. Maybe even friend." Except that I love your wife and hate your business style, he thought. "I would like to help." Because of Alice.

Fanning put his cigar across the ashtray and leaned on the desk towards Mack. He was sweating. "Listen to me, Scott. That thing got away from me. Completely away. The Chinks were there, I was weak, I know it now. I certainly didn't want to kill Mapeltharp, just make him leave the territory to us. And that's what happened of course. I don't think he actually knew I was involved. He thought he got caught in some crossfire in the Chinese gang wars. But then the girl—and all these other killings." His eyelids were blinking rapidly.

"I believe you. But I'm not important. The police may eventually get wind of this—"

"Oh God. Alice and Chad and the business." Mack edged to a place about two feet from him now, and patted his sleeve in a gesture that showed sympathy. Why? Was he feeling sympathy for this man whose ruthless greed had been responsible for a woman's death? Alice, certainly some of it was because of Alice. Or maybe it was because the man had some good in him—somewhere.

"If the authorities come, you can tell them the truth. Accessory charges probably wouldn't stand because all you ordered was a beating.

Still—"

Fanning was rubbing at his mustache, his feelings obviously in disorder. "I knew it would catch up to me. Mapeltharp almost died, and then he was terrified and went west to recover. But the sing-song girl died. Behold your sins will find you out. I kept going by the window of Lee Huang's laundry, wondering if he had told anyone. Afraid to travel where I might meet Li Ting, though they were sworn to secrecy about my part in it. And now they're both gone. Who did it?"

"Fook Soy, the cousin of Lee Huang, is a Chee Kong. The word is out that the Chee Kongs in Indianapolis may have been hired by the Hip Sings in Chicago to revenge the botched hatchet hit."

"One tong hire another to carry out a hit?"

"Well, the Hip Sings probably wouldn't have been able to get a Hip Sing to kill one of their own in this town. They'd have to get the rival tong to carry out the murders."

"Yes, yes indeed. Should have thought of it myself. I suspected the tongs were involved but never connected—yes, the Chee Kong must have been eager to do the killings here. Eager to be hired. Because of the opium trade, of course. They love these vendettas. Gives them more power." He stared out the window, towards where Abby was shutting the stable door for the last time that day.

"The chances that your part will come out are small. After all, the whole thing got caught up in a gang murder up there in Chicago. And now they're fighting among themselves over opium rights—if that's it. It went beyond you, and nobody may know any more of your part." Since justice is often bought these days, his inner voice sarcastically commented. Where was this all going anyway?

Fanning looked directly at him. "Except for Sidlow."

"And if we let free enterprise operate, he may let us alone. Give him his share, we take some."

"We?"

"Yes. I feel as if I'm in this too." More to divulge. "I was in Chicago asking about these murders for my friend. That's why I got beat up by a Chinese hansom cab."

Fanning looked hard at Mack for a moment, realizing for a brief time the import of what he was saying. Then his thoughts quickly returned to his own predicament. "Well, as you say, best just to hold my peace and let events take their turn," he said. Then he came out from behind the desk. "I owe you a deep debt, I think."

Mack was glad the man didn't extend his hand. He didn't really feel like shaking it. "I expect you'll suffer enough from your own conscience," he told Fanning.

Fanning took out a ring of keys. He was going to close the office. "You think so? Sounds like church. But maybe you're right. Could be indeed. Now let's go back and see what Alice is doing." Yes indeed, let's do, Mack thought, going out the door as Fanning inserted the key in the lock behind him.

They walked down Newman. "She was ecstatic about that trip you went on last night," Fanning said. "Her father came with a message, only for his bitsy babe."

"I didn't understand what it was all about and she didn't say—did you say her father?" Mack asked. They came to Tenth Street, through a misty drizzle that began to cover them. A lamplighter was lighting gas streetlights that still lined some of these obscure side streets, and a halo of light stood about each lamp in the mist.

"Yes. Old Arken. She said he called himself by name and wanted to know where the little miss was. That's what he used to call her, back in Delphi, Indiana before he deserted the family. Damned Irishman." They proceeded along the Arsenal grounds towards West Drive. "She never says anything about him, but it must be that she cares a lot that he went away and left her mother and her to fend for themselves. Now she goes around behind the iron fences in the Lockerbie neighborhood to talk to the spooks so Daddy will answer. Seems to me she'd hate him, but she doesn't. I don't get it all. What happened fifteen years ago doesn't mean a damn thing. Silly woman."

Mack nodded, not quite sure if what he wanted to do was agree with the man or paste him in the nose.

O'Shaughnessey laced a small pair of boxing gloves on Chad's hands and adjusted the punching bag to the boy's height.

"Now just let it come to you, then wait until it's at the right distance, like this"—he held it up before Chad—"and then give it a good clip." He smiled, then pushed it gently away from the boy, who stood thin and vulnerable in boxing shorts in the glaring light of the bulb.

"I'll get it. I'll pretend it's Arthur Trenton. He's always calling me cream puff." Chad hit the punching bag with surprising energy. Soon he was punching away with vigor.

Mack and O'Shaughnessey stood watching.

"Seems to have a lot of pent-up steam in him, doesn't he?" the Irishman said.

"There're a lot of feelings floating around like ghouls in the house where we live, and I suspect he senses them all," Mack said.

"Freud would say he's taking out his aggression towards his father on the punching bag," O'Shaughnessey said. "Oedipus complex."

"Freud? The mental doctor over in Austria?" Mack said absently. "I've heard of him—but I don't know much about what he says."

"Interesting, m'lad. He says we're all shaped by our youth. Sometimes warped by what we saw and felt as children. That the mind takes dark turns. As dark as that sewer out there." He pointed out the window towards the shiny manholes of the newly dedicated Pine Street sewer. "That's deep enough for a man to walk in, y'know," the older man murmured. "And Freud says that sometimes we all walk in the sewers in the back of our minds."

"And Oedipus—?" He had heard of him, vaguely.

"It's an ancient Greek myth. He was abandoned by his parents and raised by someone else. Later he met his father, the king of that country, on the road and not knowing who he was, killed him in a fight." He ran his fingers through his thinning white hair. "Then he went to the king's city and married his queen—without knowing it was his own mother. And Freud thinks down deep we all hate our fathers and want to marry our mothers."

They stood in silence for a while, watching the boy standing panting by the now-still bag.

"Did you ever know of a man named Arken? From Northern Indiana?" Mack asked in a low voice.

O'Shaughnessey sent him a sharp, sidewise glance. Then he pulled at his stubbly chin. "Joss Arken," he murmured. "He was here for a few months in '77. Lived on Irish Hill in a boarding house. Tough as cheese rind. Seemed to be hiding from something."

"What happened to him?"

"One night he was gone. We heard in a couple of months that he had been found dead in Memphis. Left a wife and child somewhere up there in northern Indiana." His voice trailed away, as if he knew nothing more about the matter and was less than interested.

And, thankfully, it seems you don't know who that wife and child were, Mack thought. For once he was glad that the layer-cake stratification of the city kept different social groups miles apart. And yet, O'Shaughnessey knew Mrs. Bascomb. They were in the same parish, lived in the Irish Hill section. If O'Shaughnessey didn't know this, when he knew other things about the Fannings, it must mean that Mrs. Bascomb didn't know her mistress' secrets. Or didn't care to tell them.

Abby was in the music room of the house on East Street the next morning, playing "Liebestraum," practicing for a violin concert at the German House, the elegant family gathering place nearby. The notes floated over the living room where Mack sat in the corner at this early morning hour, near a little table with an aspidistra plant, talking to Nate. Hearing Abby play made Mack realize he had no desire to again play the violin, the instrument he'd left behind with the rest of the things of his youth in Northern Michigan. Somehow that violin, with its plaintive, almost whining notes, seemed part of the constricting net that he felt had been woven around him by those who loved him.

Mack pulled his thoughts back to the present as Nate Nessing said, "Bee Chee, that cousin of Chiang's, has an alibi." He took out a tobacco pouch and carefully rolled himself a cigarette, picking up stray pieces of tobacco with the tip of his finger when he was done. "He and Fook Soy were both accounted for all night long the night of Lee Huang's murder."

Mack looked skeptical. "I suppose Bee Chee's wife is saying that he was in bed sleeping the night of the murder? That won't hold water—"

"No. He was at the Celestial Heaven," Nate said. Mack looked blank. "The Chinese house of ill repute. He and his brother own it. They were with Pink Orchid in an upstairs room."

Mack glanced through the door at Mrs. Nessing, standing in the hall tapping her finger in time to the violin music coming out of the music room. "You are telling me both of them were—with one woman?"

"It's the Chinese way."

"Could she be lying to cover for them?"

"Possibly. After all, they employ her. But the word is that in truth they were there, seen by others going in, seen going out a little bleary-eyed about 7:30 in the morning."

"Which is at least two hours too late for the murder." Abby had begun a Brahms score and stopped to study a passage of the music. There was a silence in the room. "What about that first murder—of Li Ting? What were they doing on that day in July?"

"They have no exact alibi. Bee Chee has a wife, one of the sing-song girls from Celestial Heaven, and she swears he was in bed with her that night. They swore Fook Soy was downstairs in that house, but they didn't actually see him all night. It all sounds weak, so probably they could have done the first killing."

"Doesn't quite add up anyway. Two killers bent on retribution, part of the Chee Kong hired from Chicago by the Hip Sing boss? But only one of them, Fook Soy, was actually a Chee Kong member. The old woman, Chiang's grandmother, said we were chasing the wrong cat when we went after the cousins. But who else in the Chinese community could Whi Ting Lo in Chicago have hired? Surely some kind of clue would have surfaced."

"That's just it. Normally the Hip Sings would have their ways of finding out if the rival tong had been hired for a hit. They don't just sit around waiting for hatchets to split their head. But nobody seemed to know anything then, and nobody knows anything now."

"Or isn't talking."

"No, that isn't it. My friend says—'no knowledge.' "

"Which means?"

"That somebody else may have committed the murders."

Mack leaned close to Nate. "Somebody outside the Chinese community? I don't believe that. Nobody's going to kill a Chinese man except another Chinese. No, the Chicago people thought it was a retribution killing."

"Did they actually say that?"

"Well, no. But everything points to it. It's a sure bet."

Nate smiled. "My father used to race horses bareback down the streets of the village in Germany. It was frowned on by the rabbi and by aunts and grandparents, but he and his brothers and friends would do it anyway a couple of times a year, bareback, and the men would place bets. My dad used to say, 'There's no such thing as a sure bet as long as there are other horses in the race who have an interest in winning.'"

There was the muffled noise of wood and strings clanking against the wooden case as Abby put away his instrument. Mack's mind, spinning with questions, barely registered the fact that it was time for him to go to work and the Nessing family to go about their business.

But the questions had to wait, because the fall hotel orders, both locally and in lower Michigan, kept everyone busy. In the next two-and-a-half weeks Mack also had to travel to Illinois to line up a young duck hunter to provide for the Chicago hotel trade Sidlow was trying to grab. He took the time to go to the house of the man, a highly recommended young mechanic named Charles Perdew, to meet his hunting friends and to go with them to a houseboat on the Illinois River flats to shoot ducks.

Perdew agreed to seek out the best of the canvasbacks, collect wild rice, and send them daily on the train to Chicago, letting Indiana Poultry Purveyors handle the accounts and pay him with a regular salary. Mack was able to return to Fanning to say that he had beat out Sidlow, after all, with nothing more than personal interest, the building of trust and an extra gift of appreciation money for a fine new employee.

More drizzling rain and a cold wind announced the coming of October, rattling the window casement in Mack's third-floor bedroom at midnight. A cross draft snapped the badly fitting bolt on his bedroom door. The door creaked open, showing the oriental rug runner in the hall, its pattern illuminated faintly by the flickering light of an old oil lamp.

The faint creak of a door made his hair stand on end in the murky darkness within his room; then, like a shadow, Alice Fanning passed his door, her hair dishevelled from sleep, her eyes blank.

Drawn against his will, he threw off the covers, quickly pulled on his trousers, and slipped down the stairs after her. Her shadowy form was disappearing out the back door. How cold it would be, he thought, with this wind and rain. She wore again that beautiful black peignoir, but it would be as a spider web in the gale. Was it just that he wished to protect her? Why did he want to witness the pain that drove her to glide through the night, sent on ominous errands by the dark side of her psyche? He did not know, but on he went, compelled by fear and longing.

Again she walked down the path, her small slippers passing over bricks covered with slippery leaves, as if the danger of falling did not exist.

Then on, past the privy—obviously she had not come on that errand. And, through the gate, into the narrow alley and south, into the face of the wind.

Sadly he turned back, uneasy but unwilling to spy further. She had given him no invitation to intrude on her life. It was cold, and he was filled with foreboding. It was he that loved, not she. Still, the dark forays strongly unnerved him. How could she still sleep with droplets of cold rain drifting across her face? Why did she rise from her restless bed some nights, while sleeping others? And why did she always head into the shadows of the back yard, instead of going out the front door? If he had the answers to these questions, he too might be able to sleep on these nights when his love arose to stride the lanes of darkness, dressed in black, looking for the father she had lost too early and whom she now tried to call from the very land of the dead.

The next morning dawned bright and clear. Mrs. Bascomb put a letter beside his plate of waffles and sausage. "Who do you know in Vincennes?" she asked.

"Well, my father came from Vincennes. His relatives are all there, and he's been writing to them about me."

"Will you want to read it to me?" she asked, smiling and sitting down across from him. "It's just that I'm curious."

He nodded and unfolded the letter.

September 28, 1895

Dear Young Cousin:

I heard from your Pa that you are in the capital city. He said you were curious about your kin down here in God's country and how we're getting along. I'll try to spell it out for you.

Well, your pa and me were good friends from the time we were younguns before the war. We're cousins, descendants of the original McClures who came from Ireland to Pennsylvania and then to Indiana in the time of George Washington. My great-grandpa was Dan'l McClure, who fought for George Rogers Clark. Your pa's great-grandma was Jenny McClure, Dan'ls sister. We keep their memory fresh down here with tales told round the fireplace, cause they are the stuff of legend.

Dan'l and Jenny were the children of John and Jane McClure. The father John died in Pennsylvania and Jane was eighty some year old when they finally got to the promised land, Knox County, Indiana. Dan'l was a fine old man, so they says and I don't know because I didn't know him or my father or mother either. But my Grandma Catherine Hogue told me all about them all the time.

She said your great-grandma Jenny was a sensitive. That means that she sensed things other people didn't, sensed them and saw things from other times. In the Indian times, it druv her into herself and she couldn't talk no more to anyone. Anyways, your pa and I fought in the war, in different units. I was in the Fourteenth Indiana Regiment along with my kinsmen and friends, now sadly gone, fallen at places like Chancellorsville and Gettysburg. Your pa was in the Eightieth Indiana, which fought in Kentucky at Perryville and chased Morgan the Raider. But you know that.

Your dad was in a prison camp in Richmond, I know he's told you about that, and when he come home he married your ma in Louisville. I went to that wedding, and it was the last time I saw your parents. Sure would like to see them again, that I would.

I had five children of my own and now my eldest gal, Nannie, is going to marry a fine boy, the grandson of my old friend Thomas Jefferson Brooks. John Niblack is the nephew of one of the veterans of the Fourteenth, my old friend Captain Lewis Brooks. Captain Brooks was also the colonel of your pa's unit, after he resigned from the Fourteenth and he is a old friend of your pa's too. This John Niblack runs his Grandpa Brooks' store in Wheatland. I was a-thinking that it sure would be nice if you and your pa and maybe even ma could come to that wedding. I'm sending you all a invite to it, a month from now, November 7 at the Upper Indiana Church on the old Bruceville Road at eleven in the morning. My wife Fannie is sending out some formal flim-flam invites, but I think I want to send you a invite personal.

> *Your cousin*
> *John R. McClure*

Mrs. Bascomb put another hot waffle on his plate and refilled the syrup container. He had been eating a few bites while he read this lengthy letter, and a drop or two of syrup had to be wiped off the last page.

"Well, will you be able to go? Sounds like a real down-home whing-ding"

"I don't see how—so many things happening, everything up in the air," he muttered. "I'd like to, though. I've wanted to get in touch with them. I've heard so many stories for so long."

Alice breezed into the kitchen, bright as the golden-green tree outside the back window. "I'm famished, Mrs. Bascomb. Must be all that air last night. My window was open all night long." Mrs. Bascomb did not look up from the stove. Did she know about the sleepwalking?

Then Alice's face darkened. "Mrs. Bascomb, you don't need to iron today. Mr. Fanning took the laundry himself. He left early. You can bring my tray to the family parlor." She went off went off muttering something about "insisting on that filthy place."

As Mack left the house Alice called after him, "Mr.—that is, McClure, will you join us tonight at the church? It is World Children's Day." Absently Mack called back an affirmation; he was eager to go by the laundry before he was due in the office.

"He was here," Toy Gum said, speaking English instead of Chinese. She was bent over, her long, wide sleeves brushing the sides of the basket she was piling clothes into. "Leave laundry, but really want to talk to me. See if I know any more about the deaths. He want to know if my son mention him any time. He feel it out, like a man casting line in water for a carp." She raised one corner of her mouth in what passed for a smile. She seemed to trust him, like a confidant.

"Thank you, Mrs. Toy Gum. Would you please tell Chiang that I was by and offered my respects?" He looked at the monogrammed shirts sitting in a wicker baby basket by the side of the counter. WAF. Walter A. Fanning?

At the door he paused and looked back, sensing she had something more to say.

"We put letters on the shirts. Guilt is a letter that writes itself on the face. So it is with Mr. Fanning."

Yes, and exactly how far did that guilt go? Was it only guilt? For there was one fact they hadn't fully faced. If there were retribution killings going on for the Chicago murders, Fanning might be next. If the murderer knew of Fanning's involvement. And there was a final chilling possibility. Fanning himself had everything to gain by eliminating those connected with the botched hit. Able to move unnoticed on the streets of Indianapolis because of his late-night dissipations, he could be the man passing through darkness to slash and kill Chinese. He could be the murderer.

The wind pierced his light coat as he left the laundry, and he reminded himself that he would have to use part of his salary to get a coat soon to keep out the increasing chill of the air. When he got to the office a letter from Sidlow sat on his desk.

The lights of Central Avenue Methodist Church were blazing in the Biblical way "even as the noonday sun," as Fanning, Alice and Chad approached in the rig with Mack driving.

A banner above the door announced "World Missions: A Christian Life for Children of the World." Chad strutted through the door, half-dancing. "I'm to get an award, I know I will," he said.

"What's this about?" Mack whispered to Alice.

"The Methodist Church has special children's missions as a part of their evangelical work around the world. In Africa, Asia—this is to tell us about it and to raise money for it."

And so it was. Different children marched down the aisles in costumes of countries like Rhodesia, Belgium Congo, Sumatra, China. They gathered in front of the altar to sing songs in small, piping voices, accompanied by a robust piano player lady with hips that overhung the round screw-up seat. Fanning seemed distracted, drumming his fingers against the edge of the pew and staring at the stained glass windows: the depiction of an open Bible and the doves representing the Holy Spirit.

Next was a speech by the District missions representative telling about the little Sunday Schools in the hinterlands, where the Bible was being taught to savages. Then hymns were sung by the whole congregation, "Am I a soldier of the cross/A follower of the lamb?" Mack was surprised at how enthusiastic the group was and how much he was enjoying himself—watching Fanning. The man pursed his lips, tapped his foot, clenched and unclenched his fist. He was sweating all over his monogrammed collar. Nate Nessing had said some of the Chinese community believed the murders were committed by someone other than a Chinaman. Was it—could it be possible—that Fanning himself had killed one or both of those Chinamen? To cover his tracks for the hatchet hit that went wrong in Chicago? And that he, McClure Scott was sitting in this pew with him, living in the house with him, loving his wife. Good God. Fanning could be an ax murderer. Mack was thinking the unthinkable, not without some relish.

Reverend Clayborne raised his hand. "And now, before the last part of our program, I'd like to give some of our own Central Avenue children prizes for their own missionary work." Earlier that month, Mack now recalled, they'd given out cans with a picture of a little Chinese baby on the side to all the Sunday School children so they could ask for donations. Chad had been carrying his offering can around to school and all of Woodruff Place.

They announced the third and second place winners for the most money collected and two little girls danced up one at a time, bows in their hair and patent leather shoes twinkling. They received packages which were obviously books. "And the winner of the contest, who collected $20.56, is Chad Fanning. Come up here, Chad."

Amidst applause Chad made his way up to the front and was soon back in the pew, tearing open the purple tissue paper. "Look! It's *The Pathfinder*," he cried.

"By James Fenimore Cooper. It's about the Indians and frontiersmen," Mack whispered. "We'll read it together! And I bet we can think of some adventures with it, too."

Several ushers wearing coolie or African tribal chieftain feather hats passed among the pews collecting contributions to the missions.

Dr. Clayborne smiled his broad, bland smile. With his bald head glinting in the electric glare of the lights, he looked like a giant baby in a long, black nightgown. "Now we're going to have a torchlight parade to three places in the neighborhood for refreshments typical of the mission fields. Mrs. Sally Pflug will have African fruit compote and sweets at her home in the next block north on Central. Mr. and Mrs. Noah Leete will welcome you to their home on College Avenue with Hawaiian coconut macaroons, macadamia nuts and punch; and Reverend Brockelhurst will serve Chinese tea and fortune cookies at his home over on Pine Street. Take your choice! The ushers will lead the way to the various homes in a torchlight parade!"

And so they trekked out of the church in a joyful mood, Chad carrying his book. "Let's go to the Chinese tea. I want to go inside his old house," Chad said. His mother shook her head wordlessly.

"Mr. and Mrs. Leete's is just over on College Avenue a bit," she said. "Dr. Brockelhurst's is a long way." Obviously she wouldn't care for the Chinese choice.

"No, I don't care if it is farther. I want to go to Dr. Brockelhurst's. I won the prize and I get to say where we go." His mouth turned petulant; he pulled on her arm, pleading. Finally she acquiesced and they began walking towards Pine Street.

Fanning smiled a little forced smile. She brightened and actually took his arm as she went. Odd how the day after she sleepwalked she seemed animated, joyous. Was she in some way purged of the demons that beset her by the somnambulant episodes?

Dr. Brockelhurst had arrived at his home before the torch-bearing ushers, and he opened the door himself. The festive churchgoers looked like elegant trick-or-treaters, rubbing their hands together to warm them, the women pulling fur stoles close around their shoulders against the cold. It was an old house of the sixties, with a captain's perch on the top, rather grim, actually, Mack thought. Out of the door drifted an odd, musty, almost rotten smell.

They were ushered, laughing and stamping leaves off their feet, into the interior, which was all dark burnished wood and shadows. A glowering cat stared at them from the gloom; it was a decoration on the top of an umbrella stand.

Dr. Brockelhurst stood in the entrance hall, a head smaller than most of them, with his beak nose shining in the lamplight.

"Beautiful house," Alice murmured to the minister, pulling off her gloves and looking around at horsehair sofas and needlepoint frames of the period of the Civil War. But then her eyes began to rove warily over the Chinese furnishings which lurked in the shadows.

They went into the parlor. "Do you live alone here?" Fanning asked the minister.

"My housekeeper lives upstairs," Dr. Brockelhurst said, pointing up a huge tier of lushly carpeted stairs disappearing into the darkness above.

The group of about fifteen sat on plush chairs. Their conversation grew quiet as they glanced about the room, to Cantonese screens, seated mahogany dogs, black wooden tables holding tiny porcelain cups.

"I forgot his father was a missionary," Alice murmured to Mack.

"Is this an old house? It looks haunted." Chad asked the minister. Fanning gave him a stern look.

"Well yes, and no, young man," Brockelhurst said, smiling faintly. "It was built by a man who made a fortune in munitions during the war. There is some silly legend about him haunting the house, actually, pining over the many men killed because of his factory." He licked his lips. "At that time, the street was on the edge of town, almost in the country. But now—progress marches on. The Pine Street neighborhood houses factories. This place seems a relic of a former age."

He poured from a large Russian tea service, handing cups around and then passed a plate of fortune cookies. People chatted politely, commenting on the sharpness of the green brew, which made Mack think of the Chicago restaurant.

Suddenly Alice Fanning stood up. "Excuse me," she said haltingly, pulling Chad to her and looking at Fanning. "Just all too much. I feel a little ill. I know you'll pardon us if we beg to be excused." Without even waiting for a response, she pulled on her gloves and headed quickly into the front hall. She strode over to the clothes rack where her fur wrap was draped under several others. Mack hurried from the parlor to see her grasping frantically for her stole, ignoring the wraps which fell on the floor, and finally tossing the mink heads over her shoulders. She grabbed Chad, who had rushed out of the parlor after her, by the hand and headed for the door.

"All those Chinese things," she said to Mack in an anguished voice as he followed close behind her. "I thought I could stand them on a social evening, but I guess I can't."

Fanning emerged from the parlor, nodding to everyone and giving his hand hurriedly to the minister. "Thanks for all, very much. She's ill," he muttered, and they were all through the door in a matter of seconds. But outside, in the cold darkness, as he led them back towards the church and the waiting rig, Fanning threw a piece of paper onto the curb.

Mack, trailing the others, picked it up. It was the Chinese fortune from the cookie Fanning had been given in the house. "Secrets held are like spent coals in the brazier. Fanned, they come forth."

At ten o'clock Mack was bathing himself furiously in the clawfoot bathtub beyond Chad's room, scrubbing the dirt from his arms with a heavy-nubbed washcloth and rosewater soap. It helped to get the surface dirt off; the dirt he felt he had mired himself while living in this house was a little harder to get rid of. He paused, sitting in the hot water he had heated on the little wood stove which sat in the corner. He hadn't written home in a while. What a letter that would be if he told the truth! He imagined the letter he would never send:

Dear Homefolks:

I'm fine and the tutoring and office jobs are going as well as can be expected. A threatening character named Sidlow has written me a letter affirming his intent to pursue all markets in the unethical and possibly illegal cartel my boss is participating in. Why he didn't write to my scoundrel boss Fanning is an interesting question. I've been to Chicago tracking a murderer. This shady Chicagoan Sidlow expressed interest in my search for clues to the murders here, but somehow the questions had an edge of nervousness, I thought. Why should he care any more about the Chinese murders in this town? That's a question worth knowing about.

I'm living in a house with a man who is a very good candidate for murderer in bloody ax and knifing murders and a woman who has "hysterical repressions." Where did I get that phrase? I went to the library with Chad and while we were there I looked up the works of Sigmund Freud, that doctor who treats diseases of the mind. None of his writing is actually translated—he's part of a group of European doctors and I had to read about their theories as a group in medical magazines.

The articles said Freud thinks certain women in our times suppress their womanly instincts and love for their fathers, especially if the fathers aren't around. Well, I guess so! This lady consults spiritualists to find her dead father and wanders the lanes at night looking for him in her sleep—guess that's what she's doing. I don't know why I stay except I love her passionately and couldn't possibly leave her with this Jack the Ripper (if that's what he is.) The biggest problem is I don't know if he is Jack the Ripper or just one of his friends—or even victims.

Fine kettle of fish, indeed, as Grandma Adalia says whenever she comes from Louisville and sees the winters in Traverse City, fine kettle of fish.

> *Don't worry about me. I'll either live or die pursuing my curios-*
> *ity and hopeless, fanatical love in the house with Walt the Ripper.*
>   *Your son*
>   *McClure*

For the next few days he went through the paces of work and tutoring and eating and speaking perfunctorily to the people of the house
until a few days later, when Sunday came. The household went off to
church without him, and he did what he knew he must do. He climbed
the stairs to the second floor.

It had haunted him since he entered this house—an entire floor
where only one man slept, where the cleaning lady did not clean, where
the child of the house did not seek his father, where the wife of the house
did not sleep next to her husband.

October sunlight slanted through a leaded glass window at the end
of the second floor hall. The carpet runner looked dusty, uncared for.
Once a year, in the spring, Mrs. Bascomb said, she came to this floor
and cleaned all but his room. That he did himself. It was locked, of
course; but he had taken a wax impression of the lock earlier, in a furtive, twilight trip when Fanning was gone at one of his endless "evenings out." He had not really looked in the room then.

Now he had the key; Chiang had it made downtown somewhere;
he had his ways. The other rooms on the floor were shut; but he gently
opened the first door and looked in. It was for storage; old lamps and
trunks and broken chairs were scattered about.

The next room had a sterile little bed in it, pitchers of artificial
flowers on a tall, three-footed table and one picture of a Dutch water
scene on the wall. Had it been Alice's when they were first married?
There was a door on the side wall; it seemed to connect with what had
to be Fanning's room. Wait a minute—could the door to the small room
open to Fanning's connecting apartment? That would be too good to
be true and an easier way than trying a key that might not fit. He walked
past the bed, tried the door and backed away disappointed. He would
have to break and enter with his furtive key. No doubt about that.

And so in a half a minute he was inserting the key in the lock, listening carefully for any sound below. It turned hard, seemed to stall, but finally clicked. He opened the door and entered into a room heavy with the odors of tobacco and musk and pomade sweat. A high-backed Lincoln bed was made in a surprisingly neat way with a dark maroon spread. A lamp table piled high with papers stood by the side of the bed, and two desks were under the curtained windows. He went to them; on one were stacked cigar boxes, each one with its own trade stamp on the top: buxom Cuban maidens in peasant blouses or portly gentlemen peering through pince nez spectacles. An odor of stale cigar butts wafted out of the wastebasket near the desk.

Memo pads, doodles, (skull and crossbone and Sidlow's name and women with large breasts) were on the second desk. Nothing very ominous here.

On the wall above the two desks was hung a calendar with a Gibson Girl illustrating September (it hadn't been turned) and a poster of dogs playing poker. Typical man's retreat. Nothing here—damn it, he'd have to go into the desk drawers.

Inside, *Police Gazettes*, and a book called *The Pearl*. Thumbed pages—Fanning must have read this often. Mack opened it inside to a story called "Miss Fotheringale's Ladies School." It seemed to be about a lady who had a school—teenaged girls, a visiting male cousin of the headmistresses' wants a little fun, so the old biddy throws an orgy with the girls, lots of specific details about young, nubile female bosoms and juicy nether parts and odd variations—same old stuff from the lumber camps in Michigan.

But, under the *Police Gazettes*, what was this? A revolver. Colt 45, mother-of-pearl handle. And bullets in a packet. And, on the other side of the desk, three drawers full of folders marked "special accounts," a dragon drawn in India ink on the front. Chinese names carefully listed, several for withdrawals and some kind of payments for Nate's suspects Fook Soy and Bee Chee and even for the first murdered man Li Ting. And beneath them all, three long, white opium pipes. He picked one of the pipes up; still fresh with the odd smell of what must be the drug itself.

He closed the drawer with a shove, looked around to be sure that everything was as it had been and quickly walked to the door and through it, being careful to lock it securely and wipe off its plate. He could not get down the hall fast enough and felt his heart beating wildly. He hoped to God he had left no trace of himself in the room where, obviously, there was more hiding than he could have guessed.

"He is what you call Chinese uncle," Chiang said. They sat the next day stirring cups of coffee in Ashby's Cafe. "He is under-the-table banker for the interests of the Chinese community. If they need money for financing the sing-song girl prostitution interests, legal fees if they get picked up or arrested, and most of all, loans for expanding the trade."

"Opium?"

"Yes.

"Illegal loan sharking?"

"Probably not really illegal. He doesn't make the deals himself, but uses a go-between, I think. Loans money, collects it with high interest. But it's immoral. Scores of people in this town are going down the sewer drains numbing their brains with some concoction or other and he uses their money to outfit his fancy house and go to brothels. And it's not just Chinese. You saw the den in Chicago—" Mack nodded. He couldn't help thinking of the young man lying in that terrible place curled up as he had in his mother's womb.

"Why didn't you tell me sooner?"

"I never knew until just now when you told me about the account books. My uncle often talked to him—and lately with—lot of nervousness. But I haven't wanted to know." Chiang's eyes were grim. "My whole object is to forget these things, to assimilate," he went on, sighing. "To be the ideal student at Indianapolis High School. President of Debate Team, talking of whether we should intervene in Cuba, you know, earning my own way in the white world. I wanted to get away from the Chinese community."

"Why?"

"You heard what Wong Woon said in Chicago. We are despised as dirty beasts. And Indiana is worst, because it stinks with intolerance."

"Intolerance? Well, I suppose so."

"You suppose so," Chiang said bitterly, setting down his spoon to look Mack directly in the eye. "This state—this town and everyone in it—is full of race hatred."

Mack felt a flash of anger. It was a strong accusation. "My father fought to free the slaves. I've never heard him say an unkind thing about another race and he's a Hoosier."

"Well, then he's one in a hundred. Most of these people, the children of the Civil War vets and the ones who stayed home because they hated the war, have no idea of giving equality to those the war freed. They would jump at the chance to become part of a—what do you call it? a lynching party if some colored person got 'too uppity' or look at a white girl. Don't frown at me like that—they would! The only jobs available in this town are as yard men and rag pickers."

Mack couldn't disagree.

"And we Chinese are one rung up. The town thinks of us right off as opium fiends and hired killers. Now they've finally got a way to keep us from even coming into the country. Under the bill passed by Congress not one Chinaman can come to land of the free and home of the brave. None of us can get a fair trial, any more than colored men can. The law won't protect us. Try to imagine how that feels, Mack Scott, if all your friends were seen as equal with monkeys and your father could be strung up for looking at the wrong man."

Mack did, and shook his head uncomfortably as Chiang went on. "No, the police won't find the men who did the murders among the Chinese."

"Because they think that you kill each other. And it may be true"

"But I don't think so. No, during the last week this worm has taken a turn. Talking to Wong Woon in Chicago opened up my mind. I need to quit denying I'm Chinese. I've gone to all the sides of town on what we Chinese call a forgiveness and honor quest, seeing old relatives and my grandmother's friends, repairing the hole in the wall."

"And?"

"And they say this is not a tong thing. Involved, maybe, but not done by Chinese. Look beyond."

"Fanning? Some things seem to point to him."

Chiang looked at him, understanding what he was saying. The tall waitress sat buffing her nails in a patch of sunlight by the window.

"There were three pipes in his bedroom. How bad is his habit, I wonder?" Mack whispered. "Did anybody know or say anything about him?"

"Nothing. But I can find out. What was he doing the night my uncle was murdered?"

"I don't know. He was supposed to be in the house, but of course, it would be easy to get out of that second-story bedroom and out of the house, because everybody sleeps above him. I suppose that's why he has that setup."

Chiang sat pondering the information, staring absently out the restaurant window.

"Your uncle was on the list Fanning had in his drawer. Involved in the opium and loan trade with him. So was Li Ting."

"Let's see—the night Li Ting was murdered was—"

"The night before I got to town. Which was July 21. So July 20. What was Fanning doing that night? It would be hard to re-trace. The trail is cold."

"Yes—but wait." Chiang looked up, thoughtfully. "If Fanning was feeding the dream pipe habit—it would be recorded. Each den owner keeps a tab."

"Which of the dens do you suppose he frequents?"

"Well, maybe more than one. The one on Lockerbie is closed. And Uncle's—" He rose suddenly. "Come, let's go," he said, throwing coins down on the table to cover the bill.

"Where?" Mack said as he got up from the table.

"To the steam pipes—in the basement back at the laundry. Maybe the trail is still fresh there."

Abby was putting shirts on hangers in the laundry, talking to Toy Gum when they burst through the door. "I came looking for you," he said to Chiang. "I wanted to see what you were finding out." They descended the steps and then filled him in.

"Chiang's convinced our man's not in the Chinese community," Mack said. "If that's the case, Fanning could be a real suspect."

"Why?" Abby wanted to know.

"Because of the Chicago hit. And because he's an opium eater."

He told Abby of his discovery upstairs.

"Maybe he's silencing the Chinese who have been involved with him in illegal narcotic operations in this town. Maybe one of them was blackmailing him, threatening to reveal his habit and connections to his fancy friends at the Commercial Club. The most important thing in his life is his place in society. He's nothing without that."

"Or—what about the Chicago connection," Abby said. "Fanning could be silencing a couple of Chinese somebodies who knew too much."

"I don't know if Uncle kept those secret dream repose customer records out here with the tong stuff," Chiang said, reaching into the steam pipe hole and fishing through documents. "But we shall see— ah, a few things are left. Some Hip Sing stuff—I didn't take the time to look at that before. And of course the Chee Kong initiation is gone now because we took that up to Chicago to give to Wong Woon." He brought out papers and looked at them. In a minute he shrugged his shoulders. "No list here."

"But it wouldn't be here, would it?" Abby wondered. "It would be in the opium den."

"Outside—" They raced up the steps. Mrs. Toy Gum looked at them questioningly as they passed on their way to the back shed.

The shed was locked, but Chiang had the key. They went inside and Chiang went to a closet at the back and used another, smaller key on it. Opium paraphernalia was here, pipes, boiling pots, small crates, pots of the sticky black residue, all in a box stored in the closet. Nate had mentioned that the old woman must have hidden the incriminating stuff—and this was where it was.

The police hadn't even considered the shed to be of material interest. Obviously the pallets of the floor were used for something, but Lee Huang had been found there, killed in his sleep, and if anybody else was sleeping there or smoking anything, they didn't care. They had come once, looked inside, and concluded the whole thing was a Chinese gang war. Case closed.

"We used the shed for the washhouse during the day," Chiang murmured "and at night—the customers came and went, using these pallets. They would be gone by daybreak. I heard them, but I didn't want to know." He looked at the floor.

"Fanning?" Mack wondered, poking around some cardboard trash on the sorting table.

"Probably. He could have easily walked over here through the darkness late at night."

"Nobody in the house would have seen him leave."

"Wouldn't the people on West Drive think it odd if they were wakeful and saw him walking along at midnight?"

"I don't think so," Mack answered. "He's known for his scandalous habits. And he's not the only one who walks around in Woodruff Place late at night. Sometimes men, never women of course, walk when they are restless, exercising dogs and smoking or whatnot. And several of these men are dallying with other women. They go openly to tête-à-tête at other houses in Woodruff Place. It's well known and accepted. Some of the names would surprise you, so McCloskey tells Miss Farquharson, dirty old gossip that he is. But if we could link Fanning in some way, either proving he was or wasn't here—"

Abby was pushing and probing around in the boiler pots. He pulled up the top lid of a built-in cabinet. "Wait a minute. Here are some closed containers." The three bent over and saw Ball jars with lids screwed on lined up in rows. "Starch" was written on a label on one dark brown jar which could not be seen through, and Mack quickly extracted it from the cabinet.

"Papers, rolled to fit inside a round jar," he murmured, putting his hand down. Quickly they spread them out on the table. "This is it!" Chiang said excitedly. "Records, but written in English in my uncle's hand of the guests who visited this shed. Organized by months."

"Why didn't he write in Chinese?"

"Names are easier in English. He was good in both languages."

They leaned close to scan dates. "May, June, July—here's the tenth." He turned the page.

"Nineteenth, twentieth," Abby read. "Look. Richfield, Osgood, whoever they are, and Bee Chee."

"Bee Chee—" Mack interrupted.

"And W. Fanning! Here it is! Doesn't say how long he stayed, but he was here, on this side of town, not over on the other. If this date is correct. But what's this beside his name?"

"A Chinese character," Mack said, tracing it with his finger. "What's it say, Chiang?"

Chiang looked at it for a long moment, then shook his head. "I don't know. It looks old fashioned. There are thousands of characters, and I only know the most common."

"Maybe it means he left early, or stayed all night? This could be very important," Abby said, standing up. "Shall we leave the jar? Or take it?" he wondered.

"It's evidence the police should eventually know about if—" Mack said.

Chiang looked apprehensive. "If we leave it here, whoever we're looking for, the murderer, could eventually come looking. If he knows of the guest list, that is."

"And if it's missing and we have it, we're in a terribly dangerous position."

"How would anybody know? No one saw us come out here. Besides, they don't even know the guest list exists," Mack scoffed.

"Not even the customers?" Abby wondered.

"Someone must know. Just because it's still here doesn't mean it isn't being watched. And information travels through the sewers here," Chiang said ruefully.

Mack thought about O'Shaughnessey. He knew Alice's father and probably a lot of other information about people in the town.

Mack finally made the decision, picking up the jar and putting it under his arm. Chiang then firmly closed the cabinet door. They went out the back door of the washhouse, locking it behind them.

"I mean the dark, murmuring gossip line," Chiang said. "The white and Chinese and black communities have their own version of it. Information, some pretty ugly, spread door to door, back fence to back fence behind hands. I don't know who knows what. So taking this jar is dangerous—"

"I realize that," Mack answered. "But I'm already in over my knees. Why not go over the belly?"

And who knows? The list might have information that could protect Alice. Or condemn Fanning, at least show him as a reprobate, maybe involved in criminal actions. Allow her to leave him—she must have wished to be free long before this. The thought had not occurred to him before. Did he want her free? He honestly did not know. It was only another strand in the web closing around him.

"I think that Chinese character is important. It could help confirm Fanning as the prime suspect. Can we ask your grandmother what the character means?" he asked Chiang as they walked towards the house.

"I don't think so. Or anyone else in the Chinese community. What if it says something about the murders? Or opium deals? Everyone is scared enough about all this. It raises too many fears." He turned and faced them at the door. "Anyway, I think it's in old Chinese—scholar language. My uncle was well taught. He probably wished to disguise his note, even from other Chinese."

"I know of someone I can ask. I'll do it and let you know later," Mack said. He said goodbye and walked south through the wan sunshine.

Chapter Nine

"You promised to read the *Leatherstocking Tales* with me," Chad said, pulling on Mack's coattails. It was Tuesday following the incident in Chiang's shed, and they were sitting on the stairs in the front hall looking at the evening paper.

"So I did," Mack said absently, eyeing Fanning as he sat in the formal library across the hall from the family parlor, smoking and reading a magazine. Next to him was the box with the buxom girl and the peasant blouse; in his mind's eye Mack saw it on the desk upstairs. Fanning had apparently noticed nothing after the breaking and entering of his bachelor's den.

"Well, shall I go get the book?" Chad wanted to know. It would soon be time for supper; Alice was out picking chrysanthemums for a pitcher in the center of the library table where they would eat. There was a fire in the grate. All very homey and family-like, Mack thought, a page out of the *Ladies Home Journal*. Except that somebody around here might be a murderer, with all of them living under his shadow. But why should we let that bother us, Mack wondered. The happy little family prepares for a supper beside the fire. It wasn't the only hypocrisy in this suburb of Woodruff Place tonight. Or the city of Indianapolis, for that matter. Out there James Whitcomb Riley was doing one of his poetry readings about the wholesomeness of childhood for a group of oohing and ahing ladies and gentlemen, all of whom knew that by midnight he would probably be lying drunk on the porch of the Lockerbie Street house where he boarded.

"Bring the book to me," Mack sighed. "But I can only read for a while. I have an appointment tonight." As he turned the pages past illustrations of noble savages, tall and stately, standing by huge oak trees, he found he was interested in spite of himself. It had been one of the favorite books of his childhood. But of course it was too difficult for a second grader to read, especially one who was a little behind. This first part was slow, about—what was it? Oh yes, the heroic Deerslayer and Hurry Harry, a tall boasting frontiersman, are going to visit Harry's lady friend who lives with her father and sister in the wilderness of New York State.

"Well, I remember this part. They come to a log castle on a beautiful lake. I'll read it to you," Mack said, settling Chad in beside him on the step.

On a level with the point lay a broad sheet of water, so placid and limpid that it resembled a bed of the pure mountain atmosphere, compressed into a setting of hills and woods. Its length was about three leagues, while its breadth was irregular, expanding to half a league, or even more opposite to the point and contracting to less than half that distance more to the southward. At its northern or nearest end it was bounded by an isolated mountain.

"It sounds just wonderful. I wish I could see it. Now read more."

Mack turned the page. "Well, I'll tell the story to you for a while. When they get up to this log palace in the middle of nowhere, they find the old man and his two daughters gone. And Hurry Harry—"

"Why do they call him that?"

"Because he is always rushing in and out of danger, bad situations. Anyway, Hurry Harry thinks that they've gone out in their houseboat, and Deerslayer and Harry get in a canoe and begin paddling up this beautiful lake. Let me read for you." He read of how the two frontiersmen searched for the creek outlets where the old man might have docked his houseboat to hunt and trap. "They find a likely creek and go into it with the canoe."

Along their whole length, the smaller trees overhung the water, with their branches often dipping in the transparent element. The banks were steep.. .

"I've never been to a lake or paddled a canoe, McClure. Didn't you say you grew up on the shores of a lake?"

"Lots of lakes. And I used to take canoes out and follow the paths of rivers and creeks for miles, to see where they led. Sometimes there are steep bends, and animals scurry away from you and sometimes you have to pick up the canoe and carry it over little rapids."

"Oh, I wish I could do that. Could we go follow a creek in a canoe? It could be our adventure this week."

Mrs. Bascomb set the food on the table by the fire and they rose from their seats on the stairs to go in. Mack asked her about canoes. "I don't think there are any canoes near Woodruff Place—maybe out north at White River," she said, "but they're putting them away for the winter. And anyway, White River would be a little too high after these rains."

"Could we just follow a small river? Or creek?" Chad persisted as he sat down on the couch and spread a napkin across his knees. "Start at its source and go along the bank, waiting for surprises? Animals darting out and all that."

Mack pursed his lips, thinking. It was the least of the things he wanted to do right now, with all the distractions of trying to unravel what the people in this house were about. But—

"How about Pogue's Run?" Chad asked excitedly.

"Pogue's Run. Oh, yes. That creek that you have to cross on Newman Street to get to the office. Then it flows through the Arsenal. Where does it go?" Mack asked, seating himself at a small table covered with a tatted doily.

"I don't exactly know, downtown I think. Let's ask Papa and Mama."

Alice and Walter Fanning entered the family parlor, completing the tranquil domestic scene from *Ladies Home Journal*. As he was served up a plate of lamb curry and mixed fruit salad, Mack did ask Papa and Mama about Pogue's Run.

"It is flowing pretty well by the time it comes to the Arsenal grounds," Fanning said, seating himself and buttering a biscuit. "Then it wanders and meanders southwest until the area at Pine and New York Streets where it turns south and goes across town. It empties into White River eventually. Why do you care?" He looked at McClure Scott with the same kind of wary speculativeness that was a constant for him since he'd found out that Sidlow had told Mack about the Chicago hatchet hit. He did not like having the secret layers of his life mined. The question was, how deep were those secret layers? Accessory to murder, certainly. Chinese uncle, evidently. Murderer of those who might talk? It was chilling to watch him put apple butter on a biscuit as if he were Goldilocks instead of possibly the murderer of the Rue Morgue.

"Well!" Mack said heartily. "Chad and I are going on an adventure, pretending we're Leatherstocking and his friend. Is there a footpath along Pogue's Run?"

Alice poured tea, holding the teapot lid on with a dainty finger. "Yes, a good one. You can fish in the creek too. But in the last few years, since the sewers started emptying into it, it's been getting messy with shoes and such."

Chad rose and went to her. "Mama, McClure is going to take me on an adventure up a wilderness creek. We are going to search for the hidden houseboat and see wild animals around the bends."

"Well, when is this fine trip?" she asked, smiling at her son.

"Tomorrow," Mack answered for him, "if the weather cooperates. It looks like it will be fair and mild, for a change."

"May I go? I love creek walks."

"Of course." His heart leapt. Fanning went upstairs to get a box of matches.

They ate their supper, chatting of this and that, and when she rose to see Mrs. Bascomb in the kitchen Alice murmured to him, "We can have a talk. I feel as if much is happening that I don't understand."

Fanning walked back into the room, carrying the box of sulfur matches. After Alice and Chad left the room, he plopped into a chair and said to Mack, "Have you heard anything more about that matter we talked of in Chicago?" So he was finally going to break the ice.

"Which matter? I gave you Sidlow's letter to me."

"Son-of-a-bitch," Fanning muttered. "I've talked to the rest and we aren't going to let it go. I was willing until he sent that insulting letter."

Mack sat rather stiffly in his seat at the table, saying nothing. He had been dismayed when the letter from Chicago had arrived a few days before addressed to him, challenging the cartel, accusing them of immoral behavior. Like a dog who keeps coming back to the fight when he should go home and nurse his wounds, Sidlow just couldn't let well enough alone, and if he didn't he was going to get Fanning in trouble.

Perhaps he, Mack, should have been glad for that. After all, feeling the way he did for Alice and scorning everything Fanning stood for—but he still was getting a salary to do a job.

"Has anybody been around asking about the Chink thing?" Fanning asked warily. "No policeman or snooping investigators have come to see me."

"They're calling it a Chinese tong matter. That the reason for the murders may remain hidden forever in the Chinese community."

"Maybe they will. Maybe they should," Fanning put a match to the end of his cigar, puffing it into a glowing coal. Rich smoke drifted about the room. As Mack was leaving the room, Fanning's voice stopped him. "I was thinking of promoting you to office manager."

"But what about Mr. McCloskey?

"I want someone I can trust with both business and personal matters in that job. You fit the bill."

"Well—let's wait until the first of the year. That might be a good time, when things have boiled down a bit."

Fanning looked disappointed, or was it wary? Mack did not stop for further conversation. He had an appointment.

The full moon was shining as he leapt down from the street car and walked west around the corner and down a couple of blocks. Coming to the Pine Street sign, he stopped a moment, looking up and down the street. Nobody was out strolling now, at eight o'clock on this October evening, but that was because it wasn't really a residential neighborhood, at least not any more. On a side street nearby was O'Shaughnessey's Gymnasium; he could see the back entrance from here. There were a few workingmen's houses on one side of this street which had been fashionable thirty years earlier; a livery stable and lumber yard and one or two old houses loomed on the other side of the street. The moonlight glinted off the new, large manhole covers in the street.

These old houses with the large windows from the time of the war looked wide-eyed and gaunt, particularly when only the light of small lamps shone out of heavily curtained upper stories. It was as if they were shielding themselves, turning inward and away from the public eye.

Dr. Brockelhurst appeared quickly when Mack rang the bell. Mack had used a neighbor's phone to ask Brockelhurst if he could spare a half hour tonight; oddly enough in this old-fashioned house there was a phone. Probably he needed it in case some member of the congregation called with an impending death or other emergency.

The two men sat in the dim parlor, on the little round-bottomed chairs upholstered in wine-red velvet. There was a portrait of a gentle-looking man dressed in a frock coat and ruffled collar popular in the forties standing beneath—what did you call those things—a ginkgo tree. With a pagoda in the background. Odd, he hadn't noticed it when they were here for the church missionary party.

"Is that a—relative?" Mack asked, gesturing towards the portrait.

"My father, a missionary to Nanking in China for some years," Brockelhurst said gravely. "He was assigned from the Cincinnati District in the fifties."

"I know you are a scholar with some familiarity with Chinese culture."

"I left there when I was nine, but I made the ways of China one of my studies in college." He rose to turn up the oil lamps on a table. As he paused a moment over the lamp globe, Mack could see his Roman countenance, not really much like the father in the portrait.

"I need a piece of Chinese writing translated." He reached into his pocket. "I've copied it exactly from the source. Even those in the Chinese community couldn't decipher it."

Brockelhurst put on his glasses and looked at the character. "It is scholarly Chinese, connected with the ancient discipline of fishing as a hobby among the elite and its spiritual implications. It is a part of a longer phrase of several characters. I think we can translate it as 'not yet hooked.' " He looked up at Mack intently. "It is about that time when the bait or line has been cast, the fish has nibbled, but he is not ensnared on the hook. Perhaps 'almost hooked' would be better."

Almost hooked. So Lee Huang in his opium den thought Walter Fanning was almost hooked. Which would mean he wasn't completely addicted to opium—at least at the time the list was notated. What kind of a man was trying to hook people without any regard for ruining their lives? Chiang's uncle was evil, no doubt about that. Or maybe just hooked himself. With a hook in your mouth, maybe you had to jump pretty hard to survive. Still—

"May I ask where you found this unusual character?" Reverend Brockelhurst asked.

"It isn't something I can tell you in detail, but a bit: I'm involved in helping a friend search through the records of his uncle, who's recently died, to settle his affairs." That was enough to say.

"Was this the man called Li Ting?"

"No, he was killed earlier. This is Lee Huang, the man who ran the Chinese laundry."

"Oh, yes. I did not know him personally. Are any of his family Christians?"

"I don't think so. Anyway, my friend is trying to go through his papers. He and his grandmother are running the laundry now. He says he doesn't always know the Chinese characters."

Brockelhurst smiled. "Perhaps I can help. I do have a fairly extensive knowledge of the written as well as spoken language."

"That'd be good, sir. We may be able to use you."

Brockelhurst returned the paper to Mack. "I haven't stayed close to the Chinese community. My mother died in China and my father brought me back here three years later and died soon thereafter himself. I was glad to be back here in America, though I was small when we left. Maybe the land of your birth is embedded in your bones. Like the Heny Van Dyke poem, you know

Tis fine to see the old world, and travel up and down
Among the famous palaces and cities of renown
To admire the crumbling castles and the palaces of kings
But now I think I've had enough of antiquated things
So it's home again, and home again, America for me.

Mack nodded. He liked that poem too.

"America automatically felt like home," Brockelhurst went on. "China seemed the alien place. But I stayed close to the study of Chinese life in divinity school in Kentucky and then in my churches—and keep a few things from the place I grew up, for which I have great affection." He gestured around the room.

They both rose. "How are you getting along with the busy Mr. Fanning and the charming Alice?" Brockelhurst wanted to know.

"Pretty well, I think. It's—hard to live as an outsider in a family. I get a little lonely sometimes for home. But I'm thinking about going to see some of my relatives at a wedding I've been invited to soon in Southern Indiana. Family is important."

"Indeed it is. Sometimes I get lonely, too."

"Do you? I've never had it happen before this."

"Yes, I do. I suppose the church is my family. I'm proud to be here. It isn't every church that can afford to have two full-time ministers." They had reached the door.

"Say hello to Mrs. Fanning for me. I'm not sure she always likes us at the church. Too fancy, too much folderol, she says. You know, sometimes I agree with her!" His smile was warm and winning as he patted Mack on the shoulder. Well, he thought as he went quickly down the darkened street, he liked the man. It was good to know you could find somebody willing to give an answer in a world increasingly full of questions.

"I'm suing Sidlow," Fanning said calmly when Mack came in the next morning to take dictation. "For breach of contract."

"Isn't that skating a little thin? The contract was concerned with restraint of trade."

"The Anti-trust law isn't being enforced. And it won't be. No, our contract was witnessed by a notary, it's legal, if you want to talk about that. Not that I'd want it made public."

Mack seated himself with his stenographic tablet ready. "Sidlow may make—things public that you don't want known."

"Let him try. There isn't anything in writing to link me to that botched hit by the Hip Sings in Chicago. It's unfortunate that the girl-friend of the chief died but I didn't plan for it to end that way. I'll deny everything, and I do have some small influence with the power structure in this town." His eyes closed slowly, then batted wide open. "Besides, perhaps Sidlow has his own cluttered-up dark closet to hide. Something I've just found out—he'll keep his mouth shut even if we get into court."

Mack looked at him, waiting for more information, but none was forthcoming.

"Now we need to set new prices for delivering prime chickens to the two new hotels downtown. Take a letter!"

Mack found Abby in the yard outside the livery stable, scrubbing out the wagon bed with a bucket of soapy water and told him what Fanning had just said. "I don't see how a man guilty of murder in this town can institute a lawsuit in court when an investigation of him would blow his secret sky-high," Mack said.

"No, it's too dangerous, because the murder would come out. Why does Fanning seem bent on suing Sidlow?"

"He can't stand to have anybody cross him. He's like an Indian whose manhood has been insulted, and he won't rest until the enemy pays."

Abby jumped down from the wagon. "It proves one thing to me."
"What?"
"Fanning didn't commit the murders."
"I don't know. Maybe he did."
"I tell you he wouldn't go to court right now in this town if he had a murder to hide. Besides, remember we found those lists that placed him in the opium den of Chiang's uncle the night of the first murder."

"Maybe so. But then who did kill those two if the Chee Kong didn't and the Hip Sings here didn't and the two cousins, Bee Chee and Fook Soy didn't. Well, at least they have alibis."

"And Fanning didn't do it. You didn't say that. Oh, I forgot. You don't believe he's off the hook yet. Well, Nate believes the answer may be in Chicago." Abby was bringing the horses out of their stalls to harness them to the wagon. He was late for the afternoon deliveries.

"What's Nate uncovering?" Mack wanted to know.

"He and his friend Sergeant Rossi have been asking some undercover connections in Chicago to find out whether the head of the Hip

Sings, Whi Ting Lo, isn't more deeply involved than we thought in the killings here. Whi Ting Lo, it turns out, was seen in Indian No Place a couple of times in the summer. Maybe, outraged over the killing of his sing-song girl, he did the killings himself."

"The leader of the Hip Sings?" Mack asked. "I don't want to encounter him again. My head still hurts sometimes." He began to assist Abby with the harnessing.

Finally Abby hopped up onto the wagon seat and took up the reins. With harness jangling, he began trotting the horses out of the yard.

Mack ran to catch up with him. "If Nate is going to do some investigating in Chicago, have him check out Sidlow."

"Sidlow? What's he got to do with this?"

"He's an ornery mutt—fighting the cartel all the way," Mack answered. "But I'm curious to know what his connection with the Chinese in Chicago is. Confucius say, 'Dog stinks worst who yelps loudest.' "

"I don't believe Confucius said that," Abby called back over his shoulder.

"Well, if he didn't, he should have."

"We can't go into the Arsenal grounds, of course, so we'll have to watch the creek through the fence here," Mack said. Chad was wearing short wool pants and heavy long stockings, as Mack had instructed him.

"So he's Leatherstocking now," Mack said, looking at Chad heading up the road ahead of Alice and himself. He could hardly bear to look at her. She wore a blue and white striped mutton-sleeve blouse, revealing a full bust and tiny waist, with a bouquet of artificial violets at the waist of her striped, lavender and white skirt. Her eyes were laughing, and ringlets of her hair escaped onto her forehead. It was true that her eyes were a little close-set, those large, hazel eyes. Still, the effect on him was startling as she cast a sideways glance at him, commenting as this dog or that cat trotted or minced by on its neighborhood rounds or bicyclists sailed past.

"We first see it close here, Chad, because we can't get to it in the Arsenal grounds," Mack said as they stopped on Oriental Avenue to look at Pogue's Run, running fairly full after the October rains. "Now we'll walk along this street and turn right, as the creek does. See the bridge as it comes out of the Arsenal?"

They descended the small hill past the bridge and came onto the path by the creek. "Those are sycamores, those are elms," Mack pointed out to his young charge.

Bounding ahead a bit, holding her skirt up, Alice called back, "And this is a sassafras tree. Mother always took the bark from this tree and made tea for me when I wasn't feeling well. Look, Chad, the leaves are all different. It's so unusual."

Chad went into the lead and so they followed, walking beside the creek as it twisted and turned to the southwest, seeing squirrels and occasionally a scurrying rabbit. Once they suddenly came upon a mother quail and her almost-grown children, whom she quickly led away. "So unselfish," Alice murmured. "Do you think unselfish love is a principle of nature? Revealing a First Cause which aims for our good?"

"I'm afraid quite the opposite," Mack said. "Rather brute instinct."

"But then," turning to look at him earnestly as she walked, "if most parents in the animal and human kingdom are that way, it must be a principle of nature. Call it instinct if you will. I'll call it love." Waxy yellow leaves fell and drifted over them as they walked, and red-yellow maples blazoned their glory on the residential streets beyond the creek bed.

"They're at the height of their color," Alice remarked a little sadly. "And soon they'll be gone. We are here such a short time. A vale of tears, that's what we're in. Mother used to read from Shakespeare to me. It makes you think about life—about living it to the fullest." They sat on the hillside where the creek formed a little pool. Chad chased insects around in the drying grass with a stick.

Mack was silent, caught in the spell created by the glory of the autumn day and her attraction for him.

"What are you doing, gone so much? I hear you are visiting the Chinese." There was a slight frown on her face as she absently smoothed a leaf on her knee.

"Yes. I know how you hate them. But I have a Chinese friend, a student at the high school. Several of us are all trying to help Chiang find out who killed his uncle. Do you remember the unsolved murders? There were two of them."

"They were in the paper," she said, refusing to look at him.

It made his heart ache to have to tell her the truth, but there was no living with this situation any other way.

"Your husband is caught up on the edge of it through the business, and he may be in some trouble. Has he said anything to you?"

"Walter never says anything to me that doesn't center around my management of the household and Chad. He does not believe I have a brain."

"He's not truly observed you in the slightest way, then. Or, he is lost in his own pursuits."

"He is like the Turks. They believe that pleasure is the only goal of living." Her face was bright pink.

"I think you should ask him about what happened in Chicago last year."

She finally looked at him, the large eyes questioning. "Why should you tell me this? You're risking your job."

"Because I care about you and Chad. Mr. Fanning and I have discussed the troubles, anyway. But I shouldn't say more. This is between you and him."

She nodded, considering what he had said. His hand lay near hers as they sat on the browning grass. She looked at it a moment, then said, "Let's climb this hill and see where this non-limpid stream goes." He gave her his hand and helped her up. And so they climbed, with Chad still playing down below.

When they reached the edge of the road above, he pointed. "Pogue's Run goes south there, on to Washington Street and then west."

"Yes. We've come more than a mile. Look, there's Pine Street and Dr. Brockelhurst's mansion, and beyond that, the spires of Central Avenue Church. You can just see the cross at the top."

"The sun is setting. We'd better walk back by the roads, I think. It'll be dark before long."

"I'll call Chad. But before I do, I want to tell you Mr. Scott, McClure, that I appreciate your staying with us. We are not a very easy family to be around. Sometimes I think I am lost in a dream." She turned away. He put his hand on her arm and she looked up and smiled, sadly at him, just as Chad climbed up the hill to find them and the sun set amidst salmon-colored clouds behind Pogue's Run Creek.

"Why-do-I-want-to-beat-the-shit-out-of-people?" Mack panted as he grappled with O'Shaughnessey on the mat at the gymnasium. "I just feel this overwhelming desire to throttle, maim and beat to a pulp. There's a white-explosion like a light bulb exploding in my mind's eye and then it comes over me. And I become another person. I might kill somebody if I didn't have this gym. Once in northern Michigan in the lumber camp, I almost did. I feel like a bottle with fizz in it."

"What's the matter with that? All young men want to explode sometimes. I make my money channelling these explosions into fist power," O'Shaughnessey said with some difficulty. He put his shoulder firmly against Mack as Mack resisted, trying to break free to begin again to pound him with the boxing gloves. "If I didn't have the likes of you, there'd be no gym."

They stood back, sweating and panting. The Irishman brushed hair out of his eyes.

"But I was brought up to turn away from violence, to be a gentle Christian," Mack said. "Drummed into me every day at Bible reading in the morning, evening prayers. One day, after my second year in high school, I just jumped ship. Disobeyed my parents. I went out to a lumber camp on the river, and I didn't come back for almost a year. Not that I went very wild there. Most of the time I just did the sawing and skidding and fell exhausted into bed. But it kept me from being smothered in cotton candy." He was silent for a moment. "So why all the fizz in the bottle?"

"I told you about that article I read at the reading room in the library."

"About those doctors in Vienna?"

"Yes. That Dr. Freud has the answer. Repression. You're pushing down part of what's supposed to be you and all your feelings are gathering inside you, compressing."

"I know. I read a little about it myself in the library."

Mack began to pummel O'Shaughnessy again with the gloves. And later, as they sat with towels around their shoulders on the bench, Mack said, "I guess the Austrian doctors think that women repress things too."

"Most of the people they deal with are women. More fizz in the bottle than men, even."

"Could that cause a woman to walk in her sleep?"

"It could have caused one named Lizzie Borden to take an ax and give her mother forty whacks. He's probably right about repression. These days between the Pope and all the Baptist ministers in the world and the mothers of America, we probably have a lot of repressed people out there. No wonder the bottles blow."

"There's a lot of odd stuff out there," Mack said. And as he walked along the lonely drive towards Woodruff Place, as the gas lamps which still lit some small streets flickered in the gusty wind, he thought that perhaps this very night the real Jack the Ripper might decide to walk the streets again in London. He had, after all, never been found, and that was only a few years ago. And, he thought, somewhere up Newman Street, where Pogue's Run was running about two hundred yards to the north, black as ink tonight, a man had walked two months ago on a mission to murder another, while the comfortable people all around slept in peace.

"Both of these murders happened in the best-patrolled neighborhoods in the city," Mack said as he stood with Chiang in front of the laundry the next day. His young friend was heading for the streetcar to Indianapolis High School. "For instance, the Li Ting murder occurred on Lockerbie Street. Access to it is along well lit main streets of town. No furtive figure could come in there to kill without being seen."

Chiang nodded. He was rearranging the books in his bag so he could swing it over his shoulder.

"This of course is at the crux of the puzzle," Mack went on, "and we've asked it before, but never seriously. I walked this route again last night. How did the killer get to Newman Street unseen? Why didn't anyone see the man who killed your uncle? Somebody was walking through the night, just before dawn."

"It's as if the killer flew in like a bat and dropped down on our laundry. Nate Nessing's friend, Sgt Rossi, had assigned extra beat cops because of the burglars last spring in these wealthy neighborhoods. The political heat is on. Just take my uncle's case. Tenth Street is one of the main streets in town, and all night long the beat cop patrols come round every ten minutes or so. Rossi can see the whole street as he walks along. Nobody would walk this street or cross to go down Newman without them seeing it. And past West Drive—the Woodruff Place police force keeps an eye on every house all night long and the place is walled anyway, so it isn't easy to pass through there. And of course you know yourself nobody gets through the Arsenal, although one or two of the duty men have been known to sleep under the trees. Baskerville patrols the little streets west of it. But you couldn't avoid all of them."

"The murderer could have come from the north, I suppose," Mack went on," but the streets are confused there, some dead end because of the railroad tracks, and the creek runs through and twists around all over the place. Our provisioners' factory has a locked fence at the end of the day. Besides, there are people's houses he'd have to avoid."

They began to walk up the street towards Tenth. "But of course the dream sleepers always come. Were they seen?" Chiang wondered.

"Their names were well known at police headquarters. They're the same ones, it turns out, who were on your uncle's list. Most all of them were Chinese and they were always watched closely as they walked along the street."

"They let them walk around this town? I never thought about it before, but why didn't the police raid Uncle's den?"

" 'A harmless Chink pursuit, keeps 'em out of trouble,' was what Nate was told when he asked the beat cops. And of course there are quite a few people who take opium because it's prescribed by the family quack. Along with morphine. Do you have any idea how much morphine and so-called tonic is sold in this town?" Mack asked dryly.

Then he had an idea. "But maybe the murderer didn't need to come into the area. What if the killer was one of those opium den regulars? Someone who was already there?"

Chiang sighed. "Uncle slept alone on his pallet that night. I know that because Grandmother asked me to take him some tea about ten o'clock. On other nights, if there were men out there—I made myself not see them and stayed inside. But that night he was alone. Until—" He looked away.

"This thing is going in circles. I'm not getting anything done."

They had arrived at the streetcar stop. "Well, you don't have to keep at it." Chiang was silent a moment. "You don't have to go on being Sherlock Holmes for me."

"It isn't only for you. I said I'd help your grandmother get to the truth about your uncle."

Chiang offered his hand. "I don't think my family can ever rest until we know. For good or bad. And I thank you."

"The problem is that Sherlock Holmes always sits around on Baker Street smoking his pipe and figuring out clues. He never has to take out the trash or go to the office and slave away to put food on the table. And I do. And you have to go to school. Fine bunch of detectives we are. But that's real life."

Chiang looked anxiously towards the streetcar which was swinging up the street from Irvington. He needed to go.

Mack clapped him on the shoulder. "I'm going to talk to Nate Nessing and Sergeant Rossi myself. It's like a circle, a charmed circle we've fallen into. We need some new leads to break out," Mack said. "And I'm going to leave Lee Huang's customer list, with Fanning's name on it with him, although there's probably nothing he doesn't already know." He was hurrying because the car had arrived.

Then, after watching Chiang go his way to his day at the high school, he headed up the street for the office.

The City Market sandwich stand was busy at lunch time every day of the week. Matrons and housemaids in practical daytime dresses with huge baskets meandered among the stands selecting the best oranges or artichokes, then sipped Coca Cola at the small ice cream tables with wire-backed chairs. Mack, Nate Nessing and Sgt. Rossi sat on tall stools eating sandwiches at the bar. The jar with the list sat near Sgt. Rossi's feet. Mack had been right; there was nothing in it to surprise the sergeant. But there were other, more interesting developments.

"Yes, Whi Ting Lo, the Hip Sing chieftain has been in Indianapolis," Sgt. Rossi said, consulting a notebook whose folds enclosed a lengthy telegram. "According to my private source in the police department in Chicago, he was here sometime the last of July, date unknown. At any rate, he purchased railroad tickets during that week, according to ticket agents who recognized his face."

"Then he could have done the hatchet job himself," Mack said, putting mustard on a ham-and-cheese on rye.

"Or supervised those who did," Nate said. He looked particularly natty in a new light wool jacket. The "off the record" investigation he was conducting on the Chinese murders had put him in positive spirits. He smiled broadly at the waitresses carrying chocolate sundaes and fruit salad plates to the tables.

"Maybe the Chinese are wrong and this is a tong murder after all," Mack said. "So he could have been supervising Bee Chee and Fook Soy, getting revenge for the slaying of—what was the name of his Chicago girlfriend? Shi Chi, that's it."

Sgt. Rossi, between Nate and Mack, was launching into the first of two big cheese-filled tubes of manicotti. He spoke between bites. "What you really have to do is establish the motive, I tell you. You have lots of small motives, but murder takes a motive as strong as steel. Look at the motives of all these suspects and see if you find any stronger than the others."

"Well," Mack said thoughtfully, "obviously if Bee Chee and Fook Soy committed the murders they were hired killers."

"They have an alibi," Nate said tiredly. "They were at the Celestial Heaven the night of Lee Huang's killing."

Rossi looked up. "An alibi from a brothel they own may not hold much water when it comes to indicting them."

"All right. Let's move to table the alibi for now and consider the motives of Bee Chee and Fook Soy," Mack said. "Even though they were in different tongs, they were brothers, and they both had a good deal to gain by accepting the job of seeking revenge for the Chicago Hip Sing boss. Their first motive would be to get money for committing a crime that didn't have much risk. How can you determine who actual culprits are when the tong moves in to kill someone? We've seen how the police treat the tong scene: individuals fade into the background, all Chinese look alike, I guess you could say. Bee Chee would also gain prestige in the national Hip Sing tong. Never mind that he would be killing members of the local city Hip Sings, he'd be in a position to take over at the top after the revenge killings were over. Biggest, meanest dog runs at the head of the pack, that sort of thing. He'd be getting even on behalf of his boss for the killing of the boss' girlfriend, so the Chicago Hip Sing rulers would be pleased and do what they could to reward him here. Fook Soy for his part would be promoting his own tong, the Chee Kongs, by the killings in Indianapolis. Both would get money and power."

Nate picked up the thread. "It seems to me that Whi Ting Lo, the Hip Sing Chief, actually stood to gain the most. He wanted those who botched the job with Mapeltharp and the hired assassins who killed his love to be punished. Let them pay. Revenge. That's one of the oldest of motives, from the time of the Old Testament. He could have done it himself. He was in town."

Sgt. Rossi unbuttoned the top of his blue police jacket and began attacking his second piece of manicotti. "The problem with this case is there're too many leads. There's also this Sidlow you asked me to investigate. Somehow you got the idea he has Chinese associations and they might connect him with the botched hit."

"Well, he knew a lot about the hit," Mack said. "And it seems his father was involved deeply with the Chinese community. He helped start a school and he seems to know all the Chinese all up there. What did you find out?"

"You weren't too far off the mark." Rossi answered. He took out the letter and read it again while they waited. "It says here that Sidlow read law in the southern suburbs of Chicago. He's the unofficial counsel for the Chinese community. He worked with some of the Chinese Benevolent Association leaders to set up the Chinese Waiters Union to get better rights for the lower income workers."

"So he's a do-gooder."

"Yes. But not a goody-two-shoes at all. In fact, he's been involved himself with the gambling interests, representing them in court. And two years ago there was a case when he represented the Chee Kong gambling interests against the Hip Sings, acting as their interpreter, even serving as legal counsel for some of the Chee Kong apparently. My contact enclosed a copy of a newspaper article telling all about it."

"The first victim, Li Ting, had a gambling den," Mack said eagerly.

"Yeah. The police were aware of that place. Rumor has it that all the local Chinese fortune and whoring dens are partly owned by Chicago hatchet men."

"Li Ting was a Hip Sing, too. Could he have crossed Sidlow's Chicago Chee Kong people? Taken business from them?"

"That we don't know."

Nate had been silent throughout this exchange. "Yes, but it's a long way from being angry against an enemy who has stolen the business of your clients to killing them."

"That's what I was saying about motive," Rossi said. "Sidlow may be connected. He knew about all of this and seemed uneasy when my undercover friend talked to him in Chicago. But what's his motive?"

Mack had finished his sandwich. He leaned toward Rossi, blue eyes intent. "Suppose he could kill two birds with one stone. If Sidlow knew that Fanning had ordered the botched hit in Chicago, and he wanted to destroy him in a business sense and personally, he could have killed, or ordered killed, the two Hip Sings from Indianapolis who had been hired to go to Chicago and conduct the hatchet hit, then messed it up."

"It would look like a Hip Sing revenge killing," Nate put in eagerly, "but really what would be happening was that Fanning's part in it all would be uncovered for all the world to see. The situation could possibly set up a criminal case against Fanning, too. Sidlow could be destroying the rival Hip Sing gambling house for the Chee Kongs he represented and flushing Fanning down the water closet at the same time."

"But we don't *know* that. We don't *know* it," Mack said, wadding up his napkin and throwing it on the bar. "It's all so complicated. We have a list of people, and all of them could have had some motive to commit two murders in this city."

They were silent a moment, then he went on. "But beyond motive is will. We need to decide if some one of these people could actually pick up a murder instrument and commit the act."

"It usually takes a certain kind of brute nature—or desperation," Rossi said.

Mack nodded. "Well, let's see who's brutal or desperate. First, there's Whi Ting Lo in Chicago. He was seen here, in the right time framework. Revenge and deep anger alone would cause him to murder these men and he's a ruthless ruffian. My bruises still tell me that. Right?"

Nate and Sgt. Rossi nodded.

"And then Sidlow—we have just connected him to the case. He might have motives of money, revenge and jealousy. But could he kill?"

"The letter says he's known for a violent, unpredictable temper," Rossi said solemnly, brushing crumbs from his huge mustache.

"That we saw in at the meeting in French Lick. He challenged Fanning to a duel and could easily have killed him that way. And when I talked to him he was absolutely obsessed with destroying Fanning," Mack said quickly. "But he didn't follow through with the duel, after all. He also has an idealistic side."

A mailman sat down next to Rossi at the nearly deserted bar, slinging his mailbag under it. Rossi turned his back and leaned closer to Mack.

"Then, there's still Fanning," Mack went on. "I'm not ruling him out. His motive: to keep the Chinese quiet and preserve his reputation."

Nate shook his head. "Fanning isn't high on my list. You've just told us about the evidence in that jar—Fanning was listed there as being pipe dreaming when Li Ting was killed. But more important to me, the very fact that he is willing, eager to go into court against Sidlow would be ridiculous if he were the murderer."

"Unless he were very, very clever or very foolhardy," Mack said. Fanning was not clever, though when driven enough he could be foolhardy. He wasn't counting the man out. He had been hanging around that washhouse. He could have planted his name there on the list.

Mack looked directly at Rossi, whose eyebrows were meeting in a bushy line of intense concentration. "Finally, Bee Chee and Fook Soy seemed desperate when I saw them," Mack said. "After all, they were the only suspects actually seen arguing with one of the victims—Uncle Lee Huang the day before the second murder. We've said they could have wanted to kill the two hit-botchers to gain power and money in the tong world. But why desperation?"

Mack hit the table with his fist. "Damn it," he said, "there are too many suspects. We have to eliminate some of these people definitely."

"And how do you propose to do that?" Rossi wanted to know.

"I'm going to call on Bee Chee myself. With Chiang. Just visit him"

"That's dangerous as can be. I won't let you do that," Rossi said. "These are tong members and opium traders. Anything can happen. You've already been beat up. I forbid you to—"

"Still, I'm going to do it. I won't rest till this is finished. My own personal peace of mind—well, I'm committed to it. Leave it at that."

"You are doing this on your own then. Don't expect anything from the police. And it's as stupid as running for a train when it's picking up speed." Rossi stared darkly at a small piece of ricotta cheese on his sleeve while Nate beckoned to the waitress for the bill.

"In this case the police department seems to be a minus factor anyway," Mack muttered.

"We could be completely off the track, "Nate said. "The Chinese community here keeps telling us that the murderer isn't among them. It isn't a Chinese So all this talk about Chinese suspects may be just smoke in the wind."

"Or, they may be covering for each other," Mack said.

Rossi waited a moment, then scrambled down from his stool to put a hand on Mack's shoulder. "Guard yourself," he said solemnly. "You are a fine young man, one my mother would approve of." He smiled and thumped Mack on the back. "I don't want to see you needing those lessons I've been hearing about at O'Shaughnessey's."

"When I visit Bee Chee and Fook Soy," Mack said, "at least we will have eliminated one or two strong candidates. And maybe proven the Chinese right."

Pushing the stools up to the bar, the three of them headed out of the light-filled building, past stalls of oxtails and pork ribs and oranges piled high for the city market customers. "When it comes down to it, it will be whoever has the most hatred in his soul," Rossi said, without looking at them. "All of these folks you mention hated; and why shouldn't they? Beneath the surface of their pleasant dealings, most people in this busy little town find somebody to hate in a newer immigrant group or of a different color.

"I'm an expert on all of this, believe me, coming from one of the lowliest families on the Italian southside. My parents landed in New York twenty years ago and then pushed on over here, and we've heard every insult in the book from time to time. If it wasn't for our own church and relatives, we'd be miserable most of the time."

"There's another side, we all know that. There's a lot of good here, opportunity for everyone eventually," Nate interrupted.

"You've hit the mark with that, certainly," Rossi nodded. "I'm going to forget we ever had this lunch; it never happened, understand? But remember what I say." He turned to point a finger at Nate. "Whoever has the strongest hatred is the killer in this case. Hate grabs the knife, mixes the poison and pulls the trigger in this and in most murder cases. And greed trails right behind."

Mack worked late to make up for his extended lunch hour, then went to the laundry. He poked his head in the door. Chiang was sitting at a small table studying. "I want just one good break in all of this," he told Chiang. "I'm going to poke through the stuff in the washhouse one more time. There must be something there we haven't seen. May I have the key?"

Chiang tossed him the key, hardly looking up. He was obviously getting weary of playing Sherlock Holmes too.

This sad little shack, Mack thought as he turned the key, the scene of so much debauchery, of people escaping into drugged dreams, unable to work, craving nothing but escape. Chiang and his grandmother weren't using the washhouse much these days, preferring to go with a small boiler and wringer in the back room of the main place. No wonder. The "father" and provider of the family was killed out here, after a life ruined by narcotics. Still, it would be good to give this family some kind of respect, or was it just finality, through finding Lee Huang's killer.

Not much left in this shed; the opium stuff was locked away again in the closet. There was the two-burner gas laundry stove, the two huge iron pots on top of it; the wringer by its side. Ivory soap and lye soap, flaked, in jars, bleach—all sat along the sill of the two tiny windows. He raised each one of the jars, looked inside, replaced it. The one he and Abby and Chiang had found earlier with the lists inside was now in the hands of Sgt. Rossi. They'd been over this before—no surprises. So what could he possibly be looking for?

He went to the miserable cots. He lifted the mattresses, ran his hands under them, pulled off the dirty sheets, shook them disdainfully, watching for bedbugs. He scanned the dirt floor of the shed, finding nothing but bits of leaves, beech nut hulls, twigs—the sort of stuff people coming in from the outside might have left. Whoever the murderer was, he must have come up the path, picking up leaves on his shoes as did so, then entered through that back door, come to Lee Huang on the cot, still asleep, and stabbed him over and over. Then he must have left, through the shaded paths again and slipped into the darkness just before the dawn, blending with it. The floor wasn't completely clean; these few scattered beech hulls and maple leaf fragments could have come from the murderer's shoes.

The only other thing on the floor was a pile of laundry debris under the boiler. It was taken from the bottom of the boiler: lint bits, strings torn from the clothes as they boiled, buttons, cotton fluff. He stopped to pick the debris pile up, to poke through it. It was what it seemed to be. What was he expecting anyway? That the murderer would leave a calling card?

He bent again to replace the pile and his eye fell on something, near the leg of the laundry tub, midway between the beech leaves and the laundry fluff. Not knowing exactly what the small object was, he bent over to see more closely, then picked it up. A button. It had been lying beneath the pile of debris, had possibly rolled there or been kicked over by one of the investigators—anyway it had gone unnoticed. It could be a button which had been at the bottom of the washer, but no, it did not seem connected to the pile. It had bits of beech leaves on it.

His heart grew as cold as snow. It was a black cloth button of the finest silk, with a flower rosette etched in gold on its front. A unique creation of an expensive designer. It was one of the buttons from the front of a peignoir—the dressing gown of Alice Fanning.

Blindly, unable to analyze what he had just seen, he stumbled out of the washhouse. From then on, his chest pounding with anxiety and apprehension, he thought of nothing else. He walked home through the gathering twilight, past the boys rolling hoops and the dogs gamboling around; he did not see them.

Alice's button. Not a coat button but a peignoir button. How could it have gotten there? There must be, absolutely had to be a reasonable answer. It was from the Fanning's laundry—this was, after all a place to wash clothes. There were probably plenty of buttons around. But no, Alice did not allow her laundry to get within a mile of a Chinese laundry, which she considered an abomination because she seemed to hate the Chinese. But Fanning had gone against her wishes and taken his laundry there a few times recently—could it have gotten attached to his shirts? Fat chance—Fanning never got to put his hand on the front of that peignoir (warmth radiated through him in spite of himself). But he, Mack, possessed one of those buttons. He had put it in his pocket that night in the darkness in back of the house. He thought he had put it inside a drawer in the bureau in his room but maybe—yes, that had to be it! It must have been in his pocket and had fallen out through a hole when he was in the wash shed earlier. Of course.

And when he got home, he would find it wasn't in the bureau.

He bolted through the front door of the house, raced up the stairs, and opened his bedroom door. He dashed to the bureau and—there was the button's twin, sitting on the flowered shelf paper at the bottom of his drawer. He rolled the two buttons around in the palm of his hand. So beautiful, so delicate. Why, then, was one of these buttons at the scene of a murder? His throat constricted, his pulse raced.

It was late afternoon, almost suppertime. He must make an appearance. Descending the staircase, he found the three Fannings in the family parlor, Mama and Papa reading.

"I wrote a composition for you, McClure," Chad piped up from the couch. He picked up a piece of paper, smiling proudly. "Signs of the Wilderness in the modern City—the Pogue's Run Trail I saw."

"Good, pal o' mine," he said, clapping the boy on the shoulder and putting the composition in his pocket. "I'm going to get some trail rations."

He slipped through the parlor door, went through the dining room and into the kitchen. Casually he approached Mrs. Bascomb, who was stirring vegetable soup at the stove.

"For supper?" he asked in a voice that was considerably cheerier than he was feeling.

"Yes. And there's corn muffins and cherry jam." He stood beside her.

"My favorites. Mother used to make the best corn muffins, and hide a gob of jam in the middle." His voice sounded hollow, his interest contrived. His nerves were shredded by the finding of the button. Combined with the mysterious sleepwalking, and the hatred of Chinese—the button was frighteningly ominous. But a pretense of normalcy was everything in his position. "How are your daughters? And your sister, in the family way?"

"Survivin'. I got her to visit the doctor to be sure. Mike has been poundin' the pavement lookin' for work, finally humbled himself and went to be a hod carrier. Maybe things'll get better. Can't get worse."

Mack cleared his throat. "By the way, I thought I might send my mother a sleeping garment for Christmas. A very special one, seeing as how she's such a special mother. That black peignoir of Mrs. Fanning's. How could I get one like it?"

Mrs. Bascomb looked at him curiously, and he could see her wondering how his mother could wear a black peignoir like that. The ludicrousness of what he had just said struck him. Dora Lavenham Scott, with the delicate frame of a little girl, the Christian Science Sunday School teacher, wearing a revealing garment of black silk and lace?

"Well, perhaps it's for somebody else." He tried to look embarrassed. "Anyway, it is unique."

"Doubt you could get one like it anywhere here. Or anywhere else for that matter. Mr. Fanning ordered her trousseau in Cincinnati, and he wanted it made by the best dressmaker in the city."

"I noticed the buttons."

Her face brightened, and she turned to him, proud to be able to teach him about high fashion. "They were made to match the silk and lace in the peignoir. Little rosettes of silk, with lace behind them. Only trouble is they come off."

He couldn't deny that.

"Be that as it may, I'd look downtown at one of the department stores for a nightie. That was a one-of-a-kind and it would be too much for the budget, I bet." She returned to stirring the soup.

God! How could he think such a thing. That Alice had gone to that place and had—what? What was he accusing her of? Of killing somebody? It was true that she hated the Chinese, but it was ridiculous. And yet something about the situation nagged him. He must prove or disprove the cockeyed theory in one way or another. Disprove of course. He loved her so much, and this idea was intolerable—he would, must go to her room. See if anything in there would show the least connection with any of this. He sat at the table eating the supper Mrs. Bascomb served him, waiting until noises died in the parlor. Then he walked through the dining room and parlor to the front window. This was not a good time to go snooping in the room—Alice and Chad were taking a walk by the now-empty fountains on West Drive and they could return any moment. Still—

He bolted up to the third story. Looking down the hall, past his own room, he saw no one. He sneaked around the corner, towards her room. He would just look inside; it should not be hard. He had never seen her lock the door. Slowly he opened the door. An electric lamp on a desk in the corner shed a soft light. There were pictures on the wall—a huge passion flower symbolizing Jesus' crucifixion and two Dutch landscape scenes with ruddy peasants staring out. Against the wall was the bed, small, tightly made with a quilt for a spread. Here she lay each night, that beautiful form, alone, like a cloistered nun. There was a clothes press with a drawn curtain, and in front of it, shoes in a neat line.

The desk. That would be the place if there was anything—really, this was absurd. A key protruded from the flip top desk. Cautiously he turned it. Piles of note-paper, envelopes, a pen and ink bottle of course. He pulled out the drawers and saw dried flowers, small bottles of scent. He felt like a burglar. Then he opened the top right hand drawer and his heart fell. He could not deny what he saw. There was a small but potent pearl-handled stiletto, its blade sharp and keen. And the point most certainly would fit the knife holes he'd seen in the drawings in Nate Nessing's notebook.

It sat on a square of newspaper. He picked up the knife, set it aside gingerly and looked at the scrap of newsprint. It was a caricature from a New York paper of an ugly Chinaman, his face angry at the prohibitive immigration law. And on the margin of the article were a few Chinese characters, practiced and scratched out.

He shut the desk and walked to the door, just as Alice was entering it. Her hands flew to her face as she almost bumped into him.

"I—was looking for you" he mumbled. "I wanted to check on the time of Chad's lesson tomorrow. I had no business barging in. Sorry."

His voice was weary, heavy with pain.

"Oh, yes," she said vaguely. Occupied with other thoughts, she seemed not to notice that he had invaded her bedroom.

She took his hands in hers, looked into his eyes. Her large eyes reflected the obsession she felt, an obsession which blocked out all other considerations at the moment. "Take me to the séance tonight," she whispered. Lamplight flickered about them, casting huge shadows over the bed and desk as he looked at her with surprise, then nodded mute affirmation.

Chapter Ten

The wind came up as they drove the rig across to Lockerbie neighborhood. Alice, wrapped in a velvet cape with a white rabbit matching fur cap, sat with her head down, staring at nothing.

Mack chose to drive a back way from Woodruff Place to the Lockerbie neighborhood telling himself, "It's only a short way, a matter of a mile or so here this way. And there, there is the house Abby said belonged to the senile old bakery owner, where Li Ting kept his opium house, where he was murdered." And, he told himself, not believing the direction this line of thought was leading him, a woman, driven by her own inner turmoil, loathing every Chinaman, could sleepwalk (if it was sleepwalking—he was doubting everything now), wearing black, and probably not be seen even in an area heavily patrolled by the police. She could conceivably have come through those back yards, there—and go to that shack back there. Carrying an ax? Never. Perhaps the ax was there. A hatchet was light enough to be carried. A woman wield a hatchet? Why not. Neither murder weapon had ever been found.

No, he told himself grimly, he was not going to return here tomorrow to Li Ting's shack and poke about in the dust and ashes of people's broken lives to see if he found an enameled flower peignoir button. He had done enough of that. Sick at heart he helped Alice down and to the door, and they entered the dusky silence of Mrs. Teitelbaum's house.

Gathered around the table sat the séance group, five of them. The Civil War veteran was not there this time, replaced by a new young man with hair that stood up in a frizzled pompadour, making him look like a carrot. The heaving breast woman, silent and stolid, was to his left, the veiled woman Mrs. Springer next to her.

Mrs. Teitelbaum got right down to business. Alice was grim, obviously suffering; the lights dimmed. Nothing happened for five minutes, and the carrot-headed young man began to get restless. Then, the odd rough voice they had heard before, said, "Little gal, go get 'em."

Then it laughed and began singing:

Ring ching ching, ring ching ching
Ta dee dee da,
Thus say the heathen Chinee

The voice was coarse, frightening. Mrs. Teitelbaum must be straining her vocal chords. And why was it so full of bravado and devil-may-
care? Didn't the afterlife improve people? Hone the rough edges into a
higher spirituality?

"Girlie mine, girlie dear, go get 'em. I care for ye, girlie dear," it
said in a wheedling voice.

More singing, silence, more rough-sounding talk. The spirit was
evidently in a good mood tonight.

Well, that should make Alice happy. If the voice was Joss Arken,
it had said it cared.

But she put her hand on his arm, there in the dark. "I hate this. I
thought I wanted to hear him but when he talks in that way—I can't
stand it. That's the way he used to be sometimes when—I want to go
home," she said.

"Now?" he whispered. A couple of people shushed them.

Mrs. Teitelbaum's voice changed. "Someone else is here, telling
me something. Yes? Oh, the skull. Yes. We will see it after we turn on
the lights. The person will see what is necessary in the skull's eyes. I
have heard you, spirit."

And the servant, as if in response, began to turn up the lights. Mrs.
Teitelbaum opened her eyes. "You will have to tell me who came to
you all." Alice was restless, fishing in her handbag in preparation for
leaving.

"You are to reveal the skull, madame," the mustachioed servant
told her. "So said a spirit at the end of the séance."

"Ah? The skull. Everyone stay put." She rose and went to a wal-
nut wardrobe in the corner. Opening its doors, she drew forth something that glinted in the lamplight. She carried the object to the table
and put it in front of them. It was a crystal skull, resting on purple velvet on a board. There were gasps around the table.

"I have not shown it yet, because I did not expect it would be necessary," Mrs. Teitelbaum said. "But since the spirits seem to be instructing me to, I shall tell you its story. It was given to me by a friend, an older mentor, who is now being nursed in serious illness."

Alice snapped her handbag shut. She settled in again, with the air of one who will stay two minutes, no more.

"Mrs. Evan Parsticle was one of the nation's great psychics. She had evolved in the science of the spirits—first as a phrenologist and later as an author. But her most wonderful possession was this ancient crystal skull evidently belonging to the Mayan Indians. She carried it with her when she and her husband used to travel on lecture tours."

"Where did it come from?" Mack found himself asking.

"It was found about fifty years ago in a hole in Kentucky, near Mammoth Cave." She worked the jaws of the skull, which seemed to be connected with a wire. "Some scientists think it was used by the priests of the Mayans to tell the future. Or perhaps it gave messages that people wanted to hear. For pay." She smiled. "But someone here is to get a message tonight without pay." There was silence as they all looked at the skull. Mustachio bent down at her side and whispered in her ear.

"I am told that the person for whom the message is intended will receive the impartation when he or she looks in the eyes. I ask each of you to rise and come to the point where you can look in the eyes of the skull." And so they did, Carrot Top, the veiled older woman, Elise Springer, Heaving Breast, Alice and finally Mack. And nothing happened.

"Odd," said Mrs. Teitelbaum. "Something is wrong. The spirits are not communicating. Well, we shall see later. And now, good night."

And as Mack escorted the clearly impatient Alice out the door, Mrs. Teitelbaum caught his arm and said to him, "I believe that message is intended for you, Mr. Scott. I feel it as strongly as I ever felt anything in my life. Something very important needs to be imparted. You saw nothing?"

"No. Just scratched quartz."

"I shall seek out the answer. You must return soon. Will you promise?"

Alice had already gone ahead, out the door, and was untethering the horse. "I'll try," he said, calling back over his shoulder. "Everything depends on Mrs. Fanning."

"O'Shaughnessey, who knows about this Joss Arken?" Mack asked the next afternoon. "I must find out about his life—and death."

Somehow he knew that if he could unravel the mystery of the Irishman who had been Alice's father, he might find what was driving her to walk in the night and offer a clue in case there was—further horror revealed. He must know, and know now. Every minute since he had found that knife in her bedroom had been torment. Worse was that, he could not tell Abby or Chiang or anyone. Never!

O'Shaughnessey was checking a stop watch near the prize-fighting ring. There was to be a tournament; ropes were being squared off around the boxing ring by his assistants, and he stood watching, smoking a cigar. Looking into Mack's disturbed eyes he answered. "'Tis in Delphi that your answers lie, young man. Go to Delphi, Indiana, as soon as possible and find Father Bernard. There your answers lie."

He could not do it, of course, as soon as he wanted to. Sidlow came into town the next day.

"He's got an Indianapolis lawyer to handle this affair, irritate us all and cause us grief, I suppose," Fanning said to Mack as the younger man took his seat in the office. "He's fighting our suit."

"Well, he thinks it's a matter of principle," Mack answered calmly.

"Principle! When he pockets money from half the Chinese gambling joints in the city of Chicago."

"When you mentioned Sidlow had shady dealing up there, I had Abby's brother look into his doings, and the police up there say he represents the Chinese in their interests, mainly in court. Nobody else will take their cases. Sometimes the police and judges don't even understand what the Chinese defendants are saying. But Sidlow has another side, too. He has financial interests in some of the Chinese enterprises up there."

"Enterprises like the Hoo Down Cosmic Entertainment Parlor and the Swamp Dragon Room," Fanning snorted loudly. "Where they play a little Fan Tan at tables in the front and drink tea and brandy and smoke opium in the rear."

"How did you find that out? You'd better be sure you have the names right," Mack asked coolly. The only way he figured he could live in this almost impossible situation with Fanning was to be absolutely, rock-bottom honest, to say what he thought.

"It's enough to say I do know," Fanning said, getting control of himself. He tamped a cigar against Mack's desk. "Now what I want you to do is to meet Sidlow downtown. We'll withdraw our breach of contract suit if he pays us something. Our lawyer has drawn up papers releasing the man from the contract for a specified sum. We'll let him go. I'm sick of the whole thing anyway. And I don't want to get the government hounds baying on our trail. But I want you to handle it, not the shysters at Colby & Markford downtown. Sidlow seems to tolerate you, and he has a temper hotter than hell. I don't want him put off by all of this. He might do anything when he's angered."

Anything? Sidlow was strongly connected to the Hip Sings. Did anybody know if he had left Chicago the nights of the Chinese murders? Perhaps he had his own motives, rooted in his gambling interests. And destroying Fanning. Damn the police department! They stayed busy monitoring parades and the breaking and entering of rich people's houses on Meridian Street instead of investigating these gang affairs and murders.

"He'll be at his own attorney's office at eleven o'clock. I'll have Miss Farquharson call with the message that you'll be by to discuss our business matters at noon. Maybe you can take him to lunch, show him our proposed agreement. You can leave now and take the rest of the day off, too, after you've seen Sidlow." Fanning disappeared into his office.

Miss Farquharson gave him an envious look. Mr. McCloskey sidled his huge backside onto the clerk's stool. "Well, it appears that the golden boy is a man of leisure. Lunching and idling while the rest of us must make a living," he sneered.

Mack had to meet Sidlow at noon. He began to clear his desk. On it was a telegram from Nate Nessing. He read it, and put it in his pocket. It was now after ten o'clock. He had about an hour before he needed to head downtown. An hour to do something he desperately wanted to do unobserved. He needed just about that much time to find out how this woman he loved could find a way to pass through the center part of town unobserved to kill two men. Racing back to Woodruff Place he reminded himself there were two or three facts that were established:

(1) A woman passing the several blocks from Woodruff Place to Lockerbie could not walk there on the main streets unobserved. Once

inside the Lockerbie Street neighborhood, she could pass unobserved from yard to yard. But to get there? Michigan Street? Impossible to traverse. Police walked beats to protect the solid citizens in town, to be sure jewelry stayed safe in the velvet chests of these homes, that the drunks and upper class adulterers got home safe from their nefarious after-dark affairs. Oh, and as we now knew, so that the frequenters of Li Ting and Lee Huang's after-hours opium dens could walk the streets to get their "Chinese fix" and stay out of worse trouble. That's how the cops saw their job, damn it. Could she use the little streets to the west of the Arsenal to get to the center part of town? She'd have to pass around the Arsenal, in full view of the main streets, or through it, and that was impossible.

(2) A sleepwalker might just possibly have killed two Chinese men if that sleepwalker hated, or was disturbed enough. The medical papers he had read at the library showed that these new European doctors were finding all kinds of hysterical cases in women, particularly—their personalities seem to split and they could kill themselves or do great bodily harm to others under the influence of their mental disturbances. So Alice Fanning might have killed in the hysterical state she seemed to be bordering on these days. Scrawled one of the Chinese letters she had been practicing beside the bodies. Upset over some sort of letdown her father had dealt the family or her knowledge that her husband was a nefarious philanderer and opium smoker—did she know that? He had told her on the walk that Fanning was involved in a mess in Chicago. But Fanning had probably not talked to her, even yet. And surely didn't want to talk to her now. Still, the evidence he'd found in her bedroom was strong. Well, she might have been driven to a horrible act, either asleep—or not. Chilling thought.

(3) It was absolutely clear, because he had seen it, that she was disappearing when she walked away on her midnight forays and was gone for two or three hours. Where? There was no place to go unless—

He reached West Drive, deserted now, with its children at the nearby Indianapolis school they attended. Alice was out of the house for a couple of hours. She had said this morning that she was going to the city market with Mrs. Bascomb. Poking his head into the house and finding, as he had hoped, no one home, he headed down the back path. It was time to explore this region in broad daylight. There must be an answer here.

The trees were golden now. As always a few leaves had fallen as soon as they turned and were lying underfoot, fading fast and not yet raked by the yard man. They provided a soft, sliding carpet on this bright day. The perennial bed she loved had faded, only chrysanthemums brightened the flower border. Flowers of China, he thought. What an irony. He stopped to admire them; soon in Michigan they would be covered with the first early snow. His father had written to say he had heard from his cousin in Southern Indiana. John McClure had invited him to his daughter's wedding at the same time Mack had been invited to come. In a couple of weeks Jacob Joe Scott would be taking the train to Indianapolis to pick up his son. Good God! In the midst of all of this he had to go to a wedding?

Now he was behind the livery stable, walking towards the gate. This led to the abandoned alley which formed the border of Woodruff Place. According to the old folks around here, when Woodruff had planned his suburb, he'd wanted an alley behind these houses, but the Arsenal wouldn't allow it. The government went to court to get an injunction and won, so the alley had to be abandoned. It was just a grass-grown footpath now. He and Chad had been able to see all of the alley's length from the inside of the Arsenal ground itself. When Alice was sleepwalking she could walk up this all the way to Michigan Street unimpeded.

He took visual measure of the wrought-iron fence with its spikes all around the grounds of the Arsenal. Looking at the grounds now, from this vantage point, seeing the buildings and thick clumps of trees from the east, he saw for the first time how easy it would be for a slight woman to cross this vast expanse, several acres, unobserved at night, with the cover of those maple trees if she could just get in. The sentries were lax these days; he and Chad had seen that well enough, and there was even talk that the Arsenal was up for disposal or sale by the government. But, with sentries posted at the front gate and that wrought-iron fence en-circling all, nobody could get into the Arsenal grounds to cross. Could they?

He began to walk the length of the abandoned alley, facing the back of the houses. No, all along here, the gaps between the pikes were too tight by far for anyone to pass through. But about half way down to

Michigan Street, he stopped. This fence had been built in sections, joined tightly about every fifteen feet. There at one of the section joinings was a gap. A huge rock had stood in the way, and instead of digging it out and moving the thing, the construction workers had placed the pike a few inches to the rear of it, leaving a gap closed by wire looped over the adjacent pike. The slack sentries inside were probably not concerned anyway, since no man could pass through that gap.

No man. He tried it himself, but his body was too thick. But a woman, a slight woman weighing little more than a hundred pounds, might be able to. Yes. It could be done; he was sure of it. The wire, there, was loosely twined, hardly together. It could be loosed, the bars pushed a little. She could have slipped through. And from there—he raced back up the alley and began pacing the front fence of the Arsenal. Yes, she would have passed along the side in darkness, up through deep groves of trees whichever way she went. But how would she get out? How could she possibly get out? The other side of the Arsenal was the heavily patrolled one, where the ammunition shack was, where the creek ran.

The creek, for God's sake. He stared at it through the fence. They had walked the path alongside the creek and there, inside the Arsenal grounds was the same path. Down those steep banks the commandants and officers walked and possibly fished when they were off-duty. And if you took that path down into Pogue's Run, shrouded by trees and bushes, you might pass either north or south out of the grounds. He walked as close as he could get to the creek as it passed into the grounds from Tenth Street. Well, you'd have to bend down to get under that fence to the bridge, because the spikes went low, but in the shallow creek itself, bent very low, yes! Someone could go beneath the fence, climb up the bank and come out on—he turned.

Newman Street. If you were going to, say, Lee Huang's opium den, you'd pass through a few short blocks of dark houses and you'd be there.

Or, going the other direction would take longer, but you could pass along Pogue's Run footpath—the same way they had gone on the Leatherstocking expedition—in what? About twenty minutes? to an area a few blocks from Lockerbie and, crossing only one main road get to Li Ting's opium den in the shack behind the big house.

Carrying your knife or hatchet. To kill Chinese men in hysterical hatred. He realized how improbable it all seemed.

Still his tormented mind drove him on. Find the person with the most hatred and you will find the murderer. So Sgt. Rossi said. It would take an inordinate amount of despising, a very disturbed mind to do such a thing awake or asleep. He had seen that Alice had the proper potential for such hysteria, perhaps. (He did not know about murder.) But why did she have such fear and hatred? What would cause it? What in the world was in her sad, odd past, that O'Shaughnessey had obliquely referred to, that sent her to the spiritualists?

He took his watch out of his pocket. Time to go to see Sidlow. But after that—Fanning had said take the day off. That meant the whole day. The train for Delphi, Indiana left at 1:30; he had checked on that yesterday afternoon. He would be on it if humanly possible.

He walked past Stewart's bookstore in the downtown area to get to the law office where he would meet Sidlow. A crowd was thronging inside the doors. He had a few moments before he was to appear; he moved in with them. People were looking up into the balcony as they walked up the steps.

"Who's up there?" he asked a matron with a book in her hand.

She showed the book to him: *Riley's Childhood Rhymes With Hoosier Pictures*. It had two charming children chasing a butterfly on the cover. "James Whitcomb Riley and a young writer who's his friend. I'm going to get Mr. Riley to sign my book."

Mack hurried along with the rest, up the well-worn wooden steps. There, in the midst of a circle of admiring friends sat two unassuming looking men: one young and handsome with slick black hair, a well brushed suit, and a wide smile, the other with a pince nez, rumpled clothing and the beginning of a portly stomach. Everybody knew that was Riley.

"Ladies and gentleman, I'd like you to meet a young pup who's due to be a real literary dog pretty soon. His name's Booth Tarkington. He's getting rejections slips from every magazine in America and working on a book about us all. It's about a gentleman from Indiana. I'd think it was about me, except for that term 'gentleman.' "

Admiring ladies, their fashionable hats bobbing on their pompadours, chatted with the two literary lights. Then a voice, from the woman who had brought the book in, "Mr. Riley, would you read 'Out to Old Aunt Mary's' to us? Please?"

"It's s'long," he demurred. Other voices joined in. "It's my favorite," "I have an Aunt Mary. Please."

So the poet cleared his throat and began.

Wasn't it pleasant, O brother mine
In those old days of the lost sunshine
Of youth—when the Saturday's chores were through
And the Sunday's wood in the kitchen too
And we went visiting, me and you
Out to Old Aunt Mary's?

It all comes back so clear today!
Though I am bald as you are gray—
Out in the barnlot and down the lane,
We patter along in the dust again,
As light as the tips of the drops of the rain,
Out to Old Aunt Mary's!

We cross the pasture and through the wood
Where the old gray snag of the poplar stood
Where the hammering redheads hopped awry
And the buzzard raised in the clearing sky
And lolled and circled, as we went by
Out to Old Aunt Mary's.

And then in the dust of the road again;
And the teams we met, and the countrymen
And the long highway with sunshine spread
As thick as butter on country bread,
Our cares behind and our hearts ahead
Out to Old Aunt Mary's.

The poet seemed to be squinting through his pinc nez at the page. Surely he knew the poem by heart. The audience was quiet, realizing that it was an emotional experience for the poet, that he was staring at the page because he was reexperiencing that walk, that greeting so many years ago.

> *And the romps we took, in our glad unrest!*
> *Was it the lawn that we loved the best*
> *With its swooping swing in the locust trees*
> *Or was it the grove, with its leafy breeze*
> *Or the dim haymow, with its fragrancies*
> *Out to old Aunt Mary's?*

The mezzanine of Stewart's Bookstore was as quiet as a church lobby before the first hymn. Even the clerks were listening, intently.

> *Far fields, bottom-lands, creek-banks-all,*
> *We ranged at will—Where the waterfall*
> *Laughed all day as it slowly poured*
> *Over the dam by the old mill-ford,*
> *While the tailrace writhed, and the mill-wheel roared—*
> *Out to old Aunt Mary's*

He read of the delightful things Aunt Mary made to eat, of the other country pleasures as the boys rambled amidst birds and woods and fields. Then he went on. . .

> *But home, with Aunty in nearer call*
> *That was the best place, after all—*
> *The talks on the back porch, in the low*
> *Slanting sun and the evening glow*
> *With the voice of counsel that touched us so—*

What was it those in the audience were hearing? Some were weeping. Even the few men present wiped tears from their eyes. Clearly Riley was helping them re-live some universal experience. The poetry was touching, he had to admit that. A relative who loved you and grew as close to you as a friend, as his Aunt Delia had, became a part of your heart. And when she was gone, part of you went, too.

For, O my brother so far away
This is to tell you—she waits today
To welcome us: Aunt Mary fell
Asleep this morning, whispering "Tell
the boys to come." . . . And all is well
Out to Old Aunt Mary's.

The poem was over. Ecstatic applause reflecting appreciation re-sounded, and Riley closed the book with a satisfied smile. Tarkington shook the poet's hand enthusiastically.

The man who had said, "I have an Aunt Mary too" whispered to Mack, "When my Aunt Mary died—well, other things happened, but I was never the same again. It was just after that I came to the city."

Watching the women wipe tears from their eyes with fine embroi-dered handkerchiefs taken from fashionable pocketbooks, Mack real-ized the truth. James Whitcomb Riley was the voice of an entire generation. Many of these people now in their thirties, forties and fif-ties would have grown up in the small Hoosier villages when Indiana was still on the frontier. All of them lived in simple houses, some, pos-sibly many, grew up in log cabins. They lived a life of societal interde-pendency before electric lights and streetcars and soda fountains had transformed America. Church box-lunch socials and hymn sings and long trips to the fishing creek were the stuff of their childhoods.

They yearned for that simple country past, he thought, walking downstairs past shelves of Riley's books. These poems re-capture the simplicity of a pioneer time that's dead—forever for them. And these poems are read and admired all over America for the same reason, he realized, not that they're great sonnets or odes, but because they cap-ture the simplicity of childhood gone, for a people, and for a nation.

And, thinking of his own childhood in a lumber town, he remem-bered fondly, too. The town was small and raw, and Indians and huge lumberjacks walked the muddy streets and nobody could stay really clean, but everybody knew everybody else's name and cared whether they were sick or well that day, and picnics on the beach seemed to be an eternal afternoon of sunlight and water and happiness, and prayers happened on your knees at sunset with mother's arm around your shoul-ders.

At least as he remembered it all. Of course there were other, harsher realities back then, and for all of these people listening to "Out to Old Aunt Mary's" today, too, but they didn't remember them that way. Childhood is an eternal noon, preserved like a rose under the glass of memory, and it should stay that way. For most people. But not all. Alice's sad, poignant face came into his mind, and he thought that the faded rose of her childhood memories was a dark empurpled one, possibly even bloody.

Sidlow was waiting for him in the lobby, looking at his watch.

He made the legal proposal to Sidlow, who sat silently across from him at the restaurant table in the lobby of the lawyer's building. Sidlow was to be allowed to withdraw from the association but pay a small settlement to each member, to sign an apology to the cartel; the lawsuit would then be dropped.

"And so he has me over a barrel," Sidlow said bitterly, not touching the sandwich which sat on the plate before him.

" A man who has hired *boo how doy*—"

"How's that?"

"*Boo how doy*. Chinese hit men to rough up his rival to eliminate the competition, and when it goes wrong, this man actually becomes an accessory to murder—this man wants to sue me."

"Well, the association contends yours was a witnessed, legal contract."

"And it was. Legal but not moral. I signed in a moment of weakness, when I wanted my business to grow to fund other investments."

Calmly Mack ate his ham salad sandwich and washed it down with a lemon phosphate. "Fanning says those investments are in Chinese gambling houses which are opium dens." He wasn't going to mention the police, naturally.

Sidlow's eyes flashed fire. "I invested in those things to help these people have something to do. Besides, only a few are opium dens. My God, man, all of the legitimate professions are closed to them. And Indianapolis has wide-open gambling. It's not the worst thing in the world."

"It treats in human misery." He stared right in Sidlow's eyes. "I see this all the time. Do-gooders are so righteous about high-flown causes, the poor in Cuba or the Philippines, the rights of the poor farmers, and then exploit people to make money in their own home towns. I don't understand it."

"Why you—I helped you try to find out about those murders, told you all I knew when you were in Chicago and now you turn on me. I thought you were a man. Can't bite the hand that feeds you, I see." He stood up, but Mack was not to be fazed.

"Sit down, Sidlow. It's to the best interest of all of us to settle this."

Sidlow sat down cautiously. He took a sip from his glass of sarsaparilla. "They tell me up here at this fancy firm that I should settle, not fight."

Mack was silent.

Then Sidlow jumped up again. "No, damn it! I won't kowtow. Apologize and pay! No! Let him sue me; I'll tell it all anyway."

Mack stood also. "You'll tell them that you own a part interest in the Celestial Heaven here in Indianapolis? Along with two or three members of the Chee Kong tong here in the city? And that the Hip Sings have just about forced you all out so they can run it? Your interests are in danger of collapsing here? You'll tell them that?" Nate Nessing had brought to the office this morning that telegram he'd received from Chicago. "Yes, and tell them you are the only white member of the Chee Kong anywhere in America. Initiated with special rites. And that you bound yourself to defend Chee Kong honor, brother for brother."

Sidlow's face was as white as a sheet. "You bastard. I'm proud to stand with them. They're more men than the weak-livered sons of bitches in the cartel. A thousand years ago, while our ancestors were pillaging villages in Normandy, these men's ancestors were composing fine poetry in landscaped gardens and debating philosophy. These are the men who fought the whole Manchu Dynasty in China. Why shouldn't I associate with them? They understand the meaning of brotherhood and loyalty while your cartel members—" he spat at a nearby cuspidor.

"To each his own, Sidlow," Mack said, picking up the bill. "But if I were you, I wouldn't risk the suit. Or go to the police about Fanning or anyone else. They might want to know just how far your loyalty goes when somebody's moved in on your Chee Kong brothers in this city. Or is it loyalty of the pocketbook?" Mack turned his back and strode away, his heart beating fast. He really didn't want to be picked up by his coat collar and banged against the wall of the back hall of this restaurant. One beating a month was enough.

The train station at Delphi was deserted when he, the lone passenger, got off. Late afternoon sunshine slanted over the benches by the side of the tracks; the ticket booth was empty. A black and white spotted dog with a twisted tail, sniffing at a puddle, was the only sign that there was any life at all in the town.

He walked a couple of streets back from the station, away from the river—and then the town seem to burst into life, as if the curtain had parted and the lights brightened on the stage of a playhouse. Children who had just left the schoolhouse for the day chased each other up Main Street, under huge, stately elms. Women holding smaller children by the hand were coming out of the Bon Ton general store and Carney's Candy Kitchen and the Suit-Your-Need Hardware Emporium.

Old Civil War veterans sat on benches by the courthouse re-fighting the Battle of Chickamauga, just like at home in Michigan. And there were the police officers, standing nearby gossiping with a pair of pretty girls, idle in this little town in the fading afternoon sunlight.

But Delphi hid secrets. All small towns did; the very closeness they bred, the concern for one's neighbor, also bred nosiness and contempt mixed with voyeurism, no doubt about that. All the foibles of human nature were being practiced behind the doors of these ornate wooden-faced front porches. The town fed on sin, alleged and otherwise, and gossip about sins. He knew that from his own small town.

More than one person on this very street must know the story he was looking for, but they would not tell it to a stranger. There was fear of the stranger in these little towns, a contempt for "otherness." Woe betide the colored family living in a town like this if they did not have several fellow families.

Beneath the Sunday School calendars on the walls and the pictures of Jesus at the door of the heart were people whose parents had been members of the Knights of the Golden Circle—and who would join the Ku Klux Klan in a moment—if it ever came north. James Whitcomb Riley's idyllic village people had dirty petticoats under the pretty little dresses.

But it did mean that if an oriental person had been here, ever—it would be etched in the town's collective memory like the names on the mausoleum of the most prestigious family in the cemetery up on the hill.

Somebody here knew why Alice Fanning walked in the night. Why she carried a knife in her room and put it on top of a newspaper carica-ture of an oriental. Someone in this town of Delphi knew, and he had about two hours to find out what was hidden in the heart of the town.

The Catholic Church, St. Joseph's, was located north, three or four streets beyond the main business district. It was that time of day that the priest of a parish might be in. No masses were needed, visits to pa-rishioners were over, and supper was on the stove at the parish house, now at about 3:30 in the afternoon.

Indeed, he could smell swiss steak, or maybe potroast wafting out as the housekeeper opened the door when he turned the bell crank.

"I have come from Indianapolis to see Father Bernard. Tell him Ray O'Shaughnessey sent me."

She brought him into the parlor, where the priest, a small wiry man with huge glasses, sat writing at a desk. He rose to greet the visitor cor-dially, and soon they were sitting before a little table, as the housekeeper served tea. Light chatter followed, about O'Shaughnessey and his lit-erary pursuits and boxing tournaments in the big city, about the good weather in Delphi and the river's rise and fall. Then Father Bernard looked at him with one eyebrow raised. "You didn't come all this way to talk about the river," he said.

Mack nodded. "O'Shaughnessey knew I was worried about the family I live with. The wife of the house seems deeply troubled, per-haps on the verge of nervous prostration. She does not know I have come, but I think you may know something that will help her."

"She is from here?"

"Yes. Alice Fanning—she was Alice Arken."

Father Bernard's eyebrows—silver with a few black hairs inter-spersed—became one line on his forehead.

"Alice Arken," he repeated quietly.

"Yes. She is a wonderful woman. I work for the family and I see the pain she is in. It is connected with her father, whom she seems to believe deserted the family."

The priest nodded.

"And there is a hatred, a loathing of orientals. She cannot bear the sight of a Chinaman. And it is causing her such mental anguish that I do not believe she can go on."

Father Bernard rose. "I believe we should be takin' a walk," he said, setting down his teacup.

They passed south again, towards the main street, and as they crossed it, Father Bernard pointed out local landmarks. It did not seem odd to Mack that they were not discussing Alice. He understood that the priest was saving his explanation for somewhere else, a point of destination in this little town.

"If you go east, out of town, here," Father Bernard said as they left the last of the houses, "you come to country roads." Good farmland, Mack noticed, riverbottom land, with a ridge above in the distance ahead of them. They began to walk, with Mack welcoming the feel of a country road stretching on beneath his feet. Corn shocks stood like Indian tents from the edge of the road to the horizon of hardwoods beyond. Oak and maple leaves seen across the fields were a splendid, mottled canvas at this time of year, and pumpkins, light yellow for cows, dark yellow for people, dotted the furrows.

These were the roads the adult generation in Indiana had walked along to school, or with fishing poles across the shoulder, to get bass or catfish for supper. In their memories they were forever on these roads, pant legs rolled up as children, on their way to Old Aunt Mary's.

"Here 'tis, the cottage. Up this overgrown lane."

"It isn't too far from town."

"No. Her mother taught in the town school, and she attended there too."

They walked along. Milkweed pods were bursting open on their long, thick stems. Orange and black butterflies batted their wings above the pods in the dying sunlight.

They came to a small cottage, deserted now. Fieldstones, fallen out of the mortar of the fireplace, lay on the ground outside, and the door stood slightly ajar. They pushed it open.

"Two rooms. This one was the sittin' and cookin' room, and in this all purpose room the folks slept, when Joss was home. He was a railroad man, built the roadbeds, hired the help. That other, little lean to room was Alice's."

"He was Irish," Mack murmured. "How did he—end up in Delphi?"

The words "end up" seemed to ring in the air.

"How much time d' ya have?"

Mack took out his pocket watch. "About an hour and a half before the last train leaves from the station."

Father Bernard smiled. "That should be enough time. The story is long."

"I want to hear it all." Absolutely, at this point.

"We can't sit down here. Let's walk up the hill to the church. It plays a part, too." Mack closed the door tightly as they left, without much hope that it would stay that way. They walked to the edge of the woods near the cottage for a moment; in between the second growth hawthorne trees and black cherries was a rusty wheelbarrow turned upside down and a doll without a head, sticking up from a pile of broken bottles and other effluvia of a series of seasons.

"There's always something so sad about a deserted house," Mack said, looking past the pile and into the woods, as if somehow the shade of the child Alice might be listening there, waiting without a voice in the depths, unable to explain what part the things in the pitiful little pile had played in her life.

They came to the "simple little country church, with its windows looking out on the fields" that Alice thought of with longing as she sat in the splendor of the new temple in Indianapolis. Out the window, rolling hills rippled downward towards the Tippecanoe River in the distance, and birds circled in the sky, gathering for their flight south.

There they were, the honored dead, within sound of the hymn singing. They lay in rows, under headstones with angels above them as guardians. Chiselled inscriptions bespoke their anguish at parting from lifelong associations made deeper by the isolation of country living.

"I don't think Reverend Blackstone will mind our goin' in. It's left open for prayer during the week anyhow. Nobody bothers it."

"I should hope not. It has a regular minister? Must be a small congregation."

"Methodist Episcopal. He has three churches and lives in Lafayette. But they don't call them circuit riders any more."

"No." They were standing in the vestibule, near a table with the ever-present fans advertising the local mortuary and offering envelopes and copies of the *Holiness* magazine. The sun, coming in through windows at the rear of the church, cast an orange glow over the room, over the curving row of newel posts which defined the small altar space. The pulpit, roughly hewn in pioneer days, was covered with an embroidered altar cloth with the fish that is the symbol of Christ, worked lovingly in purple crewel by some believer's hands.

There was no stained glass here; in fact the double hung windows had squares of bubble glass. This was an old church, from Indiana's earliest days.

The benches were new, though, polished with furniture polish, and the floor clean-swept. There was a dignity and simplicity to the place that touched Mack—no ornamentation except for the picture on the wall of Jesus in the garden of Gethsemane, bowing in agony. How often she must have looked up at it as she sat on these benches. They sat near the back to talk.

"To understand this story, we have t' go back to a far-away country. China, 1867."

Mack nodded, without surprise.

"There a Chinese peasant named Lu Fu was tryin' to take care of his starvin' family after the failure of the millet crop. To make some kind of livin', he put his thumbprint on a document which he thought made him a deckhand on a coaster ship. Instead, he was shanghaied to California."

Mack watched the birds circle, winging like a shaken sheet in one direction, then suddenly wheeling in the air.

"In California he was hired by the gang boss Joss Arken. Joss was himself a single man, still young as men on the railroad go. He became a sort of friend to Lu Fu."

"Sort of?"

"Well, he took him to get food and lodging in San Francisco. Joss spoke a little Chinese; he helped set Lu Fu up with the protective associations, which back then were really helpin' Chinese—sendin' money back home, arrangin' for Chinese brides and the likes and settin' up Joss houses."

"Joss?"

"Joss houses are the houses where the gods are honored. Joss Arken had helped pay to set one up, with images and bright paper and porcelain tributes and incense. That's how he got his name. He was intrigued with the Chinese, since he'd met the first ones in San Francisco. He liked the Chinese people on the whole, I s'pose, But he had been hired to bring workers into the desert to work on the railroad, and his one goal was to finish the section—even if it cost him the lives or health of the men on the project. He later regretted it, but he was young and ruthless. 'Twasn't easy to make your way as an Irishman in the sixties and seventies out west. Or anywhere, really."

"I suppose not." A thought struck Mack and he turned to look at the middle-aged priest with the round, deeply lined cheeks, the warm, blue eyes. He had probably been born in Ireland; his accent was still obvious. "How do you know all this?" He thought of the confessional.

"These are secrets told between two friends. He was not an active communicant; his sense of his own past by the time I knew him, his guilt, was too strong for him to come to the altar of Christ. We sat long hours in the parsonage, before the fire, and he came to trust me as one of the few Irish in the town."

"Go on."

"Though Joss pretended to befriend Lu Fu, he used him, and all the rest, through the blisterin' heat and disease of the railroad camps. Joss put Lu Fu deeply in debt to the company, and sweated him and worked him, along with the rest, until that Chinaman came to hate Joss with a hatred that was as deep as the veins of metal under the earth."

"Perhaps it was because Joss had offered Lu Fu friendship in the beginning."

"Yes. But Lu Fu was a man who, in other circumstances, had he stayed in China, might have lived out his life in the sunlight. I have seen men who could go either way, but for circumstances. But in this case—" he pointed forcefully towards the floor—"Straight down."

"When Lu Fu collapsed from overwork and lay in fever for a week and a half, Joss did go to visit him, saw the feverish eyes and heard him ramblin' in Chinese about his family. But he said not a word. He couldn't be bothered about bad water and unsanitary conditions and overwork that were makin' his men sicken and die. And worse than that, he appropriated all the money Lu Fu had earned on the section gang to pay the man's so-called debts. Lu Fu had nothin', nothin' at all to send home, and his family were cast to the winds.

"But Lu Fu beat the odds. He got well, and when he did, he left the section gang and returned to 'Frisco, tied up with some of the tongs that were just beginnin' to gain power in the Chinatown area. And his hatred for all that Joss and the railroad had done to him was fed by 'em, a stick at a time, you might say, until it turned into a bonfire. It was a time when the awe of the white man in America was beginnin' to turn to contempt as the Chinese saw the promise of the new land fade. Most of 'em had been here only a few years, ten at the most, and when they first got here, their hopes were high. But they came to see that the white men were corrupt and money-grubbin' and contemptuous of anyone but themselves. The Chinese who had admired the white man saw their heroes staggerin' around in the Chinese district, losin' their gold in the sing-song girl palaces and drinkin' places and gamblin' joints. Extortin' and denyin' even the basic justice to the Chinese. So, as they met in their association halls, they came to talk about the hatred and scorn and exploitation they felt ."

Mack nodded. He had sensed it in Chicago. The priest went on. The best of the Chinese, he said, were wise and deep thinking, and their eyes must have pierced the shallowness of society in the booming cities. There was no real welcome for them in the land which had boasted of the Statue of Liberty, any more than there was a welcome for the Negroes that the lives of so many men had freed. No wonder the Chinese turned bitter, like the alkali water out west. It didn't excuse crime, of course but—

"Lu Fu became an opium eater himself, and his drug dreams merged with the real injustices he'd faced. His family in China were scattered, ruined. He became obsessed with Joss Arken, determined to pursue him, grind him down, wipe him out for ruinin' his life."

The sun was an orange ball, dropping behind trees whose leaves were beginning to drift down in a rising wind. Still the priest spoke, in a voice which was now softer, whispered in the empty church.

"The year after Lu Fu left the gang, the sabotage of the railroad began. Shipments of supplies comin' from 'Frisco were waylaid and burned, fires were set in dormitory buildings; the safe was broken into. Joss became aware he was bein' hunted and punished; finally he quit the place.

"Where could he go? It was an awful thought, though the man clearly deserved it; being stalked for your life was one of the worst things a person could think of.

"He tried 'Frisco, where the company was headquartered and he had friends. But he discovered there was a contract out on his life—the hatchetmen were after him. One night he woke up with them castin' shadows over his pillow and he had to fight for his life. He carried a deep scar—shaped like a 'J' on his arm, from a hatchet."

"A real hatchet?"

"Yes. They use 'em in those days. Now they use pistols and knives."

Knives. In Mack's mind flashed the deadly, pearl-handled knife he'd seen in the dainty bedroom on the third floor. What did all this have to do with that knife? And the woman he so desperately loved? And now feared, or, said in a better way, feared for.

"He went to Chicago and tried to work in the railroad yards there," the priest went on. "But Lu Fu found him there and came and set up an opium den and a few weeks later, just when Joss thought he was safe in his new world. Lu Fu pursued him to his lodgin's in the night. In desperation the next morning Joss got on a train—he didn't care where, to escape and lose himself somewhere in the remote countryside."

Mack thought he understood. "The train came to Delphi."

"Yes. And word had it a new Irishman came into town—it wasn't unusual, the river brought other river rats into the bars of the city, and sometimes they stayed. He took work in the ticket agent's office—that way he could keep an eye on who was comin' into town. By this time he was repentin'. Sorry for his life, for what he'd done to Lu Fu and the others." He rose and stared out through the trees towards the river. "It's sunset. We'd better walk back. We can talk as we go."

Quietly they shut the door behind them.

"One Sunday morning he took a walk along this road. Climbed the hill, came through this very door." He gestured behind him. "He walked into the service as they were singin' the first hymn. He hadn't been to St. Joseph's—felt he couldn't come before God in the confessional, even. Later he told me he had to make his own penance before he could come to Mother Church."

They reached the main road and turned on it as the shadows deepened. "Anyway, he took off his cap and sat down in the back pew. His heart was touched and he asked for the forgiveness of God at that time. After church he was met by the members of the Epworth League—and one of them was an old maid schoolteacher named Elva Dobbs."

Mack took up the story. "From one of the old families—somebody in Indianapolis told me." Mrs. Bascomb had told him that. Some of the Irish families in Indianapolis knew parts of this story, but certainly not much. Best that way.

"Yes. Her parents had lived in the big house on Main Street in town. They had made a fortune from the canals, but it had been lost, completely. All that remained were her fine breeding and almost perfect manners. Behaving in a genteel way was a matter of pride, and still was even later, when she lived in a cottage." They were passing the forlorn path now, and Mack looked at it with sadness.

"Joss was as handsome as a man can ever expect to be, with that sort of fine physique and craggy features many women like. She was smitten, and they were married in that little church where we sat."

"Not in the Catholic Church."

"No, although shortly after that he began to pay calls on me. I think he believed he was payin' his debts and could someday patch it up with God in the church in which he was baptized. I listened, without givin' advice."

"Go on."

"Alice was born, and all did go well. There was no sign of the Chinaman; he assumed, and I did, too, as his confidante, that the man had either given up or died. I have to say that Joss was reformed. He was promoted in the railroad company, supervised everything from here to Lafayette on the West and South Bend on the North. He travelled a lot—I don't know if he ever settled down completely. There was a restlessness there—" The priest ran his fingers through his hair with some perplexity. "He drank sometimes, and he was often gone longer than he needed to be, but he always came back. The wife and little girl held their heads up about it, but I know they worried he'd abandoned them. There were many men like that at the time."

"Alice grew up, a rose in the country glen—"

"Yes, I guess you could say that, if you're a romantic," the priest laughed. "She absorbed her mother's perfect grace and religiosity and yet—her father's fire is there too. Buried deep but there's a streak of steel." Mack knew it all too well.

They walked for a few moments without the priest speaking. The first houses of the village were in sight. "When she was nine something happened."

"Lu Fu came to town," Mack guessed. He knew it was true to some extent. O'Shaughnessey had said something like that. How'd he know anything about this? Well, the Irish community was a close one in the state, he supposed. Surely he knew a good deal more of this story. It was probably safe with him.

"Yes. He was seen lookin' in a window at a bar downtown one night, stood out like a sore finger of course in this village. And word began to circulate that a well-groomed Chinaman was in town tradin' in Chinese porcelain with gift shops and general stores. Lodgin' at the hotel. Joss came to see me, white as a sheet. He had seen him on the street."

"Oh? Had he tried to attack Joss?"

"No. Quite the contrary. He saluted Joss with the same friendliness he'd shown in the first days he'd come to America. Joss was terribly nervous, but the import of the little chit-chat they had there on the street was that a lot of time had passed and old issues weren't important. Lu Fu had told Joss in Chinese that he'd found prosperity in Chicago, had a wife and so forth."

"And Joss believed him."

"Had every reason to, I suppose. A week passed, and Lu Fu seemed to be done transactin' business with all the little shops in the area, had even gone as far as Lafayette. Soon he'd be gone, everyone said." They were walking down the main street in town. The light was fast dimming; the train would be leaving soon.

"It was a gray, blustery Saturday in November. I remember because earlier two of the altar boys called in sick and I was worried about doin' the Mass without them. Eleven o'clock at night—apparently Joss and Elva were asleep in front of the dying fire; Alice was in her room. The wind was high, blowin' branches about everywhere. They didn't hear the window open in the little girl's room, because the wind was makin' so much noise. The Chinaman came to that window, pushed it open, jumped in before the girl could even wake up, covered her mouth with his hand and spirited her away in the night."

"God—" Mack said, dismayed. "Did he—"

"I will tell you. He took her to an abandoned shack by the old pickle plant and kept her there with him. He had many ways to terrorize that child. He knew it was the one way he could revenge himself on his former persecutor, and he did it exactly."

"I guess I need to know," Mack said softly.

"He stripped the poor child of her nightclothes and made her dance for him. He leered at her, fondled her all over. And then he abandoned her in that cold, desolate place, tellin' her if she left he would kill her."

Mack's heart had frozen. "Did he—" He could not say it.

"He did not do the final act of violation, though he might as well have. When a posse from the town finally found her late the next morning, she was curled up in a ball in the corner, blue with cold, talkin' to herself, half out of her head.

They had reached the station. The train was due soon. "I must finish the story," the priest said. "The Chinaman had left the village early, on the six o'clock train. The villagers didn't connect the abduction with Joss. They thought the man had just gone berserk and kidnapped the girl at random—said they never trusted Chinks any more than they did hunkies or black monkeys anyway. That's the way they put it. And Joss couldn't bring himself to explain it all to Elva—he just told her this man was after him for an offense he fancied Joss had committed in San Francisco days. They didn't call the sheriff, though I tried to get them to. Elva never really did forgive him—that's another story. Their lives were lived in fear after that. Letters came in written Chinese characters—more threats, though Lu Fu never came to town again. Finally, one night near Christmas Joss read one final letter—this time from Detroit. He came to the parsonage, refused to read it to me and threw it into the fire."

The doleful "hoot, hoot" of the approaching train echoed far away down the tracks.

"Joss left that night, without saying goodbye to either Elva or Alice.

He couldn't. Too much water was over the dam. He was found dead in Memphis two months later, with a knife in his back."

Mack rubbed his forehead, frowning. "Alice still mourns him. She's stuck somewhere eighteen years ago. She thinks he abandoned her."

"Lu Fu never came after them again, of course, after Joss was gone. Nobody connected him with Joss' disappearance, not even Elva and Alice. I knew the full story, but it was easier to treat it as just another case of family abandonment. Let them all blame Joss. Let the details of Joss Arken's past rest, I thought. This woman and her daughter had to live in this town."

The train was slowing down; Mack stood by the boarding gate. "Have you ever seen a mother quail fly away when a hunter approaches, taking the danger onto herself so the young ones can escape?" the priest asked. Mack looked at him steadily. "That's what Joss Arken did. And nobody really knows it except a couple of us." He put his hand on Mack's shoulder. "And that's the way it should stay. Best not to tell, don't you think?"

"I won't be bound by that promise, Father, though I thank you sincerely for what you've told me." The train was waiting. "Do you think the sins of the fathers are visited on the children, even to the tenth generation?" Mack asked in a quiet voice. They walked towards the steps for Mack to board.

"I think the past, especially past sin, does haunt us in odd ways. But I also think God's love is bigger than any sin you or I could even think of," Father Bernard answered.

Mack went up the steps and turned to wave.

"Tell O'Shaughnessey to stay out of the bars after midnight," he called. And, at Mack's questioning look, grinned and yelled "He's my brother."

Soon the train was hurtling through darkness, flying as if suspended in time and space, its odd, chortling whistle resounding ominously above Mack's head. The answers he'd found to his questions raised additional questions even more puzzling and portentous. Had the awful trauma the child Alice experienced turned her into a woman capable of homicidal killing? His heart still refused to believe it, though the facts were battering at his consciousness, demanding to be considered. Could horrible things be done in sleep? And, if they could, and he could prove her implication, what would he do with the information once he had it? And, finally, how could she endure the suffering that would follow if he disclosed what he knew about her? And how could he endure it, loving her desperately the way that he did?

It was after ten o'clock when he opened the door of the house with his key. All was dark. The late visit to Delphi still obsessed him, re-playing itself like an out-of-tune hurdygurdy—the deserted cottage where so much pain had transpired, the wooden church on that rise above the river, simple and good, with its hewn altar and its embroi-dered altar cloth, the terrible story of father, mother, daughter and their tormentor. Thank God he had not gotten anywhere near that awful shack on the grounds of the factory, the scene of the atrocities.

On the table in the hall was a photograph of Alice as a child, some-thing he had never paid attention to. Children, poor children! he thought, conscious of them in a way he had never been before. Of all of earth's resources, the most wonderful, given to us all communally, like the golden rivers and the mountain mists. But how some of us have used them, children of our communal heritage! How much pain has been placed on their innocent souls.

He climbed the stairs to the third floor. She had been wounded, grievously, no doubt about that. But could she have stalked by night, her pain buried and bursting forth like corruption from a carbuncle? That Dr. Freud in Europe thought many unspeakable horrors were wrought by buried pain.

His door was open a crack; it creaked on its hinges as he pushed it open. He groped his way towards the bed, pulling off his coat as he went, reaching for the cravat. Dark—he had seen so much darkness lately day and night. He froze. There was someone in the room, moving, there in the corner. Now, coming towards him. Damn it, where was the lamp? Suddenly there was a hand on his shoulder and he looked into her eyes, glowing like a cat's in the dark. Alice, was here and she was very angry.

Her fingernails dug into his arm even through his shirt; all the terrors of her life came into his mind as he turned to clasp her firmly by the arms.

"Mrs. Fanning—Alice—what is it?"

"You went to Delphi," she said. "I will never stop hating you for that. I know you mean to uncover my shame." She was breathing heavily, but it was fear and desperation he saw in her eyes, not violence.

"Let's sit for a moment on the chairs in the corner of this room," he said. "And let's speak quietly. I do not think it would be good for the others in the house to awaken now." He looked into the blazing, narrow slits that were her eyes. Then he led her to a chair near the window looking out on the silent streets and fountains, and as he did so, he felt her arm trembling as if she were freezing to death.

Chapter Eleven

"How did you know I've been to Delphi?" Mack asked after they sat down. He didn't light the lamp, but opened the portiere a little, so light from the lamps on the street filtered in. Her face was as pale as library paste.

"Mrs. Farquharson. She overheard you on the telephone calling Union Station, asking them to hold tickets for you. I was alarmed when you didn't come to be with Chad." She twisted her hands in her lap agitatedly.

"I left a letter for you, under your door. I said I would be detained by business."

"I did not return to my room, so I didn't find it until later. But you didn't say where you had gone. Business—you wished to deceive me, and I trusted you."

"I did deceive you, but if I had told you I was going to Delphi would you have approved? Obviously not. Is it because I found out something that I shouldn't know?"

She paced in front of the window. Her eyes, when she finally turned to him were full of distress. "What business of yours are the details of my life? You are often so mysterious, creeping about—and you were in my room. What reason did you have to be there, tell me that? And asking everybody questions about the Chinese murders. Why are you doing this?"

"I've told you about the murders, that your husband was somehow involved in all of it. Did you ask him what I meant?"

She looked at the floor. "No. I didn't want to know, I guess."

"Are you ready now? I doubt it. Still, I'll begin at the beginning and you can judge for yourself." He wasn't sure, but something was driving him to tell the truth, as it always did, like the young boy Confucius told of—impertinently asking, all the time what is truth? So he began at the beginning, and told her of Li Ting's murder in Lockerbie near Mrs. Teitelbaum's, and Lee Huang's opium den in back of the laundry and his murder, finally, there, with the police trying to decide if the

Chee Kongs had done it to try to gain power, or the Hip Sings, to get even for a botched hatchet "hit" in Chicago—ordered by her husband Walter Fanning. He did not tell her about Walter's opium habit—if you could call it that. It was not his place to tell that.

"Walter ordered what did you call it—a hatchet hit on the owner of what's the name? Chicago Select Game?" she said, astonished.

"Yes. It's called J.S. Sidlow now. The owner before Sidlow, a man named Mapeltharp, was gravely wounded. He gave up his business because of it and fled the area. But a young woman was killed in the attack. Sidlow has been here in town today, trying to get out of the association cartel and threatening Mr. Fanning with revealing his part in the murder to get out of the cartel free and clear."

"And you and your friends, including the one from the laundry are trying to sort out who really committed the two murders?"

He nodded.

"But why—how—what does Delphi have to do with it? Why did you need to dig around in the debris of my past up there?"

"What makes you think I was doing that? Perhaps I just wanted to get on the train and take a ride to see the Tippecanoe River."

She looked at him savagely. "No—you were after something about me, and I suppose you've found it. Not many people know my whole story, but enough do to satisfy your morbid curiosity." He said nothing in rebuttal. How could he? He must look to her like something of a stalking crazy man.

"I know you've been following me. And—you were in my room. Why? It's outrageous. You, a boarder here. I thought you were my friend. I demand to know."

He sighed. "I wanted to see if I could find anything to link you to the murders of those two Chinese men. I knew of your deep hatred of the race."

She tossed her head in anger. "Connection—what? I do hate them. And finding out what you have in your smarmy search in the town of my birth and degradation, do you not see why?"

"I see why, though one man is not the entire race."

"My innocence, my dignity, and my father—they took them all," she spat, and her eyes flashed again. "But kill them! How can you possibly think that I, so committed to the Christian gospel, would lift a finger against other human beings, even if they are members of the Race of Cain." He rose, went to the door and locked it. Mrs. Bascomb was not in her room this evening, having been called home because her own child was sick, and Chad usually slept through the normal sounds of the night. Still, what went on behind this door this night was nobody else's business, no matter what its outcome.

"You found the knife," she insisted, rising and looking out the window. "I saw things disturbed in my drawer, and the knife was in a different spot. I don't know why I keep it. Perhaps it was the fear of what happened on that dreadful night when I was a child. It never really leaves me." She turned suddenly from the window to face him. "Why, how can you think I would murder? That devastates me!"

He braced himself. "I thought—you might have done it while you weren't yourself."

"Drunk? Under opium? How can you—"

"Sleepwalking. Such things have been known to happen." He did not know whether she would show surprise, deny she walked.

She began to laugh. First she chuckled, then she threw back her head, then she sat down and put her head down on her hands, laughing so hard the tears came. "You—thought—I killed someone when I walked out back on those nights." It was a statement.

He smiled weakly, partly in relief, and she pointed a finger at him. "Well, but how could I have possibly gotten to Lockerbie neighborhood or to the shop near the office. A woman at night?"

"Look, let me show you what I think—thought—about it. It's a mild night. We can slip down the backstairs, go to the garden." Why not? He had gone this far in confronting her. Perhaps it was all a sham, perhaps she was a wonderful actress and a murderess as well, but he had to know. Full speed ahead into the unknown.

And so soon they stood by the back fence. She was nervous, almost fluttery, but there was relief in her eyes which showed she believed she could trust him. In the pale light of a half moon the drying flowers and bent-over grass and mounds of falling leaves looked ghostly. "I saw you walk down the path, there," he said, "and into the alley and then disappear. I supposed that, if you were desperate enough, you could pass in your sleep through the fence into the Arsenal at a point where the pikes don't meet, then along the creek, bend low, and go out the grounds into the area where the murders were committed. You would not have been seen."

She took his arm and walked with him into the alley. "I am never aware of sleepwalking while I do it, though there is a sort of dream-like memory which remains the next morning. I know I am subject to it. Walter never lets me forget," she went on sadly.

"You were gone so long, and the longest time did happen to be on the night of the second murder."

"Yes," she said, looking up at the moon. "That was the night I woke up in the midst of the sleepwalking."

"Oh? And where were you?"

"I was—oh, it's so humiliating. The grass was wet and I grew so cold, I guess, I must have been startled out of the sleep state. I guess you're right—I seem to think I have passed through a gap in the gate. But there I was on the grounds of the Arsenal—standing at the commandant's house up near Michigan Street, in the darkness there outside a ground level bedroom. I was looking in at a little girl, asleep on her bed. I suppose I have gone there before, into that Arsenal grounds, stood near that house, near that child."

"His daughter, perhaps. Chad and I saw children when on the day we explored."

She gently lifted the wire, moving it back and forth, as if unable to believe that it had been her passage into the mystery of the darkened, frightening grounds. Her soft blond hair, softly waving, had escaped and crowned her head like the lights around the lamps. She was so tiny, so beautiful, beyond anything in a fairy story, here in the garden on this almost balmy night. "I don't know what I was doing. Maybe I was there to warn her. 'Don't stay on the ground floor. Go up to where your parents sleep.' I know I was in absolute anguish in my sleep, as if reliving the night I was kidnapped. I felt the sort of heightened, crushing emotion one feels in sleep."

"I know the very feeling." She looked up, grateful for his understanding.

They stood looking into the Arsenal, in the shade of one of the West Drive carriage houses. "Here I came through, returning, wide awake, wet and afraid. Very afraid." She began to shiver a little; he stood close by her side and put his arm around her.

"There is one more thing," Mack said, relief coursing through him as he had told her his doubts and she had greeted them with such forthrightness and—innocence. That was it. "That black peignoir, the one you wear so often."

"Yes. What about it?"

"You do not have all the buttons."

"No. But what—"

"One of the black buttons, enameled in that unique way, was at the scene of Lee Huang's murder. I came upon it in the washhouse behind the laundry." He reached in his pocket; he carried it always with him these days. "Is this yours?"

"Yes," she said, eyeing it briefly and then turning her face towards the huge rock under the breach in the fence. "I have never been there." She faced him directly. "I want to tell you something, something that no one knows. McClure, I did not really need to ask why you are involved in our lives. The fates sent you my way—intertwined my life with yours—you've taken me to the séances, known of my distress when I believed someone was trying to reach me, stood by me and prayed the night my boy was miraculously healed—and now you know all my shame." Her mouth trembled. "That night in Delphi when that terrible man held me, something broke in me. I was like a doll whose main strings have sprung. On the outside, I prettied myself, and ran my life, and all was well. Pretty little doll. But inside, I felt as if I never had a minute's peace. In the midst of all happiness— my marriage, my child's birth, Christmas—I was in panic. Something, something terrible would happen, as it had before. And there was more. I could not bear to see a Chinese, but more than that, to have any man touch me. Except you. Something about you makes me trust you. When you touch my shoulder, I feel calmed, not afraid."

His mind was swirling. Was this all really happening? Had he— did he still—suspect her of murder? She was trying, succeeding in convincing him, but—he felt detached at this moment, as if he were staring down at a play from a high balcony. His mind, with all the complex details of the mystery, seemed to have gone somewhere deep asleep. Only his heart was speaking now.

"And the button?"

"Walter and I—well, I was telling you. I keep going astray." She took his hands in hers and looked into his eyes. "No living soul knows this. From the first night we were married, I could not be a wife to him. When he came to me, came into the bed—" she averted her eyes—"I fought him. It probably wasn't him then, just the idea of a man touching my body the way that awful animal had touched it. I was so young, knew nothing anyway when I was married. I kicked. I screamed; he retreated from my screams. The second night it happened again. I turned from him in the bed, weeping and when he came to me anyway, saying it was his right, that it would be all right, that I must endure as other wives had, I fought again. I seemed to be in that shed and that monster was taking off my clothes and putting his hands on me everywhere. Oh, I never told him about the shed. He thought he had married the perfect pristine princess. No—I made welts in his back with my nails."

Her voice was low and her words carefully articulated, as if what she was saying was terribly important, rehearsed within for months, years until the right time to speak would come.

"On the third night, he mastered me. He held me down and in spite of my fighting he mastered me. And ever after—whenever he wished to come to my bed, he would do what it took to achieve his will. And finally all I did was cry and grit my teeth. But when Chad was born and I was ill for weeks afterwards, it gave me the excuse I wished for. I moved up to the third floor, and took Chad with me. I warned Walter never to come up there, and hired first a servant girl and then Mrs. Bascomb. And I had a new key made for the butler's pantry on the first floor that he couldn't ever get, so I could retire there if I needed to. Then I bought the knife. I showed it to him."

"And, he never came up the steps after that?"

"Only one night. It was just before the long sleepwalk—in the summer."

"The night before the second murder."

"Well, or two nights before, perhaps. Anyway, he came and he was drunk. Of course you know how dissipated he is. Perhaps he fills his nights with whiskey and—other things—because he has no wife in his bed. I don't know." A tear appeared on her eyelash. "Anyway, he is as strong as a bull."

"I've seen—and I heard through the wall that night."

"Did you?" She seemed genuinely surprised. "He all but mastered me again, but I kicked him where I knew it would hurt. As he pulled away from me, he grabbed at the peignoir." She looked away, thought-fully. "The next morning I saw the buttons were almost all gone. I picked some up off the floor, but two were missing. They could have gotten into his clothing—he was fully clothed. Into his shirt cuffs or pocket, probably when I lunged at him and he grabbed me."

Well, that was logical. The button could have fallen into Fanning's suit cuff, and he could have carried it into the laundry washhouse.

Silence hung between them. Finally she said with emphasis, "How could you have thought I could kill?"

"I see I was wrong. But—how could I know?" he asked, as anguished as she was.

"Why didn't you just ask me?" She had his hands again, her eyes brimming with tears. He took his hand and brushed them from her cheek.

"I couldn't. I had to find out for myself," he said simply. "Because I love you." And now he had said it, and it was all over, and of course he would have to leave this house where he was a guest, and this woman who was his life, and never know the answers he had sought. He had said it and opened a door they could not re-close.

But improbably, against all logic, she put her arms around his neck. "I love you too, my dearest one." Her lips were on his, gently, longingly. They clung together in the wan light of the half-moon and the shadow of the livery barn. She stroked his hair, outlined a cleft in his chin; he wrapped his arms hungrily around her waist. They kissed deeply, over and over, and she leaned up towards him, her body pressed to his. His heart was in his throat when she pulled back.

"No! We will not go this direction," she cried. "Walter has wronged me in many ways as a wife but the worst is that he has broken his mar-riage covenant with others, many others, some on this very street." She looked disdainfully towards West Drive. "I will not do him likewise; it would lower what you and I are feeling to the level of the gutter."

Mack took a deep breath and pulled back to regain his breath. They stood, his arms still around her. "What will we do?" he asked. "It will be hell in the same house with you. I should resign, leave this town."

She looked up at him, her eyes wide. "We will go on, living life as before, and wait for all the events in this nasty situation to dispose them-selves." She kissed his cheek tenderly. "Now that I have found you, I cannot live without you near me. After all, you loved me before, didn't you, and still honored me and my son and my marriage?"

"What you ask is difficult," he muttered.

"There are murderers loose. Walter is connected with them, so you say. I'm afraid. Please—stay near us."

"Of course. I will." He kissed her once more, tenderly, as one would kiss a child.

She told him she would go into the house first. He gave her time to get upstairs and then he crept up the stairs himself, collapsing into bed and into the deep sleep of exhaustion.

Chiang and Abby were waiting at Tenth Street for him. "God— I hoped you would be here before the streetcar came. I could have missed my first class," Chiang said.

He looked solemnly at Mack. "Bee Chee was murdered last night. And the police in Chicago have arrested Whi Ting Lo as he got off the train in Chicago. Revenge killing, they say, part of a three-part string of killings here to revenge his dead girlfriend."

"Bee Chee Killed? And the head of the Hip Sings arrested." Mack looked at Chiang with a mixture of surprise and—he had to admit it— satisfaction. He still had sharp aches and sticky scabs from the beating he'd taken in Chicago from that son-of-a-bitch. And of course, had he any shred of suspicion left about Alice—she had been with him.

"Nate's getting plaudits down at the police department," Abby added eagerly. "He gave them the whole story—the shooting up there which killed the sing-song girl last year, the connection with Indianapolis Hip Sings and the Chee Kongs maybe hired here in Indianapolis to carry out the revenge. He thought it was time."

"And Fanning's part?"

"The person hiring the hit men originally hasn't come to light as yet."

"Well, but Whi Ting Lo was in Indianapolis again last night?"

"Yes, He left on the six o'clock train this morning to return to

Chicago. Says he was visiting relatives here in Indianapolis, but no one believes that."

"Does he have relatives here?"

"Yes. Over by Fook Soy's house," Abby told him.

"He was in town for one of the other killings, too." Mack said.

"The night of Li Ting's murder he was here. Not the night of Lee Huang's—but they're investigating."

"Finally."

"To answer your earlier question—Fanning may be eventually be questioned for his part last year, but the police seem ready to think of this series of events as another tong war, only this time in the Midwest," Chiang added.

"But won't Whi Ting Lo tell the police who ordered the hit?" Mack wanted to know.

"Nate says he's not admitting anything," Abby told him. "And he may not even know. Lee Huang could have handled the hit directly."

Mack was adamant. "I don't think Fanning should get off scot free. After all, he took the steps to get the hit men in the first place. And he was bankrolling the Chinese opium dealers here. That was what I found in his journal the day I was in the room."

"They probably can't prove that," Chiang said. "And it's not illegal anyway."

"Anyway, Big Walter's a member of the Commercial Club downtown," Abby added. "They don't usually touch them. If the *Indianapolis News* finds out, that's a different story. Everybody else 'll probably leave him alone. The Chicago police have wanted to get Whi Ting Lo for a long time. To nail him for the gambling palaces the Hip Sings operate in Chicago."

"And down here." Mack was silent a moment. "Is Sidlow still in town?"

"Who?"

"J. S. Sidlow—the man from the poultry association I saw in Chicago. You remember him at French Lick. He was in town yesterday talking to his lawyers."

"How should we know?" Abby demanded. "And what does he have to do with this?"

"He's a part owner of the Celestial Heaven—the gambling and

prostitution joint owned by Bee Chee and Fook Soy. He was supposed to be negotiating to get out of his contract with the Poultry Purveyors, but I suppose he was also seeing to his interest in the Chinese Chee Kong gambling place. I half suspect he was connected in some way to the killings."

"That's too far-fetched," Abby said. "The police have their man. Bee Chee must have helped Li Ting—been involved too. Just another tong war, like in San Francisco and New York. Revenge killing after a hit went wrong. The streetcar lumbered up; Abby and Chiang hopped aboard and disappeared among the passengers.

Mack walked down Newman Street towards the office. Well, so that was that. Just another Chinese intrigue. Man in custody; affair closed. He need no longer worry about anything—why was Chiang coming around the corner. He must have gotten off the streetcar.

"Hello, friend of mine. I have changed my mind and am going to pay a courteous call on my mourning cousin, proprietor of the Celestial Heaven gambling joint. I think you should go. In spite of having right man in custody, we still can—how do we say it—cover all baseball bats?"

"Bases." Mack told him he couldn't possibly go—had been gone the day before, then, grumbling, thought again. He went in to Fanning and said he had important business concerning "your Chicago affair" to investigate and would be back by noon.

The Celestial Heaven was over by White River, in the area where Mack had seen the funeral parade that first day in town. The Paris Pleasure Palace it was not, he thought as they approached a run-down, two-story frame building. A black funeral wreath hung on the door with Chinese characters written on the ribbon. They knocked and were admitted by a beautiful young woman with a chrysanthemum in her hair. Chiang nodded to her, whispering to Mack, "That's Pink Orchid, a girl of great repute."

"You mean ill. That's ill repute."

"No. Her fame is great in Chinese community." He told them she was the local madame of the sing-song girls in this town, few as they were in Indian No Place.

She ushered them in and went to get Fook Soy. He was dressed in formal mandarin clothing: wide bottomed pantaloons and a long, buttoned jacket of silk. His hair was cut in a barber-bowl short cut, and he wore very thick glasses, with his eyes crossing slightly behind them.

"Honored cousin, I shall march late this afternoon to escort the mortal remains of my cousin Bee Chee to their final resting place," Chiang said, bowing low.

"An appreciated favor, younger cousin, following his unfortunate death." Fook Soy wiped his glasses and looked at Mack. "I recall this face. It was at the laundry shop, on the day we came to see your uncle."

"He is a trusted friend of our family, my cousin."

Fook Soy, looking at them coldly, said nothing.

Three battered old parlor tables stood in the room; Chiang had already told Mack that these were fan-tan tables. In the rear was a curtained room where "suspicious activities" (as they were described in police reports) were pursued. If the police raided, it was easy enough to exit by the back door or, if someone was too dopey from the pipes to sit at the fan-tan tables supposedly playing the game. Upstairs were rooms for assignations with the two or three girls who lived here. Fook Soy lived next door.

"And so, my cousin," Chiang said, "they have found the perpetrator of this crime against your brother Bee Chee. The terrible assassin Whi Ting Lo is in custody in Chicago."

"And so he is," Fook Soy said. More silence. Finally he cleared his throat, a sound which echoed hollowly against the discomfort in the room. "But I think you do not believe he is the murderer. And you come to see if I am involved. I think we are playing children's game—Find the Swamp Dragon," Fook Soy finally said. "There are fifteen questions to discover where Swamp Dragon is at the moment, to get the candied ginger and the next turn."

"I know the police have been here more than once, cousin," Chiang said.

"The problem in the game is when nobody know what are the right question to ask."

"And what may they be?" Mack asked.

Fook Soy leaned against one of the fan-tan tables. "Well, for start, young stallions sniffing the wind, why *you* involved in all this?"

"Cousin, we are trying to clear up the mystery of Uncle's death for the honor of the family."

"Sure you are!" He began stalking back and forth agitatedly, his voice harsh. "You nosy pricks. That what you are. Come around here, nose in the air, blame us for something we not do. And you—" he pointed at Mack—"you work for the oily man with hair on face—" he searched for the word. He had been raised in China and English sat uncomfortably on his tongue.

"Mustache—you mean Mr. Fanning," Mack suggested.

"You no tell me how to talk, prick. You are ass kisser of the man who start all this." His finger pointed right in Mack's face. "What in it for you?" Mack was nonplussed. He couldn't say to a living soul that he was in love with the man's wife and needed to straighten out the mess for her. Well, there were other reasons, too, but they weren't this belligerent idiot's business.

"I wish to help a friend," he said, gesturing at Chiang.

"Police want to know why we argue with Lee Huang by his wash shed. You tell them that, is it not true? As if we want to take over his dream pipe trade, mebbe."

"Well, it did look bad," Mack said, gathering courage. "And that isn't a sarsaparilla fountain in the back room there, either," he said. "You must be able to service four or five pipe dreamers a night back there. And they can always head for the alley if the cops come. If there's any swamp dragon, it's probably inside your opium den." Fook Soy frowned, his mouth becoming a long, threatening line.

"What you know about the dream pipe trade, you water buffalo pizzle?" he said, leaning in Mack's face. "Police get Hip Sing chief from Chicago this morning. But last night, hot on another trail, police come here say murders about tongs fighting—*boo hoy doy*. They say Brother and I come to threaten our uncle Lee Huang for tong reasons day before he died. Mebbe kill him? They wrong. If it a tong war thing over dream pipes and girls how come we come together to Lee Huang? Bee Chee is in the Hip Song while I am a Chee Kong? The two enemy tongs dance arm in arm over together to argue with the uncle?"

"Well, we weren't sure Bee Chee was a Hip Sing. We didn't see his name on the Chee Kong list and we assumed—"

"Assumed. You are holes in the posterior with lizard breath farting out. Since you Shylock Holmes, tell me why if a tong war Brother and I waging war in, why Brother and I are of different tongs?"

Chiang was visibly uncomfortable, not looking at his cousin's thick glasses but at the funeral wreath instead. "They think," Mack went on— "the police think here and in Chicago—that there was a hatchet hit that went wrong, killing Whi Ting Lo's sing-song girl. And that—I guess—that some Hip Sings from here botched the hit in Chicago, and Chee Kongs were hired by Whi Ting Lo to do the revenge hit here in town. Lee Huang hired the hit, and Li Ting was the one who shot up the girl up there.

" It's likely some people were hired down here by Whi Ting Lo to carry out revenge for the girlfriend killing. And if you are Chee Kong, it could be you that was hired. And your brother Bee Chee was probably conspiring with you. Just for money, not for tong glory. Isn't it possible that first you got rid of Li Ting, the gunman? You collected the money for him and then you went after the contractor—Lee Huang. You were in the laundry that day to size up your opportunity." Chiang was madly signalling him to lay off, but he didn't intend to. He needed to see this feisty little terrier of a man's reaction.

"Oh, I see clear now," Fook Soy sarcastically intoned. "We come calling at the laundry, we prime suspects, we join forces to get payoff. Veddy evil Chinks, like in the plays at English Theatre. We play the devil god, get together to murder everybody offends the Chicago Hip Sing boss."

"Stranger things have happened," Mack said.

"Or mebbe there another answer here." He looked directly at Chiang. "Mebbe the true one. Mebbe we come on family protection matter. I, Bee Chee my brother, come to tell Lee Huang our uncle, brother of our father who fought in the Taiping Rebellion to free China from the Manchus and who died there. We two mebbe come to tell Lee Huang of grave danger to him."

Chiang tried to take in what he was saying. "But you were arguing."

"And what, manure brains, if the dear uncle refuse to listen, if he think we make up fancy fairy tale, not wish to heed warning."

"Warning—of what?" Mack demanded, suddenly following the train of thought.

"That someone chop head off in the Chinese community, of man connected with dream-pipe trade. Put characters by him that say in Old Chinese, 'Chinese demons' ".

"I don't think I heard what those Chinese characters beside Li Ting meant," Mack said.

"Not even police know. But Bee Chee and I did. And we go to Cousin Lee Huang. Say to beware of someone who hate Chinese worse than death."

No, Mack thought. We do not need that theory anymore. We now have the suspect in custody—it's a tong war, nothing else. We have disposed, thoroughly disposed of the theory of someone passing through the town unobserved, impelled by poisonous hatred of a race to kill— We must have disposed of that, have to have. But perhaps—

"There is a man who has come into town," Mack said.

"Yes? Many men have come into town," Fook Soy replied.

"His name is Sidlow. From Chicago. He is involved in some of your interests. Presses you to sell him more of the gambling interests. What about him?"

"So? You also wish to know what size underwear I order from Sears Roebuck catalogue? How often I take my wife to bed each week?"

The old thing snapped in Mack—the lumbercamp let's-get-drunk and-fight-feeling, the lightbulb popping. He pulled the slightly smaller man up by his mandarin collar. "Listen, you," he said. "If you have any idea who is committing these murders, killing people in this town, tell me, you son-of-a-bitch. I'll teach you what it means to call me a prick."

"I—don't—know *who*," the man articulated in strangulated gasps. "I only—know—somebody is deep in blood of Chinese. Whi Ting Lo— not right man."

Mack let him go.

Chiang bowed slightly; Mack straightened his shirt and tie.

"If I guess where Swamp Dragon is at this very moment, I will tell you, so you can win game," Fook Soy said with false bravado. They began to walk towards the door, when his voice called them back.

"Wait. There is something. By Brother Bee Chee body, here in the back." They turned and followed him through the room of tables into the back. There was a dark black stain on the floor; Chiang turned away. There were the familiar cots—the cabinets with hidden dope things behind their fronts, the whole place swept rather clean.

"This was written in ink, not blood, by his side, last night. Nobody else knows." He showed them four Chinese characters on tissue paper, copies of what he had obviously effaced from the floor.

"It say 'Kill the demons.'"

It was a couple of days before Mack could think more about the signs that had been written on the floors, or even the murders at all, days in which he needed to catch up on work, tutor Chad, who was feeling neglected and test his feelings at living as close as the next breath to the woman for whom he had declared his love.

It was the oddest form of torture he could imagine, and yet the necessity of it all forced him to pass her in the hall without reaching out to touch her hand, to eat at the table or in the family parlor before the fire, with Fanning on one side and Alice and Chad on the other, as if he were somebody's brother. Fanning believed him when he told of the arrest of the Chicago Chinese gang head and the possibility of Fanning's implication in the matter, which might or might not stick.

Mack discovered Sidlow had remained in town Tuesday night, the night of Bee Chee's murder, and had left on the six in the morning Monon to Chicago without having settled his case with Fanning, although his attorney said he expected him to do so. And Fanning was like a dog who has found a friend in a friendless world. He had in short, put his entire trust in Mack—leaning on a broken reed, if you put it that way. It did make it a little easier to be near Alice and not caress her: her husband trusted him.

Shylock Holmes, Fook Soy had called him. Well, unlike at Sherlock Holmes' Baker Street abode, his own mundane life continued with unexpected necessities for him—taking care of the horse out back when the freckled boy couldn't come, driving the rig to the city market, talking to Mrs. Bascomb about the never-ending dime novel that was life at her home on Irish Hill.

And, as if they were acting in some ridiculous farce in which bizarre little interludes had to break up the tragedy, a letter arrived for him; his father was coming to join him the following weekend to go to Southern Indiana for the wedding of his cousin John McClure's daughter, who was marrying the son of Jacob Joe's old and dear acquaintances Susan Brooks and her husband Sandford Niblack. "Remember, son," his father Jacob Joe Scott had written, "it was Tommy Brooks, this young man's uncle, who was in the Eightieth with me. He died as a result of wounds at Perryville in 1862. I feel a special obligation and joy in attending this wedding and am glad you'll be there with me."

They were to catch a train a week from today to Vincennes. Then they would take a couple of days to visit the Perryville battlefield and the home of the McClures in Kentucky. Fanning had said it was all right; he supposed it was. After all, it would take him far from the tension of seeing Alice's face by firelight and in the first rays of the morning—and of the uncertainties about the murders that would not leave him alone, waking or sleeping. Abby no longer cared about the killings, saying that the murderer would be arraigned in Chicago and would be extradited for trial in Indianapolis; Fanning had not been asked as yet to furnish a deposition in the grand jury investigation. If Whi Tong Lo knew anything about Fanning he wasn't talking.

The next day Mack stopped off at O'Shaughnessey's. He could not spar because several young men were preparing for the Youth Boxing Tournament, coming up in a few days. O'Shaughnessey stood by his side as they watched two fifteen-year-olds pummel each other till bruises stood on the shoulders and faces of each.

O'Shaughnessey asked about Mack's trip to Delphi.

"Why didn't you tell me Father Bernard was your brother?" Mack demanded. "I felt like a fool. And—how much did, do you know about Miss Arken of Delphi and her troubles?" That was a delicate way of avoiding saying her name. After all, the Fannings lived only a few blocks from this gymnasium.

O'Shaughnessey sighed, taking off his glasses and wiping them. "I have found being Irish in this town that it's best not to know anything about the folks who live on Meridian Street or in Woodruff Place. There's a lot of business flowin' out of the Commercial Club and its doin's these days, and it doesn't pay to gossip about the members or their families. The business interests are hirin' masons and hod carriers and electricians, and we folks from Irish Hill are the ones who are gettin' hired. 'Tis biting the hand that feeds you. And anyway, as Shakespeare says, 'What's done is done and can't be undone.' "

"You knew and kept it quiet. And yet you sent me to your brother up there. To find out—what I needed to know."

"It don't hurt to lift the stone and see the snakes, so long as you put it down again. Perhaps you've thrown the sunlight on them for a minute and at least you know where they crawl." It was a comment which didn't exactly rest Mack's mind as he heard it, but when he thought about it, he believed perhaps that was what those Viennese doctors were talking about—therapy to uncover the errors of the past and perhaps redeem them. A little sunlight never hurt anything.

The next day, Sunday, with the Fanning family at Central Avenue Methodist Church, Mack found his mind wandering during the sermon. If there had been three murders and they were the work of some sort of fanatic as Fook Soy believed, and not of the tong wars, as the police believed, then perhaps there might be another murder. There were more Chinese in this town. And the police weren't worried about further murders—they thought they had their man. They were trumpeting their victory around in the newspapers. Through it they could give the impression (false) that they were just as interested in finding justice for the yellow and black races in the city as they were for the white man. Had Bee Chee come close to finding out who had murdered his uncle and Li Ting? Was that why he had been killed? And—"Kill the Demons." What did that mean? He looked up at the altar, where Dr. Brockelhurst was holding forth on the concept of atonement in the world's religions. What a theoretical preacher he was, full of intellect, somewhat devoid of heart-felt spiritual message. Mack decided to see him after the minister had raised those scrawny arms in benediction and see if he could find out more about the inscription which had been left by the body of Bee Chee as some sort of warning.

"Kill the demons. It was the cry of the Taiping Revolt. That cry shook China to the core," Brockelhurst was saying as they sat in his parlor, drinking the coffee his aged housekeeper had sat on the little enameled table in front of them. "Yes, those are the characters. I suppose whoever it was that found these at the—scene of a murder, did you say?—didn't recognize them. Probably took it in a general way, get rid of whoever it was, but it is a part of history."

"How so?" Mack wanted to know, carefully scrutinizing the face of the man before him, the tiny, fastidious man in this museum of a house. The man who could interpret all this oddness, perhaps furnish a clue that would finally unravel the tangled net.

"Do you know anything about this? Not much? Well, during the 1830s the opium trade in China had expanded at a rapid rate, and white men were making a lot of money off addicted Chinese people. Dissatisfaction over the way the Manchus handled the European intrusions caused the Tapiping Revolt. That, and the Manchus' disgusting decadence and lack of care for their people. After the first opium war, in 1843 I think it was, a visionary named Hung Hsui Ch'uan believed the entire nation of China had been degraded by foreigners and the Manchu Dynasty. Hung was a schoolteacher—after collapsing and shouting 'Kill the Demons,' he had forty days of visions. It was after seeing Shang-Ti, whom he took to be God, that he felt the call to lead the poor people of China to drive out the Manchus and other demons."

"I think someone told me before that he led a revolt to Peking."

"Yes. The rebels took over and enacted what they considered to be reforms. It was a sort of quasi-Protestantism. Really antagonistic to the traditional Chinese religion. It didn't last, but it weakened the Manchus and you can see the results in the chaos in China today."

"You were in China then?"

"I was a young child. I heard the story, of course, later and studied the events in college. The Taiping revolt convulsed the land."

"And all of these Chinese in America today were involved in this political struggle?"

"Many were. And their children were taught to take sides—either for the upstart Manchu emperor or for the Old China—of the Ming Dynasty in the days of culture and peace. The Chee Kong, for example, represent the old Ming supporters."

Mack was still mystified. He set down his coffee cup and the half-blind, stumbling old woman housekeeper, wearing a long Victoria skirt from an earlier era took it away. "How could this message be part of murders of Chinese people in this city?"

The minister's eyes were intent. "I do not know but—if they're all three connected, there's a strong likelihood that some group—or some-one—thought the three dead men were dangers to their entire society, as the Manchu emperor was. The victims are seen to be demons and must be wiped from the face of the earth."

Mack felt a sudden chill; he sensed the truth of Brockelhurst's insight. "Will there be more?"

"This murderer is a fanatic, and a fanatic is like an energized top, spun out into his own orbit of hatred and dark action. He must spin, spin, until the momentum that sent him forth dies."

What an odd old tomb of a house this is, Mack thought, as he let himself out the huge, etched glass front door. Even the walls seem to smell of decay, rot, really, like China today, the emperor living in deca-dence and rot behind the sacred city walls of a dying dynasty. And that rot has stretched beyond the ocean, touching us here in this unlikely place in mid-America.

The next day was a bright one for the first of November. After work at the office Mack took Alice and Chad again to Pogue's Run for an adventure he had promised Chad earlier in the week, when the boy had complained about the lack of attention he'd been getting lately.

"We'll race boats in the creek," Mack had said. Now he tossed his hat on the hat tree, took the Sunday paper and helped Chad construct a small fleet of boats. Each one was painted with a special color and its own name on the stern. Then they melted some of Mrs. Bascomb's canning paraffin and waterproofed the boats. "*Voila!* A flotilla!" he said, winking at Alice.

"Did you sail as a child?" Alice asked as the three of them headed for the creek. She had on a short coat topped with a fox fur and a match-ing hat; her eyes sparkled.

"I grew up on one of the most beautiful bays in America," he said. "My mother, oddly enough, was the one who took to the water. Weigh-ing less than a hundred pounds—she's a little mite of a woman—but she took sailing lessons at the yacht club. She took me and my sisters out in a sailing dinghy on calm days. But she hated the waves. The minute the wind sent the chop into waves, she headed us back in. I remember one day a trumpeter swan attacked the boat and turned us all over. We had to swim for shore. I had to help my sister—all of us were pretty good swimmers, but she was the poorest. Luckily it wasn't very far."

"A man who builds newspaper boats and helps his sister swim to shore," Alice murmured, taking his arm. "I love everything about you, Mister McClure Scott." She put her hand around the back of his neck, touching the nape gently.

"Don't," he said. "Don't do that."

And so they decided on the race course: they would launch near the Newman Street crossing of the creek, run along the street to watch the boats proceed along the course of the creek through the Arsenal, then follow them a few blocks as the creek went west. With Chad shouting encouragement "Onward, Blue!" and Alice laughing and urging her choices on, they ran along the creek's route, descending on the path after it left the Arsenal and walking the route they'd gone before until finally, they declared the winners near Pine Street. Only two boats had finished; the rest had turned over on rocks or gone onto the opposite shore.

"My blue prevailed," Chad shouted. Then he felt faint, and his mother sat down with him, making him put his head between his knees. He had overdone. After all, he was still recovering from pneumonia. Mack climbed the hill for a look while they rested. Yes, they'd traced the creek almost to its southern turning again—there was Pine Street over the hill—O'Shaughnessey's and Brockelhurst's in sight—and the Central Avenue Church spire away off there and the downtown building silhouette to the south. And yes, they'd enjoyed a good afternoon in a world where there didn't seem to be many good afternoons lately.

Wednesday morning Fanning was elated; Sidlow's attorney reported that he would sign the agreement to desist selling select game in the Chicago market in return for the Association's termination of its breach of contract suit. He was reported to still be seething but he had agreed. No apology would be required of him, and a modest cash settlement would be given him, instead of requiring he pay the cartel.

That afternoon a letter arrived at the office for Fanning.

He opened it in his inner office, then roared in a strangled way for Mack. "What does this mean?" he asked, shoving the special delivery sheet across the desk to Mack.

Mack stared at the same four Chinese characters he had seen on the sheet given him by Fook Soy.

"Do you know what they mean?" Fanning asked, perspiration beading his forehead.

"It says 'Kill the demons.' It's supposed to be a Chinese death warning."

"How do you know?"

"It was scrawled in ink beside the body of Bee Chee over near the poultry plant. Fook Soy, his cousin, translated it and then I checked with an expert on Chinese writing to be sure."

"My God, my God," Fanning said, framing his head with his hands. "They're catching up with all of us."

"All of whom?" Mack asked.

"Li Ting, Lee Huang, Bee Chee—and now me."

"Fanning, listen to me. What do all of you have in common? Why is some group or individual singling you out?"

Fanning was silent a long moment. Then he looked up, cupping his head in his hands. His eyes were despairing. "We're all—to greater or lesser extent—opium eaters."

"You must tell me about it, in detail. I have been in touch with the police investigator and you know I have been poking around on my own. I think I know more about this than almost anybody—I must know what you know to put this all together."

And so Fanning told him of his recent—within the year—beginnings with the opium habit. "Damn it, I have been so lowbrow my own mother would be ashamed of me, I know it, and yet—it seemed to me I could do what I want to. I've earned money and power in the community, and I can spend both in the way I wish. And Alice and I—well, we didn't get on after Chad's birth, and I got desperate, I guess, devil-may-care and careless and began to frequent the Paris Pleasure Palace. There I met people who went to the dens sometimes. They said you could go and just sample it, it was exotic, and not like being drunk, like a trip to another planet. And they scoffed about getting hooked on it."

He opened a candy dish on his desk and took out a bonbon. He looked at the lines on it, then set it down on the desk. "I started going to three houses—went once or twice to each."

Mack nodded, finally understanding. "Li Ting's in Lockerbie, Lee Huang's across the street, and Bee Chee's."

"Yes. Naturally Lee Huang's laundry hangout was the most accessible, but I couldn't go there much for fear of being seen by someone I knew, perhaps the night watchman. I already knew Lee Huang because, of course, I own the laundry building and because of the plot against Mapeltharp in Chicago. Lee Huang had arranged the details of that hit, hiring the Hip Sings."

"That I knew. But—how addicted are you?"

"I'm not addicted." Mack looked skeptically at him. They said that a pipe dreamer always denied it. And yet, in the months he'd observed him, Fanning did not often seem to be out all night or foggy brained. Only occasionally.

"I began to realize, about six months into it all, that it was catching me, and I fought. I fought, I tell you, Scott. The last time I went was the night Li Ting was—decapitated." So. Lee Huang's notebook had been right!

"But you were bankrolling them."

"How do you know?"

Mack's eyes were cold, unyielding. "I saw your notebook."

"You did? Been snooping around haven't you?" His eyes were narrow and unhappy, but he was not ready to pursue Mack's intrusion. "But then you must have seen that those entries were a year old. I stopped doing it, got afraid. And then when the first murder happened, it scared me further. It did occur to me, I must tell you, that in some way the people who frequented the dens were being punished."

"Who? Who else went?"

"When I was there, there were orientals. It was a tradition that they came earlier in the evenings, in ones or twos. I joined them, and sometimes the ones who owned the dens would move about, visiting other dens. So Li Ting would be over here at Lee Huang's and so forth. All the dealers were buying the stuff when they ran out of it."

"How about Fook Soy?"

"He isn't an opium eater that I know of. But his concubine, Pink Orchid was there, enjoying her dreams. And some of the older women in town, nobody of note."

"Toy Gum, the old grandmother across the street?"

"No. Never. She hated it. And hated me, whenever she saw me looking in she turned her back in scorn."

"And how about—others in the community. Did you ever see anybody else you'd recognize?"

"No members of the Commercial Club, if that's what you mean. No, most of the respected members of the community took their dissipation with the bottle. Like Jim, James Whitcomb Riley—it was only a very few of us most decadent, lost souls who sneaked over to these filthy places before midnight. And I think the two other white men I knew have left town.

"I always left about midnight, and after a while, I went no more. So I suppose any of the people there, Chinese or other clients, could be a madman none of us recognized. Any of them could be stalking the streets murdering those he knew who frequented the dens." He was thoughtful for a moment, then finally he did take a bite of the bonbon. "But I do know there were other visitors after midnight, secret ones; sometime they'd refer to the late clients. Some from out of town, too, to get their pipes and supply."

"Out of town," Mack echoed. "Fanning, do you have any intimation that perhaps—Sidlow might have been one of the out-of-town visitors, ever?"

"Sidlow?" If a wall of bricks had crashed towards him, Fanning couldn't have been more surprised.

"He has Chinese connections in Chicago, grew up among that community. Did you know that? It's rumored that he has friends among the Chee Kong, even is a white member."

"God, no. Well, he has been in town from time to time, when we were getting him organized in the association. But I never—"

"Well, at any rate, you've told me what we need to know. I'm going to talk to my contacts on the police force."

"No! That you must not do," Fanning all but shouted, then lowered his voice again and strove for patience. "So far none of this has touched Alice or Chad. I have recently formed the resolution to lead a different life. To be what I profess to be in that church every Sunday. Honor my mother's memory—something like that."

"But this threat," Mack pointedly gestured towards the paper with the Chinese characters. "You're in real danger. Marked out for some reason with the other opium eaters. And as for Alice and Chad—"

Fanning came around to Mack's side of the desk. "Scott, please, I implore you. See your investigator friend. Tell him they're dead wrong on the idea of the Chicago Tong chief. That all of these people are opium eaters and being punished, by something or somebody. Don't mention me, please, Scott, please."

"What will you tell Al—Mrs. Fanning?"

"What can I tell her?"

"How about the truth." He stood staring right into Fanning's eyes. Confucius seemed to work for everybody else; maybe it would work for Fanning.

"I suppose I owe it to her. Damn it, it's going to be hard."

"She's going to have to be extra alert for herself and Chad. You don't have any option."

"Kill the demons! My God!"

So now, Alice Fanning would hear the details of her husband's descent into the sewers of Indianapolis, though she dreaded to have confirmed from his own lips what she already knew.

But by Tuesday, Fanning had not spoken. He went about the house and office silent, morose, and Mack felt stymied. If Fanning would not act on his own, there was nothing he could do. On Tuesday night Alice Fanning asked Mack to take her to Mrs. Teitelbaum's.

"Something's terribly the matter with Walter," she said. "A while back you told me about the trouble in Chicago. But he hasn't spoken, and I'm afraid."

"It's more than that."

"I must know. It's like a sullen cloud is on the family."

"I told you before; he's involved in something fierce. I'm not the one to tell you; he has to. Why don't you just ask him?"

"We don't talk—about anything important. You know that. And

I do have my own problems. Perhaps they're just as important as his."

He looked calmly at her, waiting for the rest of what she wanted to say.

"I want to go to Mrs. Teitelbaum's. I've received help there before. I need to see her, to see if there's guidance." Mack turned from her, shaking his head. His nerves were so taut that the thought of the spiritualist flim-flam seemed especially trying tonight. But he would do it. Of course, what could she ask, particularly under these circumstances and in such danger, that he would not grant? And anyway, he had promised Mrs. Teitelbaum he'd return.

No moon or stars tonight, Mack thought, and the coal-oil lamps on this rig seem dim. They passed along Lockerbie Street, the horses hoofs echoing, and he thought: Ten or twenty people are out there, part of the opium eaters' ring who visited these three spots in this town, and any of them could be a maniac. A clever maniac, like Jack the Ripper, who could pass among his fellow beings on three separate nights, without being seen to do the mayhem, driven on by his tortured, deluded mind to become a shadow, a fatal shadow over the city. Because now that Fanning had received a threat, there was no other conclusion.

No gang warfare, no rivalry to buy gambling dens in the town could cause a string of murders—what Fook Soy and Fanning had said added up. They were dealing with a homicidal maniac. The air was misting, with the cool, dreary early November dampness. It was a chill that grabbed the heart. He had remembered the cold creeping in when they were out in the lumber camps, between the very boards, through chinks in the windows, and their efforts to stay it off in the small cabins where they slept with liquor and song—in the cook shanty with food and drink and ghost stories around a fire that was never allowed to go out. And the fevers would sometimes come then, the lung fever and the rest, and men would die and the bodies would be stored because the ground was like granite. They'd be singing songs, and out there in the shed the bodies of their former campmates were lying, silent. There was something about cold and death that were indissolubly linked, and, for Mack, the coming of the first of November every year brought the chill of man's mortality.

He smiled wryly, though, as he helped Alice out of the buggy. Maybe the spirits could help. Nobody else was doing much of anything.

"A message, A message tonight." Mrs. Teitelbaum's voice pierced the gloom around the table as the only lamp in the room flickered. "It is about—the skull on the chiffonier," she said in a hesitating voice, as if listening to someone who was instructing her from the other side. Mack was having trouble staying awake; he had not slept for two nights, haunted by the events of the week and his life in general.

"I hear the words eighty. No, eightieth, it is. My guide says the message is for Jacob or Joe." Mack roused himself. "For Jacob Joe," the medium said. "The only one who can see in the skull is Jacob Joe."

For some reason Mack did not feel like announcing to the group that his father's name was Jacob Joe Scott. He wasn't a part of this; it was none of their business, was it?

Then the lights went on, Alice disappointed that no message had come for her from the singing railroad gang chief.

On the way home, she sat silent as a stone. Something about her detachment, the constant search she made for this man who was her father irritated him. "He didn't desert you, you know," he said without looking at her. "I guess the only ones who knew wouldn't tell you—he was drawing the Chinaman away, so you and your mother would be safe. The Chinaman had written terrible letters threatening you. He fled, and finally the Chinaman caught up with him in Memphis. He loved you."

"How do you know that?"

"I was told. In Delphi. And I believe it. I think you should too. Quit looking for your answers from the dead. The answers lie with the living." He took her in his arms and kissed her almost roughly, before releasing her.

As they were coming into West Drive, Woodruff Place, she suddenly thought to ask, "Who in the world do you suppose Jacob Joe is? What an odd name. But only he can see into the skull."

"Jacob Joe, a veteran of the Eightieth Indiana Regiment is my father. He will be here Thursday and, against my rational impulses, we shall go to Mrs. Teitelbaum's that night. You may come if you wish. The experience may be able to prove what I've always suspected—that all of this stuff is charlatanism. She certainly found out my father's name ahead of time. I was talking once to the Civil War veteran about him and she may have overheard us. Or—I don't know. We'll go and see. It

242

isn't half as crazy as the life we're living now, anyway." She moved away from him as they drove into the side drive.

"Father, I'm glad to see you," Mack said, solemnly shaking the hands of the distinguished, gentle-eyed man who had just climbed down from the train at Union Station.

"Finally I'll get to survey the stamping ground of the professional man, " Jacob Joe Scott said, smiling with pride at his son. "I told the school superintendent that I needed to have a few days for a family celebration. He's a Catholic himself, very big on family events."

Everything about his father was connected to religion. It permeated his consciousness, like salt water absorbed into a sponge from the ocean floor. Introduce any topic, squeeze the sponge a bit, and out came Christ, the meaning of the universe, God's will.

They walked to the center of town to catch the streetcars, and on the way Mack pointed out the churches. "Oh, so big," his father said. As the electric car proceeded in lurching leaps forward, Mack stared out at barren trees and gray grass. How was he going to get to the odd topic of the spiritualist meeting that, against his soundest judgment, he'd decided to attend tonight.

"There's one of the finest old neighborhoods over there—Lockerbie. That's where the poet James Whitcomb Riley lives and other artists and writers too. And—I've been taking Mrs. Fanning to meetings there at night."

Jacob Joe looked in the direction Mack was pointing. "Perhaps the temperance society? Or one of those new women's literary clubs?" Mack shook his head.

They clambered down the steps to transfer; then, sitting and swaying as the car picked up speed heading to Woodruff Place, Mack picked up the conversation. "Noo, Mrs. Fanning isn't going to any of those usual lady meetings. She visits a spiritualist." He thought that would be the beginning of a lecture on the un-Christian background of spiritualism. Of how Saul in the Old Testament had gotten into major trouble because he consulted wizards that peeped, of how often the Bible commands us not to call up the familiar spirits. Here it came.

"Interesting. I don't think all of it's good, but—our family's had some marked experiences along that line."

"Well, I've heard you mention your grandmother Jenny McClure Scott. The pioneer lady from Kentucky. You said she could see things."

"Yes. She could sense things—a sensitive, they called them in the last century." He sighed, raised his bowler hat off his head and replaced it, smoothing his hair. "There are more things in heaven and earth than are dreamed of in your philosophies, for certain. I've had some very strange dreams. Some of them came true."

Mack looked at the man next to him. Somehow since they'd been apart these four months, it seemed as if he'd just met him—noticed new lines in his cheeks, the streaks of gray in hair that had once been as blond as sunlight. "I've never heard you mention spiritualists."

"No, not that. It doesn't take a lady in a spirit closet to conjure up the world beyond this one, for those of us who have the gift."

"Those of us?"

"Well—this is supposed to be inherited. Like some other gifts or curses."

"I don't have it at all. That I know. But, it sounds like you've had some experiences."

"There were two remarkable ones. The first was in the war. I saw—well, Grandmother Jenny appeared to me. I don't feel like saying more. We're going to the Perryville battlefield site, aren't we?"

Mack nodded. "It's in the plan." *If the world doesn't fall apart before tomorrow afternoon.* They climbed off the car, and it moved on towards Irvington.

"Anyway, the main one happened after the battle, while I was on leave, actually visiting your Grandmother Lavenham's family and doing a little courting."

"Of Mother?" Mack smiled.

"Actually of your Aunt Sophie. But that's another story. We went to a performance of some phrenologists. Mr. and Mrs. Evan Parsticle—odd names—that's why I remember them, I guess. She was a great-busted woman and he a puny little man with a piping voice."

Evan Parsticle? That name—Mack had heard it before. Where?

"My, this is a lovely street, son. Looks like Sixth Street in Traverse City, only there are blocks and blocks of these fine houses here. The big city is full of rich people, I've always said, and it impresses this poor farm boy. Anyway, there in Louisville during the war, it was stuffy and I felt the need for fresh air, so I went out of the auditorium and found myself looking at an exhibit of curiosities in a little room off the lobby. I was all alone." He stopped and coughed, as if remembering with emotion, then went on .

"There was a skull, a crystal skull supposedly used by the priests of the ancient Incas or Mayans or somebody—"

"Did you say skull? A crystal skull?" Mack could scarcely believe his ears.

"Yes? Why?"

"Well, nothing, nothing really. Go on. I want to hear this."

"The lamplight was dim in the room, but I stared into the interior of that skull, and I saw her. Again. Grandmother Jenny. This time she made a serious gesture to me. She put up the forefingers of both hands and brought them together. Then she faded from view."

"What did it mean?"

"I don't know, exactly. Except that your Uncle Zach and I were not close at the time, and you know the story of how he came to save me in the Southern prison camp." His eyes seemed far away. "Went right through the Southern lines and risked his life to bring me out when I was near death from fever. So perhaps Grandmother Jenny's gesture forecast that we would be reunited in my brother's great unselfish deed. I also thought it meant the North and South would eventually come together."

"Perhaps," Mack said thoughtfully. They had reached the front steps of the house, and it would be time to introduce his father to Alice and Walter Fanning. Alice, ever aware of hostessing duties, had planned a little early supper for a few people. Knowing his father taught English, she had invited Mr. William Fortune of the Commercial Club, and a guest of Fortune's the nationally famous librarian Charles Evans and— James Whitcomb Riley was available and said he could come. It had all been cobbled up at the last moment, but Mrs. Bascomb said she would do a simple buffet. And it was to be a man's party—Alice would help with the serving. Fanning was hardly going to play the hearty host well—he was distracted and morose. Why in the hell didn't he take the bull by the tail and tell his wife about his opium habit and criminal activity? Alice and Chad were in danger, too, with the letter Fanning had received. He'd have to tell her soon himself. Mack had the distinct desire to put his arm around the man's neck and shake him off his feet.

There was a spread on the mahogany sideboard fit for a prince of the orient. And all in such a short time, Fortune marvelled in his booming basso profundo. Sweetbreads, sliced ham with raisin sauce, gelatin with canned strawberries, hot pocketbook rolls. And a giant Lady Baltimore cake with maraschino cherries on top!

The talk rolled on around the table as they tasted the fine food and raised goblets of venetian glass filled with sherry. Mack's father told of the lumber city he lived in, where giant boats came to the docks to take away what was a rapidly declining supply of white pine and steam it down to Chicago, of plants working round the clock to make wood by products like baskets and furniture, of the fine new high school where he taught.

And Mr. Fortune talked of the literary accomplishments of the Hoosier state, of Mr. Lew Wallace, whose *Ben Hur* had made him the toast of America.

"Such fine religious sentiments, tasteful sentiments," Mr. Jacob Joe Scott nodded. "And I have read Edward Eggleston's *The Hoosier Schoolmaster*," he said. "It's very humorous, although I must say it makes Indiana look like quite a rural place indeed."

"If rural means old-fashioned values and simple pleasures, we look at ourselves that way with pride," Mr. Riley said, looking down over his pince nez.

"You know, Jim," Fortune said, rising to get seconds from the buffet. "Your poem 'Little Orphant Annie' scares my children. I was reading to Evelyn the other night at bedtime, and she began to cry, when I said 'The goblins'll get you if you don't watch out.' "

"I've read that, Mr. Riley," Jacob Joe said, "Everybody has. But it is frightening. Aren't you afraid you may cast fear into innocent minds?"

"I'm sometimes asked that, Mr. Scott," Riley answered. "But I have an idea about that. I think children need to know of the dark side of life." He cleared his throat and leaned back a little in his chair. "Something in us all wants to understand horror and death. We are repulsed and frightened by the dark and unknown, but instinctively we know we must come to terms with them. And children need to know that there are horrible things out in the streets, that these realities exist, but that there are people who love them who will protect them, help them through the bad things in life."

"Bravo, Jim," Evans said. "I am not opposed to having Grimm's fairy tales in the library for that very reason, though many of the newer lady librarians say they are too awful—wolves threatening people, murders of children in the forest and huge bears that tear people limb from limb."

"And yet, Mr. Evans, if I may say so, you banned books in the library," Riley ventured.

"Yes, and I think I got in trouble for it." He had left Indianapolis Public Library three years ago because of controversy. A woman had replaced him.

"I think young people are more harmed by fictions about salacious intrigues and silly stories and degenerate values than by knowing that there is danger in the streets to watch out for," he said.

Mrs. Bascomb could be seen exiting the room, not batting an eye, though her favorite dime novels were being discussed.

"In the streets," Fortune said, staring into his goblet, where reflected lights from the gas chandelier danced, "We have had murders in this city, Mr. Scott. Some not far from here."

Jacob Joe raised his eyebrows.

"Yes, nobody important," Fortune went on. "Just some Chinese men. It seems to have been a tong war situation."

"They have arrested the murderer in Chicago," Fanning said in a hollow voice. "A tong chief."

"Well, I'm glad that's solved. One doesn't want the goblins to snatch us away to the spirit world on the very streets of this fine city," Jacob Joe said with all seriousness. Everyone laughed but Mack and Fanning, who shifted uncomfortably in his seat.

Alice Fanning appeared with a bowl of the wonderful custard and meringue floating island dessert, which she served out with a silver ladle into etched glass berry bowls.

"I understand this lady is pursuing the mysteries of the world beyond at spiritualists," Fortune said. "My wife has gone to a séance or two at Mrs. Teitelbaum's. Many of the ladies in town have frequented her discreet séances."

Alice Fanning set down her ladle and placed the floating island bowl on the buffet. "Yes, and as a matter of fact, gentlemen, I'm giving you just fifteen minutes to enjoy your cigars in the library. We have an appointment at Mrs. Teitelbaum's this very night, and I am inviting, rather urging, our guest, Mr. Scott's father, to join us." Her eyes met Mack's.

"Please, Pa, you must come," Mack whispered to his dad. "There's something there you have to see. It'll surprise you."

"Nothing surprises me any more, son," Jacob Joe said quietly as he rose with the others to go into the library for the cigars and liqueurs, though he would probably touch neither one.

The assistant seemed restless tonight. He passed coffee and then stood by the fireplace, twitching his mustache, as thunder began to rumble outside. Soon Mrs. Teitelbaum made her grand entrance, and was beckoned over to the side of the assistant. A discussion began; it was taken to the hall and soon turned into an argument. Words drifted in,

"Don't like starting late tonight. . .isn't safe any more. . .murdered as I walk home."

Mack, Alice and their guest Jacob Joe Scott mixed with the assembled group for the séance. The Civil War veteran, who had already summarized his experience in the Western Army for the visitor, and the veiled woman Mrs. Springer, were the only other visitors on this cold, rainy evening. They sat trying to ignore the conversation, which seemed to hedge on whether the assistant was being paid enough for the risks of walking in Indianapolis late at night. Finally the door closed with a bang, and Mrs. Teitelbaum entered a little agitated, but in control.

"My dear," she said to Alice. "Would you mind serving as the assistant? I hate to ask you, but there must be someone to stay near my body while the spirit communicates with the world beyond this one. It will be a difficult séance, with so much electricity from the coming storm in the air. The bridge to the spirit world will be agitated."

Alice nodded and rose. Mrs. Teitelbaum beckoned her to the large chair in the corner, where she intended to conduct the séance. "Pull up a chair, dear, that's right. Now you'll hold me down as the bridge is formed, grasping my hand, that's right." She sank in her chair gratefully, as if she were very weary. "When I start to speak, receiving the communications, you go immediately to stand four feet away from me at all times. Don't come near. But if I get into trouble—"

"What would that be?" Alice wondered apprehensively.

"If I start to move in agitation or cry out with emotional disturbance, or, God forbid, fall out of the chair, you must be there to physically restrain me. It can get violent, though it never has with this group." The Civil War veteran looked concerned, Mrs. Springer shuddered.

"Turn out the light now, and return it immediately when I come back from communication." Alice did as she was told and the room became immediately almost black, with only the faintest of lights coming from the kitchen.

"I don't really like all of this," Jacob Joe muttered. "The Bible says 'consult not familiar spirits,' and yet—"

"Shh, Pa," Mack warned. Mrs. Teitelbaum was silent in her chair. As their eyes grew accustomed to the inky blackness, they could make out the outline of her face. It looked smooth and stony, like certain granite monuments Mack had seen with Abby in Crown Hill Cemetery just north of Indianapolis.

Nothing for three or four minutes, but no squirming this time.

"A child is here at the portal, begging to see Mama." Mrs. Springer unveiled her face, weeping again.

More silence, finally the woman prompted, "What does the darling girl say?"

Mrs. Teitelbaum seemed to grumble to herself.

"What? This is torture," the woman cried.

"She seems a long way off, and I see her kissing her hand to you and leaving. But—here is someone, dressed in a full-length cape of the olden days." Her voice grew warm, blandishing. "She is beautiful. I can see her clearly, as she is one of the shining spirits with strong powers. She chooses to speak tonight through me. She is admonishing, and has messages for someone here tonight. 'Can you hear?' she asks the one who has been selected."

"I am here, Grandmother Jenny."

Mack started. The hollow voice answering the call from the spirit world was Jacob Joe Scott's.

"She says there is danger, great evil here nearby." There was a gasp. "Fading a bit, difficulty, will send the message another way, important."

"Jenny, I hear you. We will do as you say. Tell us," Jacob Joe said. Nothing.

Then Mrs. Teitelbaum's voice again. "And now a man, very pushy, wishing to be heard, older with snow white hair. And, as Mack's hair stood on end the voice of a man, the railroad man's Joss Arken's voice but this time harsh and pleading. "Little miss, I'm sorry. Beggin' your pardon for all I did. You know now 'twaren't my fault. Forgive me and cease your search. I loved you ever." Alice was on her feet, her hands in the air. "Danger, danger, for you and the child, too," the harsh voice called out.

Then Mrs. Teitelbaum began to shake. "Cross currents, difficulty," she muttered, then began to sob, her whole body shaking. She leaned to the side of the chair, seemed ready to lurch out of it and began shrieking. Alice went to her side, righted her and called for the lights.

Soon the medium was sitting, bewildered, wiping tears from her eyes and shaking her head.

The Civil War soldier, Alice, and the mother, Mrs. Springer, gathered around her, asking in wonder if she recalled nothing. But Mack had taken Jacob Joe to the corner cabinet, which he opened. In the light of the oil lamp he carefully took out the crystal skull.

"My God, I have lived to see the thing a second time in my life. It is a great mystery."

"Not really, Pa," Mack said. "Mrs. Teitelbaum said she was a friend of that Mrs. Parsticle that you said had the skull. It had been buried long ago up in Kentucky and was dug up and came to the Parsticles and they carried it around—"

"I don't mean that. I mean mystery in the way things happen, not the details. You live too much in the world of the senses, boy." He was touching the skull with one finger, outlining the exquisite contours of its cheekbones.

"Is that wrong, Pa? After all, we aren't in heaven yet!" Mack spoke with exasperation. His father was suddenly aware of what his son was saying.

"For me it would be wrong. But for you—I don't know." Mrs. Teitelbaum was being offered water. Nobody was paying attention to the little scene between father and son at the back of the room.

"Ah, something's forming here," Jacob Joe said, intently staring into the skull. "There, there she is, dressed as a young woman as I saw here on the battlefield first. Beautiful of body and spirit. She is saying, and I can hear it, 'Chaucer. Chaucer?' She is forming something with her lips. And I can hear it in my mind. What? 'Shitten shepherd.' How odd. That's it. Now she is fading. And I see other things." He was silent for half a minute, then turned around.

"What was it, Pa?" Mack wanted to know.

"Things I didn't see before when she appeared, in Kentucky the night of the lecture." Mrs. Teitelbaum was feeling better now, and was heading for them. "I can tell them these last things I'm seeing. It'll keep 'em from prying," Jacob Joe said. Alice came to stand by Mack's side.

"Well, I seem to have been the recipient of a special message," Jacob Joe said, beaming at the group that was standing around him now in a circle. "In this skull I saw, quick as thought, several things swimming about each other and fading into mist. I saw—men attacking a frontier fort, looked like Kentucky and a dying Indian who looked into my eyes, and—let's see—the battle I fought in, and some odd Indians wearing skirts standing on a hill near what looked like the Mississippi greeting Cortez or somebody like him."

"Anything else, old comrade?" the Civil War vet wanted to know.

"Well, strangest of all, and clearest, I saw a cave somewhere in the midst of lush plants, like the jungle, and inside it a young man, angry as it seemed, in the dark, with this skull in his hand. I think he must have been the owner of the skull."

"Well, it was found in a hole about three feet under the ground in Kentucky, perhaps near the fort you've seen. Anyway," said Mrs. Teitelbaum briskly, "we've had quite an evening of it. Many messages from what Mrs. Springer has told me." The veiled woman had taken off her veil. She was no longer crying but seemed quite serene, perhaps because of the kisses blown to her from the other side.

"Everybody as happy as kiddies at the birthday party," Mack said, unconvinced, drawing a long look from both Mrs. Teitelbaum and his father.

Jacob Joe wished to drive the beautiful buggy back home to Woodruff Place himself, leaving Alice and Mack in the back seat. "I understand my own message from my father except for the part about danger," Alice said. "All this talk about murderers stalking the streets—I thought they had the killer of the Chinese men in jail in Chicago. So you can be off the case." Jacob Joe looked back over his shoulder at her questioningly.

"I wrote you a little bit about it, Pa," Mack said. "Some friends and I were doing a little amateur Sherlock Holmes work on some unsolved killings around here. You remember—they were mentioning them at the dinner party. Well, after the third murder, the police finally got around to acting. They've arrested a gang leader in Chinatown in Chicago. You heard Mr. Fortune say it was all about the tong wars."

"But it seems that not everybody thinks they have the right man yet," Jacob Joe said.

"No, and there's a lot to be said about all this." Under the laprobe, Mack gently took Alice's hand. She did not withdraw it, and it seemed to send out shivers of fire through his palm and up his wrist. "There's a lot to be said about all of this, and I want to see if any of those messages which seemed to be for you, Pa, made any sense tonight. " He lowered his voice, spoke into her ear. "You must demand that your husband have a long talk with you, Alice. Did he say that he was in personal danger? That you may be too? Chad? No? The word 'danger' that we kept hearing tonight may mean something to you after he tells you. You can face talking to him. Hear what he can't bear to tell you. And tell him of what you now know of your own father. Of the torment of your soul in those earlier days. Tell the truth. If my love doesn't do anything else for you, maybe it will give you the courage to look all this in the eye. You must, now." He squeezed her hand. She shook her head gently, then finally looked at him with frightened, but accepting, eyes.

Chapter Twelve

"Listen, you addle-pated adolescent, I need your help." Mack had collected Chiang and they had gone to seek out Abby before school at his house. Mrs. Nessing and her sister Rachael were still in their housecoats. They offered Mack and Chiang coffee, bringing the cups into the living room and leaving so the boys could talk alone.

"You have backed off this murder thing completely," Mack said to Abby, stirring his coffee.

"Well, Whi Ting Lo is in jail without bond, and—"

"Listen to me, pipsqueak," Mac insisted. "He didn't do it. Fanning's had a threat made to his life, and Fook Soy insists it's because all the people who've frequented the opium dens are being punished. Wiped out one at a time by some sort of disturbed fanatic, a maniac."

Abby looked perplexed. "Fanning? What's he got to do—"

"He's been to the dens. And also admits to having bankrolled some of the Chinese opium interests. You knew that. He admitted it to me, but now says that's all over. Anyhow—somebody in this town knows about the opium and is pursuing him. He's scared stiff and I'm frightened for his family."

"But what about the argument at the laundry? Wasn't it rival tongs?"

Chiang put down his coffee cup and looked earnestly at Abby. "Fook Soy says the argument in the street was to try to warn my uncle he might be in danger, to go to him for the good of the family," he said. "And now someone's after Fanning."

Abby put down his cup and looked at the phone. "I should tell Nate and he can arrange for the police—"

"No!" Mack warned sharply. "Well, at least for now. I promised Fanning to keep the police in the dark about the opium den part of this. He thinks it'll ruin him."

"Is that smart?" Abby wanted to know.

"Knowing our police, it's probably less risky to try to find out who's doing it on our own for a while anyway. We know more about these murders than they do." He told Abby about the visit to Fook Soy, the Chinaman's insistence that a homicidal maniac was loose, killing the men who frequented the city's opium dens. Then he mentioned his own suspicions that somehow Sidlow was connected with the murders.

Abby was not convinced. "The police reports say Sidlow is an impetuous man who owns gambling dens here in Indianapolis. He's even a Chinese tong member. And he can be wild with anger sometimes from what you told me in Chicago, but I don't see him as a crazed killer."

"Whoever it is won't be an obvious person," Mack said. "A homicidal maniac can travel unobserved among us during the daytime, and then at night show his true colors as a monster. Some people think Jack the Ripper is one of the nobility, who can move through the streets of London unsuspected because he is always coming home from fancy parties late at night. And, if it were Sidlow, he could have method in his madness," he went on. "Suppose he'd developed some kind of hatred towards Chinese and the opium trade."

"You said he liked the Chinese."

"Well, perhaps he's pretending to care about them."

"You're getting desperate. Sherlock Holmes doesn't take potshots in the dark."

"Sherlock Holmes—I'm sick of him. It's Professor Moriarity I'm interested in, the evil night stalker. Indianapolis' Professor Moriarity is out there planning more killing." He was silent, pondering.

"Maybe this Sidlow had an angry cat fit about being stopped in his attempts to buy into Chinese gaming interests here," Chiang said.

"You could be right," Abby said, half ironically and savoring the intellectual exercise. "Sidlow could kill these people to eliminate his Hip Sing gambling rivals and protect himself and at the same time get even with Fanning. The police would see it as a tong war battle, and uncover Fanning's part in the mess (but not Sidlow's own, he'd see to that in both cases). He'd effectively finish off all his business competition in one swoop."

"On the other hand," Abby went on, answering himself airily, "maybe he's threatening to blow the whole thing up sky high just to scare Fanning."

Mack nodded. "Whatever his overheated brain conceived. But I'm getting convinced he is involved more deeply than we think in this. I want to know exactly where Sidlow has been in the last few days," Mack told Abby. "Or if he hired any couriers to take the train to Indianapolis and deliver threatening letters."

"We should find out, just to rule it out if nothing else. I think I can involve Nate without spilling the beans on Fanning," Abby said. "But he's going to find it hard to believe that the Chicago Hip Sing boss Whi Ting Lo isn't the right man."

"Not unless Whi Ting Lo is sending threatening letters from jail. But that isn't all. Your spooky Aunt Erna Teitelbaum hits the nail on the head sometimes. I'm not saying I believe it all, but there's something very odd in what went on at her séance last night. Some strange phrases were spoken there. I'm not saying they have anything to do with these murders, but I'm curious. Were we getting a clue from beyond? Don't laugh. Look—I'm going after anything I can get. I'm going to take Chiang with me today to the library to try to get some answers if I can get him to cut school."

"Why not?" Chiang said with a faint smile. "The principal's getting red-faced with me anyway about all my absences. Might as well get skinned for Peking duck as Su Chou goose."

"Clues at a séance?" Abby looked skeptical. He was on his feet now, looking for his books and bookstrap.

Mack put his hand on Abby's arm. "Listen. You may be right about police protection, at least after today. I have to go away for the weekend. My father and I leave on the train this afternoon for a wedding tomorrow. You'll be seeing your brother today, right?"

Abby nodded.

"See if Nate can get Sgt. Rossi to stay near the office and check to be sure the beat cops are nearby. Then at night he should have men near the house. The Woodruff Place constabulary can't handle this—they need help. Tell him Fanning's had a death threat. We can say he's in a legal battle over an industry monopoly. Nate has to convince the sergeant. I'm afraid for Alice and Chad."

Abby nodded affirmation, and bounded out the door ahead of them so as not to miss his first class. Then he was back. He had forgotten his violin.

Mack headed up Newman Street and through the door of the office, leaving Chiang to join him in the stable, unseen by his Old Grandmother, who would ask too many questions about missing school.

Fanning was in the inner office. "Best not bother him," Miss Farquharson said. "He's moody as a bear with a sore tail."

But Mack waved her down and knocked. "Come in," Fanning called, through the door. Carefully Mack entered and closed the door behind him.

"Any new—communications?" Mack wanted to know. Fanning shook his head glumly. "I've asked Abby's brother to arrange for police protection."

Fanning jumped angrily from his chair. Mack held up his hand. "No—wait. I've told them you were involved in a legal action with a monopoly charge. That you had an anonymous threat probably connected to that. When they come to inquire, back me up in that. It happens all the time, with J. P. Morgan and his interests. You need protection."

"All right," Fanning said, coming out to stand beside Mack. "But Scott, McClure—" His eyes were pained. He had been weeping or—surely not another pipe dream. "You are going to Southern Indiana and then on to Kentucky for three days?"

Mack nodded. What was this about? Fanning wasn't going to renege on letting him go, was he? Mack was beginning to wish he would. This was absolutely the wrong time to be going. Fanning grabbed his arm. "Take Alice and Chad with you, you and your father. Take them away from here this weekend. I think this will be the time. Yes, I'll accept police protection, and perhaps telling them Sidlow may be involved isn't too far short of the mark. He might be. But why should Alice and Chad be exposed to this danger?"

Why indeed. Fanning went on, his eyes reflecting desperation. "I've engaged at my expense a compartment for all of you to Vincennes and then on to Louisville. Miss Farquharson said she'd made the original travel plans for you."

A trip on the train with Chad and—Alice. Well, it did make sense to get them out of here.

"Then you've told her all about—your troubles?"

"Yes. This morning." Did he dare to ask how she took it? Fanning raised his eyes from the floor.

"She was dismayed, of course, but she was all right. Even responded to my suggestion that she and the boy get out of town for a while. Said she'd been calmed by the séance session last night. That she felt help was on the way." An odd look crossed his face. "And," almost talking to himself, "she finally told me—some things about her own childhood that had made her the way she was. And—she said she was worried about me, sincerely." That there was wonder in his voice did not surprise Mack; that Alice had said it did.

He and Chiang went to the downtown library and found Mr. Charles Evans at a table near the front door. "There's a woman in there," he whispered to Mack, gesturing over toward the Head Librarian's desk behind a glass partition, "Miss Eliza Browning. Not that she isn't capable, but not in the *top* position. What next?"

"Sir—I have an important puzzle to solve," Mack said. "I need to try to identify a quotation. I'm sure it's from literature."

"Are you looking for a particular reference?"

"Yes. It refers to a—pardon the language—a shitten shepherd."

"Shepherd? Well, there might be a couple of places where shepherds are mentioned. It seems to me I recall that phrase, uncouth as it is for our day and age. Must have come from the Renaissance, or before." He rose from his seat and guided the young men out into the stillness of the library to the classical authors' section.

"I seem to recall that it may be in Chaucer," Evans said. Mack nodded. That's what the Jenny vision had supposedly said.

"Chaucer was very frank in his language. Here's the newest version, just put out at Oxford. Take your time." Mack and Chiang sat under the electric lights looking through the prologue.

"Shitten shepherd—can't think we'll find anything like that," Chiang growled as he sat by Mack's side.

"No. It means, I guess-covered with shit." He smiled weakly, won-

'dering about his beautiful great-grandmother's choice of words. But if it was from Chaucer, days were rougher then. His father had told him that Jenny McClure Scott taught herself to read all the classics, from Shakespeare through the English playwrights, out in the woods in Pennsylvania. So there was a good possibility she'd read Chaucer, all those years ago.

"Perhaps it wasn't Chaucer after all. Sometimes my mind plays tricks. Could be someone else," Evans said, tweaking his small mustache. "But I'm glad I stopped by today to do some reading in my old haunts. You couldn't have asked a woman *that* question."

They thanked him and, after several minutes of poring over the book, left less informed than when they had come in.

"Let's get a bite of lunch and then stop off at O'Shaughnessey's gymnasium," Mack suggested as they walked back.

"Might as well," Chiang answered, shrugging indifferently. "This day's gone into eternity anyway." Odd way of expressing it, Mack thought.

The first round of the Young People's Sparring Tournament would be beginning in about an hour.

"Aren't you going out of town this afternoon?" O'Shaughnessey said, unloading towels from a cart to the lockers.

"Yes. I have to catch a train with my father—and Mrs. Fanning and Chad—at five o'clock. That gives me about three hours. So I have to hurry." Chiang walked over to the rings. He had told Mack he was fascinated by the brutality of boxing; it was not the Chinese way to take heavy gloves and beat an opponents face black and blue. Unless you were in the tongs of course. Balanced, almost choreographed arm wrestling, or games with sticks—he'd seen Chiang do some of that with Abby. But not boxing. Chiang watched the faces of the contenders, trying to see what emotions motivated them.

"You read a lot, O'Shaughnessey," Mack said.

"Sure I do. What else was there for a boy to do when his dad was off all day repairing' the Wabash and Erie canal? Bernard and I walked miles to get a book, any book. I read the *Practical Housewife Book of Cookery* three times just to look at the caricatures of the hogs." He was smoking a cigarette, thoughtfully, savoring its taste.

"Did you read Chaucer?"

"Yes, indeed. A great man, Chaucer! The librarian in the neighborhood thought it too coarse for good boys to read, but Bernard and I borrowed a copy from a schoolmaster who owed us somethin'. We had kept the boys in our neighborhood from carrying a privy to his front porch." He smiled at the memory.

Chiang was inspecting the gloves of a thin boy with too-long hair who was due to enter the final round of competition in a few moments. "Rather quickly," Mack said, "could you tell me whether there's any mention of a shepherd in Chaucer?"

"Shepherd, well, yes. But I can't think exactly where. Anything more to go on?"

"Yes. A shitten shepherd. Covered with—dung, I guess."

"It rings in m' mind, but I can't quite place it. Is it important?"

"Very. Perhaps a matter of life and death." O'Shaughnessey stubbed out his cigarette and looked earnestly at Mack. "If I come up with anything, I'll let you know."

Mack retrieved Chiang before he climbed into the ring and they rushed to the street car. He hoped Alice and Chad were ready to go.

The train was puffing out steam in little bursts, preparing to depart. Water dripped from its grimy underbelly; the steps looked slick and hazardous. Alice, somewhat flustered, flew along beside Mack, dragging Chad and a valise. His father followed, carrying two large suitcases. They were in a hurry; the cab they had called had been late. Mack checked the tickets and helped Alice climb the steps. "Compartment C," he said, pushing Chad up.

His father mounted, huffing a little. "Dad-burned forced march, as we used to say in the army," he growled and vanished into the aisle.

Someone was running up fast, as the bell rang for the third time. It was O'Shaughnessey.

"Shitten shepherd," he said, coming to a panting halt beneath the step. "Sure! Chaucer's Prologue to the *Canterbury Tales*. It describes the good parson, the best character in the book and then it says he isn't like a good many in England of his day—bad ministers. He's not a shitten shepherd of the sheep, a rotten priest who has sinned against God by using the gospel as a cover for his crimes."

"I read all the prologue at the library," Mack yelled down, "and I didn't see that. I read that part about the parson, too."

"All aboard." The conductor was boarding the car ahead.

"But then you were probably reading a modern version," O'Shaughnessey shouted. "I read it in the Middle English. Shitten shepherd is from the original, written in 1300. Franker in those days than we are in the age of Queen Victoria. The library version probably said 'soiled minister.'" The train took a lurch; heads inside jumped.

"I think it did. Thank you, my friend. You may have saved a life." O'Shaughnessey waved as the train glided by, picking up speed rapidly and Mack watched him, growing smaller every minute, then turning on his heel to bound up the steps which led to the terminal.

Mack stepped into the aisle of the train, looking for C Compartment. He did not want to go in yet, though, so he walked through four cars to the caboose and, passing trainmen just sitting down to play cards beside something on the stove that smelled like stew, went through to the back observation platform.

My God. A shitten shepherd. That was what the vision his father had called Grandmother Jenny had said. Could a so-called vision be right? Good God, it could not be. And yet—there were other things that added up. He should have thought of it, but how could he—it was the most illogical person of all. And he, Mack, had been pursuing Sidlow—wrong track completely.

Retracing his route, he came to the door of Compartment C.

He gently turned the handle, then sank into the velveteen seat next to his father, across from Alice and Chad. The boy had lain down to sleep exhausted.

"You remember the vision my father saw in the skull at Mrs. Teitelbaum's."

"Something about a dirty shepherd," Alice muttered, not very interested. His father looked at him with interest, though.

"Do you trust what happens when she's conducting messages?" he asked Alice.

"Of course. My son is living proof to what she does. But it didn't make much sense. Sometimes there's a garbled message."

"Maybe not. There's only one person who can be the shitten shepherd—the parson in Chaucer's tale who has abandoned his sheep to choose a life of corruption. Like the vision said, but it really makes sense anyway."

"What do you mean?" Alice asked.

"A homicidal maniac with two lives stands up in the pulpit of Central Avenue Church every other Sunday. It's Dr. Brockelhurst."

And then he watched two mouths fly open in outraged disbelief.

"No, now look at it this way," he said, as they awaited their squab supper in the first-class dining car, courtesy of the Walter Fanning travel expense fund. The sun was setting, glaring and ugly, over flat brown cornstalk plains that stretched to the west of the car. Chad had chosen to have a sarsaparilla and sandwich in the nearby club car, where they could watch him eating and playing cards at a little table.

"He has lived in China—we know our madman has to be in some way obsessed with the Orient. How many other people in Indianapolis are like that?"

"Well, it's true his house is loaded with Chinese treasures. But he is the son of a Methodist missionary," Alice protested angrily, emphasizing the last two words.

"Have you ever heard him express any love for the Chinese? The sort of love a man of the church who has been to China would be expected to express?"

"No—well, as a matter of fact he seems rather detached in his attitude towards them. But he was only ten or twelve when they left China, if I recall."

Mack persisted with her." Does this man talk about his experiences in China?"

"He barely mentions China, even at times of Missionary drives in the church. There's a coldness in his demeanor when it is mentioned,"

Alice admitted. "Not that I would have disagreed with that," she said a little sadly.

"He spoke of the Taiping Rebellion, the great Civil War incident they had in the fifties," Mack offered. "He seemed to steer me towards looking at the tong gangs as offshoots of that earlier, bloody Civil War in China. But I think that may have been to put me up a wrong road." They ceased discussion as the waiter put endive salad, squab, and roasted potatoes before them.

Jacob Joe Scott frowned. "But son, how can you think a minister of the gospel could do such a thing? No one in his right mind would take an ax to someone."

"That's just it, Pa. He can't be in his right mind. Have you read *Doctor Jekyll and Mr. Hyde?* That novel is really about the split personality—the person who has a terrible secret hidden deep within him, which bursts out as bestiality."

"Yes," Jacob Joe murmured softly. "But what would cause such a terrible warping?"

Mack sighed, picking up his fork. "That we don't know. But Pa— can we trust the vision?"

"Above all else you can. But our job is to interpret it correctly. That I hope you can do. It would be a terrible mistake to pin something so horrible on the wrong man."

"I know," Mack conceded. "I could never enter any church again if I made a mistake."

Alice persisted, "Exactly how could he have turned into—someone like that?"

"He could have developed a hatred of opium addicts, if Fook Soy's theory is true," Mack went on. "Found out who the addicts were some way and tracked them down. Maybe as a minister, he's had troubled sinners confess their habits, and followed up on the information. Ministers have a sort of carte blanche in the city."

"I can't credit your theory. Or should I call it a guess?" Jacob Joe said. "It's too preposterous."

Alice carefully cut a piece of endive in half, then rearranged it on her plate as she spoke. "I refuse to believe this either. You have absolutely no evidence that this man is doing anything wrong. You have jumped on some easy, obvious solution to avoid having to seek out the real, hard one. Why are you dropping your pursuit of Mr. Sidlow?"

Mack shrugged. His argument did sound weak. But he didn't really have anything on Sidlow except a hunch.

"Shouldn't you wire Mr. Fanning?" his father asked. "Tell him of your worries? If he's been threatened, maybe he should know."

Mack shrugged. "It would sound ridiculous as you say, with no evidence. Besides, Nate called on the telephone at the office just before we left. Sgt. Rossi will have two men in the neighborhood near the house. They will work with Constable Fitzgerald of the Woodruff Place Constabulary. Nobody will get through. I don't think the sergeant thought Whi Ting Lo was the right man anyway, so he believes the killer's still at large. Watching the house will give him a chance to screen the neighborhood."

They ate for a while, fascinated by the moving panorama outside the darkening window as the train hurtled through the night.

"You still haven't answered my question, McClure," his father finally said seriously. "What about the motive? What could cause a minister of the gospel, who has given his life to Christ, to kill three people of the Chinese race?"

"And how in the world would a man as well known as Brockelhurst travel on Indianapolis streets in the dead of night without being observed by the police force? Or somebody?" Alice demanded. "No, you are completely off the mark."

Mack put his napkin on the table. "I don't know how he traveled around. Or why. I simply don't know. And what's more, I don't know how to find out."

"Well, in the meantime I for one don't want to hear one more word of this. It's sacrilegious, almost," Alice said firmly. Mack had to agree with her. He was beginning to doubt his own conclusion. After all, there were probably fifty ministers in Indianapolis, if the cryptic message meant a minister at all. And why had he veered so suddenly away from Sidlow? More digging in Chicago might confirm how Sidlow was directly involved in Indianapolis tong affairs. Exactly when was he in Indianapolis in the summer? Was he refusing to face the truth? Was it that Sidlow had helped him, briefly there in Chicago, that he admired his spit-in-the-face attitude towards the cartel? Damn! He had jumped into deep snow on information which came out of a *séance*.

As they walked towards Chad and the club car, she whispered to him, "Whoever the killer is, I should be at home."

"No, whether tong members are out seeking revenge or, if a Dr. Jekyll is abroad and his dark self walks, it is best that you and Chad are with me, heading in the opposite direction."

Later he stood on the back platform, again, listening to the mournful hooting of the whistle as it rolled back from the engine in front of them, watching the tracks fly off in the distance, v-ing together to the vanishing point. Sparks flew off, blowing onto the track to shine in a brief moment of light before being extinguished.

The door of the car was pushed open; Alice came to stand by his side.

"He told you everything?" Mack said, taking her hand in his.

"He told me some of what I already know because you told me: that he has abused the power his company wielded by ordering a man to be roughed up. And that an innocent person was killed in the shooting. That he has dissipated his life away. That he has been taking opium. And then he told me what I did not know: the threat from the same insane source that killed the Chinamen in our town."

Her voice grew small, and he could barely hear it because they were buffeted by the wind. "And he told me that he still loved me and begged for my forgiveness. Which I am trying to give him." Slowly McClure Scott withdrew her hand from his and placed it on the back rail of the train.

"Cousin John, we've brought a couple of our friends with us to the wedding. Thought you wouldn't mind. We've taken hotel rooms in Vincennes." They stood on the doorstep of an old farmhouse on the loop of road that joined the venerable acres of four McClure brothers outside Vincennes, Indiana.

"Shore, don't mind at all." The balding, short man with a paunchy belly had hugged Mack's father till Jacob Joe complained he'd bust a button on his wedding coat, and he now shook everybody else's hand with such energetic welcome their heads bobbed and noses shook. They went in to find their places in the house.

It was a morning wedding; the bride came down the newly painted staircase, which was bedecked with evergreens. A small pump organ, played by her mother, provided the music. With a smile this girl everyone was calling "Nannie" met her groom, a short, handsome young man with mild eyes at a small altar.

Jacob Joe leaned over to whisper: "The minister's from Upper Indiana Church, where all the ancestors are buried."

Afterwards, they met the bride, Nancy McClure (now Niblack), John McClure's eldest daughter, her hair done in little curls and wearing a silk wedding dress with a bustle drawn up by miniature roses pinned to the bodice of the gown.

"She's charming and intelligent. Well educated, too," Mack said.

"Don't be condescending," his dad said in a sharp tone. "Here in Southern Indiana the old 'mountain' ways of talking and jesting and spittin' 'baccy are just now dying among the Scotch Irish folk. It's four generations since most of our ancestors left Ireland in poverty," Jacob Joe said. "I talk a mite like that, m'self, y' know. But not these new young 'uns." He smiled.

"Now again, how are you related to Mr. Jacob Joe Scott, Mr. McClure?" Alice asked the father of the bride.

"Waal, my grandma Catherine Hogue and his pa were first cousins. Children of the original pioneer McClures which come over the Buffalo Trace. But more'n that, Grandma Catherine and his pa John Robert Scott were close as brother and sister in their elder years."

Then he told how he and Jacob Joe had been young men together, how they had gone to join the Civil War and how he had the pleasure in the last year of the war, when Jacob Joe had returned from prison camp, of attending his cousin's wedding—the wedding of Mack's mother and father, Jacob Joe and Dora Scott.

"So I knew Mr. McClure Scott afore he was a firecracker in his father's eye." Everyone laughed.

Sandford and Susan Niblack, parents of the groom, were entertaining Chad with yarn from Mrs. Niblack's knitting bag.

"She knows eight kinds of cat's cradles," Chad said to Mack as he and his father approached. Jacob Joe bent to take her hand. "And I must inquire about your grandmother, Mrs. Niblack. Mrs. Hannah Chute Poore was one of the finest women I ever knew, and very interested in me. My father was a Quaker, and I was brought up in the faith. She had been a part of the underground railroad. Did she live to be one-hundred, as everyone predicted?"

"She passed on in '72 at the age of ninety-two, Mr. Scott," Susan Niblack said. "And my mother Susanna Brooks, is over there." They spoke to the Widow Brooks, who was as intelligent and welcoming as her daughter.

"So many faces from my youth are gone," Jacob Joe said a little sadly.

And after a luncheon served from a bountiful buffet table, and seeing the bride and groom into their carriage with rice and old shoes, the guests began to make their way home. John McClure patted Mack on the back. "Let me keep this young'un, Jacob Joe," he said. "He can stay with us out at the farm tonight. I've spoken to him about walkin' the fields with me and goin' up to the cemetery. You could come too, if you want, but it's your son I want to tell 'bout the fambly."

"No, no, John, I am going out to the old Scott house, there by Fort Knox. Where Grandma Jenny actually lived. It's owned by others now, but I thought I could knock on the door and take our two guests inside if the present owners are willing."

"Shore, shore." John McClure ushered them to the door. And as his wife Frances bustled about with the hired girls, cleaning up the food and drink and packing cake into a box, he took Mack outside. "These here's the fields my Great-Grandfather Dan'l McClure got from George Washington. He farmed 'em till he died, and lots more, too, but the rest of the farm is gone now. And not far from here, where your pa is a-goin', his sister Jenny lived with her husband and fambly. These are good fields, best of the bottomland. It took that fambly a long spell to get here—all the way from Ireland—and onct they saw it, they stayed."

Up the road they walked, with beech and maple tree branches arching over the road, across a bridge where a creek flowed full from recent rains, around a bend or two. They walked briskly, and finally they came to Upper Indiana Cemetery.

"They all come here, eventually, to lie in peace under the blue-grass. Your Great-Great Grandma, Jane, and her sons and their wives. Jenny Scott is buried here, and your Grandpa, John Robert and all my ancestors and the other McClure brothers and their numerous descendants. All here."

"But they aren't really here, are they?" Mack said out of his own conviction. "We all come to visit these places and honor these stones, but we are supposed to believe the people aren't here. They've gone on to be with God. So why do we come?"

"I didn't usta like to. Especially since I fought in the war and so many I knew of the cream of Southern Indiana's youth were planted in places like this, quiet country cemeteries in Virginia and Maryland and Tennessee. But I came t' understand it different." Mack looked at this humble little man with the beak nose and strong opinions. Somehow he did feel kin to him, felt the pull of blood. It was odd how it could flow undiluted and with its own marked attributes through so many generations.

"We come to these places because it's only here that we can really recall who they were. To give 'em a identity, see 'em close to their children and parents, usually." He placed some of the wedding roses he'd brought on various graves.

"I put flowers on both Dan'l's and George's because I'm descended from the both of 'em. And old lady Jane, the eighty-year-old who brought her fambly from Ireland and ended up here."

"May I have a couple for my great-grandparents?" Mack wanted to know. He found their stones. Jane McClure Scott, (Jenny) born 1759, her husband James Scott. He leaned down to put a rose on the ground before the round, worn-looking stones.

As they walked away, Mack said, "Well, I've heard so much about the McClures. They were true stalwart pioneers, bringing the Presbyterian faith into the wilderness, founding the first Protestant church in Indiana, serving their country."

"Waal, they did some of that, but hell, boy, they were really a bunch of hard-fighting, hard-drinking reprobates. The McClure brothers used to block the roads in Kentucky and also here, so they say, on a Saturday night when they got drunk and make people fight them to get through. And at the Battle of Piqua, fightin' with George Rogers Clark, the brothers led the troops out, then when they beat the Indians, cut off Shawnee balls to show who was boss in the Northwest Territory."

"Well, I didn't know that," Mack said lamely.

"An' my own ancestor, founder of that church we jest left, left a whole fambly of Indian half-breeds from some trip he made into the wilderness. I didn't believe it myself till it was proved to me, but I larnt from that experience that it don't do to get too high falutin' about the ancestors. They were humans, and in our case pretty rough and tough people. It's good they were. Why, I had m' own altercation the other day. Henry Badollet come out here to gas me 'bout my youngest talkin' on the party telephone line too much. I lost m' head and called him a God-damned Copperhead, a draft shirker, had no business standing in the same yard with a veteran of the Army of the Potomac. Then I put up m' fists and beat the shit out of him."

Mack was smiling broadly. He began kicking rocks in the road like a kid; he didn't know why but it made him feel happy to hear all this.

"An' it don't do to get too religious, either. It's all right in its place and we need it, but religion can smother a man. I ought to know, my wife's been a-tryin' to smother me for twenty-five years. Ever damn time the church door opens, she wants me in there."

They spoke some more, and then John McClure brought the buggy around and drove him into town. And when he left him off at the Vincennes House, he said, "Call to mind what I tole you, McClure. You got a tried and true name and you come from a line of fightin' men and that's a good thing. It's necessary to answer to the blood onct in a while."

And when Mack saw Alice, tired and distracted, walking down the hall to the water closet with Chad by the hand, he yearned for her amidst all the conflicting emotions of their situation. He all but gave up hope at that moment that he would ever be able to answer to the blood in the matter of his own choice of the woman he loved.

They had toast and coffee at seven o'clock in the morning, then they hurried to catch the train to Louisville. And from there, they caught another train to Lexington, Kentucky, and south again to a tiny station at a village called Perryville.

"I want to rent a buggy to go out to the battlefield to make a pilgrimage to Perryville," Jacob Joe said solemnly to the liveryman who met every train. "I was a soldier there." And soon, the party of four, Chad drooping in sleep on his mother's shoulder, were heading out a country road.

Jacob Joe had trouble finding the battlefield itself. At first he thought it was that section of hills and fields, then this one. But finally they found a sign. "These acres on the north and west are the site of the Battle of Perryville fought in the War Between the States, October 12, 1862."

Jacob Joe's eyes had grown intense. He was peering into the past. "We've come too far. We were coming up, marching—it was on a cross road, not this one. I don't know if you studied the Battle of Perryville in your history books."

"Gettysburg, Chancellorsville, Shiloh," Mack murmured, "not Perryville. You haven't spoken of it much."

"No. No, I haven't. If they'd put it into the textbooks, they'd say that Confederate General Braxton Bragg was trying to hold onto Kentucky, and Northern General Don Carlos Buell was trying to seize it for the North. They marched around trying to find each other. The armies of the North and South bumped into each other back there in that direction"—he pointed—"at Doctor's Creek."

Sitting in the buggy they gazed at the hillside of trees, looking like a landscape from anywhere in the Eastern part of the U.S. Chad was dropping marbles in and out of a bag, holding each up to the light before he plopped it in.

"No, I haven't spoken of that day," Jacob Joe went on. "It's odd, isn't it how we have a part of life, a hidden chapter, like in a book that's closed, that we never tell to anyone, not even our most loved people on the face of the earth. Our hidden uncertainties—that we're ugly or growing old—hatreds we can't rid ourselves of, sudden lustful thoughts about someone at church, deeply buried hopes." He did not look at them. "These lie unspoken, in consciousness, our secret stock of thoughts. But maybe sometimes one swims to the surface, shocked out of its hiding place, ripe to be told. The Battle of Perryville is like that for me."

"You've talked about your being a prisoner of war, about Castle Thunder in Richmond, the cold, the rottenness of the food, the sickness," Mack said.

"Maybe I've buried it because it was such a shock. There was another reason. We lay the night up at that crossroads we passed before the battle, along a fenceline near a cornfield. There was an eerie moon that night. I had the oddest feeling—as if we were in the world of the dead, as you feel walking in a cemetery at night. The cornshocks had been squared off, and they seemed like mausoleums, the rocks tombs. Maybe it was because we were so near the Kentucky home of the McClures, and Grandmother Jenny, Dad always said, hated this part of Kentucky for being haunted. It's only about thirty miles away. Or maybe it was a forecast. The next morning we marched; the battle had already begun and we came hurrying over that ridge, there. Let's drive up this road on this man's farm. I'm sure he's used to visitors."

They passed a small hired hand's farmhouse, with a larger one behind it, and came to a hill, finally. Jacob Joe helped Alice down; Mack followed, looking up the hill. Chad leapt out of the carriage and followed, strangely silent for once.

"We were supporting the cannons of General James Jackson," Jacob Joe said. "The Rebels were over there, all across those acres." His sweeping gesture encompassed woodlands and pastures in the opposite direction from where they'd come. "As we came up to the support of the guns, the noise would make you deaf." He was walking slowly, not looking at them, almost talking to himself. "Bullets whining everywhere—we were told to lie down, and believe me it didn't take any urging to get me to do that. The man next to me had his eye shot out and I remember the eyeball fragments running down his cheek." He stopped. Alice looked hard at him, then at Mack. It was one thing to read about the war, hear the veterans on the courthouse square chewing tobacco and outbragging each other, but to hear someone who had lived it—

"The shrapnel—it cut so many different ways. I can hear it yet, never will forget that whining, booming artillery. One of my friends had the whole right side of his head squashed in by a cannon ball. Funniest thing, I remember thinking right there in the middle of that battle, he looks like a doll some child dropped off the bed. Half his head was gone." His shoulders sagged and he sighed deeply, as if he might weep.

"Where were the Northern cannons?" Chad wanted to know, standing on the ridge of the hill.

"Right where you are standing, young man," Jacob Joe said solemnly. There were a few monument stones, marking a long, low rise at the base of the hill. "And Colonel Brooks—the older man with the long, white beard you saw at the wedding—a brave officer—rode in front of us on horseback, his hat on his sword so we could see through the smoke. 'Rush to attack!' he shouted.

"Cheatham's Confederate brigade was coming at us, wanting to take the guns, but we held longer than most of the Northern line. The troops in other brigades fell back, leaving our part of the brigade exposed in the middle of the line."

"You saw—you told me before that you saw something in the midst of the battle. Jenny?"

"Yes. There were sharpshooters in the trees over there—well, the trees have been cut down I guess now. But anyway, I was preparing to fire, with my head swimming and all the sickening smoke, when like a hallucination I saw a woman in old-fashioned clothes pointing to the trees and telling me to duck. So I did. The man in back of me dropped from a sniper's bullet, she disappeared, and the battle went on. We kept changing fronts and finally Tom Brooks, brother of the Susan you met at the wedding, was wounded. He died as a result of that wound. He was one of the best friends I ever had."

They were silent, looking at the still, peaceful countryside. Cornshocks, like the ones Jacob Joe had seen just before the battle, still stood in these Kentucky fields. Cows scavenged between them, nuzzling for dropped grains.

"There were men with their heads blown off, men with legs hanging from shreds. A horse fell on my mess-mate from Evansville and crushed his leg. His screams were like nothing I've ever heard, and only when he passed out did they stop. And in the middle of it all, a couple of men from the company were sitting behind a rock trying to get double loads out of the muzzles of their guns, when a cannon ball caught them together." He turned away from them and leaned against an oak tree. "There was a hand still holding the muzzle of a rifle, and no body attached to it. I thought it would uncurl, but it didn't."

"Pa, don't go on if you don't want to," Mack said gently.

Chad came to him and stood beside him. "Who won that battle, sir?" the boy asked.

Jacob Joe turned slowly and looked at him with a sad smile. "Nobody, son. The two armies drifted together, then they drifted apart. Bragg soon went out of Kentucky, but nothing really changed."

They began walking back to the buggy. "Was it all wasted then, Mr. Scott?" Chad wanted to know.

Jacob Joe said nothing.

"The slaves were freed during the war. Surely that made it worth doing," Alice suggested. "Although I can't say that, really. No woman can speak for the man who stood in a line of battle." They looked back one more time at the hill where the cannons had stood, where the men from Indiana and Illinois and Ohio had defended them.

"I was a Quaker—part of me still is," Jacob Joe said in a low voice. "My friend Marion Green from Richmond, where I went to the Quaker school, wrote letters saying some of our classmates were going to jail to avoid going to the war, some were going to buy out—I went because I thought it was my duty."

"That seems noble to me, Pa," Mack said.

A breeze began to ripple the trees on the far horizon. "Nobility!" Jacob Joe spat out. "I hear these men talking on the streetcorners about how brave they were and how hot the shelling was and how many jokes they played in camp and how proud they were—are because they were there." The other three looked at him, startled at the vehemence in his voice. "Why, down south of here, all across the former Confederacy, those old soldiers are proud of what they did, too! Well, I'm not." He brushed at tears in his eyes. "I should never have gone! I was a Quaker and I should have stood by it! I should never have gone!"

They drove down the road, just as the farmer came out of the house to see what they were about. They waved to him. "I would like to go to the war when I'm a man," Chad said. Alice patted him on the knee.

And finally Mack said, thoughtfully. "I guess I'm one of the ones who would have been proud to have been in the army, Pa."

His dad, turning onto the main road, looked at him sharply. "You're all McClure. Practical, physical-natured. I'm more like my strange and dreamy Scott great-grandmother and my own soft-natured Quaker mother."

They drove along towards the town. Jacob Joe kept his eyes on the road as he said, "Why do you think you enjoyed the lumber camps?

You ran off that way because you couldn't stand the confounded quiet at home. You're like the McClures—spoiling for some kind of a fight, though you cover it, as your mother taught you, with extreme good manners. It's well to know your roots, your nature, what mint turned you out. Nothing can mar that original stamp, much as we might wish it to."

He's right, Mack thought as dust floated in little puffs behind them on the road. But we all spend our lives trying to be the person we think our fathers or mothers want us to be. Sometimes that isn't the person the mint stamped out. Realization settled in: that all the restlessness he had been feeling, the angry, light-bulb shocks of brutal instinct when he was frustrated, the trip away from home—was probably about being his own person. And his father understood. He hadn't given the old man enough credit, obviously.

The horse trotted along smartly as the afternoon wore on. Chad fell asleep on his mother's arm. They would be staying the night with the Shakers at Shakertown, but on the way there they would see where McClures first lighted when they had left Pennsylvania at the end of the Revolution. "Here, this is Harrodsburg," Jacob Joe said, looking at the town limits sign. They rode down the main street of a small town with two-story houses and stores crowding right to the edge of the road, second stories overhanging firsts.

"One of the first settlements in Kentucky," Mack's father continued. "Talk about spoiling for a fight—the McClures had all the fighting they could take, so it's said, when Shawnee and Miamis besieged this area during the last part of the Revolutionary War. I'd like to see where the relatives lived." He leaned out of the buggy and asked a man in tweeds walking a dog along the street for directions.

The man pointed. "Harrodsburg Fort's in ruins back there to the west two blocks. It's on the grounds of a mansion."

"I don't think we should go, Pa. It'll soon be sundown and we're all tired," Mack said.

"It'll just take a minute," his father said, and clucked to the horses. There was nothing to see except a few bumps covered over with sod in the far corner of the yard of a large, handsome house surrounded by tall oak trees.

"I read that stream there was where the folks holed up in that fort got their water," Jacob Joe said, looking at a trickling creek near the road. "When they'd go out, the Indians would shoot at them. Some of the children were killed."

Alice shook her head. "Sometimes we yearn for the olden times, the sense of adventure. Chad keeps wishing he was with the Pathfinder. But that's too much adventure. You wonder how the women stood it."

They proceeded to Pleasant Hill, the Shaker village not far up the road. "We'll be able to leave the horse here—the livery service will pick it up. Had to pay double," Jacob Joe muttered. This trip was expensive for someone on a teacher's salary. It helped that Fanning had paid for all the train tickets and food. They would be taking the train from Wilmore, a town up the way, to Louisville and then home.

And so, just about nightfall, they came finally to the peaceful little village where Shakers had lived for almost a hundred years. The huge, barn-like buildings were made of pine, and some were in need of paint. They walked up to the meeting house, where a man in a black suit greeted them and brought their bags in. "Women in the women's residence, men in the men's," he said. Chad wasn't sure he wanted to be separated from his mother, but when Mack smilingly told him he'd be bunking in a room with Mr. Jacob Joe Scott and him, the boy let himself be led by the hand to a yellow-painted, sparsely furnished dormitory room.

Supper was eaten by candlelight with the group. Women in gray gowns and caps served delicious chicken and noodles, gelatin salad and fresh yeast rolls.

"Nobody's talking, Mama," Chad whispered, pulling on her sleeve. "And they're almost all old."

It was true. The group of about sixty were mostly in their fifties, sixties or seventies. A few children, also dressed solemnly but full of life for all that, sat with some of the women at a children's table. The visitors were allowed to talk.

Afterwards in the meeting room, sitting before a fire, Alice got up the courage to ask, "Do you still dance and sing?"

Sister Evangeline, an old woman with a saintly smile and a head held proudly high, smiled. "Only now and then. We don't have the gift of dancing much any more. Our numbers are smaller; we're waiting for God's dispensation of increase in our numbers. Thirty, forty years ago, when Mother Ann's spirit was re-visiting the group, we had hundreds of converts here."

"Who is Mother Ann?" Mack wanted to know.

"Their founder. Like Mary Baker Eddy," his father whispered.

One of the brothers, a man with kind eyes and a tic around the mouth, told of their projects: selling of seeds all over the mid and eastern part of the U.S., sheep raising, and the farming of corn and hemp to make ropes for the U.S. Navy.

"They have only the orphans to make the group grow," Jacob Joe said in Mack's ear.

They were interested to hear that Jacob Joe Scott had been raised as a Christian Scientist.

"Two of our oldest sisters, who were small children at the time of the founding, were ill last year with lung congestion," Sister Evangeline said. "They asked to have a Christian Science practitioner come out and pray for them. They were relieved. I think maybe we have some things in common."

"Being rejected as religious freaks is what comes to mind," Jacob Joe whispered back of his hand to his son.

Alice admired the sparely beautiful tables, chairs, hatracks, candlestands and hand-wrought wooden bowls, which were filled with apples the Shakers grew in the orchard and sold to much of Kentucky. The sisters and brothers escorted Jacob Joe and Chad, who said they were sleepy, back to the dormitories about nine o'clock, and Alice and Mack found themselves walking back alone.

It was fairly mild; the wind that had blown the bare branches at the battlefield had died. They walked along the lane a bit, and came to the Shaker cemetery. They stood there, around the bend, protected by a huge tree and out of sight of the community.

"It's odd how soon we can forget our problems," Alice said, leaning against him, "if we just fill up the day with eating many things, seeing many sights, and feeling nothing." She stared into the night.

"I left word," Mack said, "that we would be here, and that Mr. Fanning should telegraph us if there were signs of trouble."

"Except that if he were stabbed to death he couldn't do that," she said, turning her head from him.

"Alice—I feel as if I should wire him about Dr. Brockelhurst."

She interrupted him. "Not that ridiculous theory again. At a day's distance it seems sillier than ever. Shitten shepherd. Perhaps your father was having an hallucination."

"Are you saying now you don't believe he had an experience beyond this world's? You—the devotee of the séances." His tone was strident. It had been a long day, and in truth he didn't know why she should believe him. He didn't know why he himself believed that the minister was a murderer. Maybe he didn't.

"Besides, consider the source. That man who followed you to the train, shouting up that message. Ugh."

"O'Shaughnessey? What do you mean?"

Her mouth was set in a fine line. "Common Irish," she said.

"And your father? What was he?"

"Don't bring him into this." Her eyes were angry as she looked out across the gravestones. They both stared through the cemetery gate at the simple slab stones, most with only a first name and initial on them. The Shakers thought the end of the world was coming soon, and they didn't want to waste time putting away a body that would soon be raised again.

"You're a snob," he said, not knowing why he wanted to taunt her. "Chinese, Irish—you hate too much for the Christian you say you are. Irish—and you half Irish yourself!" He grasped her shoulders, pulled her roughly to him. "Get yourself together, girl! You're not the only person in the world who's had a hard childhood."

She slapped him across the face; he grabbed her hands and pulled her to him, kissed her while she struggled, murmuring, then kissed her again, deeply. She stopped struggling; tears began to course down her cheeks. She pulled away and stared into his eyes, but he held onto her hands. She ceased struggling, gave a shuddering sigh.

"You're right, of course. I do hate too much. But I do not hate you. No, you have taught me that love is more than a word on a pink valentine. It is as deep as a flooding river. You, my darling one that I can't possibly love, try not to love. But I do." She stared at him with brimming eyes; he kissed them, her cheeks, her open lips.

They walked up the road against the darkening landscape; far up at the other end of this lane voices singing a Shaker hymn drifted up to them as the small congregation gathered in the meeting hall. The last building before the cemetery, set back from the road about a hundred yards, was a barn; they headed towards it, their bodies dark against the sky. The door stood open a little; he pushed it back on the hinges, stepping into the musty, straw-smelling interior and closed the door.

He pulled her to him again, gently this time, reaching his hand inside her cloak, unbuttoning her bodice. Slowly he explored her breasts, bringing his fingers out towards the tips as if he were playing a sensitive instrument.

"No," she said. It was more of a question than a command.

"Yes," he said, firmly, extending his caressing hands down the front of her skirt, kissing her over and over.

She pulled back a little. "Have you forgotten—your father, my son a few yards up the road. This is a religious center."

"No, I haven't forgotten it and neither have you," he whispered, stroking her hair, wishing it were loose, free to flow over her beautiful shoulders. "Nor your husband and the murders back home. But none of that is here in this barn."

She softened under his touch, and he kissed her forehead, tenderly, as one would kiss a child's. "You've said I taught you that love is as deep as a river," he whispered. "Now I want to teach you what passion is, because you desperately need to know it. Your feelings are locked up inside like a note in a bottle at sea, needing, crying for help! You must learn to release them or you can never live. And so must I in a different way." He pulled, gently but insistently at her skirt, felt her helping him, tentatively, then stepping from it in a moment.

He took her hand, pulled her down beside him on the clean straw, spread the cloak over them both. "We have fifteen minutes, maybe, in a lifetime. Nothing else exists in that time except our love for each other. Deep, deep as a river." She clung to him, and arched towards him. He leaned urgently over her. "Tell me, tell me, you feel this," he said a moment later, half-pleading, half commanding.

"I do, I do, my dearest one," she murmured joyfully.

The next morning, as they headed for Wilmore and the train which would start them back to Indianapolis after some transfers, Mack was full of remorse. Not for what had happened in the barn, no, not for that. Alice had taken his hand as they had walked down the road back to the others, and didn't want to let it go when they came near the dormitory buildings. "Revelation," she had whispered, and that was enough for him.

No, he was haunted by the fact that he had deserted the quest he had accepted in his adopted city. The murderer walked the streets in Indianapolis. Went about his daily chores, ate his meals, and waited until the sun set behind White River to kill another victim. And he, Mack, had left town—with good enough reason, certainly, protecting Alice and Chad, but still left. The police were there, he told himself, Abby and his brother were worrying with him, alert, pursuing the case the best they could. He stared out the buggy at the Kentucky River, seen through trees now newly bare, far below at the foot of a magnificent, plunging gorge. His father was looking too. "Grandmother Jenny hated this river, so my father said. She felt its trees were forlorn looking, miserable, with their roots heaving up above the ground."

"Nothing mysterious about that. It's a flood plain, swampy. Trees grow that way," Mack said.

"She feared them. Said these were bloody lands."

He looked at his father, so even-eyed and handsome, sitting sedately beside him. "Well, this is where the skull was found," Mack said. "The one that you saw things in." His father nodded, imperceptibly.

"And Harrodsburg and the other Kentucky stations were right here in the years of the Indian wars, I guess. They called that time the Years of Blood."

"And the Battle of Perryville. So—Jenny was right, I think." His father's face was sad. Visiting the site had pulled at his soul, sucking energy from him. They were silent for a while. Chad and Alice were occupied in the seat ahead with a portable checkers game.

"You were out late last night, son," his father finally said in a very low voice.

"Not long, really. Alice—Mrs. Fanning—and I took a walk to the cemetery and back. She needed the air after the long drive."

"I looked out the window and saw you returning." His voice was even, but so low Mack could hardly hear it.

The Shaker driver started whistling a hymn. That, the smart

clopping of the horses hoofs, and the whispered words between mother and son, moving checker pieces in front of them, were the only sounds.

His dad cleared his throat. "There's a lot in the Bible of course about the pursuit of other men's wives. Potiphar's wife and Joseph, David and Bathsheba." Mack began to shift around uncomfortably, anger building.

"But the main thing I think of is an old Quaker saying. "He who plows another man's field reaps bitter herbs indeed.""

"Pa—" Mack looked at him in exasperation. "You don't understand." Perhaps his voice was a little loud. Alice stopped moving game pieces and chatting and sat stock still.

Mack lowered his voice to a whisper and talked into his father's ear. "I'm not you, Pa. You've always been upright—well, I'm not a bad man myself. I didn't intend to have an affair with Alice, but if you must know, I do love her. I'll be leaving Indianapolis without her soon. But in the meantime I have a job to do in the city. And I happen to live in that home and care about the people. I have to take my part in stopping these murders." His father said nothing. "You can't help it when you fall in love," Mack insisted, anguished. Thankfully, Alice had begun her low conversation with Chad again.

"I know that, son, I know. Well I should. I almost married your silly Aunt Sophie Lavenham."

"You did?" Mack's eyebrows went up in surprise.

They were coming to the outskirts of a town; the two men looked out at the baseball diamond and fairgrounds that marked its edges. "The heart sometimes jumps around like a bird trying to decide where to land. And where it's going to settle in and build a nest, who can tell? But I just warn you, son—"

"Pa, in spite of what you say, you've always had it so easy. No temptations." His father snorted, but Mack went on. "I'm restless. My fists itch to whop people I can't stand. And my passions rose early and remained hot, though I'm just now beginning to acknowledge that. Still, I know I'm not a doomed sinner."

Jacob Joe reached out to pat his knee. "You're a McClure, as I said yesterday. I knew it long ago, when those fights used to happen out at Hannah Camp Number Six. And Mrs. Votruba said she saw you late one night in spring going up the stairs at the Cass Street Tavern with a girl on your arm."

"What was Mrs. Votruba doing near the Cass Street Tavern at that hour, anyway?" Mack asked evenly after a moment. They both began to laugh.

"Well, I remember my father telling me an old McClure saying, passed down through the generations," Jacob Joe said. " 'Just do the best you can and things will generally turn out better than you think.' Simple but true."

"Here we are," the driver said cheerfully. "We're passin' the Methodist College now, soon be to the train station. You have a four hour wait, sorry to say. Had to bring you when I was a-comin'!"

"Methodist College?" Jacob Joe looked at the cluster of brick buildings with interest.

"Asbury College," the man said. "Brand new school trains Methodists. An' they got records of the Methodist Church Missionary Society there for safe-keepin.'"

"What did you say?" Mack asked.

"It's what-chew-call-'em a archive. Got some international records of the Africa missionary fields and all that there stuff."

"Stop the buggy, sir, if you will," Mack said suddenly.

Alice looked back at him, a question on her face. He jumped down from the buggy.

"I am going to do some research, if I can," he said, excitement in his eyes. "I have a few questions to ask about missionary life in China in the 1850s."

His father shook his head from side to side. There was too much he didn't understand about his son these days.

"Ma, is there an ice cream parlor hereabouts?" Chad asked, bending over to pick up the tiny checkers that had fallen to the floor of the carriage. "I'm powerful hungry for a soda."

Chapter Thirteen

The woman at the front desk of the library was turned away, sticking a coiffure pin through the bun of her hair. She studied her image in a Tiffany memorial glass window set in the wall of the library. A plaque beneath it read, "Bishop Asbury of the Methodist Episcopal Church." The subject of the memorial window was a determined-looking man on horseback, wearing a black felt hat, with a snowy mountain pass as background. The librarian took her position behind the circulation desk.

He pointed to the window. "Bishop Asbury?"

"That's who the school is named after. He was our great circuit rider minister in America. He rode round the mountain trails and through storms and hardships to bring the Methodist Church to the new nation. He was a man who sacrificed everything for Christianity."

"And the other man, in the portrait over there, with the curly wig and sharp nose. That's John Wesley, isn't it? I recognize him from pictures."

"Yes. That's Wesley as a minister of the Episcopal Church."

"Episcopal? Not Methodist? I've never understood that."

She smiled, putting her pocketbook under the counter. "Wesley never left the Episcopal Church. He was considered a firebrand by them because he rode about England healing people, telling them they had to stop sinning, and preaching a simple gospel of practicing Christianity each and every day."

"I wondered. I'm not a Methodist, so I didn't know. I'm here from Indiana to do a little research—for a friend. Do you have an archive room where files of the missionaries in China are kept? And—may the public use them?" he asked.

She directed him to a rotunda-like room with rectangular tables. "The files are kept in boxes by year and missionary field," she said. "And the name of the missionary family or the church which sent them to the field."

"His name would be Reverend Brockelhurst. I don't know the first name. He would have come from Ohio, I think, and served with his family in Nanking in the 1850s. I doubt if you have anything, but I thought I'd check."

Soon, to his surprise, he was sitting before a box tied with a black ribbon. Brockelhurst, 1851-1857. Inside, on top of the papers, lay a photograph. He studied the picture of a tiny, winsome woman with her head cocked and a questioning look on her face and an equally tiny man, dressed as a clergyman, with a Bible under his arm and a stoic expression, obviously the head of the family. It was the portrait of the man he had seen in Brockelhurst's parlor. And by their side stood a small boy who looked almost like a girl, with curls, wearing a velvet suit. Well, at least that explained why the minister was so small in stature. It certainly ran in the family.

With a certain nervousness he lifted the photograph. A red-bound book was under it. The library had affixed an identifying sticker: "The Journal of Reverend Pinckney R. Brockelhurst, China Mission Fields, Nanking China 1851-1857." He opened the small, leather-bound volume and began to turn pages at random.

June 10, 1851. We are here, at last, oh laborious and tedious journey! May we dedicate all the horrible crosses it put upon my dear wife, especially, to the glory of our Savior. I pray our Christian labors amidst the heathen, most of whom have known only degradation, may prosper. . . .

Typical missionary talk. A thick book—he must have written every two or three days.

June 15 Nanking a splendid city, enclosed with high, thick walls. It is teeming inside, streets full of children and dogs and chairs bearing important people and people cooking pungent and delicious things on small burners. And the freight porters carrying things on their backs—hard-packed tea in huge bundles, scarves, chickens and ducks in cages. Trade is everything, and every man a trader. Men travel about with huge loads on their back, and guilds are formed exclusively for these traders—the tea bearers' guild, the rice bearers'. There are no guilds, though, for the starving, for the old, or those infested with illness and vermin in miserable propped-up shacks. And in the inner city, oh ironic contrast, live the noblest "relatives of heaven"—the

Manchu Dynasty—behind their own walls, uninterested in the poverty and suffering of the people who surround them.

July 8, 1851. Horrible heat. Frances and I sometimes falter under the sight of so much suffering, while the rulers seem to have no care about it. We see poor creatures with scrofulas and foul diseases roaming the streets, and women who have no mission in life except to bear children until they drop and to wait on the men in the family. They are ruled by officials who make their salaries from bribes of the people who wish governmental services. . . I have asked if it were always so, so much poverty and corruption. A new man I have met, Li Fu, a just and good person from the country, who has become our servant, says no, not under the former Ming Dynasty. The Manchus now cause the trouble. That, and the opium trade. He showed me an opium pipe in a shop, with its plug of dark poison, its matches to heat the stuff.

July 12 Fascinated with the subject of opium, I asked Li Fu to take me to visit an opium den. Squalid cots crawling with lice lined the walls, while shrivelled-up skeletons of men and women drift off into dream land. Sailors from the British navy, too. The only thing more despicable or pitiful than a Chinese addicted to opium poison is the white man who encourages the trade, be he politician or ship captain, and the fellow white addict in Paris or London who stimulates the trade. Truly the harvest fields for Christianity are ripe here.

February 1852. After several visits, Li Fu's family of six went to their knees in a rice field to become our first converts, after several visits. I am pleased my son could be with me. Simon held the Bible as I baptized them, though he is only six. They will help to build the chapel.

April 24 Group has grown to twenty-four.
Mack scanned with interest the details of the growth of the congregation in the city, the focus on building a small chapel. Descriptions of Chinese culture. . the joss gods' house for expressing reverence to Chinese deities, fancy stucco work on the houses and shops, all with

gaudy coloring. . .Chinese wedding parades, the bride dressed extrava-
gantly, flowers and jewels in the hair, carried in sedan chair with cel-
ebrants accompanying, playing instruments. . . nothing here to help.

July 1 My dear wife ill, I suppose from the water, and discouraged.
Congregation growing but opposition from the mandarins noticeable and
wearing on her. Li Fu and his wife persecuted and mocked because they are
called "traitors to the Book of the Grand Study of Confucius" which all
Chinese revere.

Not much personal—he must have thought he needed a diary for
official reports. But here—

August 5 My dear Frances Ellen has been giving little Simon lessons in
English, lest he forget it. He is exceedingly bright but very quiet, always
observing rather than commenting on situations around him. We wish him
to grow up among our flock of new Christians, to know their ways. They
adore him and lavish much affection on him, perhaps because he is so di-
minutive and more like them than most European children.

More pages inscribed in the round, even script: descriptions of a
rare family excursion on the river in a Chinese boat, the cabins as wide
as small rooms with mahogany cabinets and carved doors, and more
luxuriously furnished than European river boats. . . little Simon allowed
to go to the home of Li Fu, where he was treated like a little pet, given
sweetmeats and admired for his curls and precocious use of the Chinese tongue. . . he can recite the twenty-third psalm in both Mandarin and dialect and they cheer him and give him kisses.

No, probably nothing here. Just a waste of time, Mack told himself. But as he turned the pages, mentions of the word Taiping came
out at him from the pages. The Taiping Revolt, which all the Chinese
still remembered as cataclysmic and which still affected the tongs. With
growing interest, Mack read on.

September 1852. Rumors are everywhere, and here in the outer city we try to learn the truth. Riders seem to be bringing word to the inner, sacred city of the mandarins that the rebellious army continues to grow. The Manchu nobles live in fear that their hated dynasty will be deposed, corrupt, lethargic parasites that they are. Can this revolt have any Christian principles? The Taipings claim they follow Shang-Ti—God, they have services daily with doxology, hymn, Lord's prayer which they celebrate with firecrackers. But they go to war in the name of purity in China and kill as they go. . . 18,000 have joined the ranks. They keep men and women separate, with co-habitation strictly punished except, so it is said, for the ruling leaders. . . .

December 1852. In every city that they enter these Taipling rebels cut off the "submission" pigtails that the Manchus have forced upon all the people. They conscript the men into the army and teach the women to join the Women's Army of Heaven, to prepare food and make clothing for the soldiers who will free China in the name of God. . . All I hope is they do not come here! They leave destruction in their path. My little flock is relatively secure and though persecuted, surviving. And should there be civil war here, I must be able to protect Frances Ellen and Simon. My son asks about the war; he is more of a little man with a man's intellect than any child I have ever seen. . . .

Mack read, enrapt now, as the months went along. Of the continuing strength of the revolt, as recorded in the diary, of Simon's joy in being able to roam the city with his servant and Christian friend, Li Fu, wandering among the shops, speaking fluent Chinese, and of the continuing frailty and illness of the missionary's wife. When he noticed the schoolhouse clock on the wall, he saw an hour had passed.

He reached a place in the diary where the entries grew more specific and detailed, in darker ink, as if the writer were deliberately recording what he realized were portentous events:

Feb 23, 1853. Taiping Army is moving on Nanking. They may be half a million strong, so the rumors say. I am anguished—torn between staying to be with our Christian flock or fleeing with the family. Li Fu says it would be dangerous to join the fleeing mob in the streets. Christians as they say they are, the Taipings will not harm us. I hope he is right.

February 25 The soldiers of the Manchu dynasty are disorderly, deserting. I have come to believe that this corrupt "House of Heaven" deserves to fall! Seemingly unaware of their danger, they are lounging inside those walls, smoking opium and indulging in their disgusting deviancies. The officials are sneaking out of town, not taking steps to defend the city. I, of course, am half-frantic for my family's safety. I have spoken to Frances Ellen and we went on our knees for guidance. We shall stay; Simon asks, anxiously I think, about the soldiers and confusion in the streets. We are holding services to beg God's protection.

March 6 The first troops of the Taiping Army are arriving. The people, who hate the Manchus, were yet willing to protect the city as the invading force approached. There was a spontaneous resistance to the Taiping advance by the rice carriers inside our city at the south gate. Brave men, one of them our communicant. They were willing to defend the city and requested aid from the Imperial Manchu troops but Lu Chien, who is in charge in the palace, had the rice carriers dispersed with cannon fire. He did not want common people involved with army work!!

March 8 Waterborne troops are arriving from up the Yangtze. Much disruption. Our terrorized communicants find comfort in our daily services.

March 15 The huge army is encamped outside the walls of this city. The Women's Army of Heaven have planted millions of bamboo poles, sharpened to knife-like points, outside the walls of their camp as emplacements. Simon begged to go with me to see them from the wall observation points and I let him go. His curiosity is intense, but he is so sensitive I fear for him knowing such warfare. I am apprehensive, but not despairing. Surely God, and those who call themselves Christians in the Taiping Army, will keep us from harm. Missionaries have been protected wherever the Taipings have conquered, but I fear for the people in the streets.

March 18 This night we have witnessed history, grim as it is. Several hundred Taiping soldiers rode on horseback towards the walls, and the Manchu government guard was called out to repel them. When the riders drew near, the guards discovered the horses carried not soldiers but paper effigies. In the confusion, though, which included a dynamite charge, the walls were breached.

They are entering the city! I am reading the first psalm with those of our flock who have gathered here. "God is our refuge and strength, a very present help in trouble." Simon seems highly nervous, constantly asking questions which his poor mother, now confined to bed, does not have the strength to answer.

Later that day. . . . Helped by a fifth column of anti-Manchu Buddhist monks who have infiltrated the city, the Taiping army has breached the north wall. Generals Ch'eng San Kuang and Shen Nai of the Imperial Army have fallen in the defense—small loss, I suppose, to mankind. The army has deserted their posts . . . . Much rushing around in fear on the part of the populace here in the outer city. And what of the Inner Imperial City? We cannot know. But it appears our congregation and my family are in no danger. Thanks be to God!

Mack put down the diary, wiped his brow with his handkerchief because he was beginning to perspire, and eagerly picked the book up again.

March 20, 1853 The attack on the Imperial City has begun. Our congregation is gathered here in the chapel to pray. We do not know whether to be jubilant or anxious. Posters have been put up everywhere by the invading army which read, "Everybody worships God. Everybody goes to Heaven. Come quickly. Come quickly to worship God" It is very strange, but since we are already doing that, we are safe. Simon begs to go out and see the army marching. It is a sort of fatal fascination with him; he is frightened but terribly drawn to it all. But of course it is not safe as the soldiers besiege the inner city. He is obviously distressed and enervated by the events and confusion all about us.

My God! Aid me in my distress! Our son is gone, lost out there somewhere in the confusion which is the town of Nanking under an invading army. Cannons were going off—some gun firing as the attack on the Inner City continued and he begged his mother to go see. She had taken to her couch, dizzy and quite ill, I was occupied with the congregation, attempting to secure our chapel. I sent Li Fu, my faithful right-hand man and lay preacher to get food so we could all stay together in the chapel, when Simon apparently left his mother's side and followed Li Fu.

Li Fu has not returned after two hours and Simon is out there, in a city of riot, of wanton killing and looting. I shall search.

March 21. At last Simon has been brought back to us, mute and as dazed as if he had been hit over the head with a board. Thank God he is alive. My poor wife is half dead with worry and illness, blaming herself. Here is the sequence of events. My search yesterday was fruitless; I went to the imperial and foreign provisioners' streets, and returned in despair. Li Fu tried to make his way through the chaos of the streets to the street of the common provisioners, instead, to get the foodstuffs I'd sent him for. That street is near the gates of the Imperial City, which made the turmoil in the streets worse as the last remaining Bannermen of the Emperor defended the walled citadel and the rebels surged towards it. Just as he came from one of the last shops still open, he turned to see Simon behind him, calling his name. He had followed him in the distance all the way from the chapel. Just at that moment the Taiping rebel army arrived in force to storm the walls of the Imperial City. Transfixed and petrified, Li Fu held Simon against the wall of the shop. Amidst the cannonading and gunfire soldiers literally threw themselves at the ancient and sacred gate, venting all of their hatred on the foreign dynasty which had forced the admired Mings from this sacred citadel.

Oh, horrible tale to put on paper. At that point a stray bullet felled Li Fu, and he was carried senseless into a building as my poor Simon stood transfixed, alone in the midst of the horror.

The gates gave, the few guards left fled. The "holy" "Christian" soldiers rounded up and slaughtered men inside the walls for a while; then they drove out the females from the imperial city and their relatives and there, nearby, began to slaughter them. I can hardly record the atrocities. Bonfires were built and some were tossed, bound, live into them. Others were hacked to pieces. Some were thrown into the ponds and streams nearby and held down until they drowned. The screaming hideousness of the massacre—we think it is of several thousands—my son witnessed in full detail. When Li Fu finally came to consciousness after some hours he sent someone to look for Simon and that person, one Hsiang, brought him home and told the tale.

Simon will not speak to any of us and his eyes are glazed and dull. We are keeping him in the back bedroom, away from everyone, because he screams with fear and—is it hatred?—whenever he sees a man of Chinese blood. What can it mean for the development of his mind to have seen such a thing? I fear for the future.

Mack slowly closed the diary, returning it to its box. He put the picture of the family back on top of the diary.

Carrying the box, he returned to the circulation desk. The librarian was sorting through books in a closet behind the desk and called over her shoulder for him to set the record box down. The noonday sun shone through the Tiffany window, showing Bishop Asbury in golden glory on his horse. His eyes were on the mountain pass ahead. There was an inscription Mack hadn't noticed before; in leaded glass in the corner it said, "Francis Asbury: Father of the American Methodist Church, ever Christ's Faithful Shepherd."

The librarian came forward to take the box. "Where is the telegraph office in town?" he asked her. "I have an urgent telegram to send and only a short while to do it."

It was very late in the afternoon when Mack helped Alice and Chad down from the train at Union Station in Indianapolis; Jacob Joe Scott had parted with them in Louisville to visit his wife's relatives for a day or two. He would return to Michigan mid-week.

"I'll hire a hansom cab for you two," Mack said. "I need to take care of some business right now." Alice looked puzzled; he had been silent all the way back, absently glancing at the front page of the newspaper on his lap or gazing out the window at the November country scenes.

After he had seen the two off, the horses hoofs clopping off down the street, he went to the side entrance of the depot, where he found Chiang and Abby waiting with a buggy.

"How are things in Woodruff Place?" Mack asked as he climbed inside.

"No atrocities to report, thank God," Abby said. "My Aunt Erna Teitelbaum said we could have the buggy until nine-thirty."

"Let's park near the Circle. You can fill me in there."

Abby headed north, soon driving through the Commercial District past the tower of the Commercial Club on Meridian Street, climbing skyward and looking for all the world like the Waldorf Astoria in New York City. It had been built to show the arrival at the top of the power structure of businessmen like Fanning and Colonel Lilly and William Fortune. But the Chinese and the colored people on Indiana

Avenue? The ladder they had to climb to even survive was a tall one, and they were still standing near the bottom rung. People around here weren't very willing to see them attempt the climb. And these murders seemed somehow sadly symbolic of the rejection the lower rungs of this social ladder were experiencing.

They drove around the Circle, looking at blocks of stone which would eventually be statues representing "Peace" in front of the new Soldiers' and Sailors' Monument. Then they pulled up just beyond, on north Meridian, letting the horse drink from the trough by the side of the road. They had not spoken; Abby had been busy driving and Chiang seemed oddly distant. Mack was eager to tell them what he'd found, but wanted to know what they had to say first. He felt reluctant to plunge right into his bizarre story, to have unbelieving eyes on him again, although he now knew a good deal more than when he had told Alice and his father that a Methodist minister was murdering people in town.

Abby turned to Mack. "O'Shaughnessey gave Nate your message to watch the house, that Fanning was in real danger. Nate has been over himself two or three times, just walking up and down West Drive. Fanning's been holed up like a squirrel. The cops on the beat have knocked on the door to inquire about his health every couple of hours. He hasn't been out of his dressing gown all weekend and they said he seemed scared, relieved they were around. The housekeeper was there Friday and Saturday, so at least he didn't starve."

"Mrs. Bascomb," Mack smiled. The woman would put her adopted family above her own, sacrificing the one time she had to see her girls.

"But she had to leave today," Abby added. "I talked to her and she was very upset. Her sister was rushed to the hospital. She almost died, I guess. Some sort of internal women's problem." He was embarrassed. An abortion that went wrong. That was what it was, and Abby knew it too.

"They think she'll live but Mrs. Bascomb was beside herself. Said she was never there when her own family needed her, felt torn apart."

"The telegram," Chiang said abruptly. "You sent a wire telling us to meet you here; you had a strong lead on the killer. What's the story?"

"Yes, I'm sorry. I know it's on your mind. When I tell you what I found, you're going to think I've had a fit of insanity."

"Try anyway," Chiang said, obviously tense.

"We agreed before," Mack began, "didn't we—not the police but us—that our killer is a homicidal maniac. Someone who probably walks among us undetected, like Jack the Ripper. Right?" Abby nodded, Chiang took out a cigarette, lit it with a sulfur match and began blowing smoke out into the night air.

"I didn't know you started smoking," Mack said.

"I have been strung as tight as a drum since we talked to my cousin and he called us pricks," Chiang said. "He came to see me yesterday, called me a Chinaman in a herringbone tweed. A traitor to the tradition."

Mack just looked at him, not knowing what to say. "Well, about the murderer. If these things hold true to form, the person could be highly deceptive. Functioning daily, perhaps, in a position of respect or even power."

Abby and Chiang both looked at him expectantly. "Some—recent—things have made me ask who is connected with China and among those, I came, finally to—Dr. Brockelhurst."

Chiang was astounded. "The minister at the Central Avenue Church? Why, he has tea parties for all the church guilds and is a member of the Literary Club downtown with all the swells. Are you crazy?"

"I know that. But—to start with—I've gotten to know the town a little. Brockelhurst seems to be one of the only people closely connected with the Chinese. His father was a missionary and his house is full of Chinese furniture and brassware."

They both looked at him skeptically. The streets were almost deserted; Christ Church on the Circle, however was taking up Evensong services, and handsomely dressed couples made their way up towards the doors and into the warm interior, richly resonating with organ music.

"I thought you had something real," Chiang said scornfully. "I'm about at the end of my rope with my relatives dead and the Chinese community upside down. Toy Gum has taken to her room, and you go flying like a kite in the sky on a stupid theory." He tossed the cigarette butt in an arc towards the horse trough.

"Now just listen," Mack pleaded. "Just assume that the killer is someone people know and respect."

"Dr. Jekyll?" Abby snorted." We've already talked about this."

"Yes. And remember, Robert Louis Stevenson says in that book, All of us are two people, not one. And that has to be true with killings like these. In the daytime the murderer plays his role of respected citizen. In the night, his dark urges, buried deep in his psyche—arise."

"Thank you, Viennese mind doctor," Abby said scornfully.

"Buried deep in his mind, unconscious even, these urges come out and he turns into Mr. Hyde. If we have such a man, any respectable person is a possibility. Do you concede that?"

"Well, lots of people are, maybe," Abby conceded reluctantly. "But I can't think that my Aunt Rachael is a candidate."

Mack wanted to build his case. "Remember that Nate's mentor, Sgt. Rossi, said the motive was everything? We've assumed that the motive would be some sort of tong war—revenge—takeover of Chinese business. Those would be motives, but they've led us nowhere."

"Unless Sidlow is the murderer. You led us down his track. And you always thought Fanning was involved. But you didn't!"

"Well, obviously it's not Fanning now. I saw him receive that note; unless he's the best actor in America he couldn't have written it to himself. But Sidlow is still a possibility."

Abby slapped his forehead. "Sidlow and Brockelhurst—and—how about James Whitcomb Riley and Meredith Nicholson. They're prominent. They could have a secret life."

"I always thought Riley must have one anyway," Chiang growled.

"Let's get back to motive," Mack said. "We were looking for a logical motive in the tong wars. But in the case of a homicidal maniac, there is no logic. The motive has to be warped, bent, buried like an old tin can rusting underground, which waits to hurt somebody when its edge pokes through."

"Well, maybe," Abby admitted.

"So you have to look for some sort of warped, hideous reason to act, based, maybe, on a horrible experience in the past? " He had their attention now.

He sighed. "I found myself at Asbury Theological Seminary over the weekend. They keep all the Methodist missionary records there. I looked up Brockelhurst—his father was in Nanking in the early 1850s. During the Taiping Revolt."

Chiang was instantly attentive. "Brockelhurst was there during the Taiping Revolt? He's not old enough!"

"When little Simon Brockelhurst was six, the rebels marched on the Imperial City and took it. The boy Simon ran away to see the sights and ended up seeing them, by himself, near the palace of the Manchus."

"The massacre at the walls of the inner city?" Chiang said softly.

"The person who was attending him was hit and rendered unconscious. This child saw it all, right near the walls—the women torn to pieces, the drownings, the human immolations—"

"Stop—" Chiang said, obviously disturbed. "It was a terrible chapter in Chinese history. The country was torn apart."

"And so was this child, I think," Mack said quietly. "His father's diary said he could not bear to look at a Chinese face."

They looked at him silently. "But," Chiang said, "suppose he had a warped motive for hating the Chinese people. That he could have come to hate all Chinese—opium dens—all connected with the race, how about means? The police say that nobody could go along those streets at the times of the murders, late at night, without being seen. They make reports every night for the public safety committee. Everyone down at the Police Department is very nervous. This is a hot political time right now, with all the charges the cops are bought and sold. Beat cops and the few draymen out at night saw nobody the nights of the murders except a few doctors and drunks, and it's their job to know them all. There were no suspicious people."

"Well, maybe it was a night when they weren't really looking," Mack said. "Too cold, too rainy, the police stayed inside."

"No. Nate checked that out," Abby told him. "All of the murders occurred on perfectly dry, pleasant nights. This murderer doesn't like to go through the cold rain, I guess."

"I thought we could try to re-trace the main streets which surround the murder areas," Mack said. "Drive around, look to see if he could have evaded the police, slipped through yards—you know. Let's go first to the west side, where the last murder happened." Abby jiggled the reins and clicked his tongue to the horses and they were off, to the sound of hearty voices raised in song coming out of Christ Church. A man had suddenly pushed open the door wide. "Piety must be heating up in there," Mack mused.

"Either that or the furnace," Abby said.

But the route yielded no clues, not on the west side, over by the river at the gambling-opium den, where Bee Chee had met his fate. Police patrolmen were less evident here, but it wasn't clear how someone could sneak around at night. Two police stations sat right in the middle of the district, and people were walking around under bright streetlights.

They drove to Lockerbie Street and got out to walk around."

It would be possible to sneak through back yards here once you came into the street," Abby said. "It's probably the easiest of all to be stealthy in."

"We won't go to the office on Newman Street—Indiana Purveyors because we all could walk it blindfolded," Mack said, as Abby turned the corner and trotted the horse north towards the College Corners neighborhood.

"But the problem still remains. I've asked myself a lot how someone could miss the cops on Tenth, Michigan or Massachusetts Avenues. Those beat cops know it will cost the police chief his job, and maybe theirs, if they let a vagrant slip through." Without speaking of it, they were proceeding towards Brockelhurst's mansion, drawn by dark compulsion to stare at it, to wonder if the man inside, amidst the Chinese mahogany and bronze was, improbably, a killer.

"Let's stop here so we can look at it. You can see it a long way off there, up the street. Hide the buggy among this clump of tall bushes. Here—by the creek," Mack directed.

"Do you suppose he's in there—in that old haunted house?" Abby wanted to know, as they sat staring up Pine Street towards the mansion, seen at a distance through the increasingly murky darkness. "I can see only one light in the downstairs windows."

"He may be at Sunday evening services," Chiang muttered. "I think they start about now."

"I told Aunt Erna we'd have her buggy back by nine-thirty. That's an hour and a half from now."

Mack was insistent. "I want to know if he's home. If—just if—he's the maniac we're after, he sent a very threatening note and he hasn't carried it out yet. He won't wait much longer to rove these streets."

"Fanning," Chiang snapped his fingers. "Chinese hatred yes, but why Fanning?"

"Because of the dream repose. Fanning has been to the opium dens. So had the others—often. They are being eliminated one at a time," Abby said, still staring down the street. "Intense hatred for the opium habit could be driving him on."

"If it's Brockelhurst," Chiang said. "Talk about dream repose—I think it must be a nightmare that we are even suspecting this man. But we could observe him. Something makes me want to."

They left the horse tied to a tree near Pogue's Run and went up Pine Street toward the house. After slipping behind factory buildings for about three blocks, they came to Brockelhurst's house and went around back to look through the huge downstairs windows. "I don't think anyone can see us," Abby murmured. Night was falling fast; probably the housekeeper would be lighting the lamps and having supper, if she were in there. They peeked in through cracks in the portieres.

"Look there she is, taking a lamp up the stairs," Chiang said. "No sign of Brockelhurst."

"He must be at the evening service," Mack said. "It's usually the only time he gets to preach without Dr. Clayborne there."

"Look, there's all kinds of Chinese stuff in there," Abby said. "Chairs with dragons on them, those heavy tables with animal heads on the legs."

"Interesting. All Ming Dynasty," Chiang whispered. "But just because he has Chinese stuff in here doesn't make him a killer of Chinese. In fact, it seems it would be the opposite."

"Unless you had a warped mind," Mack reminded him. They proceeded around the house, looking about furtively, peeking through to see the different rooms of the old mansion.

"What a rat-trap," Abby said. "Why anybody would want to live on this street I don't know. Time passed Pine Street by twenty years ago. The old place looks like Count Dracula is using it for headquarters."

"Warped mind," Chiang said, straightening up as they retreated into the shadows of a tree. "If—and I say if—he is the man how awful it must be. Preaching about a gospel of love in the daytime, comforting the sad and dying, having everyone look up to you and then at night, going back into a horrible world of shame and killing." He spat into the bushes. "I don't know why I care how he feels," he said bitterly.

"If a homicidal maniac feels shame," Abby mused. "Mr. Fechtman, our English teacher was reading us some Russian stories about men compelled to kill. He said they are taken over by the dark sides of their personalities, and they can't resist doing something horrible."

"But do they know in the morning?" Mack wondered. "Dr. Jekyll did. That was the awful part—to know you were turning into a monster and to secretly wonder if anyone else did."

"If it were Brockelhurst, it would be enough to make you Christians lose your faith," Chiang said scornfully. "A minister of the gospel, a homicidal maniac. Anyway, somebody is out there. It doesn't matter what warps his mind, it's an extremely dangerous one. I don't want to walk the streets on this night."

Mack turned to Abby suddenly. "I wonder if anything more has happened at Fanning's house since you last heard?"

"How could it, with Sgt. Rossi watching the front door all weekend? They have a watch posted in a shed across the street. And the south beat cop, on Michigan Street, is watching from that direction to guard the avenue there and the entrance to the alley down on Michigan Street. Nobody comes up to that house without being seen. And Nate's over there now."

"Do me a favor," Mack said, as they re-traced their steps through the trash dumps and backyards of the manufacturing plants on Pine Street towards the buggy. "Go to Woodruff Place. Find out if there are any new developments. Meet me up there at the creek in about an hour. I have to know."

"I hope we can make it. It'll be about time for the buggy to be returned," Abby said doubtfully.

"Where are you going?" Chiang wanted to know.

"To evening services at Central Avenue Church. They should be about half over, and if I hurry, I can catch the sermon and meet you back here."

They stared at him. "They'll probably be singing 'Safely Through Another Week.' " Abby offered. "Isn't that the name of it? Can't say that in Indianapolis these days. Take care of yourself."

"Bring me a small coal-oil lantern. The smallest you can find. Don't come without it! It's important!" Mack called after them.

The interior of the church was gloomy, dimly lit, with only a few older people from the neighborhood in the pews, looking lost in the immensity of the domed sanctuary. The overhead "firmament" lights were not on, perhaps to save money on the electric bills which the church board no doubt complained about.

Yes, there was Brockelhurst at the pulpit, standing on a little stool so he could loom out over its height. Mack had slipped through the huge doors, trying not to make any noise, and was sitting amidst the dark shadows of the back pews. What was Brockelhurst talking about in his sermon?

Odd topic for a sleepy autumn evening. "The Seven Last Plagues," from the book of Revelation. Nobody preached on that anymore, it was too nasty to think about—all that wrath and blood and vengeance. But it was like Brockelhurst, who loved Old Testament retribution.

Brockelhurst had his small New Testament in his hand, holding it high. He was reading:

> *And I heard a great voice out of the temple saying to the seven angels, Go your ways, and pour out the vials of the wrath of God upon the earth.*
> *And the first went, and poured out his vial upon the earth; and there fell a noisome and grievous sore upon the men which had the mark of the beast and upon them which worshipped his image....*
> *And the third angel poured out his vial upon the rivers and fountains of waters; and they became blood.*
> *And I heard the angel of the waters say, Thou art righteous O Lord, which art and wast, and shalt be, because thou has judged thus . . ..*

Why was he using this text in the somnolent evening service? To wake the congregation up?

"John goes on," said the preacher, "to equate the city, split by the plagues at the end of the world, with Babylon, the great whore, the greatest of places of sin on the face of the planet."

Well, that was true enough. The Apostle John did hate Babylon. But it stood for all sin, didn't it?

"Babylon can be any city today in America, steeped in the proud faith that material progress can bring success. Listening to the siren call of the business merger, the capital investment, the vision of venture."

Any up-and-coming city? The capital city of Indiana?

And so, the minister, his congregation not really listening, ranted on about the corruption of the police force in the city, about the pleasure palaces and fine hotel dining rooms, the secret sins behind the doors of fashion.

"But my friends, this is not the end. Because the Lord is a Lord of justice, and these places will be destroyed in his good time. Yes, they will all be gone. All of them. 'For they are the spirits of devils, working miracles, which go forth unto the kings of the earth and of the whole world.' "

Indian No Place gaskets and rubber bands and cigars and poultry—going forth to the kings at the ends of the world. Or maybe just Dubuque, Iowa.

"Gone, all of them, sin uncovered by the angels of justice, pouring the vials of truth on them—the splashing fountains and gabled mansions and carriage houses." Splashing fountains and gabled mansions? Wasn't that hitting a little close to home?

"Gone, the crystal chandeliers reflecting illegal card games and tête-à-têtes outside of marriage! Gone, gone, the bribery at the police station, as Rome 300 A.D. is vanished, as the House of Rameses, as King David's halls themselves, be-smirched with the corruption of his own weak and sinning spirit."

Not bad. The man had intelligence and preaching ability. He was too intellectual, but the basic talent was there.

Mack sighed. He was beginning to feel drowsy. The lights along the walls seemed to dance, then swim. Chiang's statement rang in his mind, jolting him awake. If Brockelhurst were what they thought him to be, it would be enough to drive a Christian out of the church. He stared at the stained glass window of the Holy Spirit as a dove. If Brockelhurst was a shitten shepherd, then this whole church, this whole beautiful, fashionable end of town was darkened. The mark of the beast in a hideous form. The man was preaching about himself.

He opened one of the Bibles which had been placed in the pew rack and turned to Revelation Chapter 16. There it all was, all the stuff about the vials.

> *And I saw three unclean spirits like frogs come out of the*
> *dragon, and out of the mouth of the beast.*

He read on for a moment, but his mind was not on the scripture.

If this man who stood before them, ordained in the same church as John Wesley and Francis Asbury, had the unspeakable effrontery to wear the robes of a minister of God during the daytime and then sneak through the streets at night as a murderer, then he darkened the spirit—made it as black as the night outside that window. Maybe that's why the lights were so low tonight, this man didn't like to stand in the light. And how would the lights be turned on again? Only if someone were willing to fight for the light.

Sometimes it took fighting. He'd been brought up by his Quaker-bred father to believe that fighting was never right, but even in the faith somebody had to fight sometime. Didn't Jesus get angry and turn over the tables of the moneychangers in the temple? Well, somebody was going to have to fight to turn on the lights again in this church. The police hadn't really cared—Brockelhurst was right about that—because the men already killed were "of the lower groups in the town." Now the killer had informed the world, sent a note, that he was ready to pounce again, this time on a member of the downtown establishment of power. The police, who had to care now, had let it slip too long. They were far behind, completely in the dark. Darkness compounded. It looked like the job fell to him. He hadn't asked for it, but there it was.

The sermon was over; the seven vials sealed; the closing hymn announced. He needed to slip out before it was finished. The old usher opened the door, and cold air rushed in. He went out into the night, chilled by more than the late fall air. It was something he hadn't wanted to think about, but which was quite obvious: if he suspected Brockelhurst, then Brockelhurst had to suspect him. He had gone to him for help, and the man knew he was involved in solving the murders. The only solace was Brockelhurst thought he was completely safe. He had to believe that as a minister of a powerful church he was as yet completely unknown to the whole town, secure in his sanctified position, able to do what he wished. If he were the murderer.

Then, as Mack reached the bottom of the steps, he knew what he wanted to do. Turning and walking quickly around the building, he entered another door, one which opened into the minister's study. He found Brockelhurst with his robe folded on his desk, sitting in the darkness, the study illuminated only by light filtering in from the sanctuary.

"Mr. Scott. I thought I saw you slip in the back." So. He had seen after all.

"Yes. I was returning from the train station after a trip out of town and decided to stop by. My church-going has not been regular of late."

"Yes, that is true. True indeed. But then you are of one of the fashionable new offshoot denominations. There are a good many of them, a little strange—you seem to be spitting in the eye of the established churches." Mack ignored the comment, watching the man. Brockelhurst's eyes, bright as embers glowing in the dark, seemed far away, distracted. He stood to shift through some papers, seeming for an instant to forget Mack's presence. It didn't fit—certainly if he were guilty, he'd have reason to be wary of Mack. Brockelhurst knew what the Sherlock Holmes boys were about. Did he not think their questions important?

"I have a question relating to the sermon," Mack said evenly.

Dr. Brockelhurst stopped fiddling with his papers and focused his attention on Mack.

"The Seven Vials in Revelation. I've always thought John was talking of the end of the world. But you seemed to think the Seven Vials will be poured out in our time."

"I think it can happen both ways. At the end of the world, surely. But the destruction of sinful places today happens as part of God's punishment. It is clear that he pulls down perdition."

"I suppose you won't mind if I disagree. How do we know that destruction of sinful places is God's work? It may be man bungling. How can we be sure it's God that destroys the palaces and places of sin? That Rameses and the Roman Empire didn't fall because their people were stupid or evil and cause and effect at the human level made their societies die out?"

Brockelhurst did not answer, making some sorts of little humphing noises.

Mack went on. He must stick an ice pick into the minister's consciousness, now, at this moment, if they were correct that the man was preparing to kill again. "I don't think it's Armageddon at work when a bar burns down. Maybe somebody just left a cigarette burning in an ashtray. I can't believe it's because of the pouring out of the Seven Vials, with God tilting the pitcher deliberately to cut sin down."

"What are you getting at, Mr. Scott?" the minister asked dryly.

"Just this. Every bordello that closes doesn't show God's anger at the prostitutes inside. And, second, Armageddon is a result of man's failures, not God's punishment. I don't believe in a punishing God."

"Well, I do. There is no sense in the new good-feeling religions like yours that preach there is no sin. If there's no sin there's no goodness, either! Just use your own eyes and see how we're heading for destruction like a repair cart down a railroad track. What has the Age of Progress brought us? The robber barons make their immoral business killings and then buy pleasures with the money—brothels, gambling places, bars on every corner. You think there are many churches in this town? Count the bars. There are double the amount of bars in this downtown area than churches of the Gospel. I was saying tonight what I believe—that these institutions of sin will be destroyed within our own time! Fall by their own corruption! And by the arm of a vengeful God!"

Mack cleared his throat. "Perhaps it isn't only bars and bordellos that are vulnerable to the Seven Vials. Maybe churches can be corrupted by the Age of Progress too. The church may be in more danger of Armageddon than the bars."

"How so?"

Mack forced himself to go on. "Well, I suspect these new worship palaces may be able to be bought by the rich people who built them. I don't know. He who pays the architect calls the hymn tune."

"If they worship Mammon, they will fall, too. We know that."

" Or they may have clearer dangers." Mack narrowed his eyes, feeling strength now in the direction the argument was going.

"Yes, churches fail," Mack went on, "and sometimes it is because they are given in sacrifice to Mammon as you've said—to fashionableness and piety and power struggles and the substitution of good-seeming deeds for personal growth in Christ. But sometimes they fail only because of the passing of time and fashions in worship. If you stop to think about it, all of these beautiful churches downtown, First Presbyterian, Second Presbyterian, First Baptist, will probably be gone in a hundred years—at least as places of worship."

"Well, I doubt that much masonry is going to crumble into White River," the minister growled.

"Not the masonry, just the mission. The downtown will grow, the industrial devils you talk about will spread all around, offices will rise higher than the Commercial Club, up twenty, thirty stories! We already have a fourteen-story skyscraper here! They will surround the churches, patterns of living will change, and people move out as they are already doing. And they will take their churches with them. We can build churches but we can't keep them. Mrs. Fanning believes her little church on the countryside road is the most spiritual place to worship. And yet all those little country churches are for all practical purposes dead, rotting into the cornfields. The times outgrew them, too."

"If the churches are to survive these natural processes and the corruption of the world—they must be strong, I suppose," the minister offered in a calmer voice, perhaps tiring of the discussion.

"Yes! But what we see today, I think, is just a foretaste. In a hundred years the forces of the seven vials you spoke of will be very strong indeed! Materialism, Mammon—will be the God worshipped on every street in Indianapolis and every city in America. Why? Because Mammon is so much more attractive and easy to worship. Easy results. No sacrifices. The cross of Christ is hard to carry, you know."

Now the minister seemed fully engaged, if only at the intellectual level. "What then do you think will save the churches in the materialistic age to come that you—and I think I—were speaking of? What can prevent the Seven Vials from pouring over the churches as well as sinful institutions?"

"What always has saved the church. The simple faith of the parishioners who have felt Christ move in their hearts and who will find a way to take His faith into their own lives and the streets of the town. Who do not let their worship become formalism and their churches social clubs. Who open the doors for the outcast and the poor, as it said in the cornerstone-laying ceremony of this very church. And—" here he averted his eyes, lest what he needed to say next seem personal. He had led the discussion in this direction and he did not want at all costs for his comments to sound personal, for that would be very dangerous.

"And, of course, the leaders, priests, ministers of the gospel. They above all must stay pure and consecrated. But of course we all know that."

"Of course." The voice coming out of the darkness was hollow.

"I remember Jesus saying that anyone who led one of these little ones astray would not be forgiven," Mack said, adding, "But that danger is small." He hoped the bitter sarcasm he felt had not shown in his voice.

Mack turned to walk towards the outside door.

The minister's voice followed him. "By the way, Mr. Scott, on another subject, I have not spoken with you since you came to see me at the house asking about the note you found. Have you solved the answer to your Chinese riddle?"

Mack turned at the door, looking through the darkness at the form of the man behind the desk. "Not yet. But I'm convinced I soon will."

He knew now that his intuition was not based on some phantom he'd dreamed up but a real man, eyes glowing through the night, his mind deep and unfathomable, but somehow troubled and troubling. Yes, Simon Brockelhurst was the man. Mack knew it. And, in spite of his own intentions to test the man, he might have revealed too much. Fallen ministers who would ruin the church, he'd said that, hadn't he? He had been surprised at how much had come into his heart and mind at the time he spoke. And now the man could know he suspected him. How could it be otherwise? He had said too much—the comment about the Chinese riddle probably showed that. Still, if insane compulsion was driving the man, it didn't matter anyway. Was he crazy to have bearded the lion in his own den? Maybe he just wanted to hasten the pouring out of the seven vials. Destroy the demons! It wasn't a half-bad idea, depending on who you thought the demons were.

He slowly walked to the rendezvous point agreed upon with Abby, avoiding the streets which led directly to the minister's house and over which Brockelhurst would be walking soon. He came to Pogue's Run by a roundabout route and, watching up the street, saw Brockelhurst arrive home, pass over the front porch, open his door and go in. He stood by his tree and in a few moments, the buggy bearing his friends approached.

Abby jumped down. He was alone. "Another note was delivered to Fanning's tonight. Actually left on the privy seat with a hatpin. It said, 'Tonight's the night.' Then more Chinese characters. Alice Fanning is a wreck and—"

"Another note? How can that be?" Mack asked sharply. "You said all access roads to the house were being watched."

"Nate doesn't know how anyone could approach," Abby offered lamely. "The note must have been flown in by carrier pigeon."

He handed Mack the small coal-oil lantern and matches. "I have to take this buggy back to Aunt Erna's," he said. "I left Chiang back in your neighborhood."

Mack waved him on. "How will you get home?" Abby asked a little apprehensively. "You're not going to do anything silly are you? This is a crazy man—if there's even a shred of truth to what you think. The police—"

"The police would box me up and cart me off to Seven Steeples Asylum if I told them what we suspect. And going to that church tonight just confirmed it. His sermon was wild-eyed and he seemed terribly nervous when I spoke to him afterwards."

"What you suspect, well—I'm half convinced." He hopped back onto the seat of the buggy.

"I think it would be good if you just told Nate to have Sgt. Rossi have this neighborhood patrolled from now till morning. I don't know what you'll tell him, but it has to be done."

"You are going to do something silly. I can see it. I'm going to call Nate and Sgt. Rossi right away." Abby tipped his cap and, with obvious reluctance, trotted off towards Lockerbie Street and his home neighborhood.

Mack walked along the back route, through the broken glass and discarded wagon wheel rims of the industrial plants' back lots to the old mansion up the street. Choosing a spot far to the rear of the yard, he sat down behind a giant cottonwood where he could see both front and back doors. He could spend the night here, chilly though it was. And if nobody came out of those two doors, he would be assured that he was on the wrong track—or at least that nobody had been murdered in Woodruff Place from this house anyway.

Not that he could be sure about that, even if he saw no one pass out the doors. If Brockelhurst were the killer, he was coming and going in a way that human eyes could not detect. How could that be? All along that had been the sticking point. In an area heavily patrolled by policemen who knew everyone in the residential areas of the north and east sides of Indianapolis, the killer had passed, over and over again, it appeared. Like a spirit, or a bird. But how?

An underground passage? Sometimes these older places had them. Servants twenty years ago were housed in outbuildings and sometimes there were tunnels to get to them. He looked around. Had there been a servants' cottage here? Could it have been connected to the Lockerbie House where Li Ting was murdered? Well, that was a longer distance than he could imagine, but what about out to Newman Street? And to the West Side? Over a mile each way? Ridiculous.

But could the minister have come out of the back cellar entrance? He could see it up there by the back door and by the look of the open doors, it seemed as if it was in use now. But where would he go then? How could someone disappear from this back yard to go to places of infamy in the neighborhoods around the downtown? He shook his head. He sat for what must have been an hour, growing colder by the minute. He settled into his greatcoat, then in spite of himself, dozed.

He awoke with a start. Something in the very still air of the night must have awakened him, thank God. There was a form coming from the back door of the house, slowly slinking across the yard. It was the figure of a slightly-built man, and he was moving from tree to tree, looking over his shoulder. Then, he took the very route Abby and Mack and Chiang had taken earlier in the evening, across the back fields of the deserted factories! But where was he going? Mack arose stiffly and hastened after him, taking great care not to step on the pieces of glass on the ground, and to stay far enough behind not to be noticed.

What if the man looked around? But the shadowy figure pressed on, with some haste now, pausing behind a tree before venturing across the side street, as if he were accustomed to watching for observers. Then both he and Mack passed into the shadow of a building, and when Mack came up, very cautiously, to the spot he'd last seen the shadow passing, the form was gone! Vanished! Into the darkness.

How in the name of God had the man disappeared? There was no one in the street ahead, no one heading back towards the house—where was there to go? He had arrived at the spot from which the buggy Abby was driving had left earlier. He was still carrying the small coal-oil lantern his friends had brought him, and he stuck it in his greatcoat pocket. Where—then he knew. Brockelhurst had gone down the bank and into Pogue's Run. Suddenly, as if light had broken over the windows of his mind, he understood it all.

Pogue's Run. The man had taken the paths along its edge as a highway, as he and Chad and Alice had. And that highway passed from Pine Street all the way through the Arsenal Grounds to—my God. To the gap in the gate and West Drive, Woodruff Place. He quickly lit the lantern, scrambled down the bank, still trying to pass as quietly as possible. Pogue's Run. The minister was small enough to navigate the bridges, evade the guard as he and Chad had done. He would pass through, in the dark of the evening, when few were out, to the small gap in the gate nobody knew about (except Alice). He was free to slip into the privy in the obscure part of the yard and leave the note, passing out again and onto his waterpath out of sight. The men were watching roads leading to the house, even the entrances at the main streets to the Arsenal path. But they could not know this man could come through the Arsenal grounds and right to the house.

He reached the creek, crept along as fast as he could and sure enough, there ahead, a city block or so, was the figure, sneaking along the path he and Alice and Chad had so happily trod a month before.

This, of course was the way the murderer had passed to Newman Street without being seen and had been able to kill Lee Huang, Chiang's uncle. This man had left his house while it was quite dark and arrived in the dark, passing up the bank north of Tenth Street and moving unobserved for the last yards between the buildings near the Purveyor's

Plant. He had stabbed the sleeping Lee Haung. Then he had retraced his path quickly, just gone down the bank again into the creek path, bending low. Using the shoreline trees for cover, he had disappeared from sight and pursuit before the sun rose.

Could he be stopped? This man was clearly insane and reckless and quick enough to come to the back door of the Fannings', slip the lock, enter and kill Fanning in a couple of minutes. Alice and Chad would be on the third floor by now. The Woodruff Place house was being watched, of course, but only one guard was on duty Sunday night, now, they had said. The chances were poor that he could really murder— but wait. The figure had stopped and plastered himself against a tree, listening. Had he heard the twigs snapping as Mack advanced, trying to be careful? He shrank against the bank.

Suddenly the shadowy shape turned, looked back and peered through the darkness. Clearly he suspected something; he splashed through the low-running water and pulling onto a tree, hoisted himself up the other side of the bank and made his way through the underbrush.

Mack was perplexed. There was no path along the other side, but he had gone over there anyway—which way? He had best try to follow. He splashed across and quickly tried to go up the slippery other side of the creek. Noises, up ahead, to the right. The shadow-man was fleeing back towards Pine Street, returning the way he had come. Mack pursued, through wild roses bushes and poplar saplings, finally coming to an old deer path. He held up the lantern now; no sense in trying to mask his pursuit. He saw the figure darting ahead, through trees, then masked by them for a moment, then emerging again.

The thought hit him that he didn't really want to catch what he was chasing. What in the name of God was he going to do if he met this man, who was probably armed with a brutal knife or even hatchet? Had he thought of that? He had best turn back, tell the police now what he had found—suddenly he saw the dim lights of Pine Street. He recrossed Pogue's Run, climbed and came to the spot from which they'd started. The form had started up the street towards the house; it disappeared in shadows. He ran to pursue towards the back of the buildings again, and as he did there was an odd, soft, bell-ringing sort of sound. He couldn't have been more than thirty seconds behind, and yet the figure was gone. He had been at the side of the street; no building was really nearby for him to hide behind. No one was anywhere on the street. What had that odd sound been?

He raced along nearly to where Brockelhurst's house stood, looking, in front, in back, his heart hammering from the exertion of the run. He walked to the side of the street, staring apprehensively up and down it. The man could jump out at any time. Then he saw it. The large manhole cover to the central sewer system, dedicated only this summer. It was the central trunk line for Indianapolis, so Fanning had said, and collected all the stormwater and the small amount of waste from houses connected to sewers from the north and east parts of town.

He went to the cover and lifted it. He took his lantern and swung it down the steps. Yes, they went down, five feet or a little more. Large enough for a man—a small man—to stand up in. Of course! That was the smell he had smelled in the minister's house—the smell of a sewer. Cautiously he listened. Up ahead, the furtive sound of muffled footsteps resonated softly. They could not be heard above ground, but here you knew. A man was passing through the sewer. Quickly he began to descend the ladder steps, not taking time to replace the cover.

Ducking uncomfortably, he passed quickly along, unable to conceal the sound of his footsteps. Recklessly, he pursued. Now what did he know about this sewer? Not much. But someone at the office had said that it went straight towards the downtown with some key branches. Which would have made it lead directly by Lockerbie Street—certainly there was an offshoot within yards of Li Ting's house. Yes, he could see what must be the branch right ahead, hear water coming in. Whew! The place smelled wretched. It wouldn't explain how this sewer murderer got to Bee Chee's, but he could use any connected line in the city to go west and emerge when he couldn't walk farther.

As he neared what must be the Lockerbie cutoff, he paused a few seconds. He had been timing his steps to those of the man ahead of him. Then they stopped.

Mack halted, fearful for the first time. This man—monster—knew he was being chased, but did not know by whom. Or did he? How much had he sensed in the confrontation in the church study? If—as it seemed—he had decided to meet the pursuer, he would likely be in a cool, murderous rage. Insane with his perverted hatreds—how could he, Mack, hope to stop him—he decided to turn around. Suddenly, from nowhere—a dark form confronted Mack from the sewer cutoff. Though the face was shadowed, the hand carried a small lantern—light glowed through dim glass framed by dark mahogany carvings. It was a Chinese lantern.

With a few slight steps the sinister form covered the escape routes forward and to the side. Mack could run back, of course, but he didn't. Something compelled him to stand stock still.

"And so, it is you. I did not know who pursued me but it could have only been you. " The voice, though low, echoed hollowly.

Mack said nothing. He must determine how mad the man was. If he were hysterical, it would be easier to overcome him, or to escape. He should proceed cautiously, but indignation made him bold.

"You are the shitten shepherd of the sheep."

"Am I?"

Mack raised the lantern to show the face of Dr. Brockelhurst. He did not seem to be in a hysterical rage.

"I saw a portrait in glass of Francis Asbury, one of the church's greatest ministers. You don't look like him at all. The character lines in the face, especially."

The minister leaned a little closer, and suddenly lurched so that Mack was pinned against the wall of the sewer. A Chinese knife in Brockelhurst's hand glinted in the light of the lantern which he quickly set at his feet. He was, clearly, near enough to spring, lithe enough from his night forays to cut the wrists or throat in a slash or two.

"How can you know what the charge and call are?" he sneered. Now Mack could clearly see the hatred in his face. "You, an apostate."

Mack said nothing.

"Non-believer—one of the new religionists. I thought of it again when we spoke. The glorious agony of this new age of science. All of us rising from the monkeys with no need for Divinity. Well, I do not suffer it. The Almighty I know of is a God of vengeance. And I am his right arm! The purveyor of the seven seals!"

Mack's heart beat so loud it seemed to resound through the darkness of the tunnel, but something kept him emboldened. He could not go back now; if he darted around, the knife could be plunged deep before he could escape. "And so, you pursue every Chinese devil you see. Kill the demons!" he said.

A bitter laugh sounded through the tunnels. "Of course not. It's not the Chinese of course. They are the victims." His tone was oddly confiding. "It is the greater evil."

"The greater evil?" Mack asked, hollowly.

"The Anti-Christ. That is what the Book of Revelation is really talking about at Armageddon., when the seven seals are broken. It is the beast which will be destroyed."

"Well in our time that has been called everything from the Anarchists to the Pope himself." How odd this theological argument sounded in the depths of the night in a sewer redolent of human excrement. He was able to shift his position slightly, evading Brockelhurst's knife by a few inches. They began circling around each other, testing, like two wrestlers looking for the best place to put on the hold and talking disarmingly as they did it. But the stakes in the match were life and death.

The minister's voice took on an agitated tone, higher than usual. "No. The beast—the Anti-Christ, is slimy and black and lives in a pipe. It promises to deliver God and freedom and gives instead the sleep of death."

"Opium." As he and Chiang and Abby had supposed. How much longer would this odd hiatus continue? How long would they bandy words? If he could just get to that knife, wrestle the man to the ground.

The man's eyes turned away slightly, his voice grew softer. "I saw the Anti-Christ on his home ground. Old women, children eleven years old, caught in a torture more horrible than the Manchu prisons devised." His voice was growing agitated. "My friend Li Fu, my father's best convert—his heart was broken when his two sons became opium fiends, their bodies shrunken, their families destitute. And he asked me and Father, why? Why did God let such a plant on the face of the earth? I shall never forget Li Fu."

"Nor the massacre at the Gates of the Inner City in Nanking?" Mack said softly.

"You know of that?" the minister said sharply, then seeming to lose interest in Mack's presence, said in that odd, far-off tone again, "Yes. All of them in there—lying on the silk couches. Taking the pipes until it deadened all morality. The women, dull and unable to care for their children in even the simplest ways. Leaving their husbands, prostituting themselves to other women, killing for the drug, finally. The Army of Heaven punished the dope fiends all, but they could not kill the evil."

The light in the lantern on the floor flickered; his own light would soon be gone. If Mack could distract him enough, he could get by him, run out. How fast would he be? "You are pouring out the vials on great evil. Slinking along these pipes and the river bed to the places where the addicts sleep. Killing them—and the people who dispense the Anti-Christ. Is that it?"

The other man sensed the appeasement in Mack's tone and his voice hardened. He would not be taken unaware. "It is the arm of the Lord that vanquisheth. But it is more than that." He stepped closer, holding the knife at throat-height directly in front of Mack.

"Yes?" Mack said, trying to muster courage.

For a moment there was nothing except the dripping of water through the system, and a muffled, metallic clattering that was a horse carriage going over the street above. Then the other muttered something.

"Say it again," Mack said, stepping back a little, his eyes searching for a route around the man.

The minister stepped before him, grabbed his collar, putting the knife up between them. "Expiation, I said. To pay. When all of them who feed the habit here are gone, then I will be free."

Mack's mind racing, seeking the second to make a move, if he could muster it. The minister, though small, had him in an iron grip; to try to wrench free would be to risk a slashed face at the least. The man was strong and skillful enough to hit the jugular in one stroke. "So you killed the men who fed the habit here—Li Ting and Lee Huang and Bee Chee of course, the opium den keepers, but what about Fanning? Why threaten him?"

"Worse than the Asian den keepers, most of them victims themselves, are the white men who feed the trade with their riches. The dilettantes who pay well feed the opium dragon that keeps us in bondage!"

"Us?" Mack wondered, astonished in spite of his fear.

The minister pushed him hard against the rank, wet wall of the sewer, putting the knife against his throat, finally done with words. "My mother became an opium eater to combat the pain of cancer of the womb. And I drank from her laudanum bottle secretly, as I sat day after day by her bed. My habit claims my life and the only—way—I—can—eradicate—" his voice became strangulated; he coughed, then began again, spitting words into Mack's face.

"Those are wrong who say that the God of the Old Testament was superseded by the New Covenant of Love. No, there is a God of vengeance, a God who sends the purging fire to pay the price of sin. I am the instrument of the seven vials." Mack frantically looked into the man's mad eyes. Could he spring with any hope of breaking free before his throat was slit?

"And now you, apostate, know—you who toy with the Almighty, you will stop the purging fire? You must perish in it!" His wrist tightened around the knife; Mack felt the forearm muscles pushing against his chest, straining, bringing the knife closer to his throat, and he strained back against the knife; the man's superhuman strength astounded, terrified him.

And suddenly all the rational, religious arguments he'd pursued meant nothing and the animal in him rose. White-hot anger, distilled from the blood of generations of fighting ancestors, bubbled in his gut and shot through his veins and he pushed the man down and found himself on top of him on the fetid floor of the sewer.

He pushed the minister's arms up, banging them against the muck to make him drop the knife, but the minister, maddened himself, thrashed around until he lay on the uppermost side. The man seemed to have a strength beyond the physical. He raised the knife to plunge, Mack's hands reaching high on his arms to stop him. The lanterns were both flickering on the floor, sending ghastly shadows; the minister's eyes flashed fire and his teeth were bared, fang-like.

Grunting, calling on all the images of past blood battles in the lumber camps and at O'Shaughnessey's, Mack heaved with his legs and thighs and threw the man off and pinned him. Then, side by side and half covering him and holding him down, he wrestled, inching towards the knife, finally wrenching it from the man and tossing it as far up the tunnel as he could.

Then he began pummelling, beating the other's head into the floor of the tunnel until the minister lay senseless. A few more blows to the head—the son-of-a-bitch deserved it—but no.

Picking up the Chinese lantern, he and stood above him, panting and gasping for breath. He looked at the chiselled, intellectual features, now bloodied, the open, flaccid lips, and the flickering light fell on the minister's collar, torn and spattered with blood. Bending, he ripped the clerical collar off the shirt and tossed it into the muck. He searched for, then found the manhole cover for the Lockerbie Street extension. He could not budge it. Then using the lantern's failing light, he walked painfully, then made himself run, the way he had entered at the manhole cover on Pine Street.

And, though no one was there when he emerged into the still city air through the manhole, he soon heard the clatter of horses' hoofs and saw the police wagon. Sgt. Rossi and Fitzgerald, the goateed officer for Woodruff Place, and a worried Nate Nessing were soon in the street beside him.

"When Abby and I came by, we saw the manhole cover and your coat," Nate said. "We climbed into the sewer and heard a commotion; I ran to meet the police wagon and they picked me up on Tenth Street. Where is he?"

It was a moment before Mack could get his breath. Then, chest heaving, he said, "Down there, down by Lockerbie Street, in the sewer. Take lanterns. You'll find him. I beat him insensible. Here's the knife." The two officers, carrying a large lantern and pistols, began to descend the steps. Nate followed.

Somehow Mack did not have the heart or stomach to wait to see the criminal brought forth. Painfully, he took himself to the police wagon, almost in a daze.

And when they returned a half an hour later, having found only a broken lantern and a bloody collar in the spot where the minister had lain, and nothing in the tunnels ahead, he shook his head.

"He can't get away in this town now," Mack said, as they drove towards Woodruff Place, and home where he went inside and collapsed on the sofa, too tired to say anything to Alice and Walter Fanning except "It's over. It was Brockelhurst. He's still at large."

It was five o'clock in the morning when Fitzgerald banged on the door of the house. Mack, having slept a fitful sleep on the parlor sofa for a while, answered the door and was told that Dr. Brockelhurst, the minister of Central Avenue Methodist Church, had been found dead, floating in White River, not far from the outlet of the Indianapolis storm sewer system.

Chapter Fourteen

Alice pulled the curtain aside in her bedroom the next day as Mack came to stand beside her. Sergeant Rossi was completing his investigation with Walter Fanning downstairs. Fanning had admitted to being a frequenter of the opium dens. The other connections with the Chicago tong killings did not seem to be of interest to the police; anyway, they weren't raising them now, with Brockelhurst the admitted murderer.

"Whi Ting Lo's been released from custody," Mack said, putting his arm around Alice's shoulders.

"From what everybody's saying, he has to be one of the evilest men alive," Alice said. She turned to trace the past and present scars on Mack's face with her finger. "Can't they hold him on anything?"

"They don't want to. He's too hot a firecracker, with too many connections in high places beyond the Chinese Community. Remember, the killings in Chicago occurred under the present administration."

"You've got to quit fist-fighting," Alice told him, shaking her head.

"Why? It saved my life. And maybe yours or your husband's."

Mrs. Bascomb had bathed Mack's wounds, telling him in the process that her sister was out of danger. The terrible husband had left town.

Mack felt no exultation, only dull relief now that the cycle of murders had run its course in the murky waters of White River. He had met with Dr. Clayborne and the Methodist bishop at Central Avenue early in the morning to tell him of the awful convoluted path of Simon Brockelhurst, minister of the gospel, ending in suicide. How many years had he been addicted to opium? No one could know, because according to the coroner, the habit had stablized itself so that with daily maintenance the minister could continue some sort of life on the outside. But inside, his mainspring had snapped, and like a crazy watch, all the inner workings had flown apart.

"Look out there. Woodruff Place is preparing for winter," Alice said. The fountains had been turned off, and children walking to school with bookstraps were wearing coats, chattering and blowing on their hands. Chad, looking stronger than he had for a while, was heading up the street towards school with a chum from down the street. His teacher had said that he was now at, or ahead of other children in second grade.

"Brockelhurst last night in his crazy sermon said that all of these mansions in Woodruff Place—at least that's part of what he meant— all of these palaces of grandeur and sometimes hypocrisy will be gone a hundred years from today. I wonder if he's right."

"They're pretty well built," Alice said doubtfully.

"So were the houses on Pine Street just before the Civil War. But they're torn down—or mouldering. Now there will be another unoccupied one up for sale there."

"No, I don't think these mansions will go. But I think that just like the Pine Street neighborhood, Woodruff Place will change. Who knows whether it will go downhill like that one did."

"Brockelhurst believed that opium was the Anti-Christ, the form of Satan among us that. That it claimed men's hearts and souls as well as their bodies."

"I don't believe that kind of addiction is going to grow in the future. People are too rooted in the church and its commandments."

"And should the church lose its hold? What I said to him I do believe, living in the city as I have now these months. It's in the city where the plagues grow—danger and crime and dissipation but also the worship of Mammon. Easy materialism. All that's been held in check, and I think it's always been that way, by the church, or synagogue, or ritual worship. Whatever turned people's eyes to what they ought to do to contribute to the good functioning of the universe. But if that goes—"

"Then I guess we ought to be wishing Central Avenue Church well! Prosperity! And a new assistant minister." She smiled a sad smile.

"Which it will have in a couple of months, when people stop talking. No, I think we're going to need every one of these places, whatever their persuasion or architecture in the age that's coming with the new century. We'll be glad for every church we have when progress replaces the Lord of the Universe."

A group of women were strolling the street, pointing at lamp posts, putting down notes on pads. "The Christmas committee," Alice mused. "They're trying to see where Christmas trees and wreaths should be hung, where the carolers' stand should be erected."

Ignoring what she said, he turned to her. "Marry me," he commanded. Without waiting for her to open her mouth, he shut it with
two fingers, then kissed her, long and ardently, holding her close to him,
in spite of the pain he felt as she pressed his bruises.

"You know I can't," she murmured. Then, contradictorily, she put
her hand behind his head, drawing his face to hers again.

"Why not? All you will need to do is accept the nasty word—let's
say it. It starts with D."

"Divorce?" Her eyes were large, beginning to mist.

"You have plenty of reason. He's been an adulterer with half of
the ladies of the night and in this neighborhood."

"Don't. I took my vows. And what about Chad? It isn't done."

"And that is, of course, why Walter Fanning took you into his life,
to tell him what is and isn't done in Indianapolis society. And why you
accepted his hire, isn't it? So you could be a lady again?"

"You're too cruel," she cried. He turned from her, towards the
window again. His bruises were bothering him fiercely and he couldn't
quite get the smell of the sewer off him, though he had scrubbed with
glycerine and rosewater till he was almost blue.

"There is nothing to keep you from doing this legally. You can get
a divorce if you wish. And he will not dare to fight you, because he's
aware of what you—and I—know of him."

"It's impossible. There are so many objections." She put her beautiful hand on his cheek and stroked it softly. He thought it was the one
most beautiful gesture of love anyone had ever given him in his life and
grasped her hand, covering it with kisses.

Then he dropped it suddenly. "Objection One. Chad. He will have
no father. But that is easy. We arrange for Walter to see him at proper
times. And Chad will easily accept me as his step-father. He adores me
anyway and I love him. Deny it, Alice. I'll be better for Chad than Fanning! Go ahead!" She shook her head, frowning at his impetuosity.

"Objection Two. Everyone will talk. But they are already talking
about a homicidal maniac who killed three Chinamen and a church
turned upside down. Nobody's going to worry about our petty little divorce."

"Objection Three. There will be nobody to care for Walter. After all he has provided you with all the husbandly amenities designed to make a little wife content: the chance to plan seven course dinners for important men, which you may not attend, unlimited charge accounts at the downtown mercantiles, the necessity of watching his philandering and wasting the family resources in his drunken forays into gaming and adultery and embarrassment over his involving you in a near-criminal action and—" he grasped her hands and looked into her eyes "marital rape." She whimpered. "You heard me. You never loved him, even in the beginning. Isn't that right?"

She nodded, mutely.

"And as far as somebody to take care of Walter, I have a perfect suggestion that will solve a couple of problems."

She put her head on his shoulder, looking up into his eyes. "And Objection Four. We will not love each other to the end of our days because we are not compatible in interests, goals and affections." He kissed the top of her head. "And our union will fail in the marriage bed because we have no mutual attraction for each other." She turned to his arms, fully, openly, and after a moment or two, he said what he had said to her before, "Tell me you don't like this. And, following a moment of silent embracing, "Objections over-ruled."

"I love you beyond all reason. Still what you say has some reason. I guess New Women can get divorces," she whispered.

They stood again together, on a hill in Delphi, Indiana, outside the lane, where a little cottage stood, its shutters flapping in the December wind. The same forlorn trash pile stood, and she went to the objects there, the old doll without a head, the broken china cup, the whiskey bottle, and she poked and pulled at them and cried a little.

"The past has strong claims on us," Mack told her, as they inspected the cracks in the wall, the leaking roof of the cottage inside. "And the Austrian doctors are right—we need to pull the sheets off the ghosts and see who's standing underneath. Then, once that's been done, the rest of our lives are up to us to live the best we can. And maybe we don't need to call up the spirit world to do that." He looked at her with a stern smile.

"You haven't been much of a mother, Alice. I expect more from you now, and you should expect to give more of yourself to Chad."

"If you don't want my problems, don't take me for your wife" she said. Gently he took her in his arms.

"Father loved me, and he did the best he could," she said in a minute. "I guess that's what we need to know about our parents after all—and hope that our children will at least grant us that when they're grown. At least I hope Chad will."

Mack pried at a lifting floorboard. "This house is still usable. It's walls and roof are strong. You own it; shall we fix it up and sell it to someone? It could house a family very nicely. You could rent it."

"Yes, and I'll—we'll need the income. I'll no longer be a lady of fashion. Perhaps I will go to Remington typewriter school too. I could do something else except have tea parties." She was silent a moment, running her hand gently over the mantel of the fireplace.

"There wasn't much in the stockings here of a Christmas, but it was all I had." She was silent a moment, then said, "Thank God Walter has seen fit to grant me the freedom I want now. And to agree that Mrs. Bascomb should move in with her two girls to be his housekeeper full-time. It will be a blessing for them, too."

"There's always a new start. But I want ours to be soon. A month is long enough for me to have been living with Abby, doing not very much each day. I need to get a new job."

"Yes, and Walter's going to have to make it on his own, too, without the monopoly structure. I rather think he can."

They closed the door after them. "We could live here, you know," Alice said. "The fixing up could be for us. There's a bedroom for Chad. We haven't spoken of where we'll be."

"No, I think not. A new start needs a new place—completely new. I think we should settle back in Southern Indiana. Near Vincennes, where the ancestors came from. I felt completely at home when I was there, where Great-Grandmother Jenny and Grandfather John Robert Scott lived. Something called to me there, from the beech trees and deep river bottoms." They headed down the lane. "I'm thinking of what a relative of mine said. John McClure."

"Yes, from the wedding. He showed you all the ancestors' graves and told you you were one of them, headstrong, with natural fighting instincts, you said."

"Yes, and he was right. 'Answer to the blood,' he said, and I did that that night under the city with Brockelhurst."

She paused as they reached the gravel road to look at him earnestly."You told me you almost killed him. And no one would have faulted you—he would have made you his fourth murder victim. Maybe your fighting McClures would have done that. What stopped you?"

"Well, I guess I don't need to beat people to a pulp every time I get angry. But then—I looked in his face and remembered what Toy Gum told me. He, too, was once some mother's child."

"As we all are," Alice said, taking his hand.

But then, in a moment, she said "Your idea of living in Southern Indiana takes me by surprise. I'd have to see it to decide. I think I'd really rather stay in Indianapolis. It's here that the battles were fought, and I don't feel like running away from the church and the neighborhood. I'll let you know what I think later."

"You'll let me know," he said, slowly, shaking his head.

"Yes, when I've decided."

"So now I think you'll be taking over your uncle's business," Mack said to Chiang. His friend was sloshing a bucket of soapy water over the floor of the washing shed. It had been cleared of everything that had stood in it. A new hot water heater and boiler stood outside the door, ready to be installed. "You'll be head of the household."

Chiang put his bucket down and turned solemnly to Mack. "I think not, my friend who presumes too much."

"Toy Gum will be depending on you. Aren't you inheritor of the family ancestor's mantel, head of joss worship—"

"As my cousin Fook Soy says you are one smart know-it-all. You understand four thousand years of Chinese culture now." He was wasn't pronouncing it "coe-chure" any more.

"I am going to college in Bloomington. I have a full scholarship. I am second in my class at Indianapolis High School."

"I know that, and you should be very proud. But aren't you obligated by Chinese tradition to become head of the house as only male?"

"That is the Chinese tradition. But there is an even better Chinese tradition, at least for those of us who live in America. Do you remember the sign we saw in Chicago?"

"Which one?"

"The one near the school Sidlow's father and my father's friend Wong Woon were involved in. It said 'It is of the utmost importance to educate children. Do not care that your families are poor or rich. For those who can use the pen, go where they will, need never ask for favors.' "

"Mrs. Bascomb told me an old Irish saying like that. 'Give a child a book and you have given him power.' I suppose both the sayings are right. If we're ever going to make Indian No Place Indian Some Place, we'd better put our energies into schools and colleges. So I'm glad you'll be going to college. But what about Toy Gum? What will become of her?"

"It will be good for her. This is America and this is the age of the New Woman."

"And of the new man who needs to know how to handle the New Woman."

They walked, laughing, through the open door of the washshed, then closed it behind them as they headed towards the street.